THE SEVEN STREETS
OF LIVERPOOL

Pearl Street in Liverpool has already seen its share of tragedy in the opening years of the war, and as the residents prepare for Christmas 1942, it is the spirit and friendship in adversity which binds them together. Since her RAF husband was seriously injured, Eileen has worried about the growing distance between them. While Kitty has hidden away, too ashamed to return to Pearl Street in disgrace with her baby, after discovering her American lover was already married. As the final years of war are played out, Pearl Street sees friendships forged, hearts broken, babies born and the most joyful of reunions.

THE SEVEN STREETS
OF LIVERPOOL

THE SEVEN STREETS OF LIVERPOOL

by

Maureen Lee

Magna Large Print Books
Long Preston, North Yorkshire,
BD23 4ND, England.

British Library Cataloguing in Publication Data.

Lee, Maureen
    The seven streets of Liverpool.

    A catalogue record of this book is
    available from the British Library

    ISBN   978-0-7505-4081-0

First published in Great Britain in 2014 by Orion Books,
an imprint of The Orion Publishing Group Ltd.

Published in Large Print 2015 by arrangement with
Orion Publishing Group

Magna Large Print is an imprint of Library Magna Books Ltd.

Printed and bound in Great Britain by
T.J. (International) Ltd., Cornwall, PL28 8RW

For Lord Alan and Lady Eileen Jordan

Prologue

Bootle, Liverpool
Millennium Eve

Penny was lost. Although the sign told her she was in Pearl Street, it was nothing like the Pearl Street she'd known more than half a century ago. Instead of two rows of terraced houses facing each other, now the street consisted of small semi-detached bungalows with tiny gardens front and back. There had either been massive redevelopment or she was in the wrong Pearl Street, the wrong Bootle. Had she come to the wrong city altogether? How many Liverpools were there on the planet?

A young woman was approaching with a stroller. The small child inside was snuggled inside too many clothes to tell if it was a boy or a girl.

'Excuse me, but do you know how long these houses have been here?' Penny enquired as she neared. 'And what happened to the bar on the corner? The King's Arms, I think it was called.' Or it might have been the Queen's Arms; she wasn't sure.

'I dunno, luv,' the woman said vaguely. 'I've only lived here a couple of years. You need to ask someone older.'

'Oh yes, I should have. But thank you anyway.'

'That's all right, luv.' The woman began to walk

11

away, then turned. 'Are you from America?'

'Yes; New York.'

'I thought so. I'd recognise an American accent anywhere.' She walked a few more steps and turned again. 'Is that coat mink?'

'Yes.'

'Jaysus.' She rolled her eyes. 'I never thought I'd see a mink coat in Pearl Street.' She laughed, and the child in the pushchair laughed with her. 'Can't stop or I'll be late picking up me little girl from the party. Ta-ra, luv.'

Ta-ra! The word was familiar. Mom used to say it sometimes. 'Ta-ra,' Penny called, though the woman was already out of earshot. It sounded odd on her tongue.

What was she supposed to do now? It was a horrible day and the sky was already growing dark. Despite the coat, she felt cold. She had expected to find the street exactly as she remembered, and had thought that if she knocked on enough doors she would be bound to find someone she knew from old – or who knew her or someone who remembered her. When she'd lived there, it had seemed as if everyone in Bootle knew everyone else – was even related in some way. But the world is a very small place when you're a child. She'd been a fool to come. Caitlin had told her to wait in the city centre hotel by Lime Street station, from where she would collect her.

'We're meeting for a party in the cottage in Melling later,' she'd said on the telephone when Penny had rung from America a few days before. 'You and I can have dinner first.'

12

Penny could vaguely remember the cottage. It seemed an appropriate place for a party on Millennium Eve. She imagined the new century dawning over the trees in the garden where she'd played with Eileen's little boy, Nicky. Eileen had been Mom's best friend in Bootle.

Her father had lived around here too, though not in Pearl Street. Mom had told her years ago, not long before she died, that Arthur Fleming, her husband at the time Penny was born, who had later been killed in the war, hadn't been her father. Her real father had had other children, so she had half-sisters in the area, a half-brother, nieces and nephews.

Penny turned a corner and there was a bar – a public house, they called them in England. But it had been closed down and was a horrible sight, with lengths of wood nailed across the smashed windows and the broken door. Its name was no longer visible.

'Are you the King's Arms?' Penny asked the building, but there was no answer. She would have died of shock if there had been. She wandered like a lost soul around another corner and found herself in a wide road full of neglected commercial buildings. This run-down place had played no part in her long-held memories of Bootle – until something familiar about the huge walls on the far side reminded her that it was the Dock Road, the 'Docky'. It had once been the busiest road on earth, bursting with traffic, bustling with strangely dressed individuals from all five continents, and thick with the various aromas from exports and imports of every description that came and went in and out of the mighty docks.

And this was the Docky now, empty of everything; deserted. It was all very depressing.

Why had she come to Liverpool anyway? Penny asked herself. It was just that the girls, her daughters, had gone to welcome in the twenty-first century from the snowy slopes of Breckenridge, Colorado, taking with them husbands, kids and even a few in-laws. Penny and Steve had been invited, but had refused.

'Your father and I will do something together,' she had told them. Like throw a dinner party, go out with friends; something.

Except that Steve, her husband of thirty-two years, eight months and three weeks, had decided to treat himself to a new wife now that there was about to be a new century and hadn't bothered to tell his current wife until the week before. Penny was aware that their marriage had gone stale a long time ago but hadn't thought they were the sort of couple who got divorced.

Well, she wasn't going to spoil the girls' holiday by informing them that their father had decided to make a fool of himself with a girl younger than themselves. Nor did she fancy spending Millennium Eve alone in New York. No, she'd go to Bootle instead. Also, there was the vaguest memory of a promise made at a party the day the war had ended nearly fifty-five years ago.

'Let's all meet on the eve of the next century,' someone had said. Penny had been very young and couldn't remember who, only that it had been a man's voice. He might be dead by now, or at least very old. There were others, like her, too

14

young to make the promise, but maybe, like her, they remembered the words.

In Pearl Street, the woman with the stroller was returning, holding the hand of a little girl of about five who was carrying a giant red balloon. Another woman was accompanied by two boys who were somehow managing to have a balloon fight.

When she saw Penny, the first woman said in a loud voice, 'I told everyone at the party I'd just met an American woman in Pearl Street wearing a mink coat. I don't think they believed me.'

Penny smiled and pretended to pinch herself. 'I'm quite real,' she said.

Someone else had appeared in the street, a woman of about Penny's own age, formally dressed in a grey suit, walking quickly, grinning widely. To Penny's astonishment, she was also waving furiously, as well as shouting at the top of her voice.

'Penny Fleming! I just knew it was you. "An American woman wearing a mink coat." Who else could it be? Why didn't you stay at the hotel? I would have come and collected you. You were bound to get lost around here. All that's left of the old Pearl Street is the name.'

The woman stopped in front of Penny and she was seized in a strong pair of arms and almost hugged to death.

'Are you Caitlin?' Penny asked. They'd started writing to each other about five years ago. 'Your snapshot doesn't do you justice.' She was a rosy, jolly woman with a glorious smile.

'We must get computers, start emailing each

15

other,' Caitlin said. 'Did you know you can send photos by email? Only if you're very clever, mind, but we can always learn.'

'I'd like that,' Penny said with enthusiasm.

'And you're not the only one who remembered what was said at that party the day the war ended, about meeting up on Millennium Eve. It was Uncle Sean's idea; he's seventy-six but still going strong. We're expected at Nicky's house in Melling at seven o'clock. It's where we went to shelter in the worst of the Blitz. Do you remember? Nicky's me Auntie Eileen's lad, still living in the same house, like.'

'I do remember, yes. But what are you doing around here anyway?'

'I thought I told you, I'm head of St James's School in Marsh Lane. We've just had a kids' party in the church hall.' She hugged Penny again. 'Oh, isn't this the absolute gear!'

Chapter 1

Pearl Street, Bootle
Christmas Morning 1942

It was still dark, though the misty half-moon provided a little illumination and the shape of the apparently lifeless street was just about visible, the damp slates gleaming slightly. A stranger cut off from humankind for the last three and a half years would have found something odd about the windows – every single one dead black and decorated with some sort of tape stuck to the glass in a diamond pattern. The tape was to protect the glass, to keep it in one piece even if shattered by a bomb exploding in the vicinity. In fact, a bomb had landed where numbers 19, 21 and 23 used to be, making a neat gap and providing extra space for children to play. Someone had planted a tree right in the middle, and people were waiting anxiously for it to grow.

Muffled sounds were coming from the docks by the nearby river. Bangs and bumps, voices, as if activity of some sort was being carried out in the darkness, most likely a ship being loaded or unloaded. An occasional seagull squawked.

There was an air of permanence about the way every door in the street was firmly closed, as if they would never open again.

But one did, and a small child, a boy, appeared,

17

wearing striped pyjamas and carrying a scooter. His feet were bare. With an air of quiet determination he put one foot on the toy and began to scoot up and down the pavement like a tiny ghost, until a woman in a nightdress came rushing out of the still open door and shouted something in an outraged voice. She grabbed the boy by the scruff of his neck with one hand and the scooter with the other and pushed them both inside, then closed the door gently, without a sound, not wishing to disturb the neighbours any further.

And so the street remained, showing no sign of the people who lived there, until fires were lit inside, the first flames turning into narrow ribbons of smoke that puffed out of the chimneys. Children opened their presents while the grown-ups got dressed. Seeing as it was Christmas Day, most were in excellent spirits.

At number 16, Sheila Reilly was watching her house gradually being turned into a rubbish tip as her six children unwrapped their presents and let the paper and boxes drop to the floor. Fortunately, being wartime, there was little wrapping paper to be had, or the tip would have been even bigger. Sheila was nursing eighteen-month-old Oona, currently the baby but about to be overtaken by a little brother or sister who was expected to arrive very soon.

Old paper chains decorated the walls and a home-made Christmas tree stood on the sideboard. These, like everything else in the house, had previously belonged to Sheila's sister Eileen, who now lived in Melling, a village on the outskirts of

Liverpool. Sheila and her ever-increasing family had once lived at number 19, where the tree now grew, or attempted to. Fortunately, no one had been at home when the bomb had dropped.

The kids' pressies weren't up to much. It wasn't only wrapping paper there was a shortage of, but just about anything else you could think of, unnecessary things like children's toys being top of the list.

Sheila's dad had made the lads a truck out of orange boxes – Lord knows where he'd got the wheels from. He'd rubbed it down and painted it bright red. Ten-year-old Dominic, the eldest child, had decided it was a fire engine, and was now pushing it in and out of the kitchen, through the living room and into the parlour while his younger brother Niall provided the sound effects and four-year-old Ryan tried to climb inside it.

'Honestly, Sheil, I don't know how you stand it.' Brenda Mahon lived a few doors away. She and Sheila had been friends since school. Brenda had a nice face, though she knew she was no oil painting. Sheila, on the other hand, was as pretty as she had always been, though rather plumper – and it wasn't just because of the forthcoming baby. Despite her normally placid nature, the current noise was setting Brenda's teeth on edge.

'You can go home if you like,' Sheila said. 'Me, I'm used to it.' In fact, she loved it. The only thing that was stopping Christmas Day from being perfect was the fact that her darling husband wasn't there to celebrate with them. Calum Reilly, a merchant seaman, risked his life on a daily basis on foreign seas where thousands of men had already lost their lives in the freezing waters.

'I only came to make sure you're all right, Sheil,' Brenda said, hurt. She had brought her girls, Monica and Muriel, who wore identical frocks made out of a man's green velvet dressing gown that Brenda, an expert dressmaker, had bought from a jumble sale. The frocks had cream crocheted collars and cuffs. The girls cowered behind their mother, unused to such close contact with boys.

The boys had so far ignored the ribbed scarves and matching hats that Brenda had knitted for them. She'd made dolls for Sheila's girls, Caitlin and Mary, who were playing house underneath the table, where the dolls had already been fed and put to bed twice.

Turning to her friend, Sheila said, 'I was only joking, Bren. You know I love having you here.'

'I worry the baby'll come in the middle of the night or something.'

'It doesn't matter if it does. Our Dominic knows to wake up Aggie Donovan and she'll fetch Susan Lane from Coral Street. They've brought all of me kids so far into the world without a hitch.'

'I think I'll make a move then.' Brenda longed to go home. 'Are you sure you can manage, luv?'

'Sure I'm sure. You be off and start on your dinner. I can cope here.' Sheila got clumsily to her feet. 'I'll just put this one in her high chair.' Sometimes she forgot the children's names.

Brenda stood too. 'I'll be round later to help you peel the taters.'

Sheila laughed. 'Just because I'm up the stick, Bren, it doesn't mean I can't peel me own taters.

And me dad'll be round soon. He can give me a hand.'

'Your dad's not likely to peel the taters, is he? Him being a man, like.'

'I suppose not. But he'll keep the kids in line while I peel them meself.'

By now, a few children had come into the street to play with their new toys. The little lad with the scooter was riding it legitimately, properly dressed. The toy was obviously second-hand, made to look newish with a bit of spit and polish. A girl with plaits and a skipping rope was charging up and down the pavement, rather dangerously, Brenda thought, and a boy was playing with a diabolo, obviously for the first time. She herself had been asked to make the clothes for a baby-sized doll being pushed along in a pram that had been spruced up with a coat of brown paint. A couple of women had come outside for a jangle. They waved at Brenda.

'Morning, Bren. Merry Christmas,' they called.

'Merry Christmas.'

Brenda didn't go home after leaving Sheila's, but knocked at the house next door. With most houses you just pulled out the key on a string through the letter box and let yourself in, but with the Tuttys you were expected to knock.

Thirteen-year-old Freda Tutty opened the door. Her thin cheeks were red and there were tears of what looked like rage in her eyes. 'What?' she snapped.

'I've brought you and Dicky a pressie each,' Brenda explained, feeling as if she'd done something wrong. 'It's only a Juliet cap for you, luv, and a nice long scarf for Dicky. The wool's not new, like, it's from something I undid.'

'We don't want them, thanks.' The girl was about to close the door, but Brenda put out her hand to stop her.

'What's wrong, luv?' Freda wasn't inclined to accept anything that might be regarded as charity, but she'd never been this rude before. Brenda wasn't surprised when she burst into tears.

'Me mam's only come home with a fella,' she sobbed. 'She hasn't done that in ages.'

'Oh dear!' Until three years ago, Freda's mother Gladys had been a hopeless drunk, selling herself on the streets night after night; anything to get her hands on a bottle of gin, her favourite tipple. Her house was a pigsty, while her children, Freda and six-year-old Dicky, were mainly left to be fed and clothed by the neighbours.

When the war started, the children were evacuated to Southport, where Freda had learnt there was a different way of living. It was much better to be clean than dirty, for example, and wearing nice clothes was a pleasure. It was a miracle how lovely her hair looked after it had been shampooed and combed. She hadn't known it was such a nice colour. She returned from Southport with Dicky determined to change their lives.

And by sheer willpower she had done it. Her mother had more or less been forced to get a job – she worked in the Co-op grocer's on the vegetable counter – Dicky went regularly to school for a change, and Freda had done so well there that she had passed the scholarship for grammar

22

school and had been at Seafield Convent since she was eleven.

But now it seemed Gladys had returned to her old ways.

'Where did she go last night, luv?' asked Brenda. Freda usually kept a close eye on her mother's activities.

She was surprised at the girl's reply.

'Midnight Mass,' Freda said sullenly.

'She can't have picked up a fella at Midnight Mass, surely!'

'Well he's upstairs in the box room. I heard him coughing.'

'And where's your mam?'

'She sleeps in the room with me. She's still there.'

'Would you like me to come in and sort things out, Freda?'

'No, ta. I'll do it meself.' Freda reached out and took the parcels containing the Juliet cap and Dicky's scarf out of Brenda's hands. 'Thanks for the presents,' she said, closing the door.

'Merry Christmas,' Brenda wished the empty air. But she had forgotten that she still had her daughters with her.

'Merry Christmas, Mam,' they said together.

'Look, Mam, the sun's come out,' observed Monica. 'On Christmas morning an' all.' They couldn't remember it having happened before.

They held on to her skirt as they walked back to their own house. Inside, they took turns looking at themselves in their new frocks in the mirror in the parlour where their mother made clothes on her Singer sewing machine for people

23

from all over Liverpool. They stood on their toes and fluttered their arms – they'd recently started having ballet lessons.

Brenda sang happily as she began to peel her own potatoes ready for dinner. This was what she liked best, order and a quiet atmosphere. And unlike most women in the street, she didn't have to wait until after three o'clock when the pubs emptied before sitting down to eat. Xavier, her louse of a husband, had left home and would hopefully never return.

After an early dinner, seeing as the sun was out, she'd take the girls for a walk along the Docky, and when they got back they'd play snakes and ladders or ludo – she'd bought them a fairly decent set of games from a second-hand shop.

Who should she wake up first – her mam or her fancy man? Freda bit her lip. And had Mam actually gone to Midnight Mass, or had she passed some pub that had stayed open after it should have closed and been unable to resist nipping inside for a quick gin that turned into several gins, giving Mass a miss, as it were?

Halfway up the stairs, she stopped and thought. She could hear Dicky moving around in his bedroom – probably looking at his pressies. She'd managed to get him a few nice things: a little boat with a sail that he could take to the pool in the park in the summer, a bow and arrow, and a *Dandy* annual – he wouldn't mind that it was a few years old and more than a bit well thumbed. It was a pity that Brenda woman hadn't brought the scarf earlier; she could have put that by the

24

bed with the other things.

Whoever was in the box room coughed again. Freda wanted to throw open the door and order him to leave, but was worried what state he might be in. She didn't want to end up seeing things she'd sooner not. After some urgent consideration, she decided to hammer on the door and shout at him to sod off, but before she could move, the door opened and he came out.

'Good morning,' he said politely when he saw her hovering on the stairs.

'Good morning,' Freda stammered. He was nothing like the seedy individuals her mother used to bring home. He was young – about twenty-five – and wore thick working trousers, a shirt without a collar, and only socks on his feet; clearly he was not yet fully dressed. But unlike those other men, he didn't smell of alcohol or anything else disgusting.

'If I could just have some warm water for a shave, then I'll be on my way,' he said, smiling.

'Do you want to do it in the kitchen?' Freda asked, surprising herself. She wasn't usually so courteous or helpful. But his smile was really nice – charming was the word.

'Well, I'd make less mess than in here. Thank you. I'll just get my stuff.'

She returned downstairs and he followed a minute later. 'Would you like some tea?' she enquired, surprising herself again.

'Thank you. You're being very kind.' Another smile.

She pulled out a chair and indicated for him to sit at the table, thankful that nowadays the room had curtains at the windows and the furniture wasn't falling to bits. Then she fetched the teapot along with two cups and saucers. The crockery was cheap, but there wasn't a single crack in anything. There'd been a time when the Tuttys had drunk out of tins.

'I suppose you're wondering why I'm here,' he said. 'Or has your mother told you?'

'She's still asleep.' He had an accent, something northern, though she couldn't tell from exactly where.

'We met at Midnight Mass. I was expecting to stay with a friend who lives by the church, but he wasn't home. I should've gone straight into town, there's a seamen's hostel there, but I wasn't feeling so good, if the truth be known. I just had to get in out of the cold. By the time Mass was over, the trams had stopped running. Your mother asked if I was all right and offered me a bed for the night when I told her how I felt. She's very kind, your mother.' The smile again. 'My name's Tom Chance, by the way.'

'I'm Freda Tutty.' Gosh, this was civilised, just like people behaved in books. 'So you'll be off to the hostel once you've had a shave, then?'

'Straight away,' he promised.

Freda had no idea what came over her. 'Would you like to stay for your Christmas dinner?' she offered. 'We've got chicken.'

Sheila Reilly was to be disappointed if she expected her dad to arrive early and help with the children. At that moment, Jack Doyle was standing with his big feet planted in the soil of his other

26

daughter's garden in Melling, having ridden over there on his bike as soon as there was a hint of daylight. He was a man who'd lived all his life in a house without a garden, and it was like a gift from heaven to find himself in charge of half an acre of land, most particularly in wartime, when food was rationed and he could grow stuff for his friends and family. Right now, he actually felt a thrill when he bent to cut the stem of a Brussels sprout plant and carried it into the cottage where his daughter was washing dishes.

'Look at that,' he said proudly, laying it on the draining board. 'Must be at least fifteen sprouts on it – look like little green roses, don't they?'

'I suppose they do, Dad,' Eileen conceded.

'Lovely and firm.' Jack pressed a couple of the sprouts between finger and thumb, then burst out laughing. 'I've done a lot of things in me life – fought in a war, married your mother, fathered two daughters and a son – but I don't think I've ever been as pleased with meself as having grown me own sprouts and picked them on Christmas Day.'

Eileen finished washing the dishes and began to dry them. 'You're a daft bugger, Dad,' she said fondly. She looked at the sprouts. 'I can't wait to eat them. They'll probably taste better with a little lump of margarine on.'

Jack nodded. 'If you don't mind, I'll take these to Sheila's and another lot for our Sean's lot. There's plenty more out there for you – I'll pick more before I go.' He'd promised some to a couple of mates, too.

'All right, Dad,' his daughter said serenely. 'Take

27

whatever you like.'

He looked at her and frowned. 'You can always come back and have your dinner with us, girl,' he urged. He was having his at Sheila's. 'It's a bit lonely here; too quiet.' Jack was used to being surrounded by people, usually very noisy and argumentative. All that could be heard here were the birds and the very occasional car passing, though the fresh air was almost as inebriating as fine wine. He sniffed to remind himself.

'Dad!' She looked at him indignantly. 'I've got me husband here, fast asleep in bed at the moment, and Nicky is in his play pen with the blocks you made him. Nick would've been up by now if he hadn't got back so late last night – you can imagine what the trains were like from London on Christmas Eve. Then he had to walk from Kirkby station carrying a suitcase.'

'All right, luv.' He couldn't very well point out that Nick hadn't been himself since his plane crashed and he lost his arm, and the little lad was too quiet by a mile.

'Would you like some brekky, Dad?' Eileen enquired. 'The people next door with the hens gave us half a dozen eggs for Christmas. D'you fancy scrambled eggs on toast?'

Jack fancied them something awful, but he said, 'No, ta, luv. Just the toast'll do me fine, particularly if I can have jam on it.' He'd sooner his grandson had the eggs.

'I've plenty of jam – home-made,' Eileen assured him. 'I'll wake Nick up with a cup of tea. Perhaps you could go and talk to Nicky for a while. I'll bring the tea in a minute.'

A cheerful fire was burning in the large, comfortable living room where fifteen-month-old Nicky sat in his play pen with the bricks Jack had made him for his birthday.

The little boy chuckled when his grandad came in. 'Ba,' he cried and sent the pile of bricks flying. 'Ba.'

'Ba yourself,' Jack picked up the child and sat him on his knee. He really should have a bit more conversation than 'ba' at his age. He was a beautiful little boy, though, the image of his father with his dark curly hair and huge brown eyes. Nick Stephens was Greek; his real name was Nicolas Stephanopoulos.

'When's he going to learn to talk?' called Jack.

Eileen appeared in the doorway. 'Whenever he wants to,' she said. 'He talks now when he's in the mood.'

'What does he say?'

'Quite long words, like "Merry Christmas".'

Jack met his grandson's eyes. 'Say "Merry Christmas",' he demanded.

'Ba,' the little boy shouted and twisted Jack's nose.

Eileen laughed. 'He's obviously not in the mood just now.'

Nicky wriggled out of Jack's arms and began to walk quite steadily around the room. Jack got up and stood in front of the fireplace. Although there was a fire guard there, the metal would be too hot to be touched by little fingers.

Napoleon, Eileen's giant ginger cat, strolled arrogantly into the room. Jack, who didn't like

29

cats, made a face at it; he could have sworn that the animal made a face back before flopping down on the mat.

He heard Eileen go upstairs, and then the voice of his son-in-law, Nick, asking, 'Is Jack here?' When Eileen replied in the affirmative, Nick said, 'I'll have that downstairs, then.'

Jack liked and admired Nick more than virtually any other man he'd ever known. At the outbreak of war he had worked as a scientist in a local munitions factory, but had argued and fought for months to be allowed to join the Royal Air Force. Eventually he had been accepted, only to crash and lose a limb mere months later.

He was wearing a dressing gown as he entered the room now, his right arm extended to shake the visitor's hand.

'Hello, Jack. Good to see you.'

'And you too, Nick, old son. How are you feeling?'

'Really well. Exceptionally well, in fact.' There was just the faintest suggestion of a nervous tremor in his voice.

Jack didn't think he looked well at all, nor did he sound it. Nick's face was tired and drawn and he'd lost yet more weight. Jack noticed that Eileen was regarding her husband with worried eyes. There was, very briefly, an awkward silence, broken by Nicky saying, 'Merry Christmas, Daddy,' and everybody laughed.

Nick scooped his son up expertly with one arm, Eileen brought in the tea, and milk for Nicky, and the two men settled down to discuss the progress of the war, their favourite subject.

There was no doubt they were winning, Jack decided as he cycled back to Bootle, the Brussels sprouts dangling from his handlebars in a string bag. It was important that he arrive home in good time – well before midday – in order to have a wash and change into his best suit for when the King's Arms opened. Most men wore their Sunday best when they went for a pint on important occasions like Christmas Day.

He whistled now as he rode, now and then breaking into song.

'Noel, Noel,' he warbled, 'Noel, Noel...'

'Born is the King of Israel,' a woman finished for him as he turned a corner.

Jack waved to her. His children would have been surprised by such behaviour coming from their rather staid father, but Jack was feeling more hopeful then he had done in months. The war was being won; there was no doubt about it.

It was three months now since the army of the German General Rommel had fallen to the Allies led by General Montgomery. Twenty-eight thousand enemy prisoners had been taken. Not long afterwards, the Japanese had been beaten by the Americans at Guadalcanal. The Japs preferred to die than be taken prisoner, and thousands had lost their lives. Added to that, the Australians were definitely on the winning side in New Guinea, Tobruk had been retaken, and following the Allied landings in North Africa, the Vichy regime had collapsed.

'This is not the end,' Winston Churchill, the prime minister, had said. 'It is not even the

31

beginning of the end, but it is perhaps the end of the beginning.'

'And so say all of us,' Jack declared out loud as he neared Bootle. A Labour man to his bones, in peacetime he wouldn't have given Churchill the time of day, but the bloke had turned out to be an ideal war leader with an awesome gift of the gab.

It was just past three o'clock and the King's Arms had closed when most of the families in Pearl Street sat down to their Christmas dinner.

Jack Doyle was slightly unsteady on his feet when he arrived at his daughter Sheila's house, and wasn't in a state to help with anything. Fortunately, Brenda, who had already eaten, arrived in time to help, quickly boiling the sprouts that Jack had forgotten to drop off earlier. Her girls had pleaded to be left at home rather than encounter those maniacal boys again. They were looking through her Simplicity pattern book, deciding what clothes they wanted made when they were grown up.

It was still sunny outside, and what sounded like a badly rehearsed male-voice choir was singing outside the pub, accompanied by Paddy O'Hara on his harmonica. Paddy was blind and usually had his Christmas dinner with one of the families in the street.

'Who's Paddy eating with this year?' Brenda enquired as she lifted the roast potatoes out of the oven. The heat made her eyes water. The lamb would be overdone if it were left in much longer.

'I think it's Alice, our Sean's missus,' Sheila said. 'Though I don't know what got into her to offer. She's not long had a baby, she's got five brothers and sisters to look after, and our Sean's in Egypt or somewhere – some place with a desert.'

'I'll take Paddy round there in a minute,' Brenda promised. 'And Alice might like a hand.' The family only lived along the street, at number 5. She sighed. She'd be glad when everything returned to normal and she could lead her own life again. And she hoped Paddy wouldn't play his harmonica in the house. She couldn't stand it.

The Tuttys had long ago finished eating but were still at the table, playing cards for balls of silver paper – each was supposed to be worth a shilling. Tom Chance had taught them how to play blackjack and rummy. They'd played snap for a while, which didn't need teaching, but it had become boring. If the silver paper had been real coins, Dicky would have won fifteen bob. Dicky didn't enjoy himself all that often and was in his element. He had a knack for cards, Tom said. 'Some people have it, most don't.'

Tom had even helped make the Christmas dinner, actually frying the chicken in pieces and making it much tastier. He'd offered to buy a bottle of wine from the pub, but on the quiet Freda had explained that her mother had once had a problem with the drink.

'If she has a glass of wine, it might make her start again.' So Tom had bought dandelion and burdock, which Freda thought probably tasted much better.

Around five o'clock, when the sun began to set, Tom said he'd best be off. 'I don't want to leave it too late to get to the hostel.'

The Tuttys looked at each other and Freda blurted out, 'You can stay with us again tonight if you want.' She'd go upstairs later and make the room more comfortable.

'Thank you,' Tom said. 'I'd like that very much.'

The street remained full of noise until late into the night. The moon came out, a perfect half, and there was no sign of a cloud in the navy-blue sky, though there were plenty of stars. The air became colder, but no one minded. It was a magical night, perfect.

As the next day was Boxing Day, the children stayed outside longer than usual. At half past six, the King's Arms reopened and was rowdier and more packed than ever. There was dancing on the cobbled streets: the 'Hokey Cokey' and 'Knees Up Mother Brown'. More songs were sung, carols, the occasional rollicking hymn.

Brenda Mahon's children had gone to bed, so Brenda went into the parlour and sat in front of her sewing machine. The place was littered with lengths of material and half-made clothes, a whole rainbow of colours. She started to sew, finding the sounds outside surprisingly entertaining alongside the regular clatter of her machine, which always reminded her of a train.

Eventually the sounds ceased and shortly afterwards next door's clock struck midnight, but still Brenda sewed, enjoying the silence as much as she had done the noise. When the clock struck one, she decided it was time she went to bed. She was tidying up when someone tapped on her window. Turning off the light – if there was an air-raid warden around and he saw the merest chink, she could be fined – she lifted a corner of the blackout curtain. Dominic Reilly was outside making faces.

She opened the door. 'Is it the baby?' she asked.

'Mam thinks so. She ses can you come straight away.'

'Are you sure she doesn't want Aggie Donovan?' Brenda was no expert on the birth of babies.

'No, she wants you,' Dominic insisted. 'She's having pains.'

'Oh, all right.' He probably meant contractions. A woman's work was never done, she thought irritably, neither hers nor Sheila's.

In the Reillys' house, Sheila was in the front bedroom, sitting on the bed.

'Is the baby on its way, Sheil?' Brenda was short of breath, having puffed her way upstairs.

'I think so.' Sheila seemed to be listening for something, almost as if she expected her contractions to make a noise. 'Look, Bren, help us change the bedding, will you. It's been on three whole weeks. If Aggie Donovan sees it, me name'll be mud all over Bootle. It'll be like she's put an advert in the *Bootle Times* saying, "Sheila Reilly's got dirty sheets." I'd never live it down. I had a set laundered specially – they're in the bottom drawer of the wardrobe. Ordinarily I'd've washed

35

them meself.'

Brenda lost her temper. 'Is the bloody baby on its way or not, Sheila?'

Sheila's shoulders collapsed. 'I thought it was, but I think it was a false alarm. I'm sorry, Bren, were you asleep?'

'I'm fully dressed, aren't I? I don't usually sleep in me clothes. Do you want the bedding changed tonight or some other night? Make it later next time, so I'll have had a few hours' shut-eye.'

Sheila grinned. 'Do you fancy a cuppa?'

'Yes,' Brenda snapped. 'And I fancy a mince pie and all.' Sheila was the only woman in the street to have managed to buy a jar of genuine mince-meat containing real fruit.

'Then go and make it and we'll drink it up here. And you can fetch me a mince pie too.'

Brenda departed, grumbling. 'I wish I'd got friendly with some other little girl when I started school rather than the one who ended up having babies every five minutes.'

In Melling, their little boy fast asleep, Eileen and Nick had drawn back the curtains so the living room was flooded with moonlight, put an Al Bowlly record on the gramophone, and were dancing to 'Love is the Sweetest Thing'.

Neither spoke. Somehow they seemed able to communicate better when silent than when attempting to hold a conversation. Eileen had curled her arms around his neck. He had his hand in the small of her back, pressing her against him.

'I love you,' she wanted to say. But it wasn't what he wanted to hear. He didn't believe that

36

she loved him, not now that he was such a damaged human being: 'a freak' was how he referred to himself. There was nothing she could say that he wouldn't think was merely sympathy because of his condition. Where did he think all the passion had gone? Eileen hadn't thought it possible to love him more, but she did now. She remembered that tomorrow, Boxing Day – actually it was already very early Boxing Day – he had to go back to London. The train would almost certainly be crowded and he wouldn't be able to sleep, perhaps not even sit down if he couldn't find a seat.

'We should go to bed, Nick,' she murmured.

Instantly he stopped dancing, his arm falling away as if she'd just told him she couldn't stand being close to him. 'Yes, we'd better,' he said stiffly. He wouldn't touch her in bed, and if she touched him he would regard it almost as an insult, because she felt sorry for him.

'Would you like some cocoa?' she asked.

'No thank you. I'll go on up now. Good night, Eileen.' She could have sworn he almost bowed courteously, as if they'd just met. It was hard to believe how much they'd once meant to each other.

Eileen made cocoa for herself and took it to drink in the moonlit room. It would give Nick time to pretend to be asleep.

At first she'd been pleased when he'd been given a clerical job in some government office in London. It was something to do with the Royal Air Force and would take his mind off things, she had thought, give him an interest. Staying in Melling he could well become bored and feel overly conscious of his injury. But she guessed he was lonely in London. There was no one there to make a fuss of him, and the weekend journey to and from Liverpool on packed trains was onerous and wore him down. She'd suggested he come home just once a month, but he'd smiled cynically as if she was saying she would prefer to see him less often.

'I'm sorry, darling, but it's seeing Nicky every week that keeps me going,' he'd said coldly.

Eileen finished the cocoa, took the cup into the kitchen to wash, then went upstairs. As usual, she climbed carefully into bed so as not to disturb Nick, though she knew darn well he was wide awake.

Next morning after breakfast, she and Nicky went with him to Kirkby station. She put the little boy in his big pram; although nowadays she mainly used his pushchair, this way Nick could put his suitcase on the pram, saving him from carrying it.

They walked down the slope to the platform. Their conversation on the way had been stilted. Eileen couldn't think of anything to say, and she assumed Nick couldn't either. She felt horribly relieved when she saw the white smoke of the train as it approached. Then horribly sick as it got nearer and she knew that she wouldn't see him again for another five or six lonely days.

Having him home was an ordeal, but seeing him leave was enough to break her heart.

Chapter 2

January 1943

There were thousands and thousands of streets similar to Pearl Street in the cities, towns and villages of Great Britain, yet each was unique in its own special way. It wasn't just the architecture but the inhabitants that distinguished them from each other.

Pearl Street had twenty-three terraced properties on each side, the front doors leading directly on to the pavement. Each small back yard housed a lavatory and a washhouse. Some of the wash-houses had been turned into basic bathrooms, tool sheds, workshops or pigeon lofts.

About halfway down the street, the row of houses on both sides was interrupted by a narrow entry that led to the neighbouring streets as well as to behind the back yards where dustbins were left to be emptied by corporation workmen. These narrow, squalid passages were used by innocent courting couples, as well as prostitutes and their clients. They were also the place where someone might be taken for a good beating, and were occasionally the scene of a murder – this had definitely been the case in some of the more violent parts of Liverpool.

There was one thing in particular that made Pearl Street and the streets nearby differ from most others, and that was the twenty-foot-high wall at one end, behind which electric trains ran to Liverpool one way and Southport the other, turning the streets into cul-de-sacs. A piece of chalk could magically turn the ugly wall into goalposts or a set of wickets. Girls could play two-balls against it, or even three-balls if they were skilful enough.

Until recently, most of the residents had lived in the street their entire married lives, had even been born there, but since September 1939, when the war began, people came and went by the minute, or so it seemed to the more permanent residents.

Eileen Costello, for example, who was now Eileen Stephens and had lived in number 16, had met a chap from Greece who'd joined the air force and had gone to live in Melling. Eileen's first husband, Francis Costello, had been killed in the raids along with their little boy, Tony. Some people thought that Eileen still hadn't got over losing Tony. Eileen's sister Sheila and her kids had moved into the house when number 19 had been bombed.

And Miss Brazier from number 10, a real sour old maid, had gone mad all of a sudden. Throwing caution as well as her old maid's clothes to the wind, she'd dyed her hair blonde, joined the army and been transferred to Scotland. Months later, it was rumoured she had married a sergeant.

Just before the war began, Mary and Joey Flaherty and their kids had gone to live in Canada, and later the Evanses had moved to Wales to live with relatives. Dear old Mr Singerman from number 3 had lost his life in one of the worst of the

40

raids. His daughter Ruth and her husband had been living in his old house ever since. The war had made a widow of Jessie Fleming, but she'd since married a Yank with a funny surname and was living in Burtonwood until the conflict was over, when she and her little daughter Penny would move to the United States. Jessie came and went from the street like a yo-yo, having lived there on three separate occasions, most recently in Miss Brazier's old house.

Now, two other women were living in number 10: the Taylors, mother and daughter. Mrs Taylor was about forty and her daughter looked as if she hadn't long left school. Both wore black a lot, as if someone close to them had recently died, presumably Mr Taylor. No one knew why they were there, or where they had come from. They were a quiet pair and were keeping themselves very much to themselves.

At least they were until Aggie Donovan managed to trap the daughter directly outside the house, where she questioned her mercilessly for a good half-hour.

'Her name's Phyllis and she's from some place near Hull.' Aggie later confided breathlessly to Brenda Mahon. 'Her mam's a nurse and she's got a job in Bootle hospital. And you'll never guess why they've come.'

'Because the mother's got a job in Bootle hospital?'

'No.' Aggie glared at her neighbour. 'It's something else. Guess.'

'I'm hopeless at guessing,' Brenda confessed.

'Her dad, Mr Taylor,' Aggie said in a hushed

41

voice, 'came to work in Bootle after the war started and has never been seen since. He just disappeared off the face of the earth,' she finished dramatically.

'I know a Mr Taylor in Southey Street,' Brenda said. 'He's about a hundred years old.'

'It's not him, they've checked,' Aggie said impatiently. 'They think he might have got caught up in an air raid and lost his memory, like. It was in a picture, *Random* something.'

'*Random Harvest*,' Brenda supplied. 'With Greer Garson and Ronald Colman. I saw it last year.'

Aggie dismissed this observation with a wave of her well-worn wrinkled hand. She had lived almost eighty years without having seen a single picture and was none the worse for it. Anyroad, real life was far more interesting. 'They're just going to wander round Bootle looking for him,' she told Brenda. She rather liked the phrase. 'Wander round,' she repeated.

'He might be dead,' Brenda remarked.

'In that case, someone would have told them; a copper, like. I mean, he'd have had his identity card on him.'

Brenda agreed that this would have been likely. She escaped from Aggie and went to relay the news to Sheila, while Aggie looked for someone else to tell.

The Taylors weren't the only new arrivals in Pearl Street. The house at the top of the street used to be the dairy, but now that the country was on rations and people were required to register with a single grocer, it couldn't exist selling nothing but milk. So the dairy closed, the farmer's son who ran it and lived upstairs returned to live on the farm, and a billeting officer in Birmingham arranged for a Mrs Lena Newton to take over the flat. It had been swiftly redecorated and some items of new furniture provided. The dairy part was left empty.

The street had already decided that Lena was as plain as the proverbial pikestaff. With her frizzy brown hair, round glasses and evidently nervous disposition she looked rather like a lost owl. Most people found this rather endearing, so it wasn't all that surprising that she'd managed to cop a fella – to prove it, there was a wedding ring on the third finger of her left hand.

Back in Birmingham Lena had been employed as secretary to an accountant, but had recently been directed by the Ministry of Labour to work for the manager of a small engineering firm in Hope Street, Liverpool, which manufactured propellers for the Royal Navy. His need of a secretary was far more urgent than that of a mere accountant – what were *they* doing towards the war?

The move suited Lena ideally. Her husband, Maurice, was a merchant seaman and Liverpool was the port to which he returned most frequently. It meant that when he was on leave they could spend more time together.

Lena was a shy person who didn't make friends easily. She willingly told Aggie her entire life story in the hope that she would pass it around and people would come and befriend her. It was Aggie who told her about Brenda Mahon being a dressmaker, and Lena decided to approach her and order two frocks, a winter one and a summer one. It was a good way of becoming part of the street.

More than anything she wanted to get to know the woman with the new baby who she'd noticed passing her flat, the infant hardly to be seen beneath its mountain of bedding. She was hoping the woman would become a friend and let her hold her new son or daughter. A baby – several babies, in fact – was what Lena wanted more than anything else in the world, but despite having been married to Maurice for ten whole years, there'd been no sign of her falling pregnant.

Tom Chance was still living with the Tuttys. He had got a job as a barman in a pub on Marsh Lane and handed over ten bob a week to Freda for his keep. He'd offered it to Gladys first, and Freda had to tell him that it was she rather than her mother who was in charge of the household finances.

'I don't want her tempted into buying gin,' she told Tom, now officially their lodger. A single bed and an extremely narrow chest of drawers had been bought second-hand and installed in the box room. Brenda Mahon had been called upon to make curtains.

'I'll have the place wallpapered when the weather gets warmer,' Freda promised.

Tom nodded gravely. He was the perfect lodger, never making a noise or a nuisance of himself in any shape or form. And he helped prepare the meals. He seemed to know ways of making the food more tasty, like mashing the potatoes and turning them into little cakes to roast in the oven, and adding a pinch of curry power which he bought from somewhere to the gravy.

At school, Freda thought about him during boring lessons like science and needlework. She had a feeling she was falling in love with Tom Chance. If he was still around when she was sixteen, she made up her mind she would marry him.

In February, Calum Reilly came home from sea with six days' leave ahead of him. For the first two, he slept solidly, waking occasionally to kiss his children, introduce himself several times to his new daughter and make love to his wife. They both realised that it wouldn't be such a good idea for Sheila to fall for another baby so soon after the last, so they reluctantly took precautions. Neither liked the idea of him having to withdraw at the very last minute, but it had to be done.

'Seven children is enough for any man, never mind the woman,' Cal said gruffly. 'And you lost one, didn't you, luv? That would've made eight.'

'I wouldn't mind eighteen,' Sheila said wistfully and not all that truthfully. The new baby, Mollie – called after Sheila's mother – was wearing her out. She'd quite like to rest for a year or so before starting again.

A few days later, Lena Newton was seated by the table nursing the new baby, now six weeks old, and marvelling at how perfect she was. It had turned out to be easy to make friends. Brenda, the dressmaker, had mentioned her best friend

Sheila's new baby, Lena had asked if she could see her, and Brenda had taken her to the Reillys' there and then. 'Sheila loves visitors,' she said.

Calum Reilly was still there and actually remembered coming across Maurice Newton, Lena's husband, on a ship once.

'He joined when he was eighteen,' Lena told Calum.

'So did I.' Calum smiled. 'It's a small world, the merchant navy.'

His children were crawling all over him, making the most of him before he went away again. Sheila was watching them, her eyes bright with happiness. Lena looked down at the tiny baby in her arms and thought how perfect their lives were. When next Maurice came home, there would be just the two of them. And although she would be pleased to see her husband, it wasn't the same without children.

She was invited to go with Sheila and the children to Melling next time they went. 'You can meet our Eileen and her little boy, Nicky. If it's the weekend, then Nick will be there, her husband, and our dad'll be doing the garden. You can meet them too.'

In London, Nick Stephens sometimes wondered if his job in the War Office had been invented specifically for him. Someone somewhere had felt sorry for him and arranged for him to sit in a room in an office in Dover Street, off Piccadilly, and make lists of statistics, as well as a record of news items from the press and the wireless and debates in Parliament that were in any way concerned with the Royal Air Force. He couldn't imagine what use the statistics were to anyone and was convinced he was being paid to waste his time.

The someone somewhere who was keeping an eye on him obviously felt the same about him as did Eileen, his wife, in whose eyes he could see nothing but pity because he wasn't a real man any more, just as he was no longer a member of the Royal Air Force.

In case this was true, he was often tempted to give up the position, but what would happen then? He couldn't get another job, not a real one, not with only one arm. He would have to live in the cottage in Melling, live with the endless pity showing in his wife's eyes.

One evening late in February he emerged from the office in Dover Street and made for Piccadilly and the basement bar where he would spend the next hour – or possibly two or three – getting totally plastered before making his unsteady way back through Green Park to his lodgings in Birdcage Walk. There he would fall into a drunken slumber, waking up with a hangover that wouldn't disappear until lunchtime the following day.

God, this was an awful life! Was he destined to live like this until the bloody war was over? And the terrible thing was that even then he genuinely couldn't think of a single thing he wanted to do. Flying a plane had always been his ultimate ambition. Nothing else held any interest.

The streets were dark – properly dark, that is, as black as a night could be without a moon, a star or a single speck of light to be seen. There was something about the lack of light that made him lose his sense of balance, so that he felt lopsided. Traffic lumbered past, ghosts of buses and cars and the occasional lorry. He was worried about crossing the road, staying upright. If he wasn't careful he'd lose his other bloody arm. If he was lucky, he might be killed and there'd be nothing at all left to worry about.

Except there was Nicky, his son. He wanted to see Nicky grow up, become a man. And there was Eileen, his beautiful wife, who he would never stop loving.

'Oh, sod it,' he said out loud.

'Is that you, Nick?' A woman's voice he vaguely recognised.

'Yes,' he said curtly. 'Who's that?'

'Doria Mallory. I work in the office next to yours. Do you mind if I hold on to you? I'm absolutely lost here. Have you any idea where we are? I always lose track the minute I step outside the building.'

'Opposite Charlie's, I reckon.' If you turned left coming out of Dover Street, it was twelve paces down.

'Charlie's?'

'It's a bar. I'm hoping to go there if I can get across the road.'

'Oh, may I join you for a drink? That would be wonderful. A gin and It is exactly what I need right now.'

'Are you old enough to go to pubs?' She didn't sound it.

'I'm eighteen; nearly nineteen.'

'Oh, all right then.' He would have preferred

48

her to go away once she had helped him across the road.

She was unfortunately on his left side, which meant she had to hold on to the empty sleeve that he normally tucked in his pocket. Somehow they managed to get to the other side of Piccadilly all in one piece and Charlie's was quickly located, next door to Osborne's, an exclusive gents' tailors. Nick lifted the curtain for his companion – he had already forgotten her name – and let it fall before opening the door and being met by the sound of the music coming from below.

For Nick, the music held almost as much attraction as the drink. It was New Orleans jazz, being played at its loudest on a gramophone: Bunk Johnson, Kid Ory, Louis Armstrong. Listening to King Oliver play 'Canal Street Blues' was an experience of which he would never tire.

'Gosh, I like the music,' his companion said. 'Is this what's called jazz?'

'New Orleans jazz,' Nick told her. So far there were only a few people in the bar, but it would quickly become crowded. He led the way to a table some distance away from the entrance.

The young woman smiled as she sat down. 'You've forgotten my name, haven't you?'

'Yes,' he was forced to confess.

'Oh well, it's not surprising when I told you it under such chaotic circumstances,' she said kindly. 'It's Doria Mallory. And the Doria isn't a variation of Doris, which I hate, but the feminine form of Dorian, which is Greek.'

'My mother and father are Greek,' Nicholas told her. They had gone to Canada at the start of the war and he hadn't seen either of them since.

'My parents are as British as an oak tree, but my mother was determined to give her children names that she – and she presumed everyone else – had never heard before. My brothers are Pierce, which is also Greek, and Fabian, which is Roman.'

'I've heard of Fabian. I think Shakespeare had a Fabian in one of his plays.' He couldn't remember which one.

Doria laughed. 'I shall write tomorrow and tell her – my mother, that is – that she's not as clever as she thinks she is. Oh, and Pierce calls himself Peter, which rather annoys her.'

'I don't blame him.' Nick was actually enjoying the sheer triviality of the conversation. The waiter, Albert, who Nick knew well, came and asked what they'd like to drink. He added a knowing wink and the suggestion of a grin when he glanced at Doria. Nick had never brought a woman here before.

Nick ordered a gin and It and a Pimm's. The evening called for more than his usual whisky and soda.

'Yes, sir,' Albert said with another wink.

After he'd gone, Nick looked properly at Doria for the first time, while she searched for something in her handbag. He was taken aback by how pretty she was, how absolutely perfect. Her hair, curled tightly in childish ringlets, glinted like gold in the subdued light of the bar. Her wide, innocent eyes were bright blue and her cheeks a delicate pink. She was the ideal woman to be seen with to incite the envy of his male friends. Her picture would have looked well on an expensive box of chocolates.

50

She looked up and caught him watching. Perhaps she saw the admiration in his eyes, because she said, 'You're not so bad yourself, Flying Officer Stephens.'

He could have sworn he blushed. 'Call me Nick,' he said. 'And I'm no longer in the forces.' After losing his arm, he hadn't expected any more flattering comments on his attractiveness to women. 'How long have you worked in Dover Street?'

'Eight months,' she said accusingly, tossing the ringlets. 'I've been trying to catch your eye since my first day. In fact, I've been flaunting myself in front of you quite outrageously, but apparently you didn't notice.' She made a face. 'You didn't even know my name.'

'I do now,' he assured her. Albert came with the drinks and Nick picked up the Pimm's and drank it as easily as if it were lemonade. That was the trouble with fancy drinks; he found them impossible to sip slowly like whisky.

'I followed you tonight, you know,' Doria said, blue eyes sparkling. 'I thought to myself, if the mountain won't come to Muhammad, then Muhammad must go to the mountain – it goes something like that, doesn't it? It wasn't by chance I asked if I could cross the road with you. It was part of my plan – I only hatched it when I noticed you passing my office to leave.'

'I'm married.' He felt he ought to be honest about his position right from the start, in case her plan included having him as a boyfriend – though he couldn't imagine why any young woman would want to.

'I know,' she said. 'Your wife and child are in Liverpool. All the girls know that, but it still doesn't stop us from trying to capture the most handsome man in the office while he's living in London.' She licked her lips and looked at him slyly. 'And not only is he handsome, but a hero to boot.'

She was flirting with him! Nick couldn't remember the last time he'd flirted with a woman. His relationship with Eileen had been deadly serious right from the start. She'd been married to a man who was a beast, and her little boy, Tony, whom Nick had grown to love as a son, had died in an air raid along with his father. It had all been so tragic – and it was still tragic now. When had they last laughed? Would they ever laugh together again?

He signalled Albert and asked for a whisky and soda. He had a strong and pleasurable feeling about what the evening had in store for him, and he knew he'd need quite a few drinks in order to play his part.

He felt guilty next morning when he woke to find Doria Mallory stark naked in his bed. It had come as a shock as well as a relief to discover that she wasn't a virgin; that at the age of eighteen she had done this before – how many times? he wondered, and was glad he hadn't been the first.

His guilt, though, wasn't great enough to cancel out the pleasure he had experienced, which had made him feel like a man again.

On 4 March, the submarine *Thunderbolt* was

sunk off the coast of Sicily with the loss of all hands. It wasn't the first time this ship and its crew had been destined for an early death, for the sub's original name was the *Thetis*, and it had sunk in Liverpool Bay on its first trial voyage three and a half years before. Ninety-nine people had died that day, most of them from Liverpool. The vessel had been raised, refurbished, and christened *Thunderbolt*, but it must have been cursed and it sank a second time. It was another terrible tragedy for the people of the city.

Chapter 3

On the first Sunday in March, Sheila Reilly went to see her sister Eileen in Melling, taking baby Mollie for her first big outing. Her other six children went with her, along with Brenda and her two girls, and Lena Newton, who had been looking forward to the visit for weeks. Lena really enjoyed making herself useful by carrying Oona and helping Mary and Ryan, still only toddlers, on and off the buses and trams.

'I'm afraid Nick isn't home,' Eileen said when the guests, all twelve of them, arrived at her pretty cottage.

It was still quite early, and little wisps of mist hung over the garden, where the trees were sporting a faint coating of green, heralding the fact that spring was on its way. Lena could see a man hard at work, digging like fury and throwing the soil to one side. He was well into his fifties but ruggedly handsome. This, she discovered later when they were introduced, was Jack Doyle, Sheila and Eileen's father. They were a handsome lot, the Doyles – there was a son, too, Sean, who she had yet to meet. Lena felt over-conscious of her plainness and her ugly round glasses, though it didn't usually bother her.

Eileen, who she was meeting for the first time, had a smooth, quiet beauty, though her blue eyes were incredibly sad. Nick, her husband, worked

54

in an office in London. There'd been a bit of a crisis, she explained, and he'd had to stay for the weekend.

'Didn't the same thing happen the week before last, sis?' Sheila remarked.

Eileen's head drooped like a flower. 'Yes, apparently it's the same crisis come back to haunt them, Nick says.'

'Let's hope it doesn't come to haunt them a third time,' Sheila said bluntly. 'It must be dead lonely for you and Nicky being in this place on your own.'

'I like it here, Sheila,' her sister said quietly.

Lena felt sure they would have had an argument about it – at least Sheila would – had there not been other people present. Then Nicky, Eileen's son, came running into the room, and he was such an endearing little boy that Lena couldn't stop herself from picking him up and giving him a hug. Being among these women, all younger than she was, all with children, made her own need rise like a ball of pain in her throat. But all she could do was blink back the tears.

It was nearing Easter, and Eileen was hosting a garden party on Easter Saturday, as she had done since moving to the cottage. 'You're invited, of course,' she said to Lena. 'Are you any good at making stuff like gloves and embroidered things to sell? Mind you, food sells best – fairy cakes, scones, cheese straws – though you'll only be getting rations for one, won't you. You won't have anything to spare.'

'I can make dolls,' Lena said eagerly. 'I'm really

good at making rag dolls. The place I worked in Birmingham used to have a summer fete. One year I made a really big doll and it was a raffle prize.'

Eileen looked pleased. When she smiled, it was dazzling and made Lena feel that she would do anything on earth to please her. 'That would be very helpful, Lena,' she said. 'I'll make a note that you're providing the raffle prize. Oh, and don't forget to ask Brenda for some scraps of cloth.'

The midday meal was eaten round a big wooden table that took up almost half of the long room that served as a living and dining room. There were beams on the ceiling, lace curtains at the windows, daffodils on the sills and bottles of preserved tomatoes and plums on the table. Sheila had brought half a pound of boiled ham, Brenda a small tin of corned beef and Lena a large bag of toffees and dolly mixtures. 'I hardly ever use my sweet coupons,' she explained, and Sheila said that would certainly make her popular with the children.

There was a groan when Eileen placed a loaf in the centre of the table with a loud thump.

'Oh no!' Sheila said.

'I don't want any, Mam,' Caitlin cried.

Jack Doyle, who'd temporarily abandoned the garden for something to eat, said sternly, 'It's good for you, girl. In fact, it's full of goodness. It's called the National Loaf.'

'But it's dirty,' Caitlin argued.

'Of course it isn't dirty,' her grandad said indignantly. 'It's that colour because the husks are in there as well as the wheat. A slice of that, girl, will do your belly a load of good.'

Caitlin regarded him disbelievingly. 'Won't it make me belly dirty too?'

'Your belly will do somersaults when it sees that bread on its way down.'

'Oh Dad!' Sheila said, exasperated. 'I don't like that horrible stuff either.'

Jack reached out, cut himself a huge chunk of the offending bread, covered it with margarine, added almost a tablespoon of home-made gooseberry jam and stuffed it in his mouth. 'Mmm! It's the gear,' he mumbled.

'I think I'll just have the jam, Mam,' said Caitlin.

It had begun to grow dark when they left to go back to Bootle, not quite time for the start of the blackout. Jack had returned to the garden and Eileen, with Nicky in her arms, stood in the doorway waving goodbye.

'She looks so lonely standing there,' Sheila said sadly. 'I'm worried about Nick. He's had to stay in London a few times before, but never twice in a single month. I hope things are all right between them. Nick lost his arm when his plane crashed,' she explained to Lena.

'How awful,' Lena gasped. But so romantic too; just like a film.

That night, reluctant to stay in on her own, she went to the pictures to see *Three Smart Girls* with Ray Milland and a new actress called Deanna Durbin, who had a voice like an angel. She sang 'Someone to Care For Me,' a song with the most beautiful words.

Lena walked back to the house in Pearl Street in the blackout, singing the song inside her head and feeling as if parts of her that had been asleep before were being woken up by new emotions. She hadn't realised how dull her life had been until now.

Did that mean she considered Maurice to be dull? Surely not! Yet he didn't possess the cheerful good looks or outgoing personality of Calum Reilly, or the gritty attraction of the much older Jack Doyle. As for the absent Nick Stephens, there'd been a photo of him and Eileen on their wedding day in the cottage, and he was as handsome as a film star – as well as a genuine war hero. Beside them Maurice was – well, she couldn't say exactly what attributes Maurice had when compared to these other men.

Anyway, he was coming home next week – well, not exactly home, but to Liverpool – and Lena realised that she wasn't looking forward to seeing him nearly as much as she usually did.

She was approaching Pearl Street when a man's voice called from behind, 'Hello there. It's Mrs Newton, isn't it?'

Lena turned. The man caught up with her and raised his hat. 'George Ransome, I live quite near you,' he said politely. 'Number seventeen.'

She could just about make him out in the milky moonlight. She didn't feel nervous; there were other people about. What was more, she recognised him, having noticed him some mornings leaving his house just before she did herself. He was fifty-ish, with a Clark Gable moustache and a

58

rather wolfish air. Smartly dressed, he could have easily just stepped out of a Burton's tailors' window. Someone must have told him her name.

'Good evening,' she said.

'What did you think of the picture?' he asked.

'Oh, were you there? I really liked it.'

'So did I. It took me mind off the war for a couple of hours. I think they're called "escapist", those sort of pictures.'

'Are they really? Well, that's true enough. I didn't think about the war once while I was watching.'

'Do you go often to the pictures, Mrs Newton?' They had stopped outside the old dairy.

'Most Sat'days,' she said. She wouldn't have minded asking him in for a cup of tea, but it seemed terribly forward; he might get the wrong idea.

He tipped his hat again. 'Perhaps we'll see each other again next week. *The Cat and the Canary* with Bob Hope and Paulette Goddard is showing. It's a comedy – I saw it at the Palais de Luxe in town when it first came out.'

'When I was in Birmingham, I sometimes went to see the same picture twice,' Lena confessed. 'Good night, Mr Ransome.'

'Good night, Mrs Newton.'

He stood there until she had unlocked the door and gone inside. Lena was sure he would have appreciated being asked inside for a cuppa, though of course he might have a wife indoors who he couldn't wait to get back to.

Nick was at a party. It was being held in the top flat of a four-storey house in Queen's Gate and

59

was so crowded it was virtually standing room only. Apparently an equerry to the King or someone of equal importance lived on the ground and first floors and a woman who made clothes for well-known actresses on the second.

Everyone was drunk, Nick included. He was propped up against the wall, attempting to overcome the inclination to slither down and sit on the floor, where people would stand on him or fall over him. Though at least then he would be out of sight of the fair-haired chap standing opposite, who had been watching him for ages. If you could describe a gaze as 'truculent', then his was. He was a little younger than Nick, and not wearing a uniform. Despite having drunk far too much, Nick was trying hard to remember who the chap was. He felt sure he wasn't from the office, nor had they been in the RAF at the same time. Perhaps they'd never met and the man merely didn't like the look of him, had hated him on sight, in fact. Or maybe he just didn't like people who only had one arm.

Doria was dancing in another room. Dancing was something else that made Nick lose his balance; not waltzes, where you could hold each other up, but quicksteps and rumbas. The 'Hokey Cokey' was the worst. For that you definitely needed all four limbs.

Doria didn't mind if he refused to dance with her – quite frankly, Nick wouldn't have cared if she did. He wasn't in love with her and assumed she wasn't with him. It was just that there was a war on and it was the sort of thing that happened. People behaved in a way that, ordinarily, in peacetime, they would have avoided like the plague.

The pianist finished a tune and began to play 'We'll Meet Again'. Nick's heart almost stopped beating. It was *their* song, his and Eileen's. He closed his eyes, and there they were, back in that hotel in London, dancing together, Tony asleep upstairs.

And oh, it was heaven, an utterly perfect moment. Except ... except that was the night he'd had a word with some RAF bigwig, pleading with the chap to get him into the forces. Eileen hadn't been pleased, understandably. Anyway, the man had obliged, Nick had been delighted, and as a consequence he was now standing here minus an arm and Eileen was pretty damn mad with him for having joined up.

Someone came and stood beside him. 'Are you all right?' It was Doria. She really was a sweet little thing.

Nick opened his eyes. 'I'm fine,' he said stoutly. 'Absolutely fine. Do you mind if we go in a minute?'

'Not at all, darling. I'll just fetch my coat.'

The fair-haired man who'd been watching Nick from across the room saw them leave. He was concerned that several hours had passed without Doria, his sister, noticing he was there. She must have entirely forgotten that it was he who'd invited her to the damn party in the first place. He had not been introduced to her new boyfriend. It was obvious she was so besotted with the chap that normal civilised behaviour was quite beyond her.

Despite her young age, Doria had 'been around', to put it bluntly, though she'd never been serious about a chap until now. It was common knowledge that Nick Stephens had a wife and child back in Liverpool. The man might be a hero, but he was also a bit of a scoundrel it would seem.

Pierce Mallory, known to everyone except his mother as Peter, had been turned down for active service due to having broken both legs in a riding accident when he was fourteen. He too worked in an office in London, and saw his sister frequently, or he had done until recently, when Nick Stephens had come into her life. Peter hoped he wasn't being priggish by not liking the idea of Nick, a married man, and Doria becoming a 'pair'. He knew that it was the sort of behaviour people indulged in in wartime, but now that one of these people was his baby sister, he decided that he'd had enough of it. It should be easy enough to acquire Stephens's address in Liverpool and have a word with the wife, who was being made a fool of virtually every single day.

Lena put her heart and soul into making the doll for Eileen Stephens's garden party. Brenda Mahon had let her have her pick of the small oddments of material kept in a box in her sewing room. Lena had chosen nothing but white satin. It was going to be a bride doll!

She made the doll itself out of old stockings stuffed with sawdust acquired from the landlord of the King's Arms. She cut a little circle of white cloth and on it very carefully embroidered eyes, nose and a little red mouth, then attached lengths of brown wool over the scalp to make hair.

The long dress had puffed sleeves and a frilly neck. Lena spent ages embroidering white flowers around the hem. She made white satin shoes tied with a white bow. There wasn't a veil to be had, so she made a bonnet instead, and a little white cloak. She even managed to fashion a bouquet of sorts out of knots of embroidery silk that looked like flowers with green stems.

The day before the party, Lena laid the finished doll on the table. She would have loved to have had such a doll when she was small. Eileen would be thrilled to bits, she just knew it.

Chapter 4

The men who were fighting the war, often in horrendous conditions, would sometimes complain that the population at home, the ones they were fighting it for, seemed to have forgotten all about them. In the early days they only had to enter a pub in uniform to have drinks thrust at them from every direction. Now they weren't even noticed. Instead they were met with complaints about having to live in such a state of extreme austerity. People were hungry (only the most basic foods were available in the shops); they were cold (there was a shortage of every single type of fuel). How were they supposed to cook without saucepans? Had anyone seen a saucepan or a kettle on sale in recent years? And with the house cold due to lack of fuel, it would have been nice to go to bed under an eiderdown, but eiderdowns (and blankets) had disappeared off the face of the earth, along with everything electric, every sort of make-up, hairclips, hairnets, hot-water bottles and most children's toys. As for alarm clocks, there had never been more of a need for these, what with people working shifts that started at all different times of the day and night. Their unavailability could only be the fault of a government that had servants to wake them up when necessary and had no idea what an alarm clock was.

It was the shortage of so many ordinary things that made the garden party held this year on Easter Saturday in Eileen Stephens's garden at first glance resemble a scrap yard rather than an ordinary village event. There was a reasonable amount of mouth-watering home-made cakes and jam, bottled fruit and jars of chutney. But the main focus of attention was the white elephant stall, for which people had raided their attics and sheds, discovering the odd stone hot-water bottle, pairs of rusty shears, bits and pieces of cutlery that urgently required a good polish, odds and ends of dishes, some cracked. There was even a battered old alarm clock that looked as if it had been thrown against a wall more than once.

Items that would once have been chucked away without a second thought had become valuable beyond belief. It no longer mattered if cutlery and crockery didn't match. The rusty shears could always be sharpened; the hot-water bottle hopefully wouldn't leak; the alarm clock could be mended, or at least used as an ornament to remind its new owner what alarm clocks used to look like in days gone by. Nearly everything was sold for a good price within the first few minutes.

The second-hand clothes stall received equal attention from women looking for garments that, even if they didn't fit, could be remodelled into something else, or knitted items that could be undone, the wool washed and knitted again. Curtains that would normally have been torn up for dusters sold extremely well.

The raffle prizes were laid out on a pasting table: a single lemon, a bottle of Drene shampoo, a tin of

Fry's cocoa, a dartboard with Hitler's backside the target, a fruit cake and, sitting proudly in the middle, Lena's doll. Brenda Mahon was selling the tickets.

It was a reasonably nice day for April. A bit breezy, a bit cold, the sun in and out by the minute, but it was the first outdoor event of the year, a prelude to the summer that lay ahead. There was even a bee buzzing around to prove it. Music came from an open window – Eileen had been loaned some classical records, and a fine baritone voice sang 'La donna è mobile' and 'Toreador' and other well-known operatic airs. The atmosphere was uplifting, making everyone there feel convinced that the war could actually be won that very weekend.

In the small tent where tea was being served, people chatted gaily, unaware that any minute now the tea would run out and from then on there'd only be Camp coffee or lemonade made from the fizzy powder that cost tuppence an ounce in the sweet shop. In an even smaller tent, Madame Nirvana, who normally worked as a barmaid in the local pub, told fortunes at threepence a time, predicting the most hilarious futures.

Eileen and Sheila were in the kitchen making more sandwiches and discussing the doll, having ensured that Lena was safely outside manning the book stall.

'Everybody's making fun of it,' Sheila said. 'I mean, the poor thing is as ugly as sin and its face is all wrong. It squints.'

'Oh dear.' Eileen wanted to laugh, but it would have been cruel.

'What shall we do? I was talking about it with Brenda. The prizes aren't rated, like first or second. If you have a winning ticket you can pick anything you like. She's worried the doll might be the last thing to be chosen and Lena will be really upset. She did go to an awful lot of trouble with it. I know that if I won, I'd prefer virtually everything else on offer before I'd choose that awful doll.' She narrowed her eyes and her voice throbbed with passion. 'I'd kill for the lemon,' she said with a sigh.

'We'll just have to cheat,' Eileen announced.

'How?' Sheila looked at her sister in amazement. 'I'm not nearly as nice or as honest as you, sis, but I've no idea how to cheat in a raffle.'

'Make sure someone we know buys a ticket – they can't all be sold yet – then put a safety pin in the half that goes in the box with the counterfoils. *I'll* pick the winner, seeing as it's my garden party. I'll just have to root around till I find the one with the pin in. We can't get me dad to win it, he's far too honest, and Brenda's selling the tickets so it'll look as if something funny's going on if she wins the first time. Ask the vicar to come in, and I'll sort it out with him.'

'You're a bloody crook at heart, Eileen Stephens,' Sheila said admiringly. 'And you've corrupted the vicar an' all. You'd never have managed that with a Catholic priest.'

Most people went home at tea time, but Eileen's family and friends stayed to tidy up the garden, then sat and chatted about the day. Tea had become available again, and the remains of the

67

food was eaten.

As soon as the local pub was open, Jack Doyle went and bought a jug of cider. A rather nice young man, very handsome, with thick fair hair, who'd been one of the first to arrive at the event, was still there and went with Jack for a supply of proper lemonade for the kids. His clothes were well cut and obviously expensive: a hairy green sports jacket, flannels and an open-necked shirt. His heavy brogue shoes looked hand-made.

'What's your name and what are you doing here?' Sheila asked when the two men returned. She had three children, including the baby, asleep on her knee, and another lying on her feet. Dominic and Niall had gone on some adventure of their own and Caitlin had disappeared too. Brenda seized the lemonade and took it into the kitchen to pour it out.

'I'm Peter Wood,' the young man said. 'I came up from London to see my old uncle Jimmy, who I'd been told was at death's door, only to find he's gone to North Wales for the weekend with his bowls club.'

'And where does your uncle live?'

Peter Wood waved vaguely somewhere behind him. 'Not far from the post office. The last train to London doesn't leave Lime Street until five past ten, so I thought I'd spend a few hours in the countryside for a change.' He treated them to a winning smile. 'I'm glad I did, otherwise I would have missed your party.' He turned to Eileen. 'Is it a party or is it a fete?' he enquired.

'It's a garden party.'

'It was very enjoyable – and I think I might have

acquired a working alarm clock. It was worthwhile coming just for that.' He patted his bulging pocket. 'I also won a bottle of shampoo that my sister will appreciate.'

'Lucky old you,' Sheila said. 'You must pop in and see our Eileen if you come back to visit your uncle. If you come on a Sunday, I'll probably be here.' She might be madly in love with Calum, but it didn't stop her from appreciating other attractive men who happened to be around.

Peter Mallory (years ago he'd gone to school with a Peter Wood) agreed that he might well visit Eileen again. He'd been planning to pretend to miss the connection from Kirkby to Lime Street, spend the night in a pub somewhere and turn up tomorrow, Sunday, but had overheard Eileen tell her father that Nick was expected home in the afternoon.

'He's overwhelmed with work,' she had said, which Peter knew was a lie, not, he felt sure, on Eileen's part, but on the part of her lousy unfaithful husband. Nick Stephens and Doria had gone to Brighton for the day. Peter hoped it had rained and they'd had a perfectly horrid time. He hadn't realised the pair didn't intend to spend the entire Easter weekend together. Perhaps Stephens had a conscience after all, and realised he should spare a little time for his wife and son.

Peter was enjoying his visit. It wasn't often he mixed with the working classes, and this Liverpudlian crowd had really charmed him. They were called Scousers, he recalled, because they ate so much scouse stew, though he himself had

69

never tried it. Jack Doyle, the paterfamilias, as it were, was the salt of the earth. A docker, he was an expert on the war and all the nuances that surrounded it, though they'd had quite a heated argument about Joseph Stalin. Jack seemed to think the chap a great liberating hero, whereas Peter considered him little better than Hitler, just fortunately on the side of the Allies.

The weather had been more or less decent, and it also wasn't often that he sat outside and experienced the end of the day. With British Double Summer Time in place, darkness was late in coming. By midsummer it could still be light at midnight.

The most important thing was that Peter was in love, had been from the first moment he had set eyes on Eileen Stephens and Nicky, her little son. Okay, so she was married and the child wasn't his, but he felt convinced that fate had ordained them to be together for always. What Nick Stephens saw in Peter's empty-headed little sister compared to his own beautiful wife, Peter had no idea.

He could never, ever hurt Eileen by telling her about her husband's reprehensible behaviour, though he hoped that she would find out one day. When that time came, he would ensure that he was on hand to comfort her – and Nicky.

Chapter 5

Lena had left the garden party at the same time as most of the other guests, even though Brenda had suggested she stay behind and have a cup of tea.

'That way we can all go home together,' she'd said.

'Sorry, but I'm meeting someone later,' Lena had replied. She hoped she hadn't sounded as miserable as she felt. It had been impossible not to notice the hilarity that her lovely doll had been met with. People had pointed it out to each other and burst out laughing. She had expected when the raffle took place for not a single person to choose it, for it to be left there, ugly and unwanted.

It had been a big relief when the vicar had been the first raffle winner and had picked Lena's doll. He had actually given it a hug and kissed it, and everyone had cheered.

Once home, Lena made tea and wondered what she would do with herself tonight; she hadn't expected to be home so early. With Sheila and Brenda still in Melling, there was no one else that she could call on.

The furniture in the flat felt strangely oppressive, as if it was about to fall down on top of her. She supposed the only thing to do was go to the pictures. Although she loved the pictures, it seemed a bit pathetic to go so often on her own. In Birmingham, she'd had a friend, Enid, to go with. Enid's husband was in the army.

She went into the kitchen, where she washed her face, combed her hair and looked at her reflection in the mirror on the windowsill. How nice it would be to be pretty; or really talented like Brenda Mahon with her dressmaking. She had grown up used to being plain and not particularly clever at anything, though she was quite a fast typist and good at shorthand. As she continued to stare in the mirror, becoming more and more miserable, she was relieved to hear a knock on the door. At least it was someone to talk to, even if for only a few minutes.

George Ransome was outside. He removed his hat when she opened the door. 'I wondered if you were going to the Palace tonight?' he said with a smile. The Palace was the picture house in Marsh Lane, only a short walk away.

'Well, I was thinking about it,' Lena conceded.

'It's that picture about American politics. It's had wonderful reviews.'

'I know, *Mr Smith Goes to Washington*, with James Stewart. I saw it in the Echo last night.' She'd also read an article about it in the *News of the World*.

'Jean Arthur's in it too.' He rubbed his hands together with enthusiasm. 'She's my favourite actress. Claudette Colbert is a close second.'

'I like them too. And James Stewart.'

He shuffled his feet. 'I just wondered,' he said casually, 'if it would be a good idea if we went to see it together. We've noticed each other coming out and walking home a few times now, and it

72

seems silly, like, us living in the same street and going to the pics on our own. What harm would it be us doing it together?'

'I'm married,' Lena said simply.

'Yes, but we'd only be going to the pics. There'd be no funny business.'

'I should hope not!'

'We'd be going as friends,' he said cheerily. 'Good friends.'

Lena chewed her lip. 'I'd have to pay for myself,' she said eventually.

'That's no problem, Mrs Newton.'

'And you must always call me Mrs Newton, not Lena.'

'That's all right by me, and I will always be Mr Ransome to you.'

'Absolutely.' Lena nodded fiercely. 'If you'd like to wait outside a minute, I'll just go and get my things together.'

'I won't move from the spot, Mrs Newton.'

Lena went upstairs to fetch her best coat. She'd asked Brenda about George Ransome after the first time he'd spoken to her on the way home from the pictures.

He was a bachelor, Brenda had explained. She supposed he was about fifty. 'Before the war, every Sat'day night without fail, he'd have these dead rowdy parties lasting all night long. Christ knows what went on in there, but the noise had to be heard to be believed.'

Lena felt herself flush. 'Oh my goodness!'

'When the war started, he was too old to be called up, but he was sent to work for the censorship department in Aintree, not far from here. He takes it very seriously,' she said gravely, 'and the parties stopped. He became an air-raid warden too. It was George who found Francis Costello and little Tony when the house they were in was hit by a bomb. Both of 'em were killed, poor sods. Poor Eileen, she was devastated, and George has never been the same since.'

Brenda had folded her arms, crossed her legs and said thoughtfully, 'Me, I lost interest in men when Xavier went and married another woman down in London – became a bigamist, would you believe – but if I should ever get interested in men again, I wouldn't mind having a go at George Ransome. His moustache makes him look a bit like Clark Gable, only thinner. If he asked me out, I'd go like a shot.'

Mr Smith Goes to Washington was really inspiring. After it was over, Lena wondered aloud that it was possible for women to go into politics.

'Would you do it?' George asked. 'Go into politics, that is?'

'For goodness' sake don't be so ridiculous.' Lena laughed.

'There's a few women in the British Parliament,' he informed her. 'There's Ellen Wilkinson, Jennie Lee and Lady Astor – that's three. There's probably more, but I can't remember their names.'

'Really?' He appeared very knowledgeable. She liked men who regularly read newspapers, not just the sport like Maurice, who was mad on football.

'Do you fancy a drink, Mrs Newton?'

'Well...' Lena fancied a drink if only so they could go on talking, but she rarely touched alcohol. 'I wouldn't mind an orange cordial or a cup of tea.' She felt so uplifted and moved by the picture that she didn't care if they were seen together. As George had said, they were friends, that was all.

'I'm afraid, Mrs Newton,' he said regretfully, 'there are no cafés round here open this late. I wouldn't dream of inviting you into one of the local pubs, but there's a nice place on Stanley Road called the Crown. It's a hotel as well as a public house, and the clientele are entirely respectable. Would you care to go there?'

They'd been standing outside the Palace all this time, in everybody's way as they left. He held out his arm for her to link, and she felt it would be awfully rude not to take it, so she did.

Although Tom Chance's job as a barman kept him busy of a night, most mornings he caught the tram into town, where he stayed for hours, sometimes not coming home until it was time for tea.

Freda was unable to hide her curiosity for long, and one day just after Easter, when she was still on holiday from school, she couldn't resist asking him what he did there.

'Have you got another job in town?' she enquired. He was about to leave the house with a khaki bag like a satchel on his shoulder. Having seen him unpack it from time to time, she knew it contained a collection of pencils, some of them coloured, and a notebook.

'No.' He smiled. Freda loved his smiles. She reckoned he kept his best ones for her. The ones he gave her mother and Dicky she was convinced weren't quite so broad, and didn't always reach his eyes. 'I was thinking of writing a history of Liverpool. All I do is walk around and around making notes and drawings.'

'A history of Liverpool!' She was impressed. She'd never thought of the city having a history. It was just *there* and she couldn't imagine it ever having been different – which, now she thought about it, was rather foolish.

'Liverpool is one of the most important cities in the world and has been the first to do so many things,' Tom went on. 'For instance, it was the first to have a lending library, a lifeboat station, municipal trams and electric trains – which reminds me, the first railway tunnels in the world were built underneath you-know-where.'

'Liverpool,' Freda breathed.

'Where else?' Tom laughed. 'Why don't you get your coat and come with me? You'll be back at school soon. I'm sure your mother won't mind.'

Freda didn't give a toss whether her mother minded or not. She collected her coat, wishing it was much smarter and a nicer colour than navy blue, and they set off. They caught a tram from Stanley Road into town. Tom paid her penny fare when she realised she hadn't thought to bring money.

On the way, he told her that the Queensway Tunnel under the Mersey, linking Liverpool to Birkenhead, was sometimes described as the Eighth Wonder of the World. 'Oh, and the first British person to win the Nobel Prize was called Ronald Ross, and he worked at the Liverpool School of

Tropical Medicine – which, incidentally, was the first school of its kind...' He paused and looked at Freda, eyebrows raised.

'In the world,' Freda said triumphantly.

'Right! Oh, we're going to have a fine old time, you and me.'

They got off the tram outside St George's Hall. 'The finest neoclassical building in all of Europe,' Tom said.

'Not in the world?' queried Freda.

'No, there must be some just as fine elsewhere, just not in Europe.'

Freda had seen it before but it hadn't made any impression on her until now. As she watched Tom, hands on hips, regarding it with a mixture of wonder and admiration, a ray of light seemed to shine on her brain and she saw the building, with its long row of marble pillars, as a thing of incredible beauty, almost making her want to cry.

'Now I'm going to take you around the Seven Streets of Liverpool – these were the first important streets of the city. They're many centuries old. Some of the names have changed, but they were originally called Castle Street, Bank Street, Juggler Street, Dale Street, Chapel Street, Moor Street and Whiteacre Street.'

Freda felt quite tired by the time they'd walked all seven streets, Tom stopping from time to time to point out a particularly spectacular building. When he put his hand on her shoulder it felt lovely and warm and heavy and she wished he would leave it there for ever. He did leave it for a little while, leading her towards a café in White-

77

chapel where they had dinner, though Tom called it lunch. They both had fish and chips and peas, followed by jam tart with custard and a big mug of tea.

'That was the gear,' Freda said when she had finished. 'Thank you,' she added shyly. It was rare that she thanked anyone, but this time she did it with total sincerity.

'And thank you, Freda, for accompanying me on my trip today. In a way, you've made me see things through different eyes and I am more impressed with Liverpool than ever.'

He leant across the table and squeezed her hand. If she had been older, Freda was convinced he would have kissed her. She just knew, could sense, that she and Tom Chance were made for each other and they would get married one day.

That night she designed her wedding dress.

A few days later, the holiday ended and Freda returned to her convent school. Her class, Form 4, had their first English lesson of the term that same morning. The girls were asked to write an essay on any event that had occurred during the week-long break.

'Any small incident, a friend or relative's visit, for instance, or your visit to them,' suggested Sister Bernadette, the English teacher. 'I would like to have the work in before the end of the week.'

That night Freda went into the parlour, where it was quieter, to write the essay, taking her dictionary with her. One of the neighbours – it might have been Eileen Costello when she used to live next door – had given her the dictionary when she had passed the scholarship and gone to Seafield Convent.

Although she didn't mention Tom, she described her trip to Liverpool and the sights she had seen, using the information he had provided her with to emphasise what an important city Liverpool was, how innovative and alive, how it was famous throughout the world. She listed the seven streets and said she had walked along every single one, and that it was her intention to do it again. Dicky might like to go one of these days; even Mam might enjoy it.

The essay was returned in class marked 9½ out of 10. Sister Bernadette called Freda to her desk. She was a young nun, good-humoured and friendly. Everybody liked her.

'This is an admirable piece of work, Freda,' she said. 'Where did you get the idea from?'

'Our lodger,' Freda admitted reluctantly, unable to think of a way of claiming it was all her own idea.

'It's so good that I would like to enter it for a prize. Liverpool Corporation have asked schools to submit essays from their sixth-form pupils, the subject being the city in which they live; in other words, Liverpool.'

'But I'm not in the sixth form yet,' Freda pointed out – as if Sister Bernadette didn't already know.

The nun shrugged. 'That might not matter. No one in our sixth form has come up with this notion of the Seven Streets. I really like that. Oh, and Freda, your essay would have earned ten out of ten had you pointed out that Liverpool isn't exactly the exemplary city you describe.'

'Isn't it?' Freda was astonished to hear it.

'No, dear. It was one of the first cities to have something called a wet dock. That means it was prominent in the slave trade. Many thousands of black people were taken via Liverpool to the United States to become slaves. The conditions on the ships were deplorable, and once the slaves arrived, they were treated with appalling cruelty. Liverpool became rich through this awful business, and it's something the city should be greatly ashamed of.'

'I see,' said Freda.

She returned to her desk feeling both proud and as if she had been taken down a peg or two.

Chapter 6

Summer had arrived. On a warm and sunny Sunday early in July, Jack Doyle was thrilled to see that the lettuces he had planted earlier in the year in Eileen's garden in Melling had grown at least another inch and would soon be ready to be eaten. As someone whose lettuces in the past had always originated from the greengrocer's, growing them himself was something akin to a miracle.

Tiny apples and pears had appeared on the fruit trees and gooseberries on the bushes. There was even a handful of strawberries, strictly meted out one at a time to Sheila and Brenda's children, and of course Eileen's son Nicky. Eventually, blackberries would appear on the prickly bushes at the bottom of the garden.

It had been a hard sacrifice to make, but Jack no longer took sugar in his tea, giving it instead to Eileen to make jams and pies. The pastry was rather hard because it didn't have enough lard in it, but Jack loved to see Eileen lift a sweet-smelling crusty fruit pie out of the oven, or witness the jars of delicious home-made jam, of which he was always the first recipient.

It cheered him up tremendously, feeling that no matter what Hitler did, the British people would make the best of things. The men would fight their hardest and the women would keep the home fires burning, as the song said.

It worried him that Nick wasn't home so often nowadays. He wasn't sure what his son-in-law did down in London; something highly confidential and very important, he imagined. Perhaps it was connected with the recent invasion by the Allies of Sicily, the final step before reaching Italy and mainland Europe.

Jack knew he wasn't the only one to wish with every fibre of his being that this bloody war would soon be over. It was a wish shared by every single person in the country.

Eileen watched from the kitchen window as her father, brow furrowed, stood beside the lettuces, lost in thought. One of the few good things that had come out of the war was her marrying Nick and moving into his cottage, thereby letting her dad loose on the large amount of land that went with it.

She wondered if, having lived his entire life in small terraced houses with only a tiny scrap of back yard, he'd always missed having a garden. He'd taken to it as if it was something he was born to, growing vegetables like an expert. The fruit bushes and some of the flowers – the hydrangeas, carnations, delphiniums and poppies – came up year after year and might have been there for ever, for all she knew. Perennials, Dad called them. Their scent was heady and overpowering, as if she had entered a different land. On summer mornings, when she drew back the kitchen curtains and heard the birds already chirping madly in the trees, Eileen quite expected to see elves and fairies playing in the

82

wisps of mist on the patch of lawn outside.

Mostly the vegetables her father grew were given away – virtually every house in Pearl Street had benefited from the produce Jack Doyle had grown on his daughter's land.

Directly outside the window, Nicky was playing in his sandpit. The sand had come from the beach at Formby; a friend of Nick's had brought it before he'd had to give up his car when petrol became restricted to vitally important people like doctors. It was about time they acquired more sand and she reckoned that was Nick's job, not hers. *She* didn't know anyone with a car. But it was Sunday, and yet again he wasn't coming home.

Eileen sniffed and blinked in an attempt to prevent herself from bursting into tears. Something was wrong, it must be. It wasn't just that now-adays he only came home to Melling once a month when it used to be once a week, but once here, it was obvious he'd come to see his son and not his wife.

Could he have met someone else? Did he have another woman down in London? It was impossible to believe. Just thinking about it made her catch her breath, almost choke with disbelief. Not Nick, not the man to whom she had given herself for ever, in sickness and in health, in every single conceivable way. She had imagined them together in the cottage; extending it when they had more children, growing old here.

She watched through the window as Nicky left the sandpit and made his steady way down the garden, calling, 'Gwandad!' He was having trouble with his r's.

Her father pushed the spade into the earth so that it stood on its own and held out his arms as the little boy approached.

'You're a great little lad, Nicky Stephens,' she heard him say. He picked up his grandson, threw him over his shoulder and came marching up the garden towards her, Nicky squealing with delight.

They arrived at the open kitchen door. 'Where's that bloody husband of yours?' demanded Jack, making Eileen want to cry again, though her father would cringe with embarrassment if she did.

'He has loads of work to do,' she muttered. 'He's overwhelmed with it.'

'You said that last time I asked – or it might have been the time before.' He nodded towards the hall. 'If I call him on that thing in there, will he answer?' He meant the telephone, which he only used occasionally because it made him nervous.

'He's not allowed to take calls in the office,' Eileen said.

'Then how the hell do you speak to each other?'

'It's not really allowed, but he can call me when the woman on the switchboard goes for her dinner and some other woman takes over who doesn't mind. There isn't a phone in his digs.'

'Has he called over the last few days?' Jack put Nicky on the floor and the boy immediately tried to climb back up his legs.

Eileen hung her head as if she'd done something wrong at school. 'No,' she whispered.

'Bastard,' spat her dad. 'I never thought I'd use

that word about Nick Stephens.'

Eileen lost her temper. 'And you shouldn't now,' she snapped. 'Something might be wrong and he doesn't want to worry me. And what makes you think he isn't genuinely overwhelmed with work?'

Her father's cheeks were red with anger. 'Then he's been overwhelmed a bloody long time. What's wrong with him? Have you asked him straight? If you haven't, then next time he deigns to show himself, I suggest you do. If you won't, I'll do it meself.'

'Oh go away, Dad. Leave me alone. Anyroad, I've got to get ready for Mass.' She picked up Nicky and almost ran out of the kitchen, slamming the door behind her.

Ten minutes later, when she and her son were ready, she returned to the kitchen intending to apologise, but her father wasn't there, nor was there any sign of him in the garden, or of his bike.

Things couldn't go on like this. When Nick had first started not coming home as much as he'd used to, he'd always phoned to let her know. But now he no longer bothered. Twice he had turned up unexpectedly on a Sunday afternoon, as if he'd found himself with time to spare and thought he might as well go home and see his wife and child, even if it only left him with a couple of hours in Melling before having to return to London.

Mass over and back home again, Eileen sat down and wrote him a letter. It was the only way she could be sure of getting in touch. She had no intention of begging and making herself sound

85

pathetic. That wasn't the sort of relationship they had. If she couldn't talk to him – *write* to him – as if she was an equal partner in the marriage, then she wouldn't write to him at all.

In the letter, she merely asked, calmly and politely, what was going on – *was* something going on? She didn't ask if she had offended him, or he had gone off her – that would have been demeaning. Just a simple question: what, if anything, was wrong?

Her father had left and Sheila wouldn't be coming over today; there was something happening at Sunday School that her children and Brenda's girls were involved in. Eileen would have gone to Bootle to see them, but there was always a chance that Nick might turn up unannounced, as he had done before.

She had no alternative but to stay at home with her son for company. In fact, Nicky was jolly good company, but short on conversation. They went outside and sat on a bench together, and in a very short time, Nicky laid his head on her knee and fell asleep.

There was no getting away from it: despite the little paradise in which she now lived, she missed Bootle, where she had lived cheek by jowl with her neighbours, where the only thing that met her eye when she drew back the curtains was a brick wall, where everyone knew her business. Were she still living in Bootle, there were at least a dozen people she could have called on and the same number who might have called on her. Had Nick turned up when she was out, someone would know where she had gone and would tell him. Paradise could be lonely at times.

She'd get a lodger, she decided. She'd let out the second bedroom where Nicky usually slept; he could sleep with her for the time being. There was a munitions factory in the village. She had been working there herself when she'd met Nick, and it was where one of her best friends, Kate Thomas, was employed. Kate was in charge of the welfare of the female workers, who came from all over the country. She found them places to live and dealt with their various problems. She was bound to know someone who needed somewhere to live.

She felt guilty at the idea of taking in a lodger for company rather than out of compassion, but she would leave the woman, whoever she was, entirely to her own devices. It was just the idea of another person living in the house that attracted her.

Eileen had almost fallen asleep herself when she became aware that someone was knocking on the front door. She carefully removed Nicky from her knee and laid him on the bench, then went to see who was there.

At first, she didn't recognise the young man standing outside, though his blond hair looked familiar.

'I'm awfully sorry,' she stammered, 'but...'

'It's Peter Wood,' he said helpfully. 'I was at your garden party'

'Oh, I remember, yes.' She stood aside to let him in. 'Have you come to Melling to see your uncle again – is he at home this time?'

'Yes, but he's got friends there, so I thought I'd come and see you – and your sister with all the children – how many is it?'

'Seven. She has about one a year. But she wasn't able to come today. Look, would you like to go into the back garden? Nicky's out there, asleep. If he wakes up, he's likely to fall off the bench.'

She led him through the house, putting the kettle on to boil on the way. Peter Wood might prefer a cold drink, but she was more than ready for a cup of tea.

'Do you have just the one child?' he enquired.

'Now I do, yes. I had another son, Tony, but he was killed in an air raid when he was six, along with my first husband.' It upset her and probably embarrassed people when she said that, but she wasn't going to deny Tony's existence for anyone's sake.

'I'm so sorry.' He sounded as if he really meant it.

Peter disliked using an alias, deceiving her. He tried to remember why he wasn't able to use his real name and recalled that it was in case she mentioned to her despicable husband that a Peter Mallory had been to the house; the husband would put two and two together straight away. Today, Stephens and Doria had gone to a party somewhere in the wilds of Suffolk, so Peter had known he wouldn't be coming to see his wife and son.

His relationship with Eileen was starting off with serious complications. Lord knew how it would end. But even if he had to remain Peter Wood for the rest of his life, he was determined to make the beautiful Mrs Stephens his wife at some time in the future. He decided not to think too closely about what he would say to his parents and the rest of his family when that happened, for how could he possibly tell Eileen the truth?

An hour later, Eileen had another visitor. Having learnt that Sheila didn't intend going to see her sister today, Lena Newton had summoned up the courage to go to Melling herself. She had checked with Sheila that there was no likelihood of Eileen's husband being there. 'I wouldn't want to be in the way,' she said.

'You wouldn't be, because he's not going to be there. He's *overwhelmed* with work,' Sheila snorted. 'Personally, I think he's up to something, but I wouldn't dream of suggesting that to our Eileen. She'll be dead pleased if you go and see her, Lena. I worry about her feeling lonely, stuck out there all on her own, I really do.'

Lena was able to buy Nicky a little present, a tiny teddy bear only five inches tall that was for sale in a sweet shop for just sixpence.

She was mortified when she arrived to find that Eileen already had a visitor – the handsome young man who'd been at the garden party – but there was no denying that Eileen was glad to see her. 'I'm finding it difficult to entertain him,' she whispered when she let her in.

The conversation was much easier with three people, and just after half past two, a third caller arrived. Jack Doyle, feeling guilty for having left the cottage earlier in a huff, had returned to make things up with his daughter. He had spent the intervening hours in the King's Arms and wobbled his way to Melling on his bike.

The two men argued fiercely over the war and the way it was being conducted. Jack thought it would all be over in a year, whereas Peter considered it would take at least another three. Eileen and Lena made faces at each other and smiled. Politics aside, the men seemed to be getting on famously.

It turned out to be an exceptionally pleasant afternoon. The sun got no warmer and was ideal to sit under on a lazy Sunday afternoon. Although Eileen loved her sister visiting, her seven children plus Brenda's two could often be overwhelming – just like Nick's work, she thought ironically.

While Jack was showing Peter around the garden, she and Lena went into the kitchen to make sandwiches and were at last able to have a conversation. Lena turned out to be a big fan of the pictures and had seen all the latest films.

Eileen confessed she hadn't been for ages. 'In fact the last time I went was to see *Gone With the Wind.*'

'I've seen that twice,' Lena said. 'I could easily sit through it again.'

'Well I've only seen it the once, and even then I didn't manage to get to the end. I went with two of me friends and one only decided to have a baby right in the middle.'

'Oh no!' gasped Lena.

'Oh yes! Actually, it was Jess Fleming – she's Jess

Henningsen now, after marrying an American major. She's lived on Pearl Street on and off. Now she's in some village by Burtonwood. Once the war's over, they're moving to America – New York.' She looked at the slices of bread she'd cut that were only faintly smeared with margarine. 'Do you think cress will be enough for proper sarnies? These look awful miserable as they are.'

'They'll probably taste nice and fresh. Anyway, it's the company that counts, not the food.'

'What a lovely thing to say, Lena.'

Lena flushed. 'Well, it's true.'

'When are we going to meet this husband of yours? What's his name?'

'Maurice. He's been to Liverpool twice but couldn't stay more than a day and a bit.'

'Next time he comes, let us know and we'll have a party. We'll all help with the food.'

'Thank you.' Lena didn't say that a party was the last thing Maurice would want when he came home.

'Oh, and by the way, thank you for the teddy bear. Nicky loves it.' The bear had been christened Pip and the little boy had been nursing it all afternoon.

The men appeared, Jack Doyle bearing half a dozen bright red tomatoes. 'These are ripe, luv.' He handed them to his daughter and asked Lena if she'd like a couple to take home with her.

'You can have some too,' he added to Peter Wood, 'if you don't mind taking them all the way back to London.'

'I don't mind a bit. They look very wholesome. My London friends will be very envious.'

They sat down to cress sandwiches, tomatoes, home-made tomato chutney, and gooseberry tart. Eileen apologised for not having enough milk to make custard, and for the sparseness of the meal.

Peter declared it absolutely delicious. 'Do you mind if I come again?' he asked Eileen. 'Is it open house on Sundays?'

'Saturdays *and* Sundays,' she replied.

'What about if your husband's here?'

'Oh, Nick just loves company. He wouldn't mind. But,' she added sadly, 'I have no idea when he'll next be home.'

'I see. Would it be possible to have your telephone number? I really would like to call and make sure it's all right first.' Lord, he felt like a cad, deceiving her like this.

'I'll give it to you before you go,' she promised.

It was five o'clock when Lena got up and announced it was time she left. 'I'm going to the pictures tonight with a friend,' she said to Eileen.

Peter Wood got to his feet and stretched his arms. 'I'll come with you. I sometimes forget I have to change trains in Liverpool to catch the one to London. I won't get home until well after midnight.'

'I don't go as far as the station,' Lena explained. 'I catch a bus to Walton Vale, then the tram to Bootle.'

'I shall see you to the bus stop,' Peter said with a smile and a little bow.

Eileen frowned. 'Will you have time to say ta-ra to your uncle Jimmy?' she asked Peter.

'I said a proper goodbye earlier when I left to come here.' Peter was glad Eileen had mentioned his non-existent uncle's name; he had totally forgotten what he'd called him. He must remember for next time he came.

Lena felt as if she was playing a small part in a romantic drama set in Liverpool; either a film or a play, she wasn't sure. On the way to the bus stop, Peter Wood talked of nothing but Eileen. He waited with her until the bus came.

Throughout the afternoon, Lena had noticed the appreciative looks Peter had bestowed on Eileen. He had listened to her with such a soppy look on his face, she'd almost wanted to laugh. It was as if everything Eileen said was some sort of golden prose that demanded extra special attention. Lena would be amazed if he wasn't head over heels in love with her.

Eileen didn't appear to be aware of Peter's fascination with her. Lena supposed that men fell in love with her all the time, so much so that she stopped noticing. It had never happened to Lena, who wasn't even sure if her own husband loved her all that much. He was forty-one, ten years older than she was, and they'd lived next door to each other since Lena had been born. He'd only proposed after his mother died. Lena's own mother claimed he just wanted a woman to look after him when he was home from sea.

'Turn him down, girl,' she'd urged, but Lena was twenty-one, and until then no man had even asked her out, let alone proposed. Anyway, it wasn't so much a husband she wanted as children.

However, there'd been so sign of a baby in the ten years she and Maurice had been married. What was more, he had turned out to be a terrible crosspatch, something she had noticed even more since they had been seeing each other more frequently in Liverpool. Lena was forced to admit that her mother had been right. Sadly, Mam had died five years ago, though she'd stayed alive long enough to see her prediction about her daughter's husband come true.

The following morning, Eileen telephoned Dunnings Munitions. The factory was only about ten minutes' walk away, in the village. She asked to speak to Miss Thomas, who answered her extension immediately with a crisp 'Good morning.'

'Good morning, Kate. It's Eileen.'

'Eileen! I've been meaning to come and see you for weeks. How are you? And how are Nick and Nicky?'

'We're all fine, thank you.' After the little lie, Eileen explained the reason for her call – letting out one of the bedrooms, but only to a woman. 'I never thought about it before, but it'd be really convenient for someone working at Dunnings – but not the sort of woman who'd want to go out dancing and partying every night. The buses are few and far between and it's a bit of a walk to Kirkby station.'

Kate promised to look into it. 'I'll give you a ring back when I find someone – I might even come and see you one lunchtime, if that's all right.'

'I'm looking forward to it, Kate.'

94

On Tuesday, Nick found Eileen's letter on the doormat in his digs in Birdcage Walk, along with post for the other tenants of the building. He recognised her writing and his stomach gave an unpleasant twist. In the past, a letter from Eileen would have been a reason to feel joyful, but this wasn't likely to be a good letter, no matter what it said. If it was complaining about him hardly going home these days, it would be a bad letter. If it was as nice as pie and she was emphasising how much she loved and missed him, then it would still be bad, because it would make him feel guilty. *More* guilty. He felt guilty enough as it was.

He didn't open the letter until he was at his desk. When he did, he discovered that it was an Eileen letter. Written neatly, it didn't complain or demand; it asked in a clear and simple way if something was wrong. If there was, she would like to know what it was so that she could do something about it – 'if possible, that is', she added. In other words, she had no intention of humiliating herself.

If he was so completely overwhelmed with work, she went on, perhaps she and Nicky could come to London and stay for a few days, meet him at dinner time and after work, possibly stay with him in his digs if there was enough room.

'We could go for a walk through Hyde Park like last time,' she suggested. The letter finished 'All my love, Eileen (and Nicky).'

It was dated Sunday, and he imagined her writing it in the late evening as darkness fell on the cottage. He also remembered the last time they had been in London together, him and Eileen and Nicky.

No! Not Nicky, but Tony, the little boy she'd had with that brute of a husband. Tony, poor dear Tony, such a lovely child, lost now, just like the love he'd once had for Eileen.

But was that true? Nick groaned, then turned it into a cough when he remembered he was in the office and other people could hear. He had no idea if it was true or not.

Doria appeared at lunchtime with a picnic basket containing sandwiches, cake and a flask of coffee, which they would eat in Green Park just across the road.

'Are you all right, darling?' She touched his face. She looked smart and pretty in a green linen Utility frock.

'I'm fine.' He smiled.

'You look pale. You know, next Sunday I really do think you should go and see your wife. I could tell you were worried about it the entire weekend in Suffolk. It's not fair on her.'

'You mean tell her I'm having an affair with you?'

'Not if you don't want to. Just go and see her – and your little boy. I wouldn't mind spending a weekend at home with the family. I haven't seen Peter in ages – I think he might have got a new girlfriend that he's keeping under wraps.'

'I've never met Peter,' Nick remarked. 'At least not properly. We haven't been introduced.' They'd been at the same party once, but had never spoken. That would never have happened in Liverpool, where no one was allowed to be a stranger.

He sighed. Next week he'd go and see Nicky. And Eileen.

On Wednesday, Kate Thomas turned up at the cottage at ten in the morning – lunchtime at Dunnings, where the shift started at six o'clock, as Eileen knew from the time she'd worked there.

Kate and Eileen had met at Dunnings. Eileen had been having problems with her violent husband and Kate had confessed that her own husband, a prominent lawyer, had been brutally cruel to her. She had fled her home, leaving not only her thug of a husband but her three daughters too. The girls had had no idea what had been going on.

Kate was a tiny woman, with no idea of fashion. Today, despite the warmth of the day, she wore a too-long tweed skirt and a heavy cream blouse. Her nice brown hair looked as if it hadn't been combed for weeks.

She had brought a small amount of tea with her. 'There should be enough for a pot for two, with two cups each,' she said as they went into the kitchen. The back door was wide open to the sunny garden and Nicky was playing with his wooden blocks while clutching Pip, the teddy bear Lena had brought.

'I've found you a lodger,' Kate announced.

'Is she new? Is she nice?' Eileen enquired.

Kate made a face. 'She's me, actually, if you don't mind. You know they took my car off me? Well, not my car, but my petrol allowance. They – being those persons in authority who make

97

decisions affecting ordinary people like you and me – decided I didn't really need petrol. As you know, I frequently have to take girls to hospital for one reason or another, or to see a doctor, or to sort out difficulties they might be having with landladies, et cetera. I've been taking them on the bus, or by ambulance if it's something serious. But it's affected me personally. None of the Dunnings special buses run from near where I live, so I need to move somewhere more convenient, and what could be more convenient than here?' She waved her arm around the kitchen. 'If you don't mind, that is. You might prefer a stranger, rather than a friend.'

Eileen smiled delightedly. 'Oh, I definitely prefer a friend – especially if the friend is you,' she cried. 'When can you move in?'

'Today?' said Kate.

'Today it is.'

Lena Newton and George Ransome had continued to meet in the dark of the Palace picture house, afterwards taking themselves to the Crown hotel in Stanley Road. George had also started occasionally visiting Lena in the evenings at around nine o'clock. By then, the children of Pearl Street were safely indoors, and the men were installed in the various pubs in the area and wouldn't emerge until after closing time. With hardly anyone around, there was little chance of him being noticed.

As an extra precaution, he went down the entry and through the back of the old dairy where Lena quickly opened the door and let him in, worried that someone would notice and automatically assume that they were having an affair.

'I've brought the latest American *Cinematographer* to show you,' George would say, or he would share a titbit that he'd read in a newspaper, sometimes even bringing a cutting – he bought two papers a day, the *Daily Herald* and the *Manchester Guardian*, and read them from cover to cover. His favourite pages covered the film reviews.

A few days after Lena had spent Sunday at Eileen's house, he arrived at just past nine o'clock, smartly turned out as always in a well-laundered shirt, navy-blue pinstriped trousers and a paisley-patterned tie. It was still warm and he was without a jacket.

Lena had been acutely aware of Peter Wood's desperately obvious feelings for Eileen and the sense of unrequited passion in the air. There was a different but equally obvious feeling in Sheila's house when Calum, her husband, was home, though there was nothing unrequited about their love for each other. Lena had never experienced anything like this throbbing sensation of love and lust and need. George Ransome would probably have a fit if he thought the neighbours had somehow got the idea that he was having an affair with Lena, but now, in a funny sort of way, she didn't mind.

This time he brought with him the latest edition of the American magazine he'd brought before. A chap at work had a brother in the merchant navy who'd got it in New York, and George was allowed to borrow it for a few days each month.

He showed her pictures of various stars, including Franchot Tone, and Betty Grable with her heavily insured legs, then read out a paragraph saying that Joan Fontaine had just been signed up to star in *Frenchman's Creek*, based on the Daphne du Maurier novel. He looked up. 'Remember Joan Fontaine was in *Rebecca?* Have you seen that picture, Mrs Newton?'

'No, I missed it,' Lena said regretfully.

'They show old pictures at the Palace on Sundays. If it comes, we must go and see it. Which reminds me' – his tobacco-coloured eyes lit up with enthusiasm – '*Alice Adams* is on this coming Sunday, with Fred MacMurray. It was made years ago, but I never mind seeing a really good picture twice or even three times; in fact I quite enjoy it. Hattie McDaniel's in it too – you know, the black maid in *Gone With the Wind?*'

'I remember her. Didn't she win an Oscar?'

'She did indeed.' He slapped his knee. 'By Jove, you know your pictures, Mrs Newton. I've never met a woman so interested in them before.'

'Sometimes,' Lena murmured, 'it's hard to believe those other worlds exist, particularly in America.' She just loved the frilly curtains Americans had on their windows, the settees with flowered covers and the big airy rooms. And it would seem that almost everybody owned a motor car.

'Isn't it,' George enthused. 'You know, once this war is over, I wouldn't mind paying a visit to America, to Hollywood in California, take a gander around the studios, like.' He put his hands behind his head, leant back in the chair and stared with an expression of sheer wonder into the empty fireplace. 'I could even stay and live there,' he said. 'Get a job. There's nothing stopping me.'

'Nothing at all, Mr Ransome,' Lena murmured breathlessly. 'It would be sheer heaven – or "the gear", as people say in Liverpool.'

'Heaven on earth,' George agreed. 'Do you know, Mrs Newton, it's you what put the idea into me head. Just talking to you about the pictures. The chap at work, the one who loans me the magazines, he's more interested in the technical side of things, the cameras, the lighting, not the stars and the pictures themselves.'

Lena would have given anything to accompany him to California. What a thing to wish for! She must be going mad.

Across the road, Brenda Mahon was busy working on her Singer sewing machine when there was a knock on her front door. Despite the late hour, Brenda went to answer it. Customers often turned up at the most unearthly times if they wanted something making. Nowaday, many people worked shifts and didn't get home till midnight. Not that it was midnight now, but quarter past ten.

'Hello,' she said when she opened the door to a soberly dressed man of about forty. 'Can I help you?'

'I'd like a dress made, please, out of this.' He held open a paper carrier bag. Inside Brenda could see folds of glittering pink satin.

'Of course. Come in.'

She took him into the parlour, which, as usual,

was draped with half-made clothes as well as old curtains and bedding that would be turned into something entirely different in the very near future.

The man stopped in the doorway. 'What a wonderful sight,' he murmured appreciatively. 'It's like an Aladdin's cave.'

'People have said that before,' Brenda told him. She took the material out of the bag, spread it on her sewing table and fingered it. There was between four and five yards and it felt thick and slippery. 'This is a lovely piece of material,' she remarked. She looked forward to working with it. 'What sort of dress would you like – is it for your wife, or your daughter?'

'For my wife,' the man said. 'We're going to a dinner dance in October.'

'Do you want to borrow a pattern book so your wife can pick the style she wants?' Brenda enquired. 'Though she'll need to come in anyroad, so I can measure her.'

'She won't be able to come in, I'm afraid; she's an invalid, but I have her measurements with me. Oh, my name is Mr Lester, by the way.'

'I'm Mrs Mahon.' They shook hands. Mr Lester was very handsome, though he appeared to have a permanent frown, and wore a well-cut dark brown suit. He took a piece of paper out of his breast pocket and unfolded it. It was a pencil drawing of a headless woman wearing a long, simply styled dress, complete with measurements; from shoulder to waist, waist to hem, the waist itself, length of arm and width of wrist. 'This is the style my wife would like,' he said.

'Are these figures enough, and do you have a suitable pattern?'

'I suppose so,' Brenda said hesitantly. She didn't need a pattern, but she had never made anything before without the presence of the prospective wearer. 'I can always come to your house and double-check these measurements,' she suggested.

'She's not well enough for that, I'm afraid.'

Brenda wondered if she would be well enough to wear the dress to the dinner dance in October. Anyroad, she was perfectly capable of making the garment to the measurements supplied. It was just that she would have liked to see it on Mrs Lester before it was handed over.

'How much do you charge?' asked Mr Lester.

'A guinea,' Brenda said promptly. She charged strangers more than she did her neighbours and friends. 'How did you get my name?'

'My wife got it from someone. Her usual dressmaker has moved away.'

'As your wife won't be able to come for fittings, will you be coming yourself when I'm halfway through, like, to make sure I've got the measurements right?'

'I don't think that will be necessary,' he said smoothly. 'I have complete confidence that you will be able to turn out the garment to my wife's satisfaction. When shall I return to collect it?'

'In a month's time.'

'Good night, Mrs Mahon.'

They shook hands again and he left.

Brenda sat thinking how much she enjoyed being a dressmaker. She loved sewing and met all sorts of interesting people. Mr Lester was a bit out of the ordinary; there was something funny about him, but she couldn't quite work out what it was.

She went upstairs and checked that her girls were fast asleep, then crept out of the house and across the road to Sheila's, where she pulled the key through the letter box on its string and let herself in.

Sheila was nursing Mollie, now six and a half months old. The living room looked as if a hurricane had swept through it. In a minute, Brenda would help her friend tidy up. They often met around this hour, after the pubs had emptied and everywhere was quiet and peaceful – though it had been dead chaotic while the raids were on – to have a jangle and to bring each other up to date on the happenings of the day.

'I saw George Ransome creep across the road and around the back to Lena's,' Brenda said. 'Well, he didn't exactly creep, but he walked sort of gingerly. He goes there regularly.'

'How can you be sure he went to Lena's?' Sheila attached the baby to her other breast. Mollie gave a half-hearted cry of protest before the new breast was thrust into her mouth.

'Lena's is the only house where he couldn't go in the front – where it wouldn't look funny, like.'

'D'you think they're actually *doing* it, Bren?'

Brenda grinned. 'Doing what, Sheil?'

'Oh, you know what I mean – *it!*'

'Well I hope so,' Brenda said with a chuckle. 'George Ransome can come through my back door any time he likes. Eh, you should have seen

104

this chap who's just been to ask if I'll make a dress for his wife. He brought this lovely pink satin with him, a bit loud for my taste, but...' She paused and a look of delighted recognition spread over her face. 'I know, he wants it for himself!'

Sheila looked started. 'What?'

Brenda wandered into the kitchen, where she put the kettle on and washed two cups and saucers. 'He wants the dress for himself,' she repeated.

'Like Old Mother Reilly and Kitty you mean? They were on at the Empire Theatre last year. That woman who works in the fish and chip shop in Marsh Lane, Millie Felice, she went to see them.'

Brenda supposed Mr Lester might be on the stage. 'I dunno,' she muttered. But if that was the case, she would have understood perfectly if he had said the dress was for him. There would be no reason to pretend it was for his wife.

'In real life,' Sheila went on, 'Old Mother Reilly is a man and he's married to Kitty.'

'I know,' Brenda acknowledged. 'Would you mind if your Calum dressed up as a woman?'

Sheila shuddered. 'I'd go right off him if he did. What about you?'

Brenda narrowed her eyes and tried to imagine Mr Lester in a pink satin dress. 'I don't think I'd mind,' she said. 'It would depend who it was. Oh, and talking of Kitty; it's ages and ages since we heard from *our* Kitty.'

The women were silent as they thought about their friend Kitty Quigley, who'd left Bootle last

105

year to be a nurse on a hospital ship.

'She left about a year ago, last August or September,' Brenda continued. 'She wrote me one letter and you had one too, didn't you? Since then, nothing. Her dad hasn't heard anything either. He's worried sick.' Kitty's dad lived along the road with his two stepsons.

'I hope she's all right,' Sheila said worriedly.

'So do I,' agreed Brenda. 'The trouble with Kitty is that she's too nice by a mile.'

Sheila smiled. 'Not like us, we're horrible.'

Brenda nodded in agreement. 'Dead horrible.'

Chapter 7

Kitty could hear the woman talking about her. She was being deliberately loud, knowing that she was in earshot, standing behind Kitty in the queue outside the greengrocer's.

'She's lived there over a year and there's been no sign of a husband,' sneered the woman. She lived in the basement in the same house as Kitty – a three-storey terraced property close to the docks – and was never seen without a ciggie in her mouth. She must get them on the black market; ordinarily, cigarettes were impossible to buy on a regular basis.

'I know a woman whose hubby's in India and has been on leave just once since the war started,' another voice said reasonably. 'Mrs Quigley's hubby could be anywhere in the world.' The voice belonged to the girl who lived next door and had just had a baby, a little boy. 'And don't forget, she wears a wedding ring.'

'Huh! Y'can get wedding rings sixpence a time in Woolies,' the other woman said scornfully. 'They're made of brass. And anyway, what about letters? She hasn't had a single letter either, not before the baby, nor after.'

'You're right,' put in another voice. Although Kitty couldn't see the speaker, she knew that this voice belonged to the woman with the hairy chin who was a friend of the smoker. 'I mean, even if her husband's not in a position to write, she must have friends, relatives, but not one has put pen to paper in all this time.'

'Well I feel sorry for her,' the girl with the baby said. 'And I wish you wouldn't talk so loud, or she'll hear.'

'I hope she does hear. This is Portsmouth. We don't like strange women landing on us with their bastard kids. Why doesn't she go back to Liverpool where she belongs?'

Why didn't she? Kitty wondered when she was back in the small, dreary room in which she had lived for so long. Why hadn't she left months ago, when she still had the money for her fare, when she could have turned up in a nice new coat with her hair styled, looking eminently respectable? Why on earth had she stayed until now, when all her savings had gone and she looked like death warmed up? And out of interest, *where* would she have turned up? The only place she could go was Bootle, Pearl Street, where she knew people, where her father lived.

She'd been too ashamed to go back; ashamed of Rosie, her beautiful little girl. What did it matter how smart she looked, how elegantly her hair was styled, when she was accompanied by a child who'd been born out of wedlock? *That* was what people would notice, her child, not her clothes or her hair.

She glanced down at her four-month-old daughter. She was fast asleep, lying on her back, her tiny arms stretched upwards in a gesture of surrender, eyelids fluttering slightly, breathing steadily, not a trouble in the world, entirely unaware of the havoc she had wrought on her mother.

How was it possible for people to regard such innocent perfection with disgust?

Kitty's mind went back to the day she had left Liverpool, so proud to have a job as a nurse on a troop ship, though at the same time devastated at having discovered that her boyfriend, Dale, an American serviceman, who she assumed she would marry in the very near future, already had a wife and two children back in the States.

At first, she'd considered that her life was over, that nothing would matter any more; even now she could still collapse into tears when she thought about how much she had loved him – and how much he had claimed to love her. But for the sake of other people – her family and friends – it was essential she return to being at least a shadow of her old self.

And she had done it. But she had only been a few weeks on the ship when she realised she was pregnant. It seemed no time since she had experienced the shock of Dale revealing he was married; now there was the further shock of discovering she was expecting his child. She had thought she could manage at least another month before having to tell someone and go home. But she was living among nurses. Some were already aware of her bouts of morning sickness.

It was Matron, who wasn't just an ordinary matron but a senior officer in the navy, who had noticed her thickening waistline. Kitty was given a good talking-to and ordered to leave the ship when next it docked in England, which turned out to be in Portsmouth. She had found the place where she now lived within the first half-hour – there was a crudely written card in a downstairs window: *Room to let, 3/6d week, sherd kichen.*

She'd enough money in a Post Office account to get by on for a while. For the next few months she hardly moved out of the room, only to register with a grocer and buy the basic rations. She was allowed extra milk for being pregnant. There was a kitchen in the house where it could be warmed, and she would dip pieces of bread in it. It was virtually all she ate, all she felt like eating.

She had returned to the room after having Rosie. She felt too weak to travel all the way to Liverpool. She wasn't a properly trained nurse, but she knew enough to realise she was probably anaemic; the baby had taken a lot out of her. She needed iron – decent meat, fruit if it was available – but still she existed on milk and bread. It was easy to get and easy to eat. She breastfed Rosie and felt only half alive.

But now something would have to be done. She had a baby and scarcely a penny in her purse – not even enough to get her through tomorrow The inertia that she had felt for so long suddenly drained away and she began to panic.

She twisted the wedding ring that she had worn since leaving Bootle. It wasn't a sixpenny brass one from Woolies, but a real gold one that had belonged to her mother. She'd always known she could pawn it in an emergency, but if she just used the money to live on, then the time would quickly come when she truly had nothing. Of course, she'd

110

never get the ring back; there was no way she would return to Portsmouth to redeem it.

She sighed and got to her feet. There were quite a few things she had to do if she was leaving the next day. One thing was to plan how she could get away without the landlord, who lived on the premises, becoming aware. If he realised that she was going for good, he'd demand a week's rent in lieu of notice. She wanted to keep all the money from the ring for the train fare and other expenses on the way. She decided to leave the pram behind. It was second-hand and falling to pieces and would be a nuisance on the train. She'd carry Rosie in her arms – well, in one arm and the suitcase in the other hand.

'I'll go to Pearl Street,' she said out loud. 'Jess Fleming will let me stay with her until I sort meself out.' She had lodged with Jess for months and she had been a shoulder to cry on when Dale had broken the news that he was married.

It took two days and four trains to get to Bootle. Some of the advertised trains didn't run at all or were cancelled at the last minute because they were required by the military. Kitty and Rosie spent the night in a hotel by Euston station. Rosie, disturbed by the unfamiliar noise and movement, as well as inadequate feeds, cried for hours and other guests complained. The manager knocked on Kitty's door and demanded she stop her baby crying.

'How?' Kitty asked simply when she opened the door. In fact, Rosie had just gone to sleep and had woken up again, disturbed by the man's knock.

111

Next morning, they left at the crack of dawn, but the train they caught only went as far as Stafford. The next train stopped at Crewe, and waited there for ages until someone decided it was to go no further. It was nine o'clock by the time Kitty and her baby arrived at Lime Street station on another train. With a mixture of despair and recklessness, she paid for a taxi to Exchange station, where she caught an electric train to Marsh Lane.

She was home! Things hadn't exactly gone swimmingly, but she'd managed to reach her destination after carrying a baby and a suitcase all the way from Portsmouth, though a lot of people had been kind and had helped with one or the other. Now all that was wanted was for Jess Fleming to be in and Kitty knew everything would be all right.

A young woman answered the door of number 10; a girl, in fact, of about sixteen.

'I'm sorry, but Mrs Fleming left ages ago,' she told Kitty. 'She lives in Burtonwood now and has a different name. People often come and ask for her, but as I said, she's gone.'

'Oh dear.' The news came as such a shock that Kitty had to lean against the doorjamb for support. What was she going to do now?

'Oh heck!' the girl gasped. 'Give me the baby and come inside. Sit down a while. Would you like a glass of water? I'm awfully sorry, we're out of tea, though we have some horrible coffee.'

'I'd like some water, please.'

Minutes later, Kitty was sitting in the familiar room in one of the chairs she'd sat on many times before. 'I used to live here,' she told the girl, 'but I've been away and lost touch with everyone.'

The girl had forgotten all about fetching water and was playing with Rosie, who had just woken up. 'She's gorgeous,' she said. 'What's her name?'

'Rosie.'

'A pretty name for a pretty baby.' She chucked Rosie under her chin. 'Hello, Rosie. I'm Phyllis. How d'you do?'

Rosie smiled, and Kitty half expected her to reply, 'I'm fine, thank you, Phyllis. How are you?'

Gosh, she must be tired!

'What will you do now that Mrs Fleming isn't here?' Phyllis enquired. She was a pretty, very composed young woman for her age, with short brown curly hair and hazel eyes. Kitty wished she'd had so much confidence when she was that young.

'I don't know. I know some other people in Pearl Street; I might go there.' Her dad would die of embarrassment if she turned up at number 22 wanting to live with him. His only daughter; his only *child*, with an illegitimate baby. He'd let her stay, but would feel it necessary to change his habits and go to a different pub, for instance, where he wasn't known.

'What's your name?' Phyllis asked. She seemed to be doing all the talking.

'It's Kitty, Kitty Quigley.'

'I'm Phyllis Taylor.'

'What are you doing here, Phyllis?' Asking questions and listening to the answers would give her time to think about what to do next. 'You're not from Liverpool, are you?'

113

'No, I was born in Beverley, near Hull,' Phyllis explained. She spoke with a faint Yorkshire accent. 'My dad's a naval architect and was transferred to Bootle on a work order in 1940 to work in a laboratory testing wave power. He must have got caught up in those terrible air raids Liverpool had, as we've never heard from him since.' She transferred Rosie to her other arm and both she and the baby gave a sigh of pleasure.

'Surely someone would have written and told you if he'd died?'

'That's what we thought too – me and Mum – except no one did. Mum wrote to people like the police and the hospitals, but they couldn't tell her anything. Then one night not long ago we went to see a film called *Random Harvest*, in which this chap loses his memory after an accident, and now Mum's convinced that that's what happened to Dad: that he's lost his memory.'

'And he's still somewhere in Bootle and doesn't know who he is?'

Phyllis made a face. 'More or less, yes. I suppose it's possible.'

Despite her tiredness and the fact that this precocious young woman seemed to have taken over her baby, Kitty was fascinated by the tale. 'How do you expect to find him?' she asked.

'Well, Mum had to get a job so we'd have something to live on, which was easy seeing as she was a nurse before she married Dad. She works in Bootle hospital. I have a voluntary job helping out at local infants' schools, but they're on holiday at the moment. In our free time we hang about outside public houses and that cinema in Marsh Lane

114

and go to football grounds when there's a match and look for him. Other times we just wander round the shops hoping we'll set eyes on him one of these days. We've been here over a year, but there's no sign of him yet. He's very handsome and looks a bit like Cary Grant. I thought that might have helped a bit, but so far it hasn't.'

'What happens if he doesn't recognise you – he won't if he's lost his memory, will he?'

Phyllis rolled her eyes. 'We'll just have to cross that bridge when we come to it, won't we? Knowing Mum, she'll soon convince him who he is. Look' – the girl seemed a tiny bit embarrassed – 'Mum works on the late shift and she'll be home any minute. You've got a lovely baby, Kitty, but you're not wearing a wedding ring. If Mum comes in and guesses you're not married, she'll have a fit. She's awfully strait-laced. Me, I don't give a hoot what people get up to as long as they don't murder each other.'

Kitty nodded. Although the words were kind, they made her want to cry. She was nothing more than a pariah; people didn't want her in their homes, even really nice people like Phyllis. She took Rosie from the girl's arms. Her suitcase was in the hall.

Phyllis said, 'You go first, and I'll bring the case. Where is it you want to go?'

'Number twenty-five.'

'Brenda Mahon's house! She's making me a frock for Christmas. It's dark green with an embroidered collar. I'm sick of wearing black – it was Mum's idea. It's a sort of mourning, just in case Dad isn't alive.'

Outside, the street was pitch black. Kitty had no idea where she was. She felt sick. Somewhere a door opened and closed, but she couldn't see a thing.

Phyllis obviously could. She said, 'Hello, Mrs Newton. I've brought a visitor for Mrs Mahon.'

'She's got two customers in there, they've only just arrived,' the invisible woman said. 'That's why I left. I'm on my way home.'

'I'd best wait a while,' Kitty said. She wasn't too sure what sort of reception she would get from Brenda, despite the fact that they'd been friends since they'd started school together, along with Sheila Doyle who was now Sheila Reilly.

'Oh, but you can't wait outside with the baby, Kitty. I can smell a fog coming. Come on back to our house. You never know, my mum might be late for once.'

The invisible woman spoke. 'Whoever it is out here with a baby must come home with me this minute. I'll take you along to Brenda's when her customers have gone.'

'It's a lady called Kitty, Mrs Newton.'

'Come along with me, Kitty dear. I live upstairs in the end house that used to be the dairy.'

Kitty remembered that the dairy had closed down. 'Thank you,' she croaked.

'I'll bring the suitcase,' Phyllis offered.

'And I'll take the baby,' said Mrs Newton.

'Call me Lena,' Mrs Newton said as soon as they were inside her flat. She had lit the gas mantle and switched on the fire, while still holding on to Rosie.

'I'm Kitty Quigley.' Kitty's head was swimming with tiredness.

'I've heard Brenda and Sheila go on about their friend Kitty who was on a hospital ship,' Lena said. 'But they didn't say you had a baby.'

'That's because they don't know,' Kitty said bluntly. She may as well be honest right from the start. If Lena Newton wanted to throw her out, then let her do it now, before Kitty had a chance to settle in this comfortable chair and fall asleep, leaving the woman with the terribly kind face to look after Rosie.

'They don't know?' Lena looked puzzled for a few seconds, then her expression cleared. 'Oh, you poor thing. Something awful's obviously happened. Where have you been living? Have you been through all this on your own?'

Kitty nodded. The sympathetic tone had the effect of making her burst into tears.

Lena disappeared into another room and returned without Rosie. 'I've put her in my bed,' she said in a low voice. 'I'll go and make you some tea; the kitchen's downstairs.'

'She'll need a clean nappy. They're in my suitcase.' The napkins were merely old towels torn into squares.

'I'll see to that when I've made the tea.'

Quarter of an hour later, Kitty had drunk the tea and was fast asleep in the chair, while Rosie had been fitted with a clean napkin and was just as fast asleep in Lena's bed. Lena herself was feeling somewhat dazed at the drama taking place around her. She had never in all her life known a woman who had had an illegitimate baby, yet now she had one – and the baby – under her very own roof. And Kitty seemed quite normal; quite nice, in fact, not at all the blatantly immoral type of woman that she'd imagined the mother of an illegitimate baby would be.

Lena was ruminating on this when downstairs the front door opened and a woman shouted, 'It's only me.'

Brenda Mahon had arrived. 'Me customers had just gone when that girl from across the road, Phyllis, came and told me that Kitty Quigley was here with a baby,' she panted when she reached the top of the stairs.

'She's asleep,' Lena whispered. 'The baby's in my bed. She's a dear little thing.'

'She's lost loads of weight.' Brenda regarded her old friend asleep in the chair. 'Can I see the baby? Phyllis didn't say it was a girl.'

'Yes, her name's Rosie. Come and look.'

The two women crept into the room where Rosie was sleeping. Lena closed the door behind them. The little girl looked unnaturally tiny in the middle of the double bed.

Brenda sat down on the corner. 'Aah!' she breathed. She watched Rosie but didn't touch her. 'She's beautiful, and although Kitty might look a wreck right now, she's beautiful too, with the most lovely hair. And that boyfriend of hers, Dale, the American, was dead gorgeous.'

Lena swallowed. 'The father's an American?' The situation could not possibly become more dramatic, romantic even.

'Yes.' Brenda nodded. 'He wasn't very nice,

though. He fooled Kitty into thinking they'd get married one day.'

'Poor Kitty.'

'Yes, poor Kitty,' Brenda echoed.

Kitty woke in the middle of the night. She hadn't the faintest idea where she was, other than in a room she couldn't remember having been in before, and there was no sign of her baby.

She got to her feet, frightened, and must have made a noise because a woman in a nightdress came in and said in a gentle voice, 'I'm Lena Newton, Kitty. Your baby is fast asleep in my bedroom. Your friend Brenda fed her earlier. She found the bottle in your suitcase and used fresh milk. I put Rosie in one of the dressing table drawers just in case I fell asleep and smothered her. I heard of that happening once back in Birmingham. Come and see.' She went back into the bedroom.

Kitty followed and saw Rosie fast asleep in a drawer on top of the bed. It all felt like a dream. 'Would you like to join her in the bed, dear?' the woman said. 'I'll take the chair.'

'But I can't possibly let you do that!' Kitty had aches and pains all over from sleeping in the chair.

'It'll just be for tonight. Tomorrow your friend Brenda is coming to sort you out.'

'We'll fix you up downstairs,' Brenda said next morning, brisk and efficient. She had Kitty's life for the next few weeks all sorted out, as if she'd been thinking about it all night. They were in

Lena's flat, Lena having gone to work, and it was raining outside. 'There's a room behind the shop which is quite respectable, and Lena's agreed for you to share her kitchen. She'll help with Rosie – when she's home, like. She's got a job as a secretary at some place on the Docky. I've got a single bed in the box room which me and Lena will fetch along later when it's dark – we'll use the back entry, not the street, so no one'll see. I know a woman who'll let us borrow her pram so you can take Rosie for walks, though you'll have to do that in the dark an' all. Have you got a headscarf? Well I'll make you one this avvy out of a spare bit of material,' she said when Kitty shook her head. 'Me, I've never taken to headscarves, but then I'm a woman who can make her own hats.'

Kitty agreed meekly to everything and Brenda continued. 'You can't go on like this for ever, Kit. It can only be for a few weeks, at the very most a couple of months, before you'll have to decide what to do – live with your dad in Pearl Street and let the whole of Bootle know you've had a baby on the wrong side of the blanket, or go away somewhere, get a job and make arrangements for someone to look after Kitty. Or get married,' she added as an afterthought. 'Did you meet any decent fellas over the last year?'

'Not a single one, Bren.'

Brenda sat back in the chair and let out a noisy breath, as if she'd been wound up and had been practising what to say for hours. 'How on earth did you manage to get yourself in this mess, Kit?'

'You know how.' Kitty shrugged. 'I fell in love. And I thought Dale was taking precautions –

well, he *was* taking precautions until that very last time. It was after he'd told me he was married,' she said bitterly. 'He must have forgotten to use something and I was too upset to notice – he was upset too. We never saw each other again.'

'Men!' Brenda spat. 'They're a race apart.'

'When will I see Sheila?' Kitty asked.

'I don't think it's such a good idea to tell Sheila you're here, Kit. She's dead religious and not as broad-minded as I am – she could well disapprove of what you've been up to. She wasn't exactly sympathetic when their Eileen met her Nick when she was still married.'

'I don't think I was either,' Kitty recalled with a dry smile.

The arrangement worked well. It helped that Phyllis Taylor considered herself to be part of the plot to keep Kitty and Rosie's presence a secret. She kept Kitty company during the day, did her shopping, borrowed books for her from the library, even took the baby for walks, pushing the pram up and down back entries before emerging on the busy dock road, where she was unlikely to be seen by anyone from Pearl Street or the nearby streets.

She had only just left school when she and her mother came to Liverpool, she told Kitty. 'I passed the School Certificate with flying colours,' she said in a matter-of-fact way, not at all boastfully. 'I want to become a nurse, like Mum, but not if I have to leave when I get married like Mum did.' Her voice rose indignantly and her brown eyes shone. 'When you consider all the things women have done for

121

the war – working in factories, driving buses, joining the forces, doing *men's* jobs – surely we'll be
treated more equally once it's over.'

If it wasn't over by the time she reached eighteen, she intended to join the Royal Navy and
become a Wren. 'And they can train me to become
a nurse, like you.'

'I wasn't a proper nurse,' Kitty hastened to
assure her. 'I was an auxiliary and didn't have any
training at all.'

Freda Tutty was cross. So cross that sometimes
she felt she just had to kick something. She had
hurt her foot twice, badly; the first time on the leg
of her desk, and at home on the bedroom door.

At school, the autumn term had started and
Sister Bernadette had asked Freda for the name
and address of the man who was writing the book
about the history of Liverpool. Shortly afterwards,
a letter had arrived for Tom Chance at the Tuttys'
house in Pearl Street signed by the nun – it was the
first letter he'd received since he'd lived there.

He showed it to Freda. 'This is from one of
your teachers,' he said, looking quite pleased.
'She wants me to walk the Upper Sixth Form
around the Seven Streets later in the month.'

'And will you do it?' Freda's chest burnt with
jealousy and other despicable feelings.

'Of course. I'm flattered to be asked.'

Perhaps Sister Bernadette would ask Freda too.
Perhaps Freda should automatically expect to be
included. Perhaps what she should do was present
herself in the Upper Sixth classroom as soon as
she got to school on the day. Or perhaps she

wasn't expected to do any such thing. She was being ignored.

What was even worse, it turned out that it wouldn't be Sister Bernadette who would be walking the girls from the Upper Sixth around the Seven Streets, but Miss Bell, who'd only started in January and was the first woman in England to obtain a first-class degree in history from some posh university down south. She was small and neat, with jet-black hair that shone so brightly it could have been polished.

What was more, her first name was Linda. Linda Bell! So much nicer and easier on the tongue than Freda Tutty. The flame in Freda's chest burnt even hotter. She hated everyone in the world except Tom Chance, who was being manipulated by all these people.

When the day did come, she was unable to concentrate on her work in class for thinking about Miss Bell and Tom Chance leading a group of seventeen- and eighteen-year-old girls around the centre of Liverpool. All of them, Miss Bell included, would fall in love with him. It wasn't fair. He belonged to *her*.

Anyroad, the day passed and to Freda's relief that appeared to be that, until she arrived home from school one Wednesday, when the shops closed early, to find that her mother had laid a new white cloth on the table, as well as some pretty crockery – white patterned with little pink roses – and their meagre cutlery had been polished to death. There was even a tiny vase in the centre of the table holding a bunch of purple pansies.

'What's this?' Freda demanded. How dare her mother take a decision without discussing it with her first?

'Tom asked me to do it,' Gladys said proudly. 'He paid for the cloth and the nice new dishes. He's bringing someone home to tea.'

'Tea!'

'Tea,' Gladys confirmed. 'I've got ham, tomatoes and pickle in the kitchen, and a trifle in the yard with a plate on top. I'm having trouble making the jelly set.'

'You can't *make* a jelly set, Mam,' Freda said sarcastically. 'It'll set when it wants to and not before.'

'Of course you can, Miss Know-All,' her mother replied, just as sarcastically. 'Jellies set more easily when it's cold, so I put the bowl in a bigger bowl of cold water that I've been changing regularly since I got home from the shop. It'll probably be set by the time we're ready to eat. Tom said that him and his young lady will be here at five o'clock.'

'Young lady!' squeaked Freda.

'Young lady,' her mother confirmed. 'She's something to do with your school.'

Miss Bell! It could only be Miss Linda Bell. Freda resisted the urge to howl her head off. If only there was a magic spell available that would make her older! Make her age another four or five years within the next hour.

'Why did Tom ask *you* to make the tea?' she croaked. Why hadn't *she* known about this?

Gladys tossed her head. 'Because I'm the mistress of this house,' she retorted. 'Tom said so.

124

I'm your mam, not your bloody servant.'

'Did he?' Freda said weakly.

Her mother's voice softened. 'He thinks you're too young to be bearing so much responsibility. You're missing your childhood. They were his very words. I know I've been a terrible mam in the past,' she said abjectly, 'getting hung up on the gin and that, but I'm over it now, luv. And it's all due to you.' She smiled and patted Freda's head.

Freda jerked her head away. 'Let us alone,' she snarled.

Tom Chance arrived on the dot of five, not with Miss Bell, but an attractive young woman Freda had never seen before. She wore a pale blue pleated skirt and a short-sleeved Fair Isle jumper knitted in a dead complicated pattern. She turned out to be Sister Bernadette's cousin, Evelyn Jones, who had recently finished university and had offered to help Tom with his book.

'I took English,' she said brightly, tossing her golden curls and fluttering her eyelashes like a mad woman, 'and I intend to become a writer myself one day. I shall write murder mysteries like Agatha Christie and sell thousands of copies of my books.'

'Aren't you a clever girl,' Gladys said unctuously.

Freda rolled her eyes and didn't say anything. She was trying to work out if Tom was in any way romantically involved with Evelyn, and realised that he was when they left together holding hands.

She felt totally betrayed. Was Tom so blind that he was unable to detect how much she loved

125

him? That they were *meant* for each other?

Her mother had started to clear the dishes off the table. 'Well, she was a nice young lady,' she remarked. 'Talks ever so posh. I suppose that's only to be expected, her being related to a nun, like. Where are you going?' she cried when Freda leapt to her feet and made for the front door.

'I won't be long,' Freda shouted before slamming the door behind her.

She ran all the way to the police station in Marsh Lane, where she reported that the man living at 14 Pearl Street was a deserter from the army. Either that or he'd avoided joining in the first place. 'His name's Thomas Chance,' she informed the sergeant behind the desk.

'And what's your name, miss?' He was writing things in a book.

'Evelyn Jones.'

The sergeant came to the house the following evening. Freda hid in the back kitchen when her mother opened the door and he announced himself.

'We checked, and he's not a deserter,' the policeman informed a somewhat mystified Gladys. 'In fact he's something of a hero. It's a wonder he's still alive after what he went through.'

'Why, what did he go through?' Gladys enquired.

'He was at Dunkirk. He was rescued by a boat that the Jerries then sank, throwing everyone on board into the water. Lieutenant Chance swam around rescuing as many of his men as he could, despite being badly injured himself.' The police-

126

man's voice throbbed with pride. 'He was given a medal, but had to be invalided out of the army, his lungs being damaged, like, and there were quite a few other internal injuries. So,' he continued huffily, 'you can just tell Miss Evelyn Jones that Thomas Chance is no deserter.'

'I'll tell her,' Gladys promised.

The door closed and Gladys found her daughter in the kitchen sobbing her heart out. 'I love him, Mam,' she wailed. 'I really love him.'

'Well that's an odd way of treating someone you love, reporting him to the bobbies and pretending to be his girlfriend.' Gladys folded her arms and looked sternly at her daughter, and a strange thing happened. It seemed as if that was the minute everything changed, and Gladys assumed her natural role as a mother while Freda returned to being a child.

The following day, Tom Chance gave in his notice and announced that he was moving on. He didn't say where to. Whether he learnt about Freda's visit to the police station she didn't know, but she thought he looked at her rather sadly, as if he felt she'd let him down.

At the Co-op, her mother was promoted to assistant manageress of the vegetable section and given a five-shillings-a-week rise.

From time to time, Freda would go into town and walk the Seven Streets, hoping to come across Tom Chance, but she never laid eyes on him again.

Chapter 8

Lena didn't mind the disruption Kitty and Rosie's presence caused to her life – in fact, she welcomed it. They shared rations, and most nights Kitty would have a meal ready for when Lena came home from work. Sometimes Lena would get Rosie ready for bed and give her the final bottle of the day, which she really loved doing. When it was dark, Kitty might go for a walk or to see Brenda, or Phyllis would come and talk about women's rights and all the wonderful things she was going to do when she got older, changing her mind frequently and impressing the other women no end.

There was one part of Lena's life that remained untouched, the covert part that no one knew about: she continued to meet George Ransome at the Palace on Saturday nights, and sometimes Sundays too, depending on what picture was showing. Afterwards they would go to the Crown for a drink. Lena had taken to drinking sherry, which made her feel dizzy as well as rather sophisticated.

Naturally, she had never mentioned Kitty to George, not that she thought he would be shocked that she'd had an illegitimate child; he wasn't that sort of person. She'd got the impression from their conversations that he wasn't remotely narrow-minded – and she hadn't forgotten those notorious parties she'd been told he used to have!

One night, however, in the Crown, Lena yawned halfway through her sherry, and apologised by saying, 'Sorry, Rosie woke me up awfully early this morning.'

'Who's Rosie?' asked George.

It wouldn't hurt to tell the truth, Lena thought. In fact, it might be an advantage to have a man in on the secret.

In a low voice, interrupted by the occasional hiccup, she told him about Kitty and Rosie turning up a few weeks ago and sleeping downstairs from where she lived. 'In the dairy part,' she finished.

George frowned and said in a very slow voice, 'When you say Kitty, do you mean Kitty Quigley who used to live at number twenty – her dad, Jimmy, still does?'

'Yes, that's right.' She wondered why he was speaking in such an odd way.

'Why isn't she back with her dad? What's she doing living in the dairy? It's a dump, that place. Least the downstairs part is.'

'Well, there's Rosie,' Lena stammered, aware that something was wrong. 'Kitty isn't married and she's got Rosie.'

'I see,' George said, even more slowly. 'What are her plans?'

'Her plans?' What *were* Kitty's plans? Brenda was forever listing them for her. 'She has to make up her mind whether to go and live with her dad,' she told George, 'which means Rosie will be called a little bastard. Or she can go away and get a job and someone to look after Rose, or find a fella.' Ordinarily Lena wouldn't have dreamt of

129

saying 'find a fella', but that was how Brenda put it. The way George was speaking was making her feel nervous.

'Do you mind if we go home?' he asked.

'Not at all.' Lena fumbled with her gloves, putting them on the wrong hands and leaving behind half her sherry.

George walked home much too quickly and she had to keep running to catch up. Once in Pearl Street, he stopped outside the dairy and said, 'Will you please ask Kitty if she'll see me?'

'Yes, George,' Lena said timidly. She unlocked the door.

As expected, Kitty was upstairs in the flat. As she climbed the stairs, Lena had the strongest feeling that tonight was the last time she would go to the pictures with George Ransome.

'Now, are you sure?' Brenda made the sternest face imaginable.

'I *think* I'm sure,' Kitty said, grinning stupidly.

'You have to know you're sure.'

'All right, so I *know* I'm sure.'

'Are you really sure?' Brenda banged her fist on the arm of the chair.

Phyllis laughed. 'Now you're going round in circles. Me, I think it's terribly romantic. Have you always loved him, Kitty?'

'Not *real* love. I think it's called calf love. I had a terrible crush on him from when I was about ten.'

'We all did,' said Brenda, soppy all of a sudden. 'Me, Kitty and Sheila. We all wanted to marry him one day, or at least be invited to one of his parties when we grew up.'

130

'And now Kitty's been invited to marry him!' Phyllis clapped her hands. 'Did it not cross your mind to propose to him?'

Kitty laughed. 'Never in a million years.'

'Don't be daft, girl,' said Brenda.

Lena wasn't saying anything. She couldn't think of anything she could contribute to the conversation. It was too sudden, too unexpected, too crazy. George Ransome had asked Kitty Quigley to marry him! Apparently he had always fancied her, but she'd seemed too young for him in those days.

'There's still the same age difference,' Brenda had pointed out.

'Somehow me being thirty and him fifty seems perfectly acceptable. In a way, it's like a dream come true.' Kitty blushed. 'Much better than the other two alternatives you suggested, Bren.'

People wanted to make a scandal out of it, but found it impossible. Everyone liked George, the women because he was so attractive and the men because he'd managed to reach the age of fifty while having a whale of a time. And now he was marrying Kitty Quigley, who was young enough to be his daughter but at the same time had a daughter herself. Rumours abounded that Kitty was a widow, or had divorced the Yank she used to go out with, rumours that nobody believed; or, it was whispered, she'd got up to no good with the Yank and Rosie was the result. It was weird, bloody weird, but all everyone could do was wish the couple well and look forward to the wedding.

Kitty and George were married on the last Saturday in September. It was a beautiful, cloudless day, with the old oaks in the churchyard dressed like Christmas trees in rich golden leaves. The white, pink and yellow rose petals that were scattered over the married couple when they emerged from the church came from Eileen Stephens's garden. It seemed unfair that brides weren't allowed extra coupons for their wedding dress and trousseau, but Kitty looked beautiful in a magnificent dress made by her friend Brenda out of an old, well-bleached white cotton sheet and a piece of lace curtain.

The street could put on a show when it wanted to. Pasting tables were erected here and there, sandwiches were distributed, biscuits bought, cakes baked, lemonade made for the children, and to crown it all, not just a sliver of wedding cake for every single person, but champagne too. George was the sort of person who could get things that other people found impossible, and he wasn't short of a few bob either. Frankly, apart from the novelty, not everyone liked the champagne. It was too fizzy, not sweet enough. It ended up being mixed with beer or sherry, and the folk who were inclined to get drunk on these occasions got drunk much quicker and toasted each other to death.

The happily married couple departed for their honeymoon in London at five o'clock, leaving Pearl Street to enjoy itself until long past midnight. There was a certain coldness that went unnoticed between Sheila Reilly and Brenda Mahon when the former discovered that the latter had known about Kitty's return many weeks before, but by next morning everything had returned to normal and they were best friends again.

Eileen Stephens always got up at half past five when Kate was on the morning shift to make her tea and toast. She appreciated her bed more than usual when she got back into it after her lodger had left. She either read a book for an hour or so, or fell back asleep, to be woken by Nicky throwing himself on top of her. When she got up again, she did the housework, and usually spent half an hour or so sewing – since clothes and bedding had become rationed, women spent a large amount of their time patching and darning: 'turning' sheets so the unworn part became the middle, letting down or taking up hems, reversing collars, repairing frayed cuffs, darning socks over and over, until sometimes there was more darn than sock.

Afterwards, she would shop for the few things that could be bought locally, such as milk, eggs and vegetables, usually walking into the village with Nicky attached to his reins – he was inclined to want to stop the occasional car by throwing himself suicidally in front of it. They would pass the little school that became a Catholic church on Sundays, where Nicky would be a pupil one day. At least, Eileen hoped so. Life in the future, even the present, seemed somewhat tenuous these days. She wondered if, after the war was over. Nick would suggest they all move to London. Would they have a life together when there was no longer a war to keep them apart?

When Kate returned home just after two, they would often catch the bus to the shops in Walton Vale to get the weekly rations and have a coffee in

Sayers. If there was a film on that appealed to them they would go to one of the picture houses. Nicky had already shown a total lack of interest in any sort of film and would instantly fall asleep.

When Kate worked afternoons, from two till ten, Eileen's life did an abrupt turn-around and the morning's tasks were undertaken in the afternoon and vice versa, though the pictures were out.

She liked having a pattern to her life. Before Kate's arrival, everything had been a muddle: now it felt more ordered. She knew where she was, as it were.

In the evenings, whatever shift Kate was on, Eileen would make them cocoa and they would listen to the BBC news, then chat till midnight. Although Kate was forever vowing that she would go to bed much earlier, she never did.

Kate's daughters were growing older. They wanted to know why their mother didn't live at home, and were no longer willing to be fobbed off with their father's excuses. He had told them she had abandoned them; that she'd had numerous affairs; that she didn't care about her children. None of this was true.

The eldest, Lily, had already written to her mother, and Kate had written back. 'I tried not to be too emotional in my letter,' she told Eileen. 'I didn't want to frighten her off by saying how much I loved all three of them, how much I missed them. Because I do,' she said. 'I miss them so much it genuinely makes my heart ache. But because of Ralph, I've not been around while my three lovely girls have been growing up.'

For the first time, Eileen mentioned her suspicion that Nick might be having an affair down in London. 'Either that, or he's completely gone off me. He hardly ever comes home, and when he does, he's terribly cold and distant.'

Kate could scarcely believe it. 'But, Eileen, no couple could have loved each other more than you and Nick. It was obvious for all the world to see. I used to envy you so much.'

Eileen shrugged. 'It's because of his arm. The war brought us together, and the war is driving us apart. He thinks I've gone off him, when in fact I only love him more.'

In Pearl Street, Maurice Newton was home from sea. Lena was conscious of how dull the place was with him there when compared to Cal Reilly's occasional periods at home with his wife and family. Whereas Cal and Sheila were all over each other, in front of anyone else who happened to be there, Maurice hardly touched Lena except in bed, when it was all over in a jiffy, and he didn't so much as kiss her at any time during the proceedings.

Lena hadn't minded in Birmingham – this was what marriage must be like for everyone, she had assumed – but since coming to Pearl Street, she'd realised that wasn't true. There must be more to it than she knew. It was called 'making love', but she was positive that she had never made love with Maurice, not properly. They just went through the motions. There was nothing romantic or passionate about it. Lena yearned for passion and romance, but didn't think she would ever experience it with Maurice.

Brenda came one day and remarked afterwards how attractive he was.

Lena was amazed. 'Attractive!' Maurice was a solid, well-built man with sandy hair and light brown eyes. She had never thought that a person could be described as looking boring, but now she thought Maurice did. She'd never found him attractive. She wondered what his opinion was of her.

'You sound surprised,' Brenda said. 'I used to think my Xavier looked a bit like a rat, but other women quite fancied him, to the extent that one actually married him. She didn't know he was already married, poor thing. Her name was Carrie and we became great friends for a while. We still write to each other.'

It riled Lena when Kitty – now Kitty Ransome – asked if she'd mind babysitting one Saturday night while she and George went to the Palace in Marsh Lane.

'*The Man in Grey* with James Mason is on. I'm longing to see it. George said it got marvellous reviews. He gets this American magazine off someone at work. I can't remember what it's called, but it's all about the latest pictures – movies, they call them. We'll pay you, of course.'

'I'm afraid I already have an appointment on Saturday,' Lena said stiffly. 'Why not ask Phyllis? She'd really appreciate the money.' She was even more offended at being offered money than at being asked to babysit. It wasn't that she'd ever visualised any sort of future with George Ransome, but she had felt for a while that they had slightly more than a casual friendship. But this

136

had turned out not to be the case, and she couldn't help but feel let down.

In London, Nick Stephens discovered that the hotel off Park Lane where he'd spent a weekend with Eileen and Tony in the first year of the war had been bombed to rubble in the Blitz. In his troubled mind it felt as if their past life together was being destroyed and the present was slowly crumbling away to nothing.

One moonless evening in December, he wandered along Oxford Street in the blackout and recalled the years before the war when the West End was brilliantly lit, the shops vying with each other to have the brightest lights and the gaudiest decorations. The windows were still beautifully done, but now that night had fallen they could no longer be seen. Oxford Street had become a place of ghosts, some of the buildings turned into jagged skeletons of their former selves. Several of the big shops had been bombed, and John Lewis was a total wreck. Nick found it infinitely depressing. Perhaps everyone felt the same. The street was almost deserted; people must have hidden themselves inside shops, restaurants, bars and theatres.

The East End, where poor people lived, had suffered far more savagely. Nick never forgot that, but he worked in the West End, where the result of Hitler's bombing campaign could be witnessed every day.

He was supposedly searching for a present for Nicky, and something for Eileen too. At the same time, he wanted to buy a gift for Doria Mallory; who had recently informed him that she was expecting his child.

'I'll get rid of it if you like,' she had said after breaking the news.

'Don't do that!' he said quickly. He couldn't stand the idea of a child being murdered, *his* child; and being discussed so airily, too, as if it was no more important than wafting away a fly.

'But, darling,' Doria murmured, 'I'm not a fallen woman; I'm quite respectable, as it happens. If I have a baby, what am I to do? Where am I to go? To live? Do I give it to another woman and just go back to work?'

Nick nearly said, 'Eileen will look after it,' but swallowed the words just in time. Why had he thought that?

'When is it due?' he asked.

'If I have it,' Doria said carefully, 'if I have it, it should arrive something like the end of June or the beginning of July.'

'Let me think about it.'

'Don't think about it too long, Nick. These things have to be done early, you know.' She'd thrown her arms around his neck. 'I'm sorry; so sorry. I know it's going to worry you silly.'

'For goodness' sake, it's not your fault,' Nick said. 'I'm the one who's supposed to be taking precautions.' He had no idea what had gone wrong, though someone had told him that not every French letter was a hundred per cent secure. A certain number in each thousand were faulty, otherwise the birth rate could fall dangerously low. The population had to remain at a certain level in order for the country to have the necessary number of workers in the future.

'I've been taking precautions too,' Doria assured him. 'This must be a child determined to be born.'

'In that case, we have no right to stop him.'

'Him? It might be a her. And what I said earlier still applies. I'm not a fallen woman, et cetera, et cetera.'

Nick was thinking about it now, walking along ghostly Oxford Street. He didn't want his child killed in its mother's womb, or given away to strangers. He wanted Doria to have their baby and for them to live happily ever after.

He already had a wife and child and was making no attempt to live happily ever after with them.

He burst through a dark doorway, fumbled with a barrier of thick, dark curtains, and found himself in a large, crowded, well-lit shop. He recognised Selfridge's. He should really have asked an assistant on which floor the toy department was, but he headed for the restaurant instead. He sat for ages drinking coffee after coffee, trying to sort out his predicament in his head. The only satisfactory conclusion he came to was that he must rent a place for him and Doria to live. He would buy her a ring, and to all intents and purposes they would become a married couple, though not as far as Doria's parents were concerned. But unlike Jack Doyle, Eileen's father, John and Esther Mallory were modern, broad-minded people who would accept that morality and normal behaviour could go to hell in wartime. As long as he promised to put everything to rights when the war was over, he felt sure they would accept the situation.

Chapter 9

Christmas Morning 1943

Early on Christmas morning, Jack Doyle sat in his house in Garnet Street, just around the corner from his daughter, Sheila, drinking tea in front of a miserably small fire, wishing he were younger, much younger. The government had started calling up men in their forties, but he was closing on fifty-six and stood no chance of receiving a letter telling him to get himself along to a recruiting office forthwith.

He was anxious to do his bit – more than the fire-watching he was doing now – and felt that if he were a member of the armed forces, the war would soon come to an end. It was nigh on six months since the Allies had landed in mainland Europe and Italy had surrendered. The troops had been expected to reach Rome in a matter of weeks. In Jack's mind the war had been virtually over, but they were still struggling to make their way up Italy and were still nowhere near Rome. The German army were putting up an unexpectedly good fight and thousands of lives on both sides were being lost.

And what the hell was happening in Malta? If Jack had had the means, he would have gone there and found out, for Malta was where his son was based. Sean Doyle was in the Royal Air

Force, and Jack felt he had a right to know what was going on.

Somehow this Christmas seemed even more depressing and hopeless than the last. It was as if there was a stalemate that would last for ever.

The weather didn't help. It was cold, icily cold, and snowing quite hard. Eileen had cancelled the invitation to the cottage for dinner in case there was no transport running. He thought about cycling there, but it would be silly to risk it. He'd already collected the sprouts and taken them round to friends and neighbours. He began to worry what Eileen would do without him and Sheila and the kids for company. Was that Kate woman spending Christmas with her? Nick had condescended to come home for New Year. What the hell was he up to in London?

Jack was working himself up into a minor rage when Sheila let herself in. She was humming a carol.

'You look as if you've lost a shilling and found a ha'penny, Dad,' she told him with a cheerful grin as she came into the room. 'What's the miserable gob for?'

'I didn't know I had a miserable gob, luv,' he lied.

'Well you have. Are you coming round our house soon?' she enquired. 'Our Niall's already broken that scooter you made him, and Caitlin sat on her doll's bed and the damn thing's snapped in two. You'd better bring a hammer and nails with you.'

Jack got to his feet with alacrity. 'I'm coming straight away, luv.' This was what he needed, to be wanted and loved. To be necessary.

141

Some hours later, at number 10, Phyllis Taylor and her mother, Winifred, were just finishing their dinner. Winifred was forty years old, with a nice face and a sensible hairstyle. Nice and sensible were adjectives that could also be applied to her personality. She made an excellent nurse and was well liked by both her patients and the other nurses.

'Well,' she said, 'considering there's a war on, I think that was an exceptionally enjoyable meal.' She'd managed to get a little piece of gammon from the grocer's. There was no law to say that gammon and a bit of stuffing didn't go together, and what with a tin of peas – well, half a tin; they'd eat the rest tomorrow – and some roast potatoes and gravy, the food had tasted utterly delicious.

'That's because your standards are falling,' Phyllis informed her. 'Before the war, you wouldn't have considered it up to much, but now we expect far less, and what was merely all right then is now considered absolutely scrumptious. I mean, I could eat Spam fried in dried egg powder until the cows come home, but four years ago I would have thought it quite disgusting.'

'Do you have to analyse everything, dear? Now you've made me think the dinner wasn't up to much.'

'It *wasn't* up to much, Mum.'

'But I enjoyed it.'

'I've just explained why.'

'Well I wish you hadn't.' Winifred wiped her mouth with her napkin. 'Let's go and sit in the parlour in front of that lovely fire. We can do the dishes later.' They'd gone mad with the coal on this one special day of the year; in order to save fuel, the front room was rarely used in winter.

Winifred worked extremely hard. She'd been lucky to get Christmas Day off and intended enjoying it to the full by having a little after-dinner nap, listening to the wireless and reading a library book by her favourite author, Dorothy L. Sayers, whose latest novel featured her brilliant detective Lord Peter Wimsey.

'I think we'll give looking for your father a miss on Christmas Day,' she remarked on their way into the parlour. Once there, she plonked herself down in an armchair and picked up the novel, hoping Phyllis would go away and read a book of her own.

'I took for granted that we would,' Phyllis snorted, ignoring the chairs. 'I think we should give it a miss every day from now on. In fact, I don't think we should have even started looking for him.'

Winifred groaned. 'Don't let's have that argument again, dear. Your poor father could be living somewhere in Bootle without any idea of who he is.'

'He could also be dead, or somewhere else in the country, Mum.' Phyllis felt embarrassed hanging round outside pubs, churches and other establishments every weekend, searching the faces of the men who came out in the hope that one of them might be her father. They'd been doing it for over a year and had become a laughing stock. Some men believed they were women of ill repute – or at least pretended to – despite their respectable clothing. A couple of times Phyllis had been handed coppers by people who'd assumed that they were begging. Most folk thought they were round the bend.

Winifred sighed. She hadn't got on terribly well with Leslie, but at the same time she had loved him to distraction. She felt honour-bound to track him down. 'I'll think about it,' she muttered when Phyllis suggested that giving up the hunt should be their New Year resolution.

'If we give it up, will we go back to Beverley?' Phyllis persisted.

'There's someone renting our house, Phyllis.' Her daughter had been a relentless questioner since the day she'd learnt to talk. 'And I don't think the government will allow people to give up their jobs and move around the country for no good reason when there's a war on. I have an important job, you know, so we're stuck in Bootle until the war is over.'

Phyllis conceded that being a nurse was vitally important. She didn't mind being stuck in Bootle, as she'd made a few friends and acquired her voluntary job supervising classes at various schools in the area. So many teachers had been called up that there was a shortage. She'd also met a young man almost as intelligent as herself who'd invited her to a party that very afternoon.

'A party?' Her mother frowned when she was told.

'At a house not far away, in Chaucer Street.'

'And where did you meet this young man? What's his name?'

'Dennis. I met him in the library. He's interested in French history, same as me.'

Winifred regarded her daughter with concern. 'What sort of party is it? I mean, will they be playing games like Postman's Knock or something more chaste like charades?'

'Oh, charades, Mum. Honest.'

'I suppose that's why you're wearing the new frock the woman across the road made for you?'

Phyllis looked down at the frock as if she wasn't aware she had it on. 'I suppose,' she said casually.

'All right then, off you go. Have a nice time.' Winifted closed her eyes and was virtually asleep by the time Phyllis had discreetly applied a touch of her mother's one and only lipstick and closed the front door behind her.

Phyllis hoped and prayed that they would play Postman's Knock at the party. She had led an interesting life, but so far she had never been kissed by a man. She wondered what it would be like.

People had forgotten all about her. She was so unimportant, so uninteresting, so utterly useless as a human being and as a friend that no one had thought to invite her to dinner on Christmas Day.

In the flat above the dairy, Lena Newton wondered if she would die of loneliness before the day was out. She put a few more lumps of coal on the fire in the hope that it would cheer her up a bit, but it was useless. Useless, like her.

Actually, Eileen Stephens had invited her to the house in Melling for her dinner, asked her to her face. Everybody was to have gone – Sheila,

Brenda, all the children, as well as Jack Doyle. But it had been cancelled because the buses and trams might not be running due to the weather. So Eileen was to stay in Melling with just little Nicky for company, her friend Kate having gone to see friends in Norfolk, and the rest were going instead to Sheila's. But somehow Lena had been missed out of this invitation, and it seemed pathetic to ask, 'Am I included in the Christmas dinner, please?'

She thought about Kitty spending her first Christmas with George Ransome. If she let herself, it would be easy to become insanely jealous.

Was it likely that public transport would be cancelled just because of a bit of snow? Well, it was more than a bit, she allowed when she glanced out of the window.

She recalled how Peter Wood had mentioned coming to Eileen's by train and getting off at a station in a place called Kirkby, then walking to Melling. She looked out at the snow again and doubted if there was enough to hold up a steam train. If the trams were running and she caught one as far as Kirkdale station, she could go to Kirkby that way. There'd be someone at the station who would tell her the way to Melling. All she had to do was walk as far as Stanley Road to catch a tram. If there weren't any, she'd simply come home again. She just had to get out of this place, at least for a while.

She looked at the clock; it was nearly one. Before the meal had been cancelled, Eileen had invited everyone for half past two. Presumably she'd still be eating dinner at around that time. If

146

Lena left the house this very minute and the trams and trains were running, she might just about manage to get there. She put on her coat, scarf, gloves and woolly hat and left the flat.

The houses in Chaucer Street were bigger than those in Pearl Street, with bay windows at the front and wider hallways and stairs. The one where the party was being held belonged to Billy, a friend of Dennis's – well, to his mum and dad. The dad worked at a pub somewhere – he was Billy's step-dad, Dennis explained – and the mum was quite incredibly pretty and fashionable. She wore black flared trousers and a dramatic red satin blouse, probably the most daring outfit ever seen in Bootle. Her name was Dawn and she looked very young, a bit like an older Shirley Temple, with loads of curly hair and little Cupid lips. She'd made things for the guests that looked like sausage rolls but with a minuscule amount of corned beef in them instead. Phyllis thought them terribly ambitious and experimental and enjoyed them no end. There were also cheese straws to dip in tomato chutney that tasted a bit off, and strips of toast spread with crab paste.

'I'm sorry, folks,' said Dawn while they ate the food – not at a table, but standing up in the parlour like grown-up people at a cocktail party – 'but that's all I could manage, what with the rationing.'

Everyone was enamoured, chuffed at being called 'folks', and they assured her that the food was absolutely fine. 'Very sophisticated,' someone murmured, and someone else added, 'Hear, hear.'

147

They had played charades for a while, then Truth or Dare, and were now playing Postman's Knock. The boys were disappointed that Billy's mum wasn't joining in; she had retired to the kitchen to clear up.

Phyllis was also disappointed when it looked as if her first kiss was to be delivered by a pimply youth of about fourteen. She glanced at Dennis, and he shrugged disappointedly.

As she waited in the hallway for the kiss, the front door opened and a man entered the house. He was tall and green-eyed and looked rather like Cary Grant with a short beard. He was definitely handsome enough to be the lovely Dawn's husband.

Phyllis forgot about the kiss, her attention having transferred itself to the man, who was divesting himself of a familiar brown and cream checked overcoat.

'Hello, Dad,' she said.

Lena was going to be late. There'd been plenty of trams running, all of them packed to the gills, but she'd had to wait ages for a train. By the time it arrived, puffing furiously, the snow had become heavier, and as the train slowed down ready to stop at Kirkby station, it was so thick it was hard to see through.

She was the only person to alight at Kirkby. An elderly railway official, an oilskin cape over his uniform, braved the snow to take her ticket and wave the train off to the next station. Lena climbed the brew to a wooden building that housed the ticket office and waited for the man.

She wanted directions to Melling. He arrived puffing slightly, like the train.

'It's a bit of a walk,' he warned, 'I certainly wouldn't risk it in this weather. Why don't you wait here a wee while; see if it goes off a bit?' He entered the ticket office and closed the door.

Lena supposed she better had. She stood in the entrance to the building – there was no door – and watched the snow get thicker and thicker until it was like a fluffy white blanket blowing in front of her eyes.

There must be a public house across the road; it couldn't be seen for the snow, but she could hear singing that every now and then became louder when, she assumed, someone opened the door to go in or come out. None of the voices were female, otherwise she might have gone there to shelter. She felt ten times more miserable now than she'd done at home, where at least she'd been warm.

The railway official emerged from his office. 'I reckon you'd best come inside and sit with me, luvvie,' he said. 'That snow's showing no sign of letting up. There's a nice fire in here and a window where you can keep an eye on the weather. I'll make you a cup of summat if you like. What d'you fancy, tea, cocoa or coffee?'

'Tea, please,' Lena said gratefully.

She entered the tiny office, one wall of which was lined with shelves holding dusty ledgers and metal filing baskets full of yellowing forms. The tickets were on a special shelf of their own beside the little window through which they were sold. It seemed odd being inside a place that all her life

149

she'd only observed from the outside when she bought a ticket. An extravagant fire burnt invitingly in the fireplace with a boiling kettle on top, and placed in front were two carver chairs crammed with tatty cushions. The oilskin cape was dripping on a hook behind the door.

'It looks very snug,' Lena said.

'Sit down, luvvie, make yourself at home.' The old man fussed around spooning tea into two badly stained tin mugs. He had removed his cap and his gentle, rosy-cheeked face was surrounded by a halo of pure silver hair. 'I'm Godfrey, by the way. I retired from the London and North Western Railway more than twenty years ago, but was brought back because of the war. This sort of weather don't suit an old chap of eighty-two.'

'You don't look that old,' Lena remarked. 'I'm Mrs Newton – I mean Lena.'

'D'you take sugar in your tea, Lena?' He had a Lancashire accent rather than a Liverpool one.

'I used to, but I got used to doing without once the war began.'

Godfrey sighed. 'I wish I could do the same.' He put two heaped spoons of sugar in one of the mugs, a spoonful of tea leaves in both, then poured in the water followed by milk. 'I'll put this on the floor beside you; the handle'll be too hot to touch for a while.'

'Thank you. Don't your family mind you having to work on Christmas Day?' she enquired.

'There's only me wife, Elsie. We had six sons; one was killed in the Great War, and the others live in different parts of the country. They send us cards, tell us about our grandsons and granddaughters. We've had a couple of great-grand-children over the last few years.' He smiled ruefully at Lena. 'As for minding, it's wartime, isn't it? I'm only too pleased to have the chance of doing me bit at my age, and Elsie's pleased too. She's at home knitting scarves for Russian sailors.'

'Well, I really appreciate you being here to look after the trains.'

'I'll only be here till seven; there'll be no more trains after that.'

'Won't there?' Lena gnawed her lip. According to the big clock over the fireplace, it was half past three. By the time she got to Eileen's – *if* she got to Eileen's; it was still snowing hard outside – it'd be almost time to leave. 'I think I'd best catch the next train to Liverpool,' she told Godfrey. Home seemed so much more appealing now that she wasn't there.

'It'll be the same train you came on, going back,' he said. 'Does that mean you haven't had your Christmas dinner?'

Lena shrugged. 'I'm afraid so. But it doesn't matter. It's not the end of the world.' Although she had thought so earlier, in her flat.

There was a noise in the corner of the room, a little squeaky sound coming from a cardboard box beneath an ancient desk that she hadn't noticed before. When she looked, Lena came face to face with a black and white cat that climbed slowly out of the box and rubbed itself against Godfrey's legs, leaving behind two absolutely irresistible kittens: a tabby, and a black one with a white patch on its chest and one white foot.

'You're not going to like it out there, Beth.'

Godrey spoke to the cat in a chatty way, as if it were human. 'It's snowing something awful.' He opened the door and the cat disappeared.

Lena picked up the tabby. 'That's Tommy,' Godfrey said. 'After Tommy Handley on the wireless. The other's Patch, after itself, I suppose. Beth had seven kittens altogether and five have been given away. There's only Tommy and Patch left. Are you short of a kitten in your house, Lena? If so, we've got two to spare.'

'I wouldn't want two.' But she'd love one. Her mother had always had a cat at home.

'Tommy's the healthiest.' Godfrey said. 'Patch is the runt of the litter; I think that's what they're called. He's smaller and not as tough as the others.'

'Then I'll have him.' She put Tommy back and picked up the tiny black and white kitten, which felt as light as feathers in her hands. 'Could I take him with me?'

'Of course, luvvie. I'll get a box and a bit of rag to go in it. Have you got somewhere for him to sleep at home?'

'I'll find somewhere.' There were empty boxes in the dairy. She kissed the tiny cat on his forehead. 'Me and you are going to be best friends,' she whispered.

Godfrey must have had excellent hearing. He nodded approvingly. 'I'm pleased he's going to a good home. If you know anyone who'd like Tommy, then he's still available.'

'I'll ask around,' Lena promised. How precarious a cat's life was, she thought. Handed over to any Tom, Dick or Harry, or their female equivalents, with no guarantee that they'd be looked after properly.

'You're awfully quiet since you got home from that party,' Winifred looked anxiously at her daughter. 'Are you sure something didn't happen?'

'Nothing happened, Mum,' Phyllis replied impatiently. 'I mean, it was only a party. What could have happened?'

'I could think of a hundred things. You've been very quiet, and it's not like you to be quiet, Phyllis. *Ever*,' she emphasised.

'I'm tired, that's all.'

'It's not like you to be tired, either.'

'As we're not going out tonight, I think I'll go upstairs and take off me new dress and put on an old one,' Phyllis said, changing the subject. She left the room before her mother had the chance to ask more questions. Upstairs, she sat on the bed and relived the moment when her father had walked into the house in Chaucer Street.

'*Phyllis!*' She had never seen anyone look so shocked and frightened before. It was as if he'd genuinely seen a ghost. 'What the hell are you doing here?'

'I'm at the party. More to the point, Dad, what are *you* doing here? Me and Mum thought you'd lost your memory, which you obviously haven't or you wouldn't have known who I was. We were also worried that you might be dead.'

'Is your mother here?' His jaw, which had already fallen quite a bit, fell further.

'Not at this party; no. But she's at home in Pearl Street.'

153

'Where the hell's Pearl Street?' His face had gone completely white. Phyllis was genuinely worried he was going to have a heart attack.

'It's about five minutes' walk from here,' she told him.

'Bloody hell!'

'Don't swear,' she said sternly.

'Sorry. How long have you been in Bootle?' he enquired in a shaky voice.

'Just over a year. We've been looking for you everywhere. Is this where you've been all the time, in this house?'

'Ahem!' exclaimed the boy who had been hoping to kiss Phyllis. 'We're supposed to be playing a game.'

Phyllis opened the parlour door and shoved him back inside. 'Tell them something important has cropped up,' she ordered.

Her father grabbed her arm. 'Let's go upstairs.'

The bedroom they entered smelt of cheap perfume. Phyllis and her father sat beside each other on the end of a lace-covered bed.

'Is this where you sleep with Dawn?' Phyllis asked.

Her father's face went from white to red in an instant; and she knew she had sized up the situation accurately. 'It is; yes, it is,' he acknowledged sheepishly.

'So what happened, Dad? I mean, what name do you go under these days? Mum couldn't find a Leslie Taylor anywhere.'

'Mick O'Brien.' He groaned. 'Look, Phyll, I'll tell you what happened from beginning to end, save being cross-questioned. I know what you're

154

like when you've got the bit between your teeth.' He coughed, cleared his throat and began. 'I met Dawn at a party in this very house, as it happens. It was about the time the air raids were exceptionally bad. She'd been living with a Mick O'Brien who'd just walked out. She thinks he went back to London. He had a wife and family there.'

Dawn would seem to be attracted to men with families, Phyllis thought, though she didn't interrupt her father's explanation about why he'd apparently disappeared off the face of the earth.

'Anyway,' he continued. 'Dawn and I...' He paused. 'We fell in love. I don't know if it was her idea, or if it were me, but after the raids were over, I decided to...' He paused again.

'Die?' Phyllis suggested.

'Well, yes,' he conceded. 'Die. It so happened Mick O'Brien had left his identity card behind, so I became him instead of me. I didn't go back to work or to my lodgings.' He made a helpless gesture with his hands, as if he'd had little choice in the matter. 'Your mother and I had never got on. I didn't think she'd miss me...'

'*What!*' Phyllis interrupted angrily. 'She's been heartbroken, and desperately worried. At first we took it for granted that you'd been killed in the raids, though no one could find evidence that you were dead. Then she saw this picture, *Random Harvest*. The hero, it was Ronald Colman, has an accident and loses his memory. Mum immediately decided that that was what had happened to you, so we let the house in Beverley and moved all the way to Bootle just so she could look for you. It was literally only this morning that I managed to

155

persuade her to give up.'

Her father hung his head in shame. 'Are you going to tell her you've found me?'

'Of course not. I wouldn't dream of telling her. She's already been upset enough.'

'When will you go back to Beverley?' There was a tinge of hope in his voice.

'Not for a long time,' Phyllis snapped. 'Our place is here, in Bootle, until the war is over. Where are you working anyway?' she demanded.

'In a pub in Seaforth.' He looked downcast.

'As a barman?'

'Yes.'

'But, Dad,' Phyllis said impatiently, 'you're a naval architect; you have dozens of letters after your name. What are you doing working in a pub?'

He regarded her sadly. 'Where else could I go without giving away my real name? It's what love does to you, Phyll. I'd do anything for Dawn.'

Phyllis had left the party soon afterwards, forgetting all about telling Dennis, who had invited her there. She was outraged by what her father had told her, but there was nothing she could do. She would just go on supporting her mother, who came into her bedroom at that very moment and said that she was convinced something really awful must have happened at the party and to *please* tell her what it was.

'Nothing, Mum.' Phyllis ran across the room and hugged her mother so tightly that she gasped for breath. 'You know I love you very much?'

'Well, I rather took that for granted, Phyllis. You are, after all, my daughter and only child.'

'Aren't there any nice-looking doctors at that hospital that you could get off with?' Phyllis asked.

'I haven't noticed.' Her mother laughed. 'And as far as I know, dear, I'm still a married woman.'

'I think you should assume you are a widow from now on. Dad was never up to much, was he? You're better off without him.'

'Phyllis, what a terrible thing to say!'

'It might well be terrible. Mum, but it's also true.'

As soon as she arrived home, Lena relit the fire, found a bigger box than the one she'd been given at the station, folded an old but warm scarf inside and placed the kitten on top of it. He merely sat, a tiny bunch of fluff, and looked at her pathetically with his big blue eyes.

'Oh dear,' Lena cried. 'I expect you're badly in need of milk and something to eat.'

She rushed around and found a saucer, filled it with milk, then opened a tin of corned beef, cut off a slice and crumbled it into another saucer. She'd boil a couple of potatoes in a minute and make corned beef hash for her Christmas dinner.

The kitten drank the milk, ate the food and weed on the floor. 'I shall have to train you to do that outside,' she told him. He was probably missing his mother terribly.

Downstairs, the front door opened and Brenda Mahon called up, 'It's only me!'

She came into the room wearing a lovely royal-blue dress that she'd made for herself for Christmas. 'Where have you been?' she demanded.

'Sheila was expecting you for dinner. I came to look for you, but you were out.'

'I didn't realise I'd been invited. I went somewhere else.'

Brenda was probably about to ask where the somewhere else was when she noticed the kitten. 'Ah,' she breathed, dropping on to her knees beside the box. 'Isn't it *lovely!* Is it a boy or a girl?'

'A boy,' Lena said proudly.

'What's his name?'

'Godfrey.' It was more dignified than Patch.

'Godfrey! That's a mouthful for such a little kitten. Can I pick him up?'

'He won't always be little, and yes, you can pick him up.'

Brenda picked up the kitten and sat down in Lena's chair. 'It's been a day and a half,' she complained. 'It was murder at Sheila's. I've never known such a noise. Her dad was there and he spent half the time putting the toys he'd made for the kids back together. It was dead noisy. I'm glad I've only got the two kids and they're nice quiet little girls.'

'Would you like some tea?' Lena asked. She glanced jealously at Godfrey, who was lying, purring for the first time, on Brenda's chest.

'No, ta, luv.' Brenda placed the kitten back in his box. 'In fact, I came to see if you were in and invite you to tea at Sheila's.'

'No thank you. I wouldn't like to leave Godfrey on his own so soon. He's only just been separated from his mother.'

'Of course you can't leave him, luv. I weren't thinking proper, like. But you can't take him to

Sheila's either. Those kids'd kill him with kindness within the first five minutes.'

Lena nodded her agreement. She didn't want Godfrey going anywhere near the Reilly children, not even when he was a fully grown cat.

'If you like, you can come round ours a bit later, bring Godfrey with you and we'll have a natter and a drink – one of me customers gave us a bottle of sweet sherry. Me girls will love meeting Godfrey and I'll make them promise not to touch. Actually,' she said thoughtfully, 'they're constantly on at me about getting a cat, I might do it one of these days.'

'Well I know a place where you can get one, Bren. He's a tabby called Tommy.' How nice it would be, Lena thought excitedly, to have Godfrey's brother living just along the street. It would almost be as if she and Brenda were related.

Chapter 10

Boxing Day

At half past ten on Boxing Day morning, the village of Melling was deserted. The snow was thick on the ground and outside there wasn't a soul to be seen. The lights were on in most houses and an occasional decorated Christmas tree could be glimpsed. The snow on the pavements was mainly undisturbed; few people had braved the outdoors and left tracks.

Peter Wood had only encountered two other human beings by the time he arrived at Eileen Stephens's cottage. Not a footprint could be seen anywhere, though there was an orange glow coming from the living room, as if a fire had been lit.

He hung about, stamping his frozen feet in the snow. He should have stayed in the Liverpool hotel a mite longer, arrived here at lunchtime. It almost certainly wasn't done to barge in on people this early in the morning on Boxing Day. It was not even as if Eileen was a friend. Well, he wanted to be more than friends, but she would probably regard him as virtually a stranger. They had only met twice before, though it would have been much more than that if the circumstances had been different and Peter could have brought himself to be a bit more forward. Normally he was an extremely confident person, but with

160

Eileen he felt like an awkward schoolboy.

Nick Stephens was staying at the Mallory family home in Wimbledon, and Peter had been sickened by the chap's behaviour with Doria, who was apparently pregnant with his child. He'd shocked his parents by making himself scarce well before it was time for Christmas dinner and making a beeline for Euston station. There were plenty of trains running. After all, there was a war on and troops had to be moved.

His parents doted on Stephens. They were convinced that when the war was over, he'd get divorced and marry their daughter. The chap had been an officer in the Royal Air Force, a hero, and they believed his every word. His father had told Peter that one of these days his future son-in-law would be in receipt of a medal.

Peter was looking at his feet, buried up to his ankles in snow, wondering what to do next and unaware that the front door of the cottage had opened. He was startled when a voice said, 'Would you like to come in, Mr Wood?'

Eileen was standing in the open doorway, unaware of how beautiful she looked in a plain navy jersey and skirt to match, her blonde hair like satin. He could see the blue of her eyes from where he stood.

'Mrs Stephens,' he stammered.

'Please hurry, I'm letting in the cold.'

He almost ran down the path; almost fell over in his anxiety to not let in the cold.

'Good morning,' she said as he approached. 'Merry Christmas, if it's not too late to wish you that.'

'Thank you.' He'd had a bloody awful Christmas, anything but merry, but he couldn't very well tell her why.

'Have you been to see your uncle?' she asked.

'Uncle Johnny, yes.' He stepped inside, she closed the door and he banged his feet on the mat.

'It was Uncle Jimmy last time you were here. I think you should take your shoes off, Mr Wood,' she went on without a pause. 'I'll fetch you a pair of my husband's slippers from upstairs. What size do you take?'

'Nine.'

'Nick takes ten so they'll be a bit too big. Are your socks wet?'

'No, they're fine.' He'd sooner have frostbite in his toes than wear Nick Stephens's socks.

He had unlaced his shoes and removed them by the time she came downstairs with a pair of tweed slippers. 'Thank you.' He slipped them on.

'Come into the living room. Nicky and I have just stopped what we were doing to have a cuppa. Would you like one?'

'Please.' He loved this room, with its white walls, black beams and old pictures on the walls. A bowl of what could only be waxed fruit stood on the polished table and a nice warm fire was burning in the grate. Nicky – he must be two years old by now – was sitting on the floor in front of it drawing on a pad with crayons, while the cat, Napoleon, was stretched full length beside him. A prettily dressed tree stood in the corner, and there was a half-done jigsaw on the table, not quite childish and not quite adult either. They'd clearly

162

been doing it between them. 'Did you and Nicky spend Christmas on your own?'

'Yes, my family had planned to come for the day, but couldn't because of the snow, and the friend who normally lives here is in Norfolk. But me and Nicky enjoyed ourselves, didn't we, luv?' She ruffled the little boy's hair.

'Yes.' The smile he gave his mother was like a ray of sunshine.

Eileen went into the kitchen and returned with a cup of tea. 'This is very weak,' she said. 'I just added water to the tea leaves left in the pot and stirred like mad. I can't remember if you take sugar.'

'I don't, thank you.' He felt angry that she'd spent yesterday alone with her son in this isolated house, but remembered that the snow had been relentless.

'Me dad will probably come and see us on his bike today, now that the snow has stopped.' She drained her own cup and put it on the table. 'Tell me, Mr Wood, if you haven't an uncle living in the village, what are you doing here? This is the third time you've been.'

Just imagine if he told her the truth! Just imagine if he said, 'Well you see, Mrs Stephens, your husband is having an affair with my sister and she's expecting his baby. Initially I came to tell you what was going on, but I fell in love with you at first sight. If things were different, I would have been here a hundred times, not just three, and would almost certainly have proposed marriage by now.'

Instead, he sat there dumbstruck, not having

163

the faintest idea what to say. It was she who spoke first. 'I'm beginning to wonder if I should throw you out, Mr Wood. For some reason, you're here under false pretences.'

'At Easter...' he began, then paused, his mind having gone blank.

'Yes?' Eileen said encouragingly. 'Easter was the first time you came – to the garden party if I remember rightly.'

'That's right. I'd been to a wedding,' he continued haltingly. 'A wedding in Kirkby. It was a friend from university – we'd been at Oxford together. There was a pile of us and we all got drunk, very drunk. Next morning, I went for a walk, to clear my head sort of thing. I passed your house, saw what was going on, so came in. I paid my sixpence entrance fee,' he assured her, just in case she thought he'd sneaked in.

'That was very good of you. Why didn't any of your friends come on the walk with you?'

'They were much more drunk than I was,' he lied.

'And why the need to invent an uncle that you'd come to see?'

'It seemed rather more acceptable than the truth; that I was walking off a hangover.'

She laughed at that and he felt relieved. 'And why did you come again – why are you here now?' she asked. She was still smiling. 'Has there been another wedding?'

Peter supposed that it was time for at least half the truth. 'Because I'm in love with you,' he said thickly. 'I've been in love with you since the first moment we met.'

164

'Oh dear.' The smile disappeared and she frowned. 'But Mr Wood,' she said seriously, 'you know very well I'm married. What makes you think my husband wouldn't have been home for Christmas? What if it had been him, not me, who looked out of the window earlier and saw you hanging about outside?'

Oh Lord! He was tying himself in knots. What excuse could he give? It had to be time for the whole truth, every single bit of it. 'Because I knew he wasn't here,' he said hoarsely. It was the only possible answer. 'Because he's with my sister in my family's home in Wimbledon. She's having his baby. My sister is Doria Mallory and I'm Peter Mallory, not Wood. That was another lie.'

'No!' It was a cry of pain that seemed to have come from the very depths of her being. 'No, not Nick.' Her expression was tragic.

'I'm sorry,' Peter whispered.

'He said he was working Christmas Eve and had to be back in the office tomorrow.'

'I'm afraid he's not,' Peter said, somewhat inadequately. 'I think I'd better go.'

He was about to get to his feet when Eileen shouted, '*No!* Don't you dare leave me by myself after telling me such a terrible thing.'

'Can I get you something? More tea, perhaps. Or have you got anything stronger to drink?' He wouldn't have minded a large whisky himself.

'The last thing I want to do is drink.' She set her burning gaze on Nicky, who was still happily drawing pictures with a crayon. 'What's he going to do without a dad?'

'I think your husband is coming home for New

Year,' Peter said hastily.

'Oh yes, he is,' Eileen said bitterly. 'He has graciously agreed to spend a few days with us.' She leant forward in the chair. 'How old is your sister? And what does she look like? What did you say her name was?'

'Doria. She's eighteen and very pretty.'

'When is she expecting the baby?'

'Summer some time. June, I think. She's...'

'Don't tell me any more. I don't want to know.' She drew in a sharp breath. 'I shouldn't have asked that much. Oh, and I do think you should go. Before you know it, I'll be asking more questions and I really don't want to hear the answers.'

'I'm really, really sorry,' Peter said. He'd never felt more sorry about anything in his life before. This was the worst thing he'd ever done. 'The last thing I want is for you to be unhappy. And I know it doesn't help in the slightest, but I really do love you.'

He went into the hall and removed Nick Stephens's slippers. When he had his own shoes on again, he said, 'Goodbye, Mrs Stephens.'

'Goodbye, Mr – what did you say your real name was?'

'Mallory. Peter Mallory.'

'Goodbye, Mr Mallory.'

Peter opened the door, then turned. 'There's just one thing...' It was the most awful cheek.

'And what's that?'

'May I come and see you again?'

A slight pause, then, 'Why not?'

At previous New Years, people had told themselves that the war was bound to end before that particular year was over. They'd thought it in 1942 and 1943, and now it was about to be 1944. Surely it would finish before this year was out. It felt as if the country had been at war for ever.

They were fed up with rationing, with shortages of so many essential things, with the blackout and blackout curtains, with seeing barbed wire and sandbags all over the place, with the tape covering their windows; they were fed up with worrying that the air raids would start again and with having to live with the devastating results of the previous raids – there were places in Liverpool that resembled deserts of bricks instead of sand.

Most of all, they were fed up with their husbands, sons and sometimes daughters being posted to dangerous places where they could so easily be killed. They were fed up with getting telegrams saying that their loved ones had died, sometimes in places they'd never heard of, or with someone else in the same street or the next street getting the same sort of telegram.

In Pearl Street, and every other part of the country, on the first day of 1944, people woke up praying that this time next year the war would be behind them. One day it would become a distant memory. The time might even come when they could hardly remember it at all.

Eileen Stephens had woken early on New Year's Day with her husband asleep beside her. She was aware that she was on the verge of losing him, but she wasn't going to give up without a fight. Not

167

that Nick would be aware that he was being fought over.

She had no intention of painting her face, showering herself with scent, wearing see-through nightclothes – not that she had any, or the coupons to buy such things if they were available; her old cotton nightdresses would just have to do. Nor was she prepared to slobber all over him, paw him and kiss him in a way she never had before.

No. What she had decided was to stop waiting for Nick to come round, to be himself again of his own volition. She should have done it before; it was just that she hadn't wanted to put pressure on him. She'd felt certain that one day he would realise that she had never stopped loving him, that the loss of his arm had only made her love him more, something she hadn't thought possible.

She was angry with him too, though she couldn't imagine ever railing at him because of it; angry that he was having a child with another woman, in effect deserting Nicky as well as her. She had thought that she and Nicky – in particular Nicky – comprised his entire world.

Yesterday, when he had let himself in, she had followed Nicky when he ran to greet his dad, and they had hugged Nick together. 'We've missed you,' she had whispered in his ear.

She had told him so again after they had eaten, then sat there smiling while he and Nicky played on the mat in front of the fire with the lorry her dad had made his grandson for Christmas. The smile hid a variety of feelings. How much forgiveness did you owe a man who had slept with another woman, who was now expecting his child? How much of an allowance should be made for him losing his arm? This Doria, *pregnant* Doria, made a pretty tough competitor, plus she had the advantage of seeing Nick daily. Did Eileen stand much of a chance of keeping him?

Of course I do, she told herself. This is Nick, the love of my life, my *husband*, for God's sake. We were made for each other. Could he possibly love this other woman as much as he loves me? Or should I say, as much as he *loved* me?

Now, on New Year's Day, she lay in bed watching him sleep. She'd seduced him twice during the night, touching him until he was wild with desire. Now he was worn out. For the first time ever, she had exaggerated the effect their lovemaking was having; she had put on a bit of a show. There'd never been a need for it before; she had just lain there enjoying the feeling of utter delight building up inside her until it exploded into something that was so exquisite it was beyond description. They would usually arrive at this point together, and so they did last night; twice.

'That was wonderful, darling,' he whispered the first time.

'That was even better,' he claimed when they'd made love again at her instigation in the middle of the night.

She wondered if he was ready for a third time, but decided to let him sleep. At least by now she might have dispelled his belief that she no longer found him attractive. And it looked as if pretty eighteen-year-old Doria hadn't completely put

169

him off his wife. She would pray, light candles, do everything possible to ensure their relationship returned to the way it had been before he lost his arm.

She recalled that when she'd become pregnant with Nicky, she and Nick had only made love once and it had seemed like a miracle; last night they had made love twice. She would say more prayers and light more candles in the hope that another miracle might happen.

Sean Doyle had been spoilt for most of his life. He was a handsome lad with dark gypsy looks and an appealing disposition, and was the apple of his dad's eye. His mam had died not long after he was born, and his elder sisters, Eileen and Sheila, adored him. In their eyes he could do no wrong.

Though neither his dad nor his sisters had approved when Sean fell in love with pretty Alice Scully, who had a serious limp, five younger brothers and sisters and a mother at death's door.

They disapproved even more when Sean and Alice married not long after he had been called up and joined the Royal Air Force. He was only just nineteen and Alice two years younger. Mrs Scully had died not long afterwards and Sean had taken the entire family under his wing. By a stroke of good fortune, the family had acquired the best house in Pearl Street, number 5, which had once belonged to Jessica Fleming and was the only one with an electric stove. It was there that Alice had given birth to their first child, a boy called Edward, who was now fourteen months old, and who his father had so far never set eyes on.

Everyone missed sunny, good-natured Sean: his wife, his dad, his sisters. But, as they said to each other every time his name came up, which was usually several times a day, 'Knowing our Sean, he'll be having a grand old time in the RAF.'

They were wrong.

Sean had been surprised to find he didn't much like being in the forces. He had always considered himself to be as popular with the men as with the girls. He'd had loads of mates at work, yet he didn't really fit in the RAF. His problem was he took it much too seriously. He wasn't able to treat death as lightly as the other men.

He had trained to be an airframe fitter, and at the present time was responsible for the mechanics of the aircraft operating from Hal Far airfield in Malta, where he'd been posted almost a year ago. By then, most of the heavy raids inflicted on the island by the German air force had ceased. The siege of Malta was over and it wasn't quite such a dangerous place to be.

Not that death worried Sean; he wasn't a coward. If he was killed, then it was what fate had in store for him. His dad and his sisters would look after Alice and the son he had never seen. After all, Alice had coped before he came on the scene and she'd cope again if he was no longer there.

Sean had grown up, become a man, without realising how desperately vile and cruel war could be. It was hard to watch the Spitfire pilots, some younger than him, flying off to provide protection for the planes that were bombing Italy, knowing that a large number would not be coming back. Some even laughed as they flew off to almost certain death. There was a phrase for it, 'like lambs to the slaughter'. It upset Sean almost to the point of tears – tears that he had to keep well hidden.

It was such a terrible waste of lives. It was heinous, it was murder, it was crazy. When he witnessed the air raids, whether from close by or at a distance, he wasn't just aware of the planes flying overhead, the sound of the explosions as the bombs landed; he visualised the casualties, the blood and the mutilated bodies, the families being torn apart, the hideousness of it all. He couldn't get his head around men committing murder; not just the Germans, but his own side too, who were terrorising enemy cities night after terrible night.

After a while, he realised he should have been a conscientious objector. But he wouldn't have had the courage. His dad would never have been able to hold his head up in Bootle again if people had known how his son felt. There wasn't a single person he could confide in about his feelings.

He was regarded as a quiet young man, a bit withdrawn, who kept himself to himself. He wouldn't have dreamt of accompanying his comrades to a brothel, sleeping with another woman when Alice was waiting for him at home. Instead of the life and soul of any gathering that he had once been, he had become a rather stuffy, sanctimonious sort of person that his younger self wouldn't have cared for.

Sean didn't know exactly what date it was, only that it was early in January and the year was 1944. The dawn sky in Malta was dark blue, though the blue was fading fast along with the stars. A pink blush had appeared on the horizon. The sloppily shaped moon seemed to be blinking on and off as if it held a message for him in code. At least he could still appreciate beauty. It seemed odd for it to be so lovely and warm in January when back in Bootle it would be freezing.

By now, all was quiet. Forty-three aircraft had taken off around midnight, and thirty-seven had returned, one with a badly damaged propeller, which had been removed. The men, including Sean, who'd been on night duty would stay until eight o'clock, when the day shift took over and they could go back to their quarters and sleep. In the meantime, there was always the hope that the missing aircraft might still turn up. So far, there'd been no radio contact.

Sergeant Ellis, who was in charge, needed two men to go and collect a new propeller from the stores a few miles inland.

'If you go now, the roads will be clear and we can get it fitted by tonight. Later, you could get stuck behind a bloody horse and cart the whole way there and back. There's bound to be a religious festival of some sort.' There were religious festivals for one saint or another virtually every day in Malta.

The sergeant scanned the group of rather bored men, all anxious for a kip. 'Doyle, you can drive, and Maitland, you go with him. While you're there, you can fill the truck up with petrol.'

Sean's heart sank. He couldn't stand Alfie Maitland, a loud-mouthed individual who was incapable of having a conversation without peppering it with four-letter words. Even worse, he was a drinker and had been swigging rum all night, as was his habit, something the sergeant was unaware of.

'I'll go with Doyle, if that's all right, Sarge,' offered Bernie Roberts, who was a far more reasonable human being and also a sort of friend of Sean's. He winked at him now.

But Sergeant Ellis turned down the offer. Having made his decision, he wanted it followed to the letter.

Neither Sean nor Maitland spoke much on the way to the maintenance unit. The other man made a few remarks that Sean regarded as inane, and rather crude, while continuing to sip at his bottle of rum.

When they reached the unit, Sean drove through the open doors of a large hangar to the part where he knew the propellers were stored. The night staff were on duty, and a couple of them had appeared by the time Sean braked. He handed over the chit Sergeant Ellis had made out, and the new propeller was quickly secured on the back of the truck, a blade protruding from each side.

'You'd best get in the back,' Sean said gruffly to Maitland. 'Make sure the propeller doesn't fall off.' No matter how well it had been tied on, it could work loose as the truck was driven along the island's bumpy dirt roads.

'Get stuffed, Doyle.' And to everyone's surprise,

174

Maitland leapt into the truck and sat behind the steering wheel. When Sean attempted to drag him out, he started the engine and the truck began to move. In desperation, not wanting to be left behind, Sean managed to pull himself on to the back with the propeller.

'Hang on!' yelled one of the maintenance men as Maitland picked up speed and drove like a maniac towards the doors of the hangar. They had been opened wide enough to allow the truck in, but weren't wide enough to let it out now that it had a propeller loaded on the back.

'Stop, you bloody idiot!' screamed the man.

Maitland responded with a jubilant yell as the cab of the truck burst through the hangar doors. The blades of the propeller were caught on both sides with such force that the rope securing it snapped, and it was thrown off the back of the truck, Sean with it.

And then everything went black.

Chapter 11

Kate had had a lovely time in Norfolk, and was thrilled because she'd heard from Lily, her eldest daughter.

'I told her where I would be at Christmas and she sent a card and said she'd like to come and see me. She suggested next Saturday. Would you mind, Eileen?' Lily was twenty-one and worked as an admissions officer in a military hospital in Essex. 'She can sleep with me.'

It was Kate's second night home, and she and Eileen were sitting lazily in front of the dying fire at almost midnight. Napoleon was purring on Eileen's knee, keeping her warm. Nicky had been fast asleep in bed for hours.

Eileen said she felt offended to be asked. 'Of course I wouldn't mind. This is your home at the moment, isn't it?'

Kate happily agreed that it was. 'When she comes, I'll try and get something special for tea.'

'Would you like me to go out so you and Lily can have the place to yourselves?'

Now it was Kate's turn to claim to be offended. 'Just as if! It might be my home, but it's your house, isn't it? Anyway, I'd like you to be here in case there are any embarrassing silences, which you can fill with idle chatter.'

'I'm good at idle chatter,' Eileen said with a smile.

'Maybe so, but you're not very good at hiding the fact that something pretty awful happened while I was away,' Kate said drily. 'Whenever you think I'm not watching, you look dead miserable, as people say in Liverpool. What's wrong, love?'

Eileen sighed, but was relieved to be able to share the news about Nick with someone. 'He's having an affair with an eighteen-year-old girl and she's pregnant,' she explained in a rush. 'They're about to move in together.'

Kate literally went pale with shock. 'I can't even bring myself to imagine what you must have said when he came home at New Year. I mean, how did you manage not to kill him?'

'I didn't say anything.' Eileen was aware how inadequate she must appear in other women's eyes. There were many who wouldn't have let Nick in the house – even if it was his house. 'He doesn't know I know. I want him back,' she said fiercely. 'I'm not prepared to give him up without a fight – and I'm fighting in the only way I know how.'

'And did it work?' Kate looked doubtful. 'The fighting?'

'I don't know. I might not know until the war is over and it's time for him to choose.'

'It seems she, the girl – what's her name?'

'Doria.'

'Doria has a very big advantage over you – she's with him all the time. Whereas you...' Kate paused.

'I only see him when he feels like it.' Eileen shrugged. 'Then I'll just have to fight harder, won't I?' She had written Nick a long, tender letter, but had no idea what to do next. It all felt very limp. 'I really should go to London and face

177

him.' Or should she? 'I never dreamt I'd end up fighting for Nick.'

On Saturday morning, Kate went to the station to meet Lily. Mother and daughter returned to the cottage in tears, having experienced an emotional reunion. Lily was a pretty young woman, very like her mother must have been at twenty-one. With Nicky's help, Eileen had set the table for lunch – home-made potato soup, a one-egg omelette each with slices of fried potato, and apple charlotte for afters. It was quite a decent spread for wartime.

'We grow our own potatoes,' Eileen explained, 'so we have loads. And loads of apples too. I would have liked to make an apple pie, but we haven't any lard. Our neighbours occasionally give us eggs.'

'It was a lovely meal.' Lily patted her stomach. 'Thank you very much.'

Eileen took Nicky upstairs, where she managed to find lots of things to do, leaving Kate and Lily to discuss in privacy the tragic story of their lives so far – a mother and her daughters separated for years due to the evil nature of the husband and father. While she dusted and tidied drawers, she couldn't help but overhear snippets of their conversation.

'Dad said you kept having affairs with different men,' Lily said.

'Oh, but that's not true,' Kate protested.

Then later, 'He told us you never really wanted children.'

'I would have liked *more* children, darling, but

178

he'd already turned against me by the time I had Maisie.'

Maisie was Kate's youngest daughter. Eileen paused in the middle of rearranging the ornaments on the dressing table to reflect that it wasn't just wars that made people unhappy and turned their lives upside down: people of ill will were quite capable of doing the same thing. Her own first husband, Francis, had been that sort of man. She shivered just thinking about him.

She could have easily cried, but didn't want to upset Nicky, who was in his favourite place in the world – sitting in the middle of the double bed playing with his teddy bears. She hugged him and told him she loved him very much.

'I love you too, Mum,' he assured her. He picked up the tiny teddy that Lena Newton had brought him months ago. 'But I love little Pip best of all.'

It was a Saturday afternoon at the end of January when Jack Doyle remarked to his daughter Sheila, 'Y'know, luv, I haven't heard from our Sean for quite a few weeks.'

'Well I haven't heard from him for nearly a whole year,' Sheila complained. She was attacking a mountain of ironing. The younger children were being unnaturally quiet and the older ones had gone to the matinee at the Palace in Marsh Lane to see *Deadwood Dick*. 'In fact, I've only had about two letters since he was called up, and then they were written on a titchy scrap of paper.'

'I know, luv,' Jack said patiently, 'but he sent them on your birthday, if I remember right. The lad can't be expected to write letters to every

179

single member of his family. He writes to Alice and to me, and the ones he writes to me are for you and our Eileen too. Anyroad,' he continued, annoyed at the interruption, 'it was well before Christmas that I had the last letter, and there's been nowt since.'

Sheila looked worried. '*That* long! Maybe he's been posted somewhere else. You said, didn't you, Dad, that there wouldn't be much more need for him to be in Malta; that he'd be sent to Italy soon, or back home?'

'If that was the case, luv, he'd have written to us like a shot.' Jack frowned. He was getting really worried about Sean. He got to his feet and groaned along with his creaking bones. 'I'll go and see Alice, see if she's heard.'

Number 5 wasn't just the best house in Pearl Street; it was probably also the cleanest and the shiniest. Alice Doyle, Jack's daughter-in-law, was in the kitchen in the middle of drying the dishes when he went in, rubbing a dinner plate with such zeal he thought she could well make a hole in it. Little Edward was seated by the table, playing with a wooden train set. A delicate child of just over a year, he wasn't nearly as robust as Eileen's Nicky or Sheila's lads. Jack patted him affectionately on the head and the child blew him a raspberry. Should anyone dare to call him 'Eddie', Alice would correct them, saying in a stern voice, 'His name is Edward, if you don't mind.'

'Hello, luv,' Jack said guardedly to his son's wife. At twenty, she was less than half his age, and half his size, yet she scared him witless. A tiny wisp of a girl with the face of an angel, she had more character in her little finger than most people had in their entire bodies.

At the sound of his voice, she turned upon him like one of those whirling dervishes he'd heard about. Her long skirt flared, exposing the specially made boot she wore because her left leg was three inches shorter than the right. 'Have you come about our Sean?' she demanded.

'Yes, I have.'

'Have you heard from him, then?'

'No, I haven't, luv.'

She collapsed on a chair as if all the air had gone out of her. 'I'd've come to ask if you'd had a letter, but if you'd said no then I'd only have been more worried than I was already. I was hoping you'd had a letter and mine had gone astray. D'ye know what I mean, Mr Doyle?'

He hadn't the faintest idea what she meant. He also wished she'd stop calling him 'Mr Doyle' and call him 'Jack' instead, but he'd given up suggesting it. 'I just hope there's nothing wrong,' he said.

'There can't be anything wrong,' she cried passionately. 'I won't *let* there be. Sean's all right, I'm sure of it. The good Lord will have been keeping an eye on him.'

Jack Doyle hadn't an ounce of faith in the good Lord keeping an eye on anyone. If that was the case, then why hadn't he been keeping an eye on the millions of people who'd already died in this bloody awful war? He thought it best to keep his trap shut in front of Alice, who had a fearful temper.

181

'Our Harry got his call-up papers the other day,' she said. She already had one brother, Tommy, in the army.

'Well I doubt he'll be in for long,' Jack assured her. 'The war's bound to be over by this time next year.'

'That's what they said this time last year,' she pointed out.

Jack escaped, but not before promising to come round straight away if he heard from Sean, and Alice promised to come and see him if she got a letter first.

In London, Nick Stephens had received an item of news that had come as a bit of a shock. The bedroom of the apartment he rented in Birdcage Walk was extremely small. It had been perfectly adequate until he'd met Doria. Even then, a young, healthy man and woman having to occupy a single bed had been more of a pleasure than an inconvenience, but it was beginning to feel a bit cramped now that she was pregnant. They would certainly require a bigger space once the baby was born.

It seemed as if they'd been extraordinarily lucky when a ground-floor flat with two bedrooms became vacant in the same building directly after Christmas. Nick applied for it immediately, Doria gave in her notice at her own flat – she had long ago left the family home in Wimbledon – and she and Nick prepared to move in together.

The shock came when they were turned down on moral grounds.

'That's what it said in the letter,' an astounded

Nick told Doria later in the day. 'On moral grounds.'

'What do they mean?' Doria enquired, puzzled. For all her expensive education, she wasn't nearly as clever as Eileen, who'd left school at fourteen.

Nick smiled. 'We're not married, are we, idiot? We'd be living in sin. And the landlord of the building disapproves.' The smile faded. Put like that, it sounded rather shameful. He thought about Eileen and the time they'd spent together in the New Year, and felt like a cad. He was behaving disgracefully, but was unable to see a way out of it.

'We'll have to find somewhere pretty quick,' he said. On top of everything, he'd been given a week's notice for his present room. He was no longer a desirable tenant; they wanted him off the premises.

The flat Nick eventually found wasn't in nearly such a pleasant area. He would no longer be able to walk to the office. It was advertised as South Kensington, but was really on the edge of Fulham. Unlike the Birdcage Walk flat, it was much too big, having two huge rooms with high ceilings, a cavernous bathroom and a tiny alcove of a kitchen.

Doria, always easy-going, said she didn't mind. Each day she brought another suitcase of clothes and other possessions round to Nick's flat, ready to be moved to the new place on Friday evening when he was due to leave – or be chucked out, Nick thought drily.

They ended up having to make several journeys by bus and underground to get everything from one place to the other, taxis being rarely available

183

even in London. Not that everything would have fitted in a single cab anyway.

The enchantment of their affair hadn't completely vanished, but something had changed. Instead of being exciting and illicit, it had become immoral. Although Nick considered the landlord of his flat to be unnecessarily narrow-minded – after all, there was a war on and everything had turned topsy-turvy – it nevertheless made him feel uncomfortable being thrown out of his digs. It wasn't the sort of thing that happened to a chap like him.

To make matters worse, the Jerries had started to bomb London at night again, though the raids weren't as heavy as they had been in the early years of the war. It just made life a trial when it had been a pleasure. Doria had to leave work when the baby began to show, and there she was, stuck miles away from the West End and the shops that she loved. It was all rather unfortunate, Nick thought sadly.

It wasn't until February was almost over that Alice received a letter from the War Ministry to say that her husband, Sean Doyle, was seriously ill in St Steven's Hospital, South Promenade, Blackpool, Lancashire.

She had Edward's warm coat on him in a jiffy, along with his woolly hat and a pair of mittens, but when she reached Jack Doyle's house, he'd gone to work. Alice stamped her foot in frustration, annoyed with herself for always expecting her father-in-law to be there to help in an emergency. Years ago, Sean's dad had fought hard to get compensation when her own dad had been killed in an accident on the docks. He'd obtained £25, which had been a boon at the time, helping the family through until her mam found a job and could provide for her family of six young children. While other people had urged her to put them in an orphanage, Jack Doyle had kept them together. Since then, Alice had worshipped him, not that anyone would ever know, and certainly not Jack himself.

After some thought, she wheeled the pushchair around to Sheila's.

Sheila was sitting at the table doing absolutely nothing. 'I've just got four of 'em off to school,' she explained. 'In a minute I'll sort out the other three.' The sound of childish laughter was coming from upstairs.

Alice waved the letter that had come that morning. 'Sean's in hospital in Blackpool.'

'Is he now? Let's see.' Sheila grabbed the letter and quickly read it. 'What are we going to do?' she asked.

'I'm going to Blackpool to see him. Here and now, like. Would you mind looking after Edward while I'm gone?'

Sheila looked shocked. 'Oh, Alice, Blackpool's a long way away. Would you like me to come with you?'

Alice wanted nothing of the kind. She just wanted to be left alone to find her husband, no matter how hard it might be.

'No, ta, Sheila. I'd sooner go on me own.' There were times when Alice's confidence knew no bounds.

185

Sheila knew it was no use arguing. She nodded. 'All right, girl. Do you need some money?'

'I've got money at home, thanks.' Alice abruptly kissed Edward on the top of his head and left.

In her own house, she upturned the old tea caddy that held the cash she'd been saving for an emergency ever since she and Sean had married. There hadn't been one as yet, but now there was an emergency bigger than any she had ever imagined. She picked up the two crumpled ten-shilling notes and the assortment of copper and silver coins and counted them; she had thirty-two shillings and fourpence halfpenny.

She put the money in her purse and sat down at the table. All of a sudden, the confidence had gone. Instead, she was panting for breath and felt as sick as a dog. She had no idea how to get to Blackpool. None of Sean's relatives realised that she had scarcely been outside Bootle in her life. When Mam was alive, they'd sometimes gone on the tram to Scotland Road, where there was a market and they'd bought enough second-hand clothes to see the family through the next few months, but that, and Eileen's house in Melling, was as far as she had ever been.

She knew Blackpool wasn't far away, because it was in Lancashire, and Bootle was in Lancashire too. She reckoned if she caught a train from Marsh Lane station then she would be going in the right direction and at some point she'd find out which way to go next. All she had to do was grit her teeth and get on with it. It was what she'd done when she used to take in washing. She'd come home laden with a frightening amount of bedding that had to be washed and ironed quickly, and had worked till midnight day after day until it was done and she could return it to its owner in good time and be paid what she was owed.

Alice had never let anyone down, and she certainly had no intention of letting down her darling Sean, who was lying seriously ill in a hospital somewhere in Blackpool.

It was a relief to discover that an electric train would take her from Marsh Lane to Exchange station in Liverpool, from where she would catch another train, a steam one this time, to Blackpool.

It would have been an adventure if the reason for her journey had been less worrisome, passing row after row of streets on the way in to Liverpool. Alice knew that there were millions of people in the world and that thousands of them lived in Liverpool, but it was strange to see proof of it for the first time.

The journey to Blackpool was just as interesting, stopping as it did at St Helens and Wigan and at a place called Preston, where hundreds of soldiers were waiting for other trains to take them to places unknown.

Alice alighted from the train in Blackpool feeling as if she'd just landed on the moon. It looked so strange, with its tall houses and closed shops and not all that many people about when she'd thought it would be crowded. But perhaps that was only in the summer, when people came on holiday.

The letter said that Sean's hospital was on South Promenade. 'Just catch a tram along the front, luv,' a porter at the station told her, so Alice did, and it looked even more like the moon as she trundled past some alarming constructions and the weirdest buildings, with signs proclaiming themselves Pleasure Park, Amusements, Fortunes Told and even a Ghost Train, whatever that was.

Out of the window on the other side of the tram, the Irish Sea was a vast expanse of huddled waves the colour of mud, and the sky was full of mottled grey clouds without a patch of blue.

Alice had never felt so alone before. She was relieved when the alarming constructions ended and houses took their place, some of them extremely grand. She got off the tram in case it passed the hospital without her knowing.

Her boot was hurting badly by the time she arrived at a big double-fronted sandstone building with a sign above the glass doors saying that it was St Steven's Hospital. She limped up the steps and through the doors into a small hallway with a room marked Reception. She had no idea what that meant, but she knocked on the door anyway; it seemed the obvious thing to do.

A woman inside shouted, 'Come in.'

'Good afternoon,' she said when Alice entered.

'Good afternoon.' Alice had thought it was still only morning. She produced the letter from the hospital and said she had come to see Aircraftsman Sean Doyle. She was instructed to take a seat outside and a Dr Whelan would come and see her shortly.

The doctor turned out to be a charming

Irishman with twinkly brown eyes and a head of thick grey curls. As they climbed the stairs towards the first floor, Alice asked if her husband would be expecting her. 'I came the minute I got the letter,' she said.

Dr Whelan looked at her sadly. 'I'm afraid not, Mrs Doyle.' He didn't explain why, but opened a door, and there was the dearest husband in the world lying on a bed with his eyes closed, though they opened wide when Alice threw herself on top of him and showered his face with kisses.

The doctor took her arm and pulled her gently away, and Alice was left to stare into Sean's familiar brown eyes, which showed absolutely no acknowledgement, no familiar twinkle, no sign whatsoever that he recognised who she was.

'What's wrong with him?' she asked in an anguished voice. She had expected to see him perhaps with his arm in a sling, his leg in plaster, a bandage on his head, but not looking perfectly whole except for his empty eyes.

'He has amnesia, Mrs Doyle,' Dr Whelan said quietly. 'He has lost his memory. There was an incident in Malta.'

'Will it ever come back?'

'Hopefully; in time.'

'In time,' Alice echoed. She was regarding her husband silently, not knowing what to do or say, when a familiar voice from behind her said, 'There you are, girl,' and she turned to see that Jack Doyle had entered the room.

'Mr Doyle!' Alice launched herself at him and he had no alternative but to catch her in his arms. 'He's here, can you see him, our Sean? But he

189

can't see us.'

Jack set her back on the floor. 'He can see us, luv. He just doesn't know who we are.'

'Oh, but he will one day, won't he?' she said eagerly. 'One day soon?'

'Let's hope so.' He turned to the doctor. 'I'm Sean's father: I rang up this morning,' he said. Then, to Alice, 'Sheila managed to get a message to me at work. I came straight away.'

The doctor left, and Jack and Alice sat and talked to Sean for a good hour, though by the time they left he had shown no sign at all of recognising them.

'I reckon we'd better start making tracks back to Bootle,' Jack said eventually. 'Have you had anything to eat today, luv?'

Alice remembered that the letter had arrived before she'd had so much as a cup of tea. 'No,' she admitted.

'Then we'll go somewhere and have a drink and a sarnie, then get the train home.'

Alice didn't think she'd be able to eat again until Sean was better and had recovered his memory. She said so to his dad.

'Don't be daft,' Jack snorted. 'We don't want Sean getting better while his missus steadily wastes away. It wouldn't exactly please him, would it?'

On Saturday, Jack and Alice, this time accompanied by Sean's sisters, Sheila and Eileen, travelled to Blackpool together.

The problem of the children – Sheila's seven,

along with Alice's Edward and Eileen's Nicky – was solved when Kate volunteered to look after all of them at the cottage in Melling, as long as a few other people were willing to give her a hand. Brenda Mahon, bringing her girls, and Lena Newton offered to help. Phyllis Taylor, when she heard, insisted on coming along too. Phyllis liked having her finger in every available pie.

It was the first day of March, the sun was out, and spring was in the air. You could almost smell the forthcoming sunshine, the plants that were about to grow and the leaves that would soon appear on the trees.

Kate had drawn up a timetable showing expected mealtimes and games to play and pinned it to the kitchen door. A giant pan of scouse had been simmering on the stove since early morning; a cake missing all sorts of ingredients, fortunately none of them essential, was waiting to go in the oven; lemonade and sweets had been purchased and a few small prizes were there to be won.

The kittens, Godfrey and Tommy, had been left in the flat over the dairy as company for each other.

They arrived at the cottage like a youthful army, marching in pairs. The older ones played hide and seek, first in the house, then in the garden when a pale sun appeared mid-morning. Afterwards, they picked daisies and made chains. Dominic Reilly, Sheila's eldest boy, who was nearly twelve, became aware that Monica Mahon, Brenda's elder girl, who was approaching eleven, was outstandingly

191

pretty, with her chestnut-brown ringlets and wide-apart grey eyes. He had known her his entire life, but had never really noticed her before.

When they gathered round the big table in the cottage for their dinner, he held out the chair next to his for her to sit on. 'Thank you,' she whispered, blushing slightly. She thought what a nice lad he was, if a bit loud and extremely naughty a lot of the time, though not now.

After the meal was over, the four youngest were put to sleep in Eileen's double bed, where Lena Newton watched over them, wishing that at least one of them belonged to her. Maurice had been transferred to a ship whose job it was to take supplies to Russia, so she didn't see as much of him as she used to. She knew she should have been sorry and was ashamed that she felt glad, even though it meant there was less chance of her having a baby than there'd been before.

Dinner over, the older children went outside again. On the list that Kate had made, they were due to play rounders. Instead, they went mad, climbing trees, doing cartwheels, and running around with their arms spread wide like aeroplanes while making the appropriate noises and pretending to shoot each other down.

Halfway through the afternoon, Peter Mallory turned up. He was disappointed that Eileen wasn't there, but was willing to organise a game of cricket, 'If there's a bat around anywhere.'

Brenda said she thought there was one in the garden shed, while Kate wondered who on earth he was.

'He's a friend of Eileen's,' said Lena, who'd met

Peter before. 'But I could have sworn his name was Wood, not Mallory.'

Kate didn't care what his name was; she was just thankful that a man had turned up to keep the older boys in hand, though Dominic, who she'd thought at first was the naughtiest of the boys, showed no interest in cricket and seemed happy to share the swing with one of Brenda's daughters. Kate considered it rather touching, though by now she was longing for the mothers to come back and reclaim their various children.

They arrived, Eileen, Sheila and Alice, just after six o'clock, when the children were exhausted and had collapsed in odd places all over the house, from where they were collected and counted.

'How was Sean?' Kate asked, concerned at the sight of their miserable faces.

'Not so hot,' Sheila said with a sigh. She clapped her hands and her oldest children pretended to stand to attention. Two of them saluted. 'There's nothing funny about anything,' Sheila snapped. 'Your uncle Sean's not at all well. Fetch your coats and we'll go home.'

'He's lost his memory,' Eileen explained to everyone. 'But they're letting him out in a fortnight, see how he gets on with his family all around him.'

'He's going to get better,' Alice said fiercely. 'I'll make him better if it kills me.'

It was dark by the time everyone arrived back in Pearl Street. The children, young and old, were quite agreeable to going to bed early. Even Phyllis Taylor felt tired after spending an entire day chasing after eleven children, not that she hadn't enjoyed herself tremendously. Her mother worked disgracefully long hours and wouldn't be home until ten. Phyllis decided to listen to some music while reading a book, two of her favourite occupations.

She had turned on the gas fire and Radio Luxembourg was on the wireless, with Bing Crosby singing a collection of songs from Broadway shows, when there was a knock on the door. It couldn't be anybody local, or they would have just pulled the key through the letter box and let themselves in. Always interested in anything even faintly out of the ordinary, Phyllis leapt to her feet and went to answer the door.

A young, truly gorgeous American soldier was standing on the pavement outside, a jeep parked in the street behind him. He looked disappointed when Phyllis appeared and she wondered who he had expected to see.

'The lady who used to live here, she had red hair,' he said haltingly. 'Is she in?'

'You mean Mrs Fleming – Jessica? She's Mrs Henningsen now.' Phyllis had never met Jessica, but had heard all sorts of interesting things about her, including the fact that she had the most amazing red hair.

He nodded eagerly. 'That's right, Jessica.'

'Well, after marrying Captain Henningsen, she went to live near Warrington. He's an American, like you.'

The soldier shifted from foot to foot. 'I'm going about this all the wrong way, miss. It's not Jessica – Mrs Henningsen – I wanted to see; it's the girl who lived here with her: Kitty Quigley.'

'Ah! Kitty, well she...' Phyllis paused and a whole chain of thoughts chased each other through her head. She reckoned this must be the soldier that Kitty had fallen madly in love with and who had made her pregnant. But Kitty was living directly across the street, happily married to George Ransome and now expecting his baby. On the other hand, she had only married George while on the rebound from the exceptionally attractive specimen of manhood staring at Phyllis at this very moment, waiting for her to reply. The man was married, but perhaps his wife had died or divorced him. Would Kitty be able to resist him if it turned out he was now available? Phyllis had noticed that some people didn't think twice about dispensing with honour and integrity when there was a war on. Look at her own father! All in all, in the long run it would be better if Kitty wasn't told that her old lover had come in search of her, whether he was still married or not.

She smiled warmly at the soldier. 'Would you like to come in for a minute?'

He stepped inside. 'Why, thank you, miss. I'm Dale Tooley, by the way – Sergeant. I haven't been this way, Lancashire, for a long time. I'm normally based in Kent.'

'I'm normally based in Beverley, near Hull, and my name is Phyllis Taylor.'

She directed him into the sitting room, where she turned off the wireless and sat at the table, indicating to him to sit opposite so she could admire him – he wouldn't be there for much longer. He had lovely brown hair, slightly curly, and

195

brown eyes with enviably long lashes.

'My mum and I have lived here for about eighteen months,' she told him. 'We rented the house off Jessica – Mrs Henningsen. I've been told that Kitty was a nurse.'

'That's right, she was a nurse,' he interrupted.

'It seems she joined up and went away on a hospital ship. It sailed somewhere, I think it was Australia, where she met a doctor and they got married.'

'Did she!' His face fell, and Phyllis went off him quite a bit, despite him being utterly gorgeous. Did he think he could just break Kitty's heart and leave her pregnant with his child, then turn up and expect her to fall into his arms? 'Is that where she lives – Australia?' he asked shakily.

'Yes, I'm sure of it – in Melbourne, as a matter of fact. She has two children, a boy and a girl,' Phyllis told him, rubbing it in. 'Twins,' she added, in case there hadn't been time for Kitty to have married and become pregnant twice. 'Apparently she's extremely happy.'

'Is she really?' His shoulders hunched and he stood to leave. 'Well, thank you, Miss Taylor. It's kind of you to pass on this information. I'll leave you in peace now.'

Phyllis showed him out, wishing she'd kept him for a bit longer – offered him a cup of tea, perhaps. She heard the jeep start up and drive away and was about to switch the wireless back on again and pick up her book when there was another knock at the door, much louder than the first.

Phyllis rolled her eyes in mock exasperation:

196

she was rather enjoying the drama of having two callers on a Saturday night. 'Who is it this time?' she asked herself out loud.

She opened the door and her father burst into the house. 'What the hell d'you think you're doing entertaining a bloody Yank at this time of night?' he shouted.

Phyllis put on a bored look and glanced at her watch. 'It's only half past eight,' she said. 'And I wasn't entertaining him. He just came to ask a question.'

'What sort of question?' her father asked suspiciously.

She thought of saying something outrageous, but he looked too mad to take a joke. She strolled back into the living room and he followed. 'He was looking for a woman who used to live here.'

'How long was he here?' He still looked suspicious. 'And where's your mother?'

Phyllis lost her temper. '*He* was here about ten minutes,' she shouted. 'And she's where she is most of the time: at work. She works all the hours God sends these days. Why aren't *you* at work, Dad? It's Saturday; isn't that when pubs are at their busiest?'

'I'm sick,' he said.

'You don't look sick.' He had shaved off his beard and looked better without it. She'd always been proud of having such a youthfully handsome father. 'And what are you doing in our street?' she demanded.

'I just happened to be walking past the house.'

'It's a cul-de-sac,' Phyllis pointed out.

He scowled and looked uncomfortable. 'Oh, all

197

right, I've been keeping an eye on you and your mother. I was worried about you.'

'Huh!' Phyllis said scornfully. 'It's a bit late in the day, isn't it?'

He sat down in the chair the American had just vacated. 'Yes,' he conceded. 'I know I've been a bastard, but what's happened is Mick O'Brien has been called up and I don't know what to do about it.'

'Who's Mick O'Brien?'

'It's who I'm supposed to be, isn't it? I told you when we met at Christmas. Mick walked out on Dawn, so I moved in and took over his identity. We were about the same age. It all seemed a bit of a joke at the time. But now they've started calling up chaps in their forties. I don't mind doing my bit, but doing it using Mick's name is taking things a bit too far.'

'You could get into serious trouble,' his daughter warned him.

'There's no need to tell me that, Phyllis. I already know.' He scratched his neck and looked helpless. 'What am I going to do?'

'Are you still in love with Dawn?' Phyllis asked.

He thought a bit, looked dubious, wrinkled his nose, then said, 'Nah! I don't think I ever was. Not really.' He reached across the table and seized her arm. 'You had to be here to experience those air raids, Phyll. It was like hell on earth. Every night you feared for your life. You'd come out of the shelter next morning and there'd be houses right in front of you reduced to rubble. The world was a different place from when you went in. It made you wonder what you'd been put on earth for.'

198

'To be unfaithful to your wife and desert your one and only child?' Phyllis suggested sarcastically, wanting to rile him, but he merely shook his head and looked sad.

'Your mother always claimed I'd never properly grew up,' he said. 'That I was a sort of Peter Pan. I suppose I got ideas about being young again, squeezing more out of life than I already had; that sort of thing. Then when I heard at Christmas that you and your mum had been looking for me, I felt awful about it. Now with this Mick O'Brien business, I realise what a clot I've been.'

'So what are you going to do?'

'I dunno. Have you got any suggestions?' He regarded her hopefully.

'Not at the moment.' She jumped to her feet. 'I'll think about it, but I think you should leave. I'm not expecting Mum until after ten, but very occasionally she comes home early. The last thing we want is for her to find you here.'

'I'll be off then.'

Before leaving, he had the nerve to kiss her on the cheek.

Phyllis waited to give him time to leave the street before putting on her coat and going for a walk. She felt like getting out of the house for a while.

Men, she thought as she walked along the dark streets. What babies they were, what fools. What was the point of them?

Gosh, it was dark! There was no moon, and the clouds were great mountains of black with angry streaks of orange here and there, as if there was a fire burning behind them. Phyllis stopped walking and stared at the sky, both impressed and terrified at how vast it was, and how incredibly ugly. It made her, made the whole world, feel very small and unimportant. There must be more to *it*, more to something that she couldn't think of the word for, than just this single planet.

And why had God let there be a war like this one, with ordinary human beings helpless against hundreds and thousands of bombs dropped from aeroplanes way up in the sky? Was that why aeroplanes had been invented? To kill people, rather than fly them to other countries to see what the rest of what should have been a wonderful world was like?

Phyllis began to cry. She leant against the wall and slid down until she was crouched on the pavement. It was someone's house, the wireless was on, and she could hear Judy Garland singing 'Somewhere Over the Rainbow'.

She had gone to see *The Wizard of Oz* with her mum and dad in Hull as soon as it came out. She'd been thirteen. Oh, how she'd loved that song! It had seemed to express all the good things she wanted to do with her life, the marvellous adventures she would have, the places she would go. But the war had spoilt it, not just for her but for everyone, young and old alike.

Things would be no better on the other side of the rainbow than they were on this side, of that she was sure.

She wished now that she'd been honest with Dale Tooley when she'd spoken to him earlier. How could she have lied to him, told him that Kitty was on the other side of the world when she

200

was merely across the road with his baby daughter? It was up to Kitty; Dale Tooley and George Ransome to sort out their lives, not her. She might have done something truly terrible by keeping back the truth. Although she could tell Kitty tomorrow that her American had come looking for her, Phyllis could think of all sorts of reasons why it might only make things worse.

And was she being just as silly and selfish, thinking she was some sort of god, by not telling her mother that her husband was alive and well? It was up to Mum to decide if she wanted Dad back, not her, not their daughter.

Phyllis struggled to her feet and realised she had no idea where she was. Now she was lost on top of everything else. She began to cry again, and was still crying when two elderly ladies who'd been to a whist drive found her and took her home to Pearl Street.

She felt considerably better after turning on the wireless and lighting the fire. She boiled water so that she could make tea for her mum the instant she entered the house.

'Are you all right, love?' her mother asked later when she was sitting comfortably in her chair drinking the tea. 'You look as if you've been crying.'

'I'm fine, Mum,' Phyllis assured her. 'Just a bit tired, that's all. By then, she was fine, almost, but she also felt a little older, a little wiser, and a little sadder than she'd been before her mother had gone to work earlier in the day.

Chapter 12

On St Patrick's Day, Sean Doyle came home to Pearl Street. Strictly speaking, he had never lived in the street, but round the corner in Garnet Street with his father. He'd been away when Alice had acquired number 5.

Alice had always imagined him exclaiming with delight when he was shown around the wonderful house with the electric stove, seeing it for the first time. But although Sean could walk, he couldn't talk. He couldn't understand what people said to him, though a little part of his brain was still alive. His body told him when it was time to go to the lavatory. It told him how to use a knife and fork when he was given food or to how to hold a cup when a drink was offered.

If Edward, the son he had never seen, was placed carefully on his lap, then Sean would hold him just as carefully, but not look at him in the way a father should. His eyes were dead, without expression. They never lit up for anything. He never smiled.

Alice insisted he remain in the living room, not go to the parlour where it was quiet, which he might prefer.

'No, I want him in here, with us,' she said. 'I want him getting used to us, his family.' Alice and her brothers and sisters ate around him, laughed around him, sang to him, kissed and hugged him.

On the quiet, when only the two of them were there – oh, not counting Edward – Alice even danced for him. It was something she had done before in their old place; a crooked sort of skipping motion from one foot to the other that used to make him laugh because her left leg was shorter than the right. But even this strange exhibition did nothing to stir Sean out of his coma, or whatever it was called. Nobody, not even the doctors, knew precisely what was wrong with him.

The chair beneath the window was designated Sean's chair, just as a different chair beneath a different window had belonged to Alice's dad what seemed like a million years ago. After only a few days at home, Sean began to automatically sit in his chair whenever he entered the room.

Jack Doyle came every day to hold his son's hand. His sisters visited regularly, told him jokes and reminded him of the funny things he'd done when he was a little boy.

But nothing could make Sean smile or stir him out of his trance.

Eileen had forgotten all about the Easter garden party that had been held at the cottage at Easter for the last few years. She was reminded of it late in January by Cicily Dean, who usually arranged for posters to be made and also collected the entrance money at the gate. Cicily belonged to the Women's Voluntary Services, who used the money raised for all sorts of good purposes.

'It had slipped my mind,' Eileen confessed to Cicily when she called at the cottage. 'I'm afraid I've had lots of things to think about.'

'We thought something like that might have happened.' Cicily nodded understandingly. She was a sweet-natured woman who, at only sixty-one, had recently become a great-grandmother. 'With a war on, there's so many things to worry about. How is your husband, by the way?'

Eileen's husband was the thing she was most worried about. Not only had she not seen or heard from him since New Year's Day, her letters since had gone unanswered and the last one had been returned, unopened, and with 'Gone Away' written on the envelope.

'Oh, Nick's fine,' she told Cicily Dean.

The garden party went ahead on Easter Saturday, though Eileen didn't play much part in it. The hoop-la had been unearthed from someone's shed, and the shove ha'penny table from somewhere else. Pasting tables were set up and were laden with White Elephant items, or badly knitted garments that people might well buy to undo and knit up again. Cakes and prizes appeared from nowhere – the first prize in the raffle was a tiny wicker basket containing four bars of soap shaped like fruit.

The kitchen in the cottage was used to make drinks; Eileen's sisters and friends came from Bootle to lend a hand and her dad arrived to protect the back garden from strangers who might trample on his precious vegetable plants.

Kate wasn't there; she was spending the day in Liverpool with her daughters, the first time all four of them had been together in at least ten years.

Peter Mallory came up from London. He

hadn't seen Eileen since Christmas. The last time he'd come was the day she'd gone to Blackpool to see her brother and they'd missed each other – or at least he had missed her; he doubted she had given him a second thought.

He was surprised she seemed so pleased to see him at Easter until she said, 'Peter! I need to talk to you about Nick.' She hadn't wanted to see him for himself, but to ask about her husband.

Had the bastard told her he'd moved house? he wondered. Nick and Doria had been living in Fulham for months now. Well, he wasn't going to lie to her. As soon as he had the opportunity, he'd tell her the truth.

It seemed she wanted the opportunity to be now, straight away. And who could blame her?

She took him to the bottom of the garden, where, amidst the vegetables, there was an old wooden bench. Her father was standing not far away, but fortunately out of earshot, looking as if he was on guard for some reason. The big cat, Napoleon, was perched on his favourite tree, glaring at the visitors.

'The last time I saw Nick was on New Year's Day,' she told him in a thin, shaky voice when they were seated. 'Since then I've had a letter returned marked "Gone Away". Have you any idea where he is?'

Peter took a deep breath. His feelings were mixed. He didn't like giving her bad news, but at the same time he knew he had acquired a faintly holier-than-thou attitude when telling her about Nick's appalling behaviour.

'Nick and Doria have moved to Fulham,' he

said. He was about to add, 'and are living as man and wife', but couldn't bring himself to hurt her so cruelly. 'They need a bigger place for the baby.'

She seemed to wilt beside him. 'He didn't bother to tell me,' she whispered.

'I think he's bitten off more than he can chew,' Peter said. The last time he'd seen Nick, he'd looked vaguely frantic. 'He'd expected to just go on having a damned good time, not move to a dingy flat miles away from the West End.'

Eileen didn't speak. Peter reckoned she couldn't think of anything to say. After a while she muttered, 'What on earth am I going to do?'

He realised she wasn't expecting him to come up with a solution, but was asking the question of herself. 'Why don't you go to London?' he suggested.

She looked surprised at this. 'And what would I do there?'

'Talk to Nick?'

'I wouldn't know what to *say*.' She shrugged doubtfully. 'All I'd do is shout and yell. It wouldn't get us anywhere. It definitely wouldn't fix our marriage.' She must have forgotten until now that he and Doria were related, for she suddenly asked, 'How is your sister taking things?'

'She's six months pregnant and feeling lousy about it. She was nineteen a few weeks ago,' he added.

'So young,' Eileen breathed. 'So young to be in such a mess. Oh, Nick!' she cried passionately. 'What the hell d'you think you're up to?'

'Are you all right, luv?' her father called.

'I'm fine, Dad.' She turned to Peter and said quietly, 'Me dad admired Nick no end. He's been calling him names for not coming to see me and Nicky. If he knew what he was really up to, he'd do his nut. What do your parents think about the situation your sister is in?'

Peter recalled how things had been hunky-dory at Christmas. Lately, though, his folks had started to complain. Doria clearly wasn't happy. They wanted her to come home and live with them, at least until she'd had the baby. They were losing confidence in Nick Stephens.

He didn't answer Eileen's question. Instead he said, 'I have a few days' leave next week. You could ask someone to look after Nicky and I'll meet you in London – take you anywhere you want to go. You can't go on being upset like this. You need to know where you stand. Why not meet Nick and have a talk?'

'I should do something,' she murmured. 'You're right. I need to know where I am. I mean, is he ever likely to come back to us?'

She asked if he would let her have Nick's address in Fulham before he went, then left him sitting there and went to the kitchen to help with refreshments.

Peter stayed where he was until Eileen's father, Jack Doyle, came and sat beside him.

'Like the countryside, do you, son?' he asked.

'Well, I like it round here, sir,' Peter replied.

'Please don't call me "sir", if you don't mind,' Jack said a trifle churlishly. 'It implies that you think I'm better than you are.'

He was an awkward individual, Peter remembered. 'To my mind, it implies you're older, not better,' he argued. 'What would you say if I asked you not to call me "son"?'

'I'd say that you're someone's son, if not mine, though perhaps I was being too familiar.'

'I call my own father "sir".'

Jack grinned. 'Not very friendly, is it? Do you call your mam "madam"?'

'No, I call her Ma – sir!' It was Peter's turn to grin. 'I don't think this conversation is getting us very far, do you?'

'No, lad. Is it all right if I call you "lad"?'

'It was all right when you called me "son".'

'Well, son,' he pointed to a dilapidated shed halfway down the garden, 'how long do you think it'd take to dismantle that shed and put it back together again?'

'Would there be a point to doing that?' Peter enquired.

'The point would be I've got a few bits and pieces of sound wood, and I'd saw good bits off the new stuff and rotten bits off the old stuff, and when it was back together it'd be a decent shed again.'

'I think it would take more than a day or two,' Peter surmised.

Jack grunted. 'In that case, once all these people have gone home, I'll start taking it to pieces.'

'Can I give you a hand?' Peter asked eagerly.

'Have you ever done anything like that before?'

Peter shook his head. 'Never in all my life.' He wasn't really keen on manual work, but he fancied helping Jack with his shed.

'Then you're not likely to be much help, are you?'

'I shall do my absolute best – sir.'

'What about them poncey clothes you're wearing?'

'Oh!' Peter looked down at his poncey clothes. He couldn't allow them to be ruined, not during the war, when new clothes needed coupons and his mother and Doria used as many of his and his father's as they could get their hands on.

'Never mind, Eileen'll let you have some of Nick's old stuff. Nick's her husband; he was in the RAF.' He frowned slightly. 'We don't see as much of him these days as we used to.'

By just after six, everyone had gone, including most of Eileen's friends and relatives. Only her father and Peter Mallory were left. Peter was wearing Nick's gardening outfit and was in the process of clearing out the contents of the garden shed. Jack had already taken the door off.

Half an hour later, Eileen took them tea and biscuits and promised to have a meal ready at nine o'clock. 'Nothing heavy because it's a bit late. I suppose you intend sleeping here tonight, Peter?'

Peter's heart did a cartwheel, but Jack said, 'Where's Kate? He can't stay without Kate being here. Ye'll have the neighbours talking. Mind you, you're good at doing that. You had the neighbours talking in Pearl Street, if I remember right.'

Eileen made a face at her father. 'Don't worry, and don't be such a moraliser, Dad. Kate's going to be home late. Peter can sleep on the settee in the living room with a sleeping bag. It's quite comfortable. Our Nicky's already upstairs, dead to the world.'

By nine o'clock, when the meal was ready to eat, the shed had been completely demolished. The door and the window were leaning against a wall waiting to be put back when the building was reassembled. Jack had sawn off the rotten ends of the planks wherever necessary and all the pieces had been neatly stacked.

'All ready for tomorrer,' he said comfortably.

After the meal had been eaten – stew with mincemeat, loads of vegetables and a dumpling each – Jack climbed on to his bike and headed for Bootle.

'Is the bike light bright enough?' Peter asked Eileen worriedly. He'd become rather fond of Jack and would hate him to have an accident.

'There isn't much traffic about and he always gets out the way if he hears a car coming behind.'

'He's a grand old fellow, isn't he?'

Eileen laughed. 'Yes, but never let him hear you call him that. He doesn't consider himself to be either old or grand.'

Peter believed it. He was beside himself with joy. He was about to spend the night under the same roof as Eileen Stephens! He didn't expect anything to happen other than that they would both sleep soundly, but it would do for now.

Eileen had found Peter a sleeping bag and a pillow, plumped up the cushions on the settee, given him a pair of Nick's pyjamas and made him a cup of cocoa.

'I don't know about you,' she said, 'but I'm dead tired. I bet you're even more so. You worked really hard helping take down that flippin' shed.'

'I enjoyed it,' Peter assured her. 'I'm looking forward to putting it back together.'

'As soon as Kate comes back, we can go to bed.'

The telephone rang, making them both jump. Eileen answered it.

'Oh, all right then,' she said after a while. 'I hope you sleep well in that posh hotel.' She put down the receiver and turned to Peter. 'That was Kate. She's staying overnight at the Adelphi with her girls. She might bring them to see us tomorrow.' She gave a satisfied little sigh and moved towards the stairs. 'It means we can go to bed straight away. Good night, Peter.'

'Good night.' Peter changed into the hated Nick's pyjamas and was fast asleep within minutes.

Eileen wasn't surprised to find she was unable to sleep, despite it having been such a demanding day. It was almost impossible to believe that Nick had changed his address in London yet had not bothered to tell her. It meant that their relationship had broken down to the point that she and Nicky no longer existed for him. Did he so much as *think* about them these days? The hurt she felt was physical, as if a dagger had been thrust into her side.

Yet deep down, deeper than the hurt, she felt desperately sorry for Nick. He wouldn't have behaved like this had he not been so hurt himself.

It wasn't just his arm that had been lost when his plane had crashed, but something else. Like her brother Sean, he had been badly damaged. Neither Nick nor Sean were the men they used to be. They were still alive, but part of them had been killed in the war, and the chances were that they would never be the same men again.

These depressing thoughts were interrupted by a creaking sound. She half sat up, but realised that it was probably Peter coming up the stairs to use the lavatory. In the corner of the room, Nicky was fast asleep in his cot, breathing steadily, without a care in the world. These days, he didn't often mention his dad.

The creaking sound continued until it stopped and the handle of the bedroom door was slowly turned. The hairs on Eileen's neck stiffened and she sat up properly. 'Who is it?' she demanded in the firmest voice she could manage under the circumstances. Not Peter, surely!

In answer to her query, the door was flung open and a dark figure threw itself on top of her, seizing her by the throat and squeezing hard.

Eileen screamed; Nicky woke up and started to cry. Eileen screamed again, weaker than before. She choked for breath and tried to push the attacker away, but his hands were like an iron band around her throat.

There were footsteps, grunts and groans, a loud roar, and the person on top of Eileen was pulled away with force. When the electric light was switched on, it revealed a man lying on his back on the floor, with Peter Mallory standing over him, one foot on his chest.

212

By now, Nicky was terrified and crying pitifully. Eileen scrambled across the bed and lifted him up. She swallowed hard, her throat hurting, and said to Peter, 'Who is he?'

The man on the floor was dark-haired and wild-eyed, with a thin moustache. She had never seen him before.

'I have no idea,' Peter said. 'Go downstairs and ring the police.'

'No,' the man shouted, flailing his arms. 'No, don't do that. I thought you were someone else.'

Peter pressed on his chest harder with his foot. 'Eileen, take no notice. Ring the police – *now!*'

Eileen wouldn't have dreamt of not taking any notice. She stumbled downstairs, clutching Nicky, and grabbed the telephone. Her father had written a list of important numbers on a postcard tacked to the wall, including the nearest police station. As she dialled the number with shaking fingers, she remembered calling him an old fusspot when he showed her what he'd done.

She returned upstairs with Nicky and stood outside the bedroom. 'The police are on their way,' she called. 'They'll be about ten or fifteen minutes.'

'I don't think I'm going to be able to keep this bastard down for that long,' Peter gasped. 'He's bigger and stronger than me.'

'Let him go, then. He can't get far. Whoever he is, the police will find him.'

'Then get out of the way before I lift my foot.'

Eileen slipped into Kate's room. She heard what sounded like a brief struggle, then footsteps on the landing and down the stairs. The front door slammed, and Peter Mallory opened the door of Kate's bedroom.

'Oh God!' Eileen leant against him and he took both her and Nicky in his arms. 'Who on earth was it?'

'I don't know. But he's left his wallet on your bed, not deliberately I presume. Let's go and have a look, shall we?'

As the three of them went into the main bedroom, they heard the sound of a car starting up and driving away. Eileen watched as Peter picked up the wallet and opened it. It contained an identity card, other papers, a thick wad of pound notes and a silver propelling pencil. Peter removed the card. 'His name's Roger Thomas,' he said.

'Kate's husband,' Eileen wheezed. Her voice seemed to have gone altogether. 'Holy Mary, Mother of God, he thought he was killing Kate.'

She explained that Kate's husband, a highly respected lawyer, had been so violent that Kate had been forced to leave home. 'She reported him to the police, but they wouldn't believe a word said against him. After she left, he told their daughters all sorts of horrible things about their mother. It's only recently that they've started seeing each other again.' She made a horrified face. 'He must have decided to kill her!'

Quarter of an hour later, two policemen arrived, a sergeant and a young constable. Peter made a pot of tea, and Nicky slept in his mother's arms while she described what had happened.

'He must have climbed through the living room window,' the sergeant said. Peter winced, realising that he'd been asleep in the room at the time and not heard a thing. 'I was sleeping the sleep of the dead,' he explained, and wasn't too pleased when the constable remarked that he could well have ended up sleeping the sleep of the dead for real.

It was almost four o'clock by the time the police left an exhausted Eileen and a triumphant Peter – he considered that he had saved her from being brutally murdered – to go to bed for a second time. Eileen and Nicky returned to their own beds, but in an act of extraordinary gallantry, Peter laid his sleeping bag outside her door, where he scarcely slept a wink.

Next morning, Jack Doyle arrived on his bike at the same time as two more policemen drove up in a car. Eileen had been hoping to leave her father ignorant of the night's events – he genuinely was an old fusspot – but it turned out to be impossible. As expected, he carried on about how dangerous it was for her and Nicky to be living alone in such an isolated place, and threatened to cycle there every night after he'd finished work in order to protect her.

'But Kate's usually here,' she protested.

'If it hadn't been for Kate, you wouldn't have had last night's visitor,' he reminded her, as if it wasn't something she didn't already know.

Of course, when Kate arrived and discovered what had happened, she was distressed to the point of tears. 'I don't know what to say,' she cried. 'I can't apologise enough.'

'You have no need to apologise. It wasn't your fault,' Eileen assured her, glancing sternly across the room at her father, who looked as if he was

215

about to insist that it was.

Kate had been about to tell Eileen that she would soon be leaving the cottage to live with her daughter, Lily, who had acquired a job and a flat in Southport from which Kate would be able to travel daily by train to Dunnings. 'Oh, but, Eileen, I wouldn't dream of leaving you on your own, not after what's happened,' she assured her friend.

'Well I wouldn't dream of allowing you to stay,' Eileen assured her back. Her voice still sounded a touch rusty, but would probably be all right by tomorrow. To everyone's great relief, there'd been a phone call from the police to say that Roger Thomas had been apprehended on the road to Birmingham and would no longer be a danger to anyone.

Chapter 13

No work was done on the shed that day. Peter was too tired, Jack too angry; and Eileen wasn't bothered; one of these days the shed would be put back together and she didn't care when it happened. Nicky appeared to have forgotten the night's events and had woken up in his usual happy mood. There was nothing to be seen of Napoleon, but Eileen said he often disappeared for a few days. 'I reckon he's having an affair with a lady cat.' Peter wondered aloud if her name was Josephine, and Eileen groaned. Under the circumstances, it wasn't a terribly funny joke.

At lunchtime, Peter offered to treat them all to lunch at the local pub. Kate refused, saying she wanted to start sorting out her clothes, but the others went and enjoyed their juicy meat pie and roast potatoes. It was actually warm enough to sit outside under the trees in the garden, an indication that summer was on its way.

The terror of the night was over; everything was back to normal again.

Except it wasn't, not really, at least not for Eileen. Nick had still done what he'd done: moved to another part of London without telling her his new address. Under normal circumstances she would have written and told him what had happened, that Kate's awful husband had tried to strangle her believing she was Kate. Under the

217

same normal circumstances it would have brought him rushing home the following weekend to make sure she was all right. He would have stroked her neck and kissed it to make sure it was completely better.

But she could no longer rely on Nick – on her husband – for anything. And was she supposed to just sit in the cottage in Melling and pretend it wasn't happening?

By Tuesday, Easter was over. Peter had returned to London and her dad was back at work in Bootle. Kate was at Dunnings but would be leaving for Southport in a few days.

Eileen was standing in the kitchen, hands on hips, contemplating the pile of dirty washing in the laundry basket. Nicky was standing in the same position, waiting to see what her next move would be.

'Sod the washing,' she said. 'Let's go to Bootle and see your Auntie Brenda. I want to ask her a favour.'

'Sod the washing,' Nicky agreed. 'Go see Auntie Brenda.'

Brenda's girls were playing in the street outside, while inside Brenda was toiling away on her sewing machine, though for her, this was a pleasure.

Eileen was always fascinated by her friend's uniquely colourful parlour.

'What are you making now?' she asked as a length of turquoise wool sped under the foot of the machine.

'A dress for someone; you don't know them.'

218

Brenda replied. 'What can I do for you, Eileen?'

'Can you look after Nicky for me tomorrer?'

Brenda stopped sewing. 'Well...' she said slowly, and Eileen just knew she was going to turn her down because she was doing something else. 'Tomorrer,' she went on, 'it's still the school holidays, and me and your Sheila, plus all the kids, are going to Sefton Park to have a picnic in the fairy glen. I don't fancy taking your Nicky an' all. There'd be too many kids to keep an eye on. I'd be worried he'd run off and get lost.' She made a face at Nicky, who giggled. 'You would too, wouldn't you, you little bugger? Like an eel, he is,' she added to Eileen, 'when you try to pick him up.'

Eileen sighed. 'Never mind, there's always another time.'

'What did you want to do, Eil?'

'Go to London.'

Brenda eyed her keenly. 'Well, I can imagine why you want to go. Let's nip over the road, see what Phyllis is up to. She and Nicky got on like a house on fire that day you went to Blackpool to see Sean.'

Phyllis turned out to be a cheerfully pretty young woman with chestnut-coloured hair. 'Hello, Nicks,' she cried, bending down and hoisting Nicky on to her hip. He apparently remembered her well and tugged at her curls affectionately.

'Of course I'll look after him,' she promised Eileen. 'I'm really looking forward to it – the picnic too.'

'She's nice,' Eileen remarked when they were

219

back in Brenda's parlour. She'd promised Phyllis she'd bring Nicky at half past eight the following morning. 'How long has she lived here?'

'About eighteen months, I reckon. She's here with her mam, who's a nurse at Bootle hospital.' Brenda explained the reason for the Taylors' presence in Bootle.

'I don't like things happening in Pearl Street and me not knowing about it,' Eileen complained. 'Are there any more new people about?'

'Only Tommy and Godfrey.'

'Where do they live?'

'Tommy lives with me and Godfrey with Lena Newton.' Brenda laughed at Eileen's confused face. 'They're kittens, five months old. I don't let Tommy in the parlour while I'm sewing because he swings on the material. He's in the living room. Come on, I'll introduce you.'

Eileen could have stayed for ever playing with Tommy, a dead gorgeous tabby, and Nicky became so enamoured he had to be dragged away. Eileen wanted to call on Sheila, where Nicky was left to play with his cousins while his mother went to see Alice and Sean.

Their little boy, Edward, was seated on the mat in front of the fire playing with a wooden lorry that looked as if it weighed a ton.

'Did me dad make that?' Eileen asked her sister-in-law.

Alice smiled faintly. 'Yes, it takes two people to lift it.'

Eileen transferred her gaze to her brother, who was sitting in the corner staring at nothing. Her heart ached at the sight of him. 'Is he no better?

Not even the slightest bit?'

'No, but he will be, one day,' Alice assured her, tightening her lips purposefully. 'I can feel it in me bones.'

'Oh, Sean!' Eileen fell on her knees in front of him, wrapping her arms around his thin legs. He ate little and was becoming more skeletal by the day. As ever, his face showed no sign of emotion. She sighed and got back to her feet.

'Are you going to Sefton Park with the others tomorrow?' she asked Alice.

'No, I wouldn't dream of leaving Sean on his own for such a long time.' Alice stroked her husband's head affectionately. 'Brenda comes and sits with him when I do the shopping and go to Mass, but otherwise I stay at home.'

'But, Alice, luv, you need to get out more often than just doing the shopping,' Eileen argued.

'No I don't, Eil.' Alice gave her a dazzling smile. 'One of these days Sean is going to get better and be his old self again. I really want to be here when it happens.'

It was early afternoon the following day, Wednesday, when Eileen reached number 8 Townsend Road in Fulham, a tall red-brick house with four floors. The bricks were crumbling here and there and the paint had almost disappeared off the windowsills, revealing big patches of bare cement.

It was all so different to the London she'd seen before, when she and dear little Tony had stayed with Nick at the posh hotel off Park Lane. It was the first time she and Nick had made love, and it had been like heaven.

221

Eileen climbed the five steps to the front door. On a panel outside there was a list of names. 'STEPHENS' was printed neatly beside the button for the second floor. Eileen's heart twisted when she recognised Nick's handwriting. She pressed the bell and waited. After a few minutes she heard a woman's voice calling, 'Who's there?'

She opened the front door and entered a huge, dismal hallway with a cracked tile floor. There was a telephone with a box to put money in on the wall. 'Who is it?' the same voice asked. Looking up, Eileen saw a woman peering over the banisters on the second floor.

'It's Eileen Stephens,' she said.

There was a pause, then the woman said tiredly, 'I suppose you'd better come up.'

Eileen climbed the stairs, which were covered with a once expensive, highly patterned carpet, now dangerously frayed in places. When she reached the second floor, the woman had disappeared, but a door had been left wide open. She knocked on it loudly and went inside.

The woman half sat, half lay on a settee. She was young, heavily pregnant, and would have been pretty had she not looked so utterly wretched. She wore a smart navy-blue maternity frock with white buttons and there was a ring that looked like real gold on the third finger of her left hand. 'If you've come to have a fight, then you're wasting your time,' she said. 'I haven't got the energy. You can call me all the names under the sun, but I don't care. I probably deserve them.'

'I don't want a fight,' Eileen said mildly. 'I'm here to find out how I stand with my husband. I

222

mean, are you two going to get married one of these days, after the war is over, say? Should I expect him to divorce me?' There was a wooden chair against the wall right beside her and she sat down. 'It's Doria, isn't it?'

'Yes.' The girl frowned. 'How do you know? Has Nick told you about me?'

'No, but your brother has.'

'Peter! You know Peter? It can only be Peter; Fabian is abroad.'

'Yes, I do know Peter. Quite well, in fact.'

The girl sighed. 'Ah well. Nothing surprises me any more.' She laid her head on the arm of the settee. 'Do you mind if I go to sleep?'

'Yes, I do, actually,' Eileen said sternly. 'I've come all the way from Liverpool to have a talk. It's my intention to go back home again tonight. As I said, I'd like to know where I stand.'

'I suppose you'd like to scratch my eyes out.' Doria sat up straight and put both feet on the floor.

Eileen ignored the comment. 'I must say, for a woman having a passionate affair – I take it for granted it's passionate – you don't seem very happy. When I was having an affair with Nick, I was over the moon. Every minute we were together was wonderful.'

Doria's head fell as if she no longer had the energy to hold it up. 'It used to be like that for us, but then I became pregnant, which was absolutely the last thing either of us wanted. We had to move house and this was all we could get in a hurry – Nick was being chucked out of his old place.' She waved her arm around the drab room with its

223

much-too-high ceiling and old furniture. The walls had been distempered a curious pink, but maybe it only looked curious because it was fading. 'I *hate* it,' she said, suddenly angry. 'I had to leave work and I have absolutely nothing to do all day. There's nowhere to go except some awful market full of second-hand stuff. The other night, there was an air raid close by; one of those V-1 things. And you know what?' She leant forward.

'What?'

'Nick's started arriving home really late, ten o'clock or later. His breath smells of drink, which means he's calling in at some bar or other after work, probably Charlie's, where we met – or I should say, where I picked him up. He's stopped coming straight home.' She began to cry. 'I'm stuck here for thirteen or fourteen hours a day all on my own, wondering if he's got himself another woman, one who isn't in the club. Mind you, it's my own fault. It was me that seduced him, not the other way around.'

'Oh dear.' Eileen crossed the room and sat on the settee beside the girl. 'Can't you go back home?'

Doria looked astonished. 'And leave Nick?'

'It hardly seems fair that you're on your own for so much of the day, particularly with you being pregnant.' Anyroad, hadn't Peter said the family only lived in a different part of London; she couldn't remember what it was called. Nick wouldn't be totally deserted; Doria would be within reach – if he was still interested, that was.

'Is this just a way for you to get him back?' The girl's eyes narrowed. 'To make sure I'm out of the way, as it were?'

Eileen thought before she answered. 'I'm not sure how much I want him back,' she said thoughtfully. 'I certainly don't want him now, at the moment, on the rebound because you've left him. He's treated you terribly, but that's not the Nick I know, who I fell in love with years ago. I think – hope – that that Nick is still there, and I love him with all my heart.' If he *was* there, she'd have him back like a shot. Well, maybe.

Doria turned and looked her full in the face. 'He doesn't deserve you,' she said.

'He doesn't deserve *you*.'

For some reason, despite the drama of the situation, both women were aware that there was humour in it too, if somewhat black. They both burst out laughing, and Doria laughed so much that she began to cry again.

Eileen said, 'I understand that your parents know you're having a baby.'

'Yes, they're all right about it. Least they were; they've both gone off Nick more than a bit. They can see how unhappy he's making me.'

'Wouldn't you feel happier if you were living with them? Do they live very far away?'

'They live in London, in Wimbledon.' Doria's eyes lit up, making her look quite transformed. Eileen wasn't surprised that Nick had been attracted to her, particularly if she had made a play for him. 'It would be marvellous living with them, with Mummy there to care for me.' She clapped her hands. 'She'd even look after the baby for me after it was born and I could go back to work. I worked in the same office as Nick, you know.'

'Yes, Peter told me.'

Doria was in the process of forcing her feet into a pair of high-heeled navy-blue shoes. 'How do you know my brother so well, Eileen? Is it all right if I call you that?'

'It's fine. As for Peter, he just turned up at my house one day. I've no idea where he got my address from. We get on well. He was there at Easter.' She didn't go on to explain that he had probably saved her life.

'How strange!' Doria stood, wobbling slightly in the shoes. 'Do you know, I think I will go home, right this minute. Oh, Eileen' – she turned upon the other woman, her face radiant – 'you have no idea how happy that makes me feel, the idea that I could be back with Mummy and Daddy within the hour. I'll go downstairs this minute and phone for a taxi.'

'Be careful with those shoes on the carpet,' Eileen warned. 'Your heel might get caught in one of the holes. When I was pregnant,' she recalled aloud, 'I mainly wore flat shoes.'

'Oh yes, you have a son, don't you?' Doria remarked. 'What's his name?'

Unexpected tears suddenly filled Eileen's eyes. 'His name's Nicky, but I had another son, Tony, who was killed during the raids.'

'Oh, I'm so sorry.' Impulsively Doria threw her arms around Eileen's neck, and for a few brief seconds, the two women who loved Nick Stephens embraced.

As Eileen had no idea what time she would get back to Liverpool, Brenda had agreed to look after Nicky overnight. The taxi Doria had booked couldn't come for an hour, so Eileen had helped her pack her clothes and write a letter to leave for Nick.

'Do you want me to mention you?' Doria had asked.

'Oh no. I don't want him thinking it's my fault that you left. It isn't, is it?' she asked the other woman anxiously.

'Well, actually, it is.' Doria frowned slightly. 'It was your idea that I should go back to Mummy and Daddy, but I know you were thinking of me, not yourself.'

'I don't want him coming back to me only because you've gone.' Eileen felt a few moments of panic, praying it wouldn't happen.

Eventually the taxi arrived, Doria left, and Eileen caught a bus to Euston station, where she got on the five o'clock train to Liverpool.

As she'd had nothing to eat since breakfast, she bought a sarnie and a cup of tea on board the train. By the time she'd finished eating, they were halfway to Liverpool, it had begun to get dark and the blinds of the half-full carriage were drawn. The lights inside were merely a dismal glow, not sufficient to read by. She glanced round the edge of the blind, but there was nothing but blackness, mile after mile of it, not a single glimmer of light to be seen anywhere.

The world felt like a nightmarish place at the moment. So nightmarish that she felt nervous about catching a bus to Melling and walking along the dark lane leading to the empty cottage, particularly after what had happened only a few days ago. On reaching Lime Street, she hurried through the blacked-out city to another station, Exchange, where she caught an electric train to Marsh Lane and then walked to her dad's house in Garnet Street. He wasn't long back from the King's Arms and about to make himself a cup of cocoa.

'What do you want?' he asked in astonishment, though he was undoubtedly pleased to see her. 'Is Nicky all right?'

Eileen hadn't gone round to Brenda's to see Nicky, but assumed that he was fine. 'I've been to London,' she said. 'And I didn't feel like going all the way back to Melling. Is our Sean's old bed made up?'

'It's always made up ready for visitors. Mind you, you're the first I've had in a while. What were you doing in London?'

After he'd made cocoa for them both, Eileen explained about Nick and Doria. He was shocked, but not quite as angry as she had expected.

'It's this bloody war,' he said. 'It's knocking folks for six in all sorts of different ways. They're out of alignment, as it were. Things happen to them that they wouldn't have expected to happen in a million years. Like our Sean, for instance, him of the bright eyes and full of mischief. It's all gone – and will it ever come back again?'

'Let's hope so, Dad.'

'And Nick,' her father went on, a catch in his deep, gruff voice, 'he's an honourable chap. He'd never have been unfaithful to you if he hadn't lost his arm and his whole world was turned upside down. People can't be judged by normal standards these days.'

Eileen confessed that she had yet to make up her mind how to deal with Nick. 'I need to have a good long think about it.'

As Sean had taken over the bedroom his sisters had shared before they'd left home to get married, Eileen went to sleep that night in the bed she'd slept in as a child and a young woman. The mattress was as springy as it had ever been and her mind felt curiously relaxed, rested and free of worry as she snuggled under the bedclothes.

She woke up to the sound of seagulls squawking on the roof, instead of the quite ordinary birdsong she'd become used to. Remembering that she was in her father's house, she got up and drew back the blackout curtains, and was met by the sight of nothing but grey slate roofs and brick walls instead of trees and fields.

She drew in a breath of pure happiness. She was home!

She could hear that her father was already up, and had started to get dressed with the intention of going down and making his breakfast – it was a long time since he'd been waited on at home – when the front door slammed; he'd gone to work, leaving her to sleep in.

She had to prevent herself from bursting into tears – no matter what went wrong with her life, she would always have the best and dearest father in the world.

Downstairs, the kettle was still warm, so she added water and made herself tea. She drank it standing up in the kitchen, listening to the sounds that surrounded her. The people on one side were listening to the wireless. On the other side, dishes rattled and raised voices could be heard having an argument. Footsteps sounded on the pavement outside as men like her father made their way to the docks in their heavy boots. Although it wasn't long gone half past seven, children were playing outside, laughing and shouting as they began their day with a game of football or cricket. She'd like to bet that a girl, or even a couple of girls, was already swinging from the lamp post directly outside the house. Eileen had swung on it herself enough when she was a child, as had Sheila.

Who should she go and see first? Brenda, naturally, to make sure Nicky was all right and have a little play with the kitten. Afterwards she would call on Sheila, then on that nice girl Phyllis, to thank her for looking after Nicky yesterday. There was Kitty to visit, see how she was getting on – the baby was due in a couple of months. And there were all sorts of other people she hadn't seen in quite a while. She'd like to know how Freda Tutty was getting on, for instance.

Eileen rubbed her hands together. She was really looking forward to seeing everyone, not that she'd be able to cram all of them into a single day.

'I know,' she said aloud to her dad's living room. 'I'll have a holiday, a holiday in Garnet Street with Dad. And I'll stay as long as I like, until I feel like going home again.' She'd have to go back to Melling to fetch a few things, but she could do that this afternoon.

Nicky had enjoyed the trip to the fairy glen the day before, as well as his stay at Brenda's, where the girls had made a tremendous fuss of him. He explained earnestly to his mother that he wanted to keep Tommy the kitten, and swap him with Napoleon.

Brenda laughed and assured him that Tommy would not stay a kitten for always, but would one day be just as big as Napoleon. 'Though perhaps not quite so bad-tempered and moody. That cat was very badly brought up.'

Eileen then had to explain that she had no idea who had brought up Napoleon. 'It wasn't Nick. I think the cat was one of the fittings and fixtures when he bought the cottage.' It reminded her that she would need to make arrangements for Napoleon to be fed while she was having her little holiday.

After thanking Brenda for looking after her son, she and Nicky made their way to Sheila's, where the children were getting up slowly because there was no need to get ready for school. Nicky disappeared into the yard, where the big boys were playing football.

'What were you doing in London yesterday?' Sheila asked. 'Did you have a nice day out?'

Eileen snorted. 'No, I had a horrible day out as it happens.' She took a deep breath and told her sister the whole sorry tale of Nick and Doria and Doria's baby.

Sheila gasped with horror. 'How long have you known that?'

'Since Christmas.'

'You can't possibly take Nick back now,' her sister said firmly, shaking her head. 'Not ever.'

'I can if I want – and if he wants to come back, like. We took each other for better and for worse, didn't we?' Eileen remembered having a row about the same sort of thing with Sheila years ago. In those days, their views had been the other way around, with Sheila adamant that Eileen should never leave Francis, her vicious first husband.

Her sister looked doubtful. 'Yes, but there's a limit.'

'Don't be daft, Sheil. There can't possibly be a limit. You don't promise to take someone for better and for worse depending on how much worse it gets.'

Eileen wasn't in the mood to explain to her sister how she felt about Nick. After yesterday, and after what her father had said last night about the way the war had affected people, she thought it best to suspend her feelings for the time being, see how things went. She and Nick had loved each other so very much that it was nigh on impossible to believe it was all over.

She left Nicky in the yard with Dominic and Niall and called on Phyllis Taylor, who invited her inside to meet her mother, Winifred, a pleasant woman who was a senior nurse at Bootle hospital. Brenda had told her the reason why the pair had come to live in Bootle, and Eileen looked with interest at the wedding photograph on the mantelpiece.

'I don't suppose you've seen him around?' Winifred asked. 'We've given up looking for him, but there's always the odd chance someone has seen him.'

'I'm afraid not. He's very handsome – oh, and you are too,' Eileen stammered. 'Not handsome, I don't mean that, but very pretty.'

Winifred laughed. 'I'm not the least bit pretty, but it's nice of you to pretend I am. We think he might have lost his memory.'

'No, Mum,' Phyllis said impatiently. '*You* think he might have lost his memory. I can't pretend to guess what really happened to him.'

Minutes later, Eileen was presented with her fourth cup of tea that morning, and it wasn't yet half past nine.

Outside again, Aggie Donovan was standing in front of her house with a bucket of water, about to scrub the doorstep. Eileen realised with satisfaction that it was years since she'd scrubbed a step.

On spying her old neighbour, Aggie forgot her housework and began to relate the latest tittle-tattle, whereupon two other women emerged with buckets and joined in. Years ago, Eileen had been the subject of Aggie's vicious gossip, and as soon as the women began tearing to pieces the reputations of some of their neighbours, she wandered away.

She went to see Kitty Quigley, now Kitty Ransome, who, like some other people in the street, she'd known her entire life. Kitty was at about the same point in her pregnancy as Doria, but so much happier.

She was sitting with her feet up in front of the fire George had made that morning before he'd gone to work, both hands resting comfortably on her stomach. Her little girl, Rosie, had been taken for a walk by the woman next door.

'She has a boy Rosie's age. Me, I've been ordered not to move a muscle until George comes home tonight,' she said to Eileen. 'He knows someone'll come and make me a cuppa.' There were sandwiches on the table beside her, an Eccles cake and a bottle of lemonade.

'What's in the cake?' Eileen asked. Surely it wasn't full of currants, as Eccles cakes were supposed to be? If so, she'd like to know where they came from so she could get some for herself.

'Prunes,' twinkled Kitty 'D'you fancy half?'

'No, ta, Kitty. I don't have any problems that need solving with a few prunes.'

'I'm afraid I do at the moment.' Kitty seized the cake and took a bite.

'I hope whoever made it took the stones out.'

Kitty choked and began to laugh. 'Oh, Eileen, you shouldn't make jokes like that with a woman who's up the stick. What are you doing here anyroad? Aren't you supposed to be living in Melling?'

'Yes, but right now I'm on holiday in Garnet Street, staying at me dad's.' She looked long and hard at her old friend. 'Are you happy, Kit?'

'As a lark, Eil.'

She was alone on the bus on her way back to Melling, Nicky left behind with her sister, thinking how upside down and back to front life was,

234

the way luck could choose who it would alight upon at any particular time. The difference between Doria and Kitty was stark. Yet a year ago, it was Kitty who had been in the depths of despair, left with a child by her already married American, while Doria had not long met Nick and was madly in love.

Then there was herself, who she didn't really want to think about. Instead, she made a mental list of things to collect from home: clothes for herself and Nicky, make-up, a hairbrush, toys, a book to read, a few things from the larder so that she could make her dad's tea tonight. And while she was there, she would pick up the week's rations from the little grocer's shop.

Once in the cottage, she packed the necessary items and gave Napoleon something to eat. She remembered that her father would be there regularly now that it was spring, to attend to the garden. He could put out extra food for the cat each time he came.

While she was upstairs, she looked in to Kate's room and saw that all her belongings had gone. She had a feeling that that particular friendship had come to an end. Poor Kate had been so shocked and embarrassed at her husband's behaviour that, although she couldn't be held responsible for it, she felt unable to be Eileen's friend any more. They would probably merely exchange Christmas cards with each other from now.

She was about to leave when she noticed an envelope that hadn't quite been pushed through and was hanging from the inside of the letter box. It was from Nick. Without a second's thought,

she put it in the drawer of the little telephone
table. Now wasn't the time to read it. She'd do
that when she came back from holiday.

Chapter 14

A few days later, Eileen and Nicky caught the ferry to New Brighton. The fairground had just opened for the summer season and they went on the waltzer and the terrifying bumper cars – at least Eileen thought they were terrifying, and considered herself extremely brave for going on them twice because Nicky enjoyed them so much. He was delirious with joy, going by himself on the helter-skelter, waving madly to his mother before he slid down.

The nights were gradually getting lighter, and they sailed back to Liverpool with the setting sun reflecting a blurred image of the city skyline in the dusky water.

The following day, she took her sister's lads and Nicky to Southport, where they played football on the miles of flat golden sand before going to see *Snow White and the Seven Dwarfs* in a picture house on Lord Street, probably the most elegant street in the land.

Perhaps because she didn't live permanently in the area, while she was in Bootle Eileen was told things privately that people wouldn't have told someone they saw every day.

Lena Newton, for instance, confided how desperately lonely she was and that she didn't love her husband, Maurice, not the least little bit. 'I only married him because I was scared of being left on the shelf. I wonder why women do that?' She cocked her head sideways. 'On reflection, I'd sooner be single any day. Although,' she continued in a questioning voice, 'perhaps I wouldn't mind being married to him if we had children.'

'You won't believe this, Lena,' Eileen said gently, 'but I more or less did the same thing. Me dad didn't exactly insist, but he made it clear that he wanted me to marry Francis Costello, who turned out to be a monster. He was dead cruel, not just to me, but to our little boy, Tony.'

'Does that mean we should never try to please the people we love?' Lena wondered aloud. She was nursing Godfrey, her handsome black and white kitten, as if he were a baby.

'But your mother didn't want you to marry Maurice,' Eileen pointed out. Lena's reasoning was becoming rather tortuous.

She invited her to come and spend a weekend at the cottage as soon as she returned to Melling. 'I've got a bedroom going spare at the moment.'

One night, her dad was at the pub, Nicky was in bed and Eileen was reading the *Daily Herald* when Phyllis Taylor knocked on the door.

'I've done something terrible,' Phyllis confessed when she was seated in front of the empty fireplace – the weather was getting warmer and there was no need for a fire most days.

She had such a nice, honest fact that Eileen couldn't imagine her having ever done anything remotely terrible.

'Yes?' she said encouragingly.

'Your friend Kitty – I understand she used to

live in the house where me and Mum live now.'

'That's right,' Eileen confirmed.

'Well, an American serviceman called a few weeks ago and asked for Kitty. I told him she lives somewhere else...'

She paused, and Eileen said, 'Well, you were right. She lives just across the road.'

'I know that, but I told him she was married and was living in Australia with her husband and two children.'

'Why on earth did you tell a lie like that?' Eileen asked sharply.

'Oh dear.' Phyllis dropped her head into her hands and began to cry. 'You disapprove! I just knew I'd done something terrible.'

'Yes, but *why* did you do it?' Eileen demanded.

'Kitty seems so happy,' Phyllis wept. 'I didn't want it to be spoilt by the American – he was truly gorgeous, by the way. I imagined her leaving George for him – Dale, his name was – and being made unhappy again when it was time for him to go back to America.'

'But maybe he merely came to say ta-ra or something,' Eileen said reasonably. 'Or to tell her he was sorry for what he'd done. Any minute now, thousands of Allied troops are expected to be sent to France. Perhaps he had a premonition and expects to be killed.'

'Do you think I might have changed the course of Kitty's life?' Phyllis looked pathetically at the older woman. 'I felt terrible afterwards, as if I thought I was God.'

Eileen stared into space for almost a minute before saying, 'On reflection, I think I might have

239

done the same.' Phyllis breathed a sigh of relief, but Eileen continued. 'I think we would both have been wrong. If Kitty had given up George for the American, in my view she would have been making the biggest mistake of her life, as well as breaking George's heart. But people should be left to make their own mistakes without interference, no matter how well meant it is.' She suddenly smiled. 'Does that make you feel better?'

'Yes, it does.' Phyllis smiled back and said, 'There's something else.'

'Jaysus, Mary and Joseph,' Eileen complained. 'You make me feel like some wise old woman solving the problems of the young. Perhaps I should set meself up in a tent with a crystal ball and start telling fortunes for a living. Have you been acting like God again?'

'Sort of. It's about my dad. The thing is, he didn't lose his memory; he's in Bootle, alive and well, living in Chaucer Street with a younger woman and working in a pub in Seaforth. I only found out by accident.' She shrugged helplessly. 'I don't know what to do about it. I haven't told my mum.'

'Bloody men!' Eileen gasped. 'Look, luv, I think your dad has to sort this out himself. If he intends getting back with your mam, then he should do it in the least hurtful way possible. If I were you, I'd keep out of it, for the time being at least.'

'I'll do that,' Phyllis said meekly. 'Thank you, Eileen.'

Freda Tutty scowled when she answered the door to Eileen's knock. She was growing to be quite

240

tall, and her hair looked nice and wavy out of its usual tight plaits.

'Hello, luv,' Eileen said in her friendliest voice. 'I've been staying with me dad for a little while and I thought I'd call on you before I go back home. I just wondered how you were getting on?'

'I'm all right,' Freda said churlishly.

'And how about your mam and Dicky?' Freda and Dicky had been evacuated to Southport at the beginning of the war, and it was because Eileen had been dispatched by their mother to fetch them back that she had first spoken to Nick Stephens, a day so precious in her mind that she would remember it for as long as she lived.

'They're both all right too,' Freda confirmed grudgingly.

'Brenda Mahon said you had this dead handsome lodger for a while; Tom something.'

'Chance, Tom Chance,' Freda said through gritted teeth. 'He left ages ago.'

'Yes, Brenda said. It's just that she also said you'd written an essay at school about the history of Liverpool and it was published in the *Bootle Times*.' Eileen longed to get a smile out of the girl. 'You must have been very proud.'

Freda's demeanour changed instantly for the better, though she didn't smile. 'Yes, I was, Mrs Stephens; very proud.'

'We were wondering, me, Brenda and our Sheila, if you wouldn't mind taking us and the kids for that walk of yours, around the Seven Streets. Would tomorrer be convenient? We could go somewhere for a cup of tea when it's over.'

A smile at last. 'Oh, Mrs Stephens!' Freda cried.

241

'I'd love to.'

They left Pearl Street at nine o'clock the next morning, Eileen and Nicky, Brenda and her girls, Sheila's entire brood, Lena Newton and Phyllis Taylor. They caught a tram into the city; where the small procession marched as far as High Street.

Freda stopped. 'This used to be called Juggler Street,' she announced in a loud voice. 'Now it's High Street. The seven old streets are shaped like an H and this one is at the centre. There was a time, hundreds of years ago, when Liverpool only consisted of these seven streets.'

'Why was it called Juggler Street?' Niall asked.

'I don't know,' Freda admitted. 'I've never been able to find out.'

Niall suggested that perhaps a juggler lived there and Freda agreed that that could well have been the case.

The procession continued up Tithebarn Street, down Dale Street, along Castle Street, over to Water Street, back down Chapel Street and across to Old Hall Street.

It was a lovely day, the sort that the people of Liverpool swore only occurred in their city and nowhere else. It was as if magic stardust was in the air, making everywhere shimmer and shine. Buildings glowed, the pavements glistened, the sky looked more silver than blue.

Without thinking, the children began to march in rhythm, and every now and then people would join the little procession before eventually drifting away. Dominic Reilly and Monica Mahon, hand in hand near the front, began to sing, 'There'll be bluebells over the white cliffs of Dover...' Eileen and Lena brought up the rear, making sure no one from the group went astray.

They passed stately banks and elegant office buildings; shops selling stationery and men's clothes; the odd hotel and the occasional public house; restaurants in cellars, and bomb sites where buildings had once been and people had worked, but no more.

Whenever Freda, stopped to explain precisely where they were, a small crowd would also stop and listen. Sometimes she would receive a burst of applause. She became a different Freda altogether, taller and quite pretty, full of confidence. By the time the march finished, she was linking arms with Phyllis Taylor and they appeared to be the best of friends.

Eventually they arrived at the Pier Head, where the Mersey shone so brilliantly it looked like a river of diamonds. There was a café not far away, and Eileen treated everyone to a drink and a cake if they wanted it.

After the drinks had been drunk and the cake eaten, they all got on a tram and returned to Pearl Street.

It was sad that she and Nicky would be leaving her dad on his own again when she returned to the cottage the following day. Eileen could tell he'd enjoyed their company, and he'd taught Nicky how to play dominoes. Although Sheila did as much as she could for her dad, she had seven children to look after, as well as a husband when Calum was home. She did his washing and made him the occasional pie or cake, but she wasn't there to greet him when he came home from work or keep him company while he listened to the ten o'clock news and drank his bedtime cup of cocoa.

Eileen had really made a fuss of her dad, cooking his favourite meals – as far as rationing would allow – and even making him two jars of pineapple jam, hoping he wouldn't notice that it was made out of swedes and not pineapples.

She wondered whether, if she and Nick didn't get back together – and he didn't want his cottage back – she would choose to return to Pearl Street.

No, she decided. She could never bring herself to deliberately deprive her father of the beautiful garden.

Anyroad, she thought as she lay in bed on her last night in her father's house, Nicky snoring lightly at her side, it had been a really lovely holiday and she'd enjoyed herself no end.

She didn't realise that the best was yet to come.

Alice was getting ready for Mass. Sometimes she considered taking Sean with her. He could easily walk that far, even if he didn't know where he was going and wouldn't realise he was in a church. But people would talk to him, want to shake his hand, confuse him. They might even be rude if he didn't answer their questions. Occasionally she would take him for a tiny walk when it was dark, but only when there was moonlight and they could see where they were going.

Even though he ate little, he was getting better, but only physically. There was no change in his expression, no light in his lovely brown eyes.

That morning she came downstairs with him following behind. She sat him in his chair, made tea and gave him a cup, putting it in both his hands. Then, after removing the metal fireguard, she began to light the fire, despite it being a nice sunny day.

Lighting fires in good weather irritated Alice no end. She knew it was possible to heat water by clicking a switch in a cupboard, but not in Pearl Street, where a fire was the only method. Being Sunday, her sisters and the one brother still living at home would all want baths that afternoon.

Edward began to cry, so she went upstairs and fetched him down, placing him under the table where he liked to play, then continued with the fire, putting a rolled-up newspaper in the grate, some kindling, a few lumps of coal on top, then lighting a match and setting fire to the paper. Upstairs, her sisters, Colette and Bessie, began to squabble. They shared a double bed and had terrible fights over one or the other taking up too much space.

There was a scream, followed by a loud crash, and Alice swore under her breath. Bessie had probably kicked Colette out of bed again and really hurt her. This was proven to be the case when Colette began to cry loudly and yelled, 'Alice.'

'Coming,' Alice shouted back. Bessie was older and bigger than Colette and had always been a bit of a bully. Alice was having no more of it.

She went up the stairs faster than most women with normal legs, picked up Colette by the collar of her nightdress, threw her on to the bed, then

245

turned on Bessie and punched her on the nose. 'Do that again and you're out this house for ever,' she yelled.

Downstairs, Sean heard the sounds somewhere at the back of his mind, though they made no sense. Inside his head was made up of absolutely nothing that meant anything.

He was only vaguely aware of the shadowy figure of a small boy emerging on all fours from beneath the table. It was probably a dream – he had dreams all the time. With the help of a chair, the boy pulled himself to his feet, then approached Sean and attempted to climb on to his knee, but gave up when he wasn't picked up. He chuckled and looked around the room, still holding on to Sean's leg, but there was no sign of his mother. There was, however, something lovely and bright, something flickering playfully almost within reach.

He released Sean's leg and had taken a few careful steps towards the fire, reaching out his tiny hand towards the flames, when there came the most tremendous yell, which was heard by almost half of Pearl Street.

'*NO!*' roared Sean. '*NO, NO, NO.*'

'*Edward!*' screamed Alice from upstairs, and nearly fell all the way down to reach her son. She found Sean kneeling on the floor, crying his eyes out, with Edward clasped in his arms. The little boy looked too astonished to cry.

'Sean, darlin',' she said softly, kneeling beside them both. 'Oh, Sean!'

Sean looked at her. Nothing was making sense. 'Where am I?'

'You're home, darlin',' Alice whispered. 'Safe at home.'

An hour later, Colette turned up at Jack Doyle's house. Eileen had just returned from Mass and was packing ready to go back to the cottage later in the afternoon.

'Our Alice wants Jack round ours straight away. It would seem that Sean is himself again,' Colette announced.

Jack was upstairs preparing himself for a Sunday session at the King's Arms. 'Dad!' Eileen screeched. 'Our Sean's better. Let's get round there straight away.'

'Alice only wants Jack for now.' Colette tossed her head. 'She said you and your Sheila can come later. She doesn't want to confuse him with too many new faces – that's exactly what she said.'

Eileen believed it. Alice was a bossy little madam. Still, she only had Sean's welfare at heart. Her father came storming downstairs and shot out of the house at the speed of light, leaving Eileen to continue her packing.

Eileen and Sheila were allowed to see Sean later that afternoon.

'He received a shock to his system,' Alice diagnosed. 'When faced with Edward about to put his hand in the fire, all his feelings came back in a rush and now he's himself again.'

Not quite himself, Eileen and Sheila thought afterwards when they discussed their brother between them. His face was too pale, his brain not what it should be, his voice – after the initial roar

247

– little more than a whisper. This was Sean at a very low key, a Sean who actually cried at one point.

'Oh, but he'll get better,' Sheila said, more as if to reassure herself than anyone else.

'He's bound to get better,' Eileen agreed in the same sort of voice.

Later that evening, back at the cottage, everywhere felt slightly damp, so Eileen lit fires to warm the place up a bit. Nicky collected all his toys together, put them on the settee and played with them one by one, as if he'd missed them. Napoleon jumped on Eileen's knee and allowed her to stroke him for almost an hour, after which he jumped off and became his old arrogant, unfriendly self again.

It wasn't until she was listening to the BBC news on the wireless that she remembered Nick's letter and retrieved it from the drawer in the telephone table. She guessed he'd written it after he'd gone back to that awful flat in Fulham and discovered that Doria had left, but it was hard to tell. He merely said that he had decided to leave his job and was unsure what he wanted to do next. He advised her not to write to Birdcage Walk – she recalled bitterly that he'd never told her he'd left there, or about the flat in Fulham, – and said he would get in touch as soon as he had acquired a new address.

'Look after yourself and Nicky, my dear Eileen. I look forward to this damn war being over and life returning to normal again. Yours, Nick.'

It wasn't a romantic letter, not the sort of letter

a wife should expect from a husband when they didn't see each other very often. Well, she couldn't reply, and would do her utmost not to write letters in her head until the time came when she could put one down on paper and send it to him.

She put the letter away and went upstairs. Tomorrow morning she'd change the bedclothes in the spare room so that it would be ready for the next time someone came to stay, though she didn't envisage having a visitor at any time in the near future.

She couldn't have been more wrong.

Chapter 15

Nick wrote a letter to the owners of the flat in Fulham to tell them he was leaving. He put it on the table in the spot where last week Doria had left her letter saying she was going back to her parents in Wimbledon, then threw a few of his oldest clothes in a travelling bag; it was simpler to carry than a suitcase. He was neither glad nor sorry that she had gone. She had told him in her letter not to hesitate to join her in Wimbledon should he so desire.

Well, Nick didn't desire it, not at all. Her parents were a stuffy old-fashioned pair. Although they pretended not to care that he wasn't married to the daughter he'd made pregnant, he sensed that they cared very much, and that if it hadn't been hurtful to Doria, they would have told him to go to hell.

He thought it would probably be all right that he had packed in his job. It wasn't very important – in fact he'd always thought it had been invented as a favour to compensate him for the loss of his arm. He had telephoned the supervisor earlier and announced he was leaving, ignoring the spluttered comment that he was supposed to work four weeks' notice. He never wanted to sit at a desk again; it was slowly driving him mad, as was wearing sensible dark suits every day. It wasn't as if he needed the money. He'd been left money by his grandfather that would last for years. He supposed he should invest it in something that would earn interest, rather than just leaving it in the bank in a current account.

He'd do that very soon, he decided. He put his most important papers in the side pocket of the bag and left the flat. There was a bus stop across the road where a few people were waiting. A bus approached and he ran to catch it. He had no idea where it was going, or where he wanted to go. Were any farms interested in taking on a one-armed labourer? He climbed the stairs, sat at the front and wondered where it would take him.

It was a lovely sunny, blowy day. Eileen had washed the bedding from the spare room and was pegging it on the line when she heard the knock on the door. She dropped the remainder of the sheets in the laundry basket, checked that Nicky was happily riding his little three-wheeler bike up and down the concrete path, and went to answer it.

At first she didn't recognise the very pregnant young woman standing outside, until she said, rather impatiently, 'Hello, Eileen.'

'Doria!' she gasped. 'What on earth are you doing here?'

'Can I come in first?' the girl said irritably. 'I've walked all the way from the station for the second day in a row and I'm tired out. They don't seem to have taxis in this neck of the woods.'

'Come in.'

Doria picked up a suitcase and entered the house. 'I came yesterday,' she said, somewhat aggressively, 'and you weren't here.' She was clearly in a very bad mood. 'I had to stay in a horrid hotel, the Railway Inn, or something.'

'Well I didn't know you were coming, did I?' Eileen was dismayed at her attitude. Last week they had parted friends. Why had it changed?

She soon found out. 'Mummy and Daddy were thrilled to have me back,' Doria explained after she had collapsed into an armchair with a sigh, 'but they insisted I have the baby adopted. When I found myself pregnant, I actually considered getting rid of it, but after us living together all this time – me and baby, that is – I wouldn't dream of parting with him, or her. And I had to keep myself hidden while I lived at home. No one must know I'm "in the family way", as Mummy put it. I never realised they were so old-fashioned. If we had visitors, I was supposed to take myself upstairs.'

'Has Nick been in touch?'

'No, Nick has not been in touch,' Doria said crossly. 'I telephoned the office the other day and was told he had left without working his notice, just a phone call, that's all. They're very angry with him there, as are Mummy and Daddy.'

'That's not like Nick,' Eileen murmured.

'No,' Doria conceded. 'I must admit it isn't like him at all. Until recently, he was always very reliable. I think, between us, we've got him down.'

'*I* haven't done anything to get him down,' Eileen said angrily. 'I have always been exceptionally patient with him. It was losing his arm that's got him down.'

'Perhaps you shouldn't have been so patient. Perhaps you should have given him a good shake

252

and told him to pull his socks up.'

'Perhaps *you* shouldn't have seduced him – that's what you told me you'd done when I was in London. Without you around, he might have been his old self again by now.'

'Mum!' Nicky entered the room accompanied by Napoleon, his tail erect and bristling with indignation at the sight of a stranger in his house. Nicky looked shyly at Doria. 'Hello.'

Doria's ill temper vanished in an instant. 'Hello, little boy. What's your name?'

'Nicky.'

'My name is Doria.' She held out her hand for him to shake. 'It's nice to meet you, Nicky.'

Nicky grinned and shook her hand, very grown up. 'It's nice to meet you, D...' He looked at Eileen. 'I can't remember her name, Mum.'

'It's Doria, love.'

'Why have you come to see my mum?' he asked the visitor – a very unwelcome visitor, Eileen thought sourly, but an attractive one all the same, with her mass of ringlets and her lovely blue eyes. She wore straight black slacks and a dark pink maternity smock with an embroidered yoke. She hoped the woman would go away soon – but why on earth had she come all this way in the first place?

'Why have I come to see your mum?' Doria put a finger to her chin and pretended to wonder. 'Because I'm her friend and she's invited me to stay until my baby is born in June.'

'I have done no...' Eileen spluttered, 'no such thing,' she added more quietly.

'No, you're right,' Doria said airily, 'but it was

253

your idea I go home to my parents. It's your fault I'm in the position I'm in. The least you can do to make up for it is to let me live here for a while. I honestly have nowhere else to go.'

Eileen could think of numerous arguments against this, as well as suggestions for places she could go, but she knew Doria wouldn't be prepared to accept them. Anyroad, if the girl refused to budge, she couldn't very well physically throw her out or demand that the police come and do it. All she could do was let her stay and put up with it.

'Are you wearing your wedding ring?' she asked.

Doria held up her left hand, showing the ring on her third finger.

'You'll have to invent a husband. Me sister and her friend know the truth, but I don't want the whole world knowing you're on your way to becoming an unmarried mother.' People would ask her all sorts of questions. Just imagine if she told everyone that Nick was the father of Doria's baby, who would be Nicky's half-brother or sister!

'My, you're frightfully narrow-minded, Mrs Stephens,' Doria said in a dead posh voice.

'I'm not, actually, but some of me family and friends are.' Her dad would be shocked to the core. 'Oh, and another thing. You'd best think up a name other than Mallory. Peter has become a family friend. It'll confuse everyone no end if they find out he's your brother.'

Doria's jaw dropped. 'I know you said you knew Peter, but how on earth has he become a family friend?'

'You'll have to ask him that.' Just at the moment, Eileen couldn't be bothered to explain.

'What,' Leslie Taylor enquired of his daughter, 'were you and a crowd of other people doing last Saturday morning marching through the business area of Liverpool?'

Phyllis gave him a look of contempt. 'Were you following us?'

'Yes,' her father conceded miserably. 'I saw you leave the house and went upstairs on the tram you caught into town. And please don't give your poor old dad a horrible look like that, Phyllis. It's not a very nice thing to do.'

'I wouldn't give you horrible looks if you weren't such an idiot and acted like a proper father.'

'Don't call me an idiot, either.'

Phyllis gave him a truly awful look. 'Fathers don't spy on their daughters.' She had gone back to work at her various schools on Monday, and her father had been waiting outside the house when she arrived home today. Her mother was on the afternoon shift at the hospital.

'Can I come in, darling?'

Phyllis stood aside to let him in. 'Kindly don't call me "darling", Dad. You've never did it when we lived in Beverley.'

He stamped his way along the hall into the living room, where he threw himself into a chair. 'What am I going to do?' he pleaded. 'I can't go back to Dawn's. The police are threatening to come and take Mick O'Brien away by force. Can't you think of a way I can get back in with your mum?'

'No, and anyway – or anyroad, as they say in Liverpool – what makes you think I want you and Mum back together? We are both very happy without you.' Actually, Phyllis would quite like him back; he was a hopeless father, but fun to live with, always cracking jokes and doing stupid things. She remembered the advice Eileen Stephens had offered. 'It's up to you to think of how to get back with Mum,' she told him, laughing. 'Perhaps you could pretend to recover your memory. It might work.'

It was a hint, and she hoped he would take it.

Leslie Taylor was deep in thought as he made his way towards the public house in Seaforth where he worked. How on earth had he managed to get himself into such a mess? The trouble was, Dawn was so provocatively attractive, and he'd felt lonesome in Bootle on his own, and petrified by the air raids. It had seemed exciting at the time, to just disappear from his old life and become someone else. He might even write a novel about it one of these days.

He stopped dead in the middle of Marsh Lane, remembering what his daughter had said. 'Why don't you pretend to recover your memory?' How about if he had an 'accident', his memory returned and he could profess total ignorance of what had happened in the meantime?

If he were going to do it, then he should do it now, not let himself think about it, risk changing his mind. He wouldn't go back to Dawn's house in Chaucer Street to collect his things. It would be more believable if he only had a few bob in his

256

pocket and wasn't carrying an identity card. He would announce his name to be Leslie Taylor and deny all knowledge of what had happened to him since 1941. Even if they produced Dawn, he would fail to recognise her and profess total ignorance of Mick O'Brien, who he had pretended to be all this time.

He turned on his heel and walked in the direction of Marsh Lane station, where he knew there was a set of steps up to the platforms.

A train had just come in when he arrived, but once everyone had gone, he climbed to the top of the stairs and looked back, ready to throw himself down. It looked awfully steep! If he wasn't careful, he could cause himself a serious injury, or even genuinely lose his memory. He walked halfway down the steps, but it still looked dangerous. In the end, he sort of let himself roll down the final three steps, banging his head deliberately so he would have a bruise.

He lay prone at the foot of the steps to Marsh Lane station and waited to be found.

'Nurse Taylor, Nurse Taylor!'

Staff Nurse Winifred Taylor looked up when she heard the cry. She was in her office in the children's wards bringing the records up to date. The ward was only half full. Children – and a goodly proportion of adults – were much healthier than they'd been when she'd started nursing more than twenty years ago. Of course, she'd had to leave when she got married – for a reason she could never fathom, only single women were allowed to be nurses.

But the war had changed all that, just as the basic rations had improved the diet of the entire population, making them healthier. The rich might complain about the limited variety of food available, little realising it was doing them the world of good.

'Nurse Taylor!' A young nurse had appeared at the door of her office, her eyes bright with excitement. 'There's a chap in Emergency who says his name is Leslie Taylor. When we told him what year it was, he claims he can't remember anything that has happened since May 1941 – you know, when we had those terrible air raids. We wondered, me and Staff Nurse Bennett, that is, if he's your husband. Staff Nurse Bennett said he's been missing for ages.' She sighed a sigh of pure happiness at the idea of being at the centre of such a drama. 'Would you like to come and take a look at him, Nurse Taylor?'

'Yes, Nurse.' Winifred Taylor got to her feet. 'I'll come now.'

The emergency ward was on the ground floor. She followed the young nurse downstairs, along corridors and around corners. 'We put him in a room on his own,' she was informed, 'once Staff realised who he was – or who he might be, like.'

An older nurse was holding a glass of water for the new patient, a remarkably handsome gentleman in his early forties. She smiled when Nurse Taylor walked in; Winifred's own face was totally devoid of expression. 'I'll leave you two alone together,' she said, and left the room, closing the door behind her.

The patient raised his head slightly to stare at the newcomer.

'Winnie?' he said weakly.

'Oh, come off it, Leslie,' Winifred said in a voice the opposite of weak. 'I know darned well you haven't lost your memory. You've been passing yourself off as a man called Mick O'Brien for the last few years and living in Chaucer Street with a woman called Dawn. Did you really expect to take me in with this charade?'

'Well, yes.' The invalid pushed himself into a sitting position on the bed. Apart from an insignificant bruise on his forehead, he appeared to be in the best of health. 'If you've known all this time, why didn't you come and rescue me?'

'*Rescue* you! Were you being kept prisoner?'

'Well, no,' he conceded. 'But if you knew I hadn't lost my memory, why did you and Phyllis come all the way from Beverley to look for me?'

'At first we thought you were dead and your body would eventually be found. Then we went to the cinema and saw a film and genuinely thought you had amnesia, like Ronald Colman in *Random Harvest* – or at least I did; I don't think Phyllis was ever convinced.'

'She wasn't, actually.'

'How on earth would you know that?' Winifred asked in astonishment.

'We've met each other a couple of times.'

'And she didn't tell me?' Winifred felt hurt.

'She doesn't want me back, Winnie, that's why. She thinks I'm bad for you.'

'You *are* bad for me. Frankly, Leslie, I wish I'd never met you. When we arrived in Liverpool, we

259

spent over a year looking for you. Then last Christmas I decided to hire a private detective. He tracked you down within a week. Ever since, I've been waiting for you to approach me. I knew you'd get fed up with Dawn, just as you've got fed up with all the other women you've had relationships with since we've been married.'

He looked at her soulfully. 'Yes, but you're the only one I've ever loved, Winnie; *really* loved.'

Despite the cloying voice and the soulful eyes, she almost believed him. He reached out and took her hand, and she wanted to collapse on top of him on the bed and kiss him to death.

'Does the bruise hurt?' she asked instead.

'Only a little,' he said bravely. 'When the hospital let me out, can I come home with you?'

Winifred sat in the chair beside the bed and thought. This Dawn person was bound to start searching for him. And initially Winifred herself had made such a performance out of trying to find him that the local newspaper might well discover he'd turned up and want to do an article about him. If he was discovered to have been lying, he could well get into serious trouble: leaving his job in a government establishment; using another man's identity card.

'I don't know,' she said slowly. 'You've got yourself into a rather dubious position, Leslie. I think the best plan would be for you to go back to Beverley and start again. You won't be able to get our own house back for a while, so you'll have to rent somewhere else for the time being.'

'Anything you say, Winnie.' He smiled obediently. 'Will you be coming with me?'

'I think you should go first, straight away, in fact, and find us somewhere to live. I can't give up my job just because I feel like it, so that will take some working out. I might be able to arrange a swap with another nurse.'

'Yes, Winnie. I'll go tomorrow.' He stared at her. 'Just now, how did you know I hadn't lost my memory?'

'I could tell by the expression on your face. You're an awfully clever chap, Leslie, but somehow you manage to be awfully silly at the same time.'

Phyllis flatly refused to leave Bootle and return to Beverley. 'I like it here,' she said defiantly. 'Anyway, I shall be eighteen in August and will be called up.'

'Women aren't called up,' her mother informed her.

'Then I shall call myself up. I'd like to join the army and go abroad.'

'Phyllis!' Her mother sat down with a thump. After Leslie turning up, she didn't think she could stand another shock. Although she was right about women not being called up, they were required to take on some sort of wartime duties when they reached the age of eighteen, like working in a munitions factory, for instance. One of her friends at the hospital had a daughter who was in the Women's Land Army.

'It might be July before I can join your father in Beverley,' she said. 'I always thought that one day you would take your Higher School Certificate, then go to university. Isn't that what you planned to do?'

Phyllis hadn't realised her mother would be so upset at her refusal to return home. Her voice was softer when she replied. 'Yes, Mum. I'd still like to do it one day, but there's a war on. Hopefully it will be over soon, but I doubt it will end before I turn eighteen. There may never be another war in my lifetime, so I really would like to do my bit while I have the chance.'

Winifred stroked her daughter's glossy hair. 'You are a lovely young woman, Phyllis,' she said fondly. 'Me and your father don't really deserve you.'

'Well *he* doesn't,' Phyllis said derisively. 'And he doesn't deserve you, either.' Privately, she was overjoyed that her parents would soon be back together again.

After about a week, Eileen and Doria weren't getting on too badly. Their conversations were becoming slightly friendlier. Now that it was May, her dad came almost every day after work to tend to the garden or just sit on the old bench at the bottom smoking a cigarette and surveying his little kingdom with a pleased smile.

She had told him that Doria was a friend of one of Kate Thomas's daughter's – he already knew that Kate had moved out – and that her husband was with the British forces in India.

'I expect he's an officer,' Jack said with a cynical grin. 'Her talking the way she does, dead posh like. You don't get made an officer if you don't talk like you've got a plum permanently stuck in your gob.'

'Oh, you're a sarcastic bugger, Dad.' Eileen punched him lightly in the chest. 'But you're right, he's a captain.'

Sheila, Brenda and their children had visited on Sunday and had been told the same thing, though they demanded more information.

'His name's Hugh,' Doria had told them. 'Hugh Kneale. He comes from London, the same part as me: Wimbledon. We met when we were children.'

'Why are you staying with our Eileen?' Sheila wanted to know.

'Because I desperately needed peace and quiet,' Doria said with a dramatic wave of the hand. 'Hugh and I hadn't found a place to live when we married, only a year ago. It was a rushed wartime wedding: you know the sort of thing.' She paused. 'I've been living with my parents and they have so many *friends!* There wasn't a moment of peace.' She glanced slyly at Eileen and winked. They had worked out the story the other night.

There was loads more information about the imaginary Hugh should anybody ask. But nobody did.

Nick's bus had taken him as far as Earls Court. It was a part of London he didn't know, so he got on another bus that was going to Liverpool Street station. He didn't know that either, but at least it was a major station and he could get a train to somewhere far away that he *had* heard of.

Norwich, he discovered when he arrived at the station and enquired about tickets. He bought a ticket; a single. Norwich was where he'd gone to meet Eileen when she'd worked for a while on a farm. It was after her little boy, Tony, had died and she was devastated. Nick had been looking forward to them all living together one day in the cottage in Melling.

Life had seemed so much more simple and straightforward in those days, yet in reality, looking back, it had been full of complications. His courtship of Eileen had been eventful; would they get married or not? Deep down, he had always known they would, because they had loved each other, 'till death us do part', as the vows they had taken at their wedding had promised. What had happened to change all that?

He laughed aloud, a sardonic laugh that had no humour in it, startling the other passengers in the carriage. For a moment, he'd actually forgotten that he had lost his arm.

Chapter 16

Phyllis Taylor turned up at Eileen's cottage one Saturday at the end of May bringing her cheese ration and a tin of golden syrup that had been given to her mother by one of her patients.

Eileen professed herself eternally grateful. 'Nicky loves syrup sarnies, the sort where the syrup soaks right through the bread, and cheese is useful for all sorts of things. I think I might grate it.'

'Can I help with something?' Phyllis enquired. Eileen, Sheila and Brenda were seated around the kitchen table drinking tea.

'Yes, luv, you can actually.' Eileen gestured through the window. 'See that girl on the bench at the bottom of the garden?' Phyllis looked and saw a very pregnant young woman nursing her stomach, on which Napoleon was curled in a ball. She looked fed up to the teeth.

Phyllis nodded. 'Who is she?'

'Her name is Doria Kneale and she's married to a captain in the army,' Eileen told her. 'She's staying with us for the time being and I'm pretty sure she'd appreciate the company of someone her own age, rather than someone like me giving her all sorts of advice she doesn't want. Go and talk to her for a while, if you don't mind.'

'Of course I don't mind.' Phyllis's face sparkled with enthusiasm and willingness to help as she

265

left the kitchen and marched purposefully down the garden.

Eileen watched her. 'I really like that young woman,' she said. 'In her own way, she's the salt of the earth. I wish there were more like her around.'

Brenda and Sheila murmured their agreement. 'Though I don't think she'll be here for much longer,' Brenda remarked. 'Aggie Donovan says her mother wants to leave and move back to Yorkshire. She's trying to find someone to swap jobs with.'

Eileen wrinkled her nose. 'I'll be dead sorry to see Phyllis go.'

'So will I,' echoed Sheila. 'I wonder who'll move into their house?'

'Since this bloody war started, people move in and out of property by the minute,' Brenda complained. 'I mean, Miss Brazier lived in that house from the day she was born, and only left when she joined the army, then Jessica Fleming took it over. *She* left when she married that Yank and moved to Burtonwood. Now Phyllis and her mam are about to move on. In the old days, people got married and lived in the same house all their lives – like me!' She folded her arms and said indignantly, 'I'm beginning to feel like a real stick-in-the-mud. I wouldn't mind moving somewhere meself.'

Doria Mallory and Phyllis became instant friends when Phyllis introduced herself that day in Eileen's garden. There was something in their very different personalities that appealed to the other.

Phyllis thought it most peculiar that although

they were about the same age, their lives had gone so differently. 'I've never even had a proper boyfriend,' she said, 'and you've got a husband in the army and are about to have a baby. It's not that I'm envious or anything, just that I think life's funny. It has no pattern.'

'How old are you?' Doria asked.

'I'll be eighteen in August.'

'I'll be twenty in August.'

'What date?'

'The fifteenth.'

Phyllis clapped her hands delightedly. 'I'm the fifteenth too. Isn't that an incredible coincidence?'

'Yes – but you know, Phyllis, two years makes all the difference. An awful lot can happen in that time – as it did to me.'

'When I'm eighteen, I intend to join up,' Phyllis told her. 'I really fancy the army.' She sat at the end of the bench and automatically picked up Doria's feet and placed them on her knee, as if was her role in life. 'How do you keep your slacks up?' she enquired.

Doria was wearing black trousers with a loose top. She lifted the top to reveal long straps that went over her shoulders. 'I haven't got a waist any more,' she said sadly.

'I expect they're called maternity slacks.'

'I expect they are.' Doria's arms went back around her stomach and Napoleon. 'I wish I'd done something more exciting when I was eighteen,' she said. 'But I had an important clerical job in London by then and I don't know if the powers-that-be would have let me leave. The girls I know who are in the forces are having a really

267

exciting time. Wherever they might be, there's at least twenty men for every girl. One girl I know is in the furthest reaches of Scotland, and another is in Italy.'

Phyllis was momentarily shocked. 'You shouldn't be thinking like that when you're a married woman about to have a baby.'

'I know, but the thing is, I shall never have a good time again.' Doria looked stricken, as if it had only just dawned on her that the list of things she could no longer do would lengthen immeasurably once she became a mother. 'I shall have to be nothing but sensible from now on.'

'Poor you!' Phyllis patted one of her feet. 'Sensible is an all right thing to be. If everyone in the world were sensible, there would never be wars. Are you up to going to the pictures in your condition?'

'Just about.' She could still probably fit in a seat.

'Then shall we go one afternoon next week? *The Glass Key* with Alan Ladd and Veronica Lake is on in Walton Vale. We could meet about half past four after I've finished work. You can catch a bus straight there from Melling.'

'I'd love to. Gosh, once I've had the baby, I won't even be able to go to the pictures without getting someone to look after him or her.'

Phyllis cocked her head on one side and said thoughtfully, 'You'll have someone to care for who is actually more important than yourself. That would be a really funny feeling. I mean, I really love my mum, but fancy loving someone even more, so that no one else really matters, not even yourself.'

'I'll *never* feel like that.' Doria shuddered. Imagine not having enough to buy a new frock from Harrods, and having to spend what money you had on clothes for the baby instead.

'You will, you'll see,' Phyllis promised, squeezing both of Doria's feet in a comforting gesture.

But Doria still doubted it very much.

It had been rumoured for months that D-Day was absolutely certain to take place any day now. No one knew exactly when. Letters were received from relatives living in the Home Counties or on the south coast telling news of never-ending aeroplanes flying over, of non-stop troop movements, of seeing hundreds, perhaps thousands, possibly millions of American soldiers whichever way you looked.

Troop carriers, lorries and vehicles of every description, all camouflaged, poured through towns and villages, where people had never seen anything like it before. All this activity was in preparation for the crossing of the Channel to France, and before you could say 'abracadabra', the troops would have reached Germany and the war would be over.

Wouldn't it?

Hopes had been raised so many times before. It was the best part of a year since the Allies had landed in Sicily, yet they still hadn't arrived in Rome.

But people couldn't help but think that the end was definitely in sight when, at half past nine on Tuesday morning, 6 June 1944, it was announced

269

on the BBC that D-Day had arrived at last. Overnight, the first of the thousands of troops had crossed the Channel as part of the Normandy landings.

That night, the King of England spoke to the nation on the wireless. 'D-Day has come. Early this morning, the Allies began the assault on the north-western face of Hitler's European fortress...'

Well, victory must certainly be in sight if the King himself believed it.

Leslie Taylor had found a pretty little cottage to rent in the very centre of Beverley. 'It's just off the main street,' he wrote to Winifred. 'I actually prefer it to our own house. It's much cosier and warmer and very handy for the shops. I'm sure Phyllis will love it.'

Phyllis had no intention of loving it, or even going to see it, at least not for a long time. She had made arrangements to move in with Lena Newton and sleep on her settee once her mother had gone.

'I'll come back to live with you and Dad one day,' she promised, 'but I did tell you, Mum, I mean to join the forces when I'm eighteen. And I want to be company for Doria for a while after her baby's born.' Doria was convinced she would be depressed.

Her mother sighed. 'I know, love. I just know you're going to have a terribly important and never-endingly busy life.' Just now, Phyllis was breaking her heart. She almost wished Leslie hadn't put in an appearance when he did or, better still, hadn't vanished in the first place. They'd still

270

be living in Beverley, and Phyllis would be about to leave school and go to university.

Eileen couldn't wait for Doria to have her baby. The girl did nothing but moan about the problems she had moving, lying down, sitting up and sitting still, going to the lavatory, climbing stairs and coming down again. She was off her food one day, and couldn't eat enough the next. Basically she had quite a sweet nature, but only when her life was going smoothly and nothing even vaguely difficult – like having a baby – was happening.

What was worrying Eileen was how Doria would feel once the baby was born. What about if the delivery hurt? (Did a delivery ever *not* hurt?) Or the baby cried a lot – or even a little? Or it needed its nappy changing more than once a day?

More importantly, how long did Doria intend to stay in the cottage with Eileen having no option but to listen to her constant complaints. Where could the girl go? Her mam and dad wouldn't want her, not with a baby.

Phyllis was an enormous help. Eileen didn't know how she would have managed without her. She came after work every single day apart from Saturday and Sunday, when she stayed from early morning until late at night, and she also announced that she had learnt at school back in Beverley how babies were delivered.

'The cookery teacher, Miss Wainwright, thought us girls should know how it was done, so she described it and made some illustrations. Oh, and she got into terrible trouble when the head-mistress found out. You'd think there was something disgusting about it.'

'I hope she didn't get the sack,' Eileen said. 'Miss Wainwright, that is, not the headmistress.'

'No, but she left to go to another school soon afterwards.'

'When I was at school,' Eileen reminisced, 'some girl got into trouble when she asked one of nuns to explain the virgin birth.'

'It's a perfectly legitimate question,' Phyllis said. 'No one should get into trouble for being curious.'

Doria's baby arrived on a Sunday afternoon at the end of June. Eileen wasn't present. It was Sean's twenty-second birthday, and a party had been planned at the cottage – it would have been his first big day out since his recovery – but rain had been predicted for the whole of that weekend, and it had been pouring down non-stop since Saturday morning.

Instead, Eileen took Nicky and the food she had prepared to Pearl Street. The party would be held at Sean and Alice's house instead. Phyllis stayed behind in Melling to keep Doria company.

When Eileen returned to the cottage that night, having left Nicky with his grandad, Doria wasn't there, but Phyllis was.

'It was about midday when she had her first contraction,' Phyllis explained. 'For a while, they were half an hour apart. I telephoned the hospital when they became more frequent' – arrangements had been made for the baby to be born in Walton hospital – 'and they said to keep a note of the pains and when they reached ten minutes apart to telephone again and they'd send an ambulance.'

'Yes?' Eileen said impatiently. She followed the girl into the kitchen, where she'd been told a kettle had just boiled for tea.

'Well, that's what I did. When the pains were ten minutes apart, I telephoned the hospital and an ambulance came. I went with her, the baby was born, Doria fell asleep and I came home. It wasn't nearly as exciting as I expected,' Phyllis said disappointedly. The kettle had boiled again and she poured the water into the teapot.

Eileen sat down and grinned. 'I bet you were hoping to deliver it yourself.'

Phyllis grinned back. 'I wouldn't have minded.'

'Anyroad, you still haven't told me whether it's a boy or a girl.'

'It's a boy, he's terribly pink. He weighed eight pounds five ounces, and he's to be called Theobald.'

'*What?*' Eileen was horrified. 'That's a terrible name to give a child, particularly in Liverpool. If he's not popular at school, they're likely to call him Baldy.'

'I think Theo's rather nice.' Phyllis put a cup of tea in front of Eileen and sat down at the table with her own. 'Can I sleep in Doria's bed tonight?'

'Of course, luv.' Eileen gave a sigh of relief. 'Oh well, I'm glad that's over. Has Doria said anything about what she intends to do next?'

'She muttered something about joining the forces with me – I shall be eighteen in August.'

That couldn't possibly be right – the girl had

273

only just had a baby – but it seemed as if Doria would be out of her hair soon in one way or another. Perhaps she hoped her mum and dad in Wimbledon wouldn't be able to resist their first grandson once they set eyes on him, then she could join up and they wouldn't mind.

Winifred Taylor discovered a nurse in Hull – the city was close to Beverley – who fancied working in Liverpool, if only for the variety it offered. Her name was Barbara Wilkinson and she was ten years younger than Winifred and didn't have children.

'My husband is in the army somewhere in Italy,' she wrote. 'I'm sure he would like to work in Liverpool when he comes home after the war. It would be a lovely change for us both, almost an adventure.'

Now Barbara had to be interviewed and approved by Bootle hospital, and Winifred by the one in Hull.

'It shouldn't take much longer,' Winifred said to Phyllis. From her record, she was sure Barbara would be an ideal nurse. 'Hopefully I will still be here for your birthday in August. Would you like a party, love?' She was dreading the day she would be parted from her daughter, even if it meant she would be living with Leslie again.

'No thanks, Mum, but I'd like a big do on my twenty-first. By then the war will be long over and I will have loads of new friends.' Though Doria would remain her best friend for ever and ever.

Doria's baby was a tough little thing. He looked more like an Albert or a Tommy than a Theo; Eileen refused to say the name in full. He didn't cry much, but used his fists and feet a lot, forever punching and kicking the air as if he was having a battle with it. His tight little face bore a permanent scowl, but she knew that very soon he would smile. Doria expressed the opinion that he was ugly.

'And I didn't think about it before,' she said, 'but I would have much preferred a girl, so I could dress her in pretty clothes. I might even have been able to make her a frock, but I can't manage little boys' clothes.'

Eileen wished with all her heart that Doria would soon go and take her baby with her. She was gradually falling in love with Theo, and Nicky was becoming fond of him too.

'Is he my brother, Mum?' he enquired.

'No, love.' Eileen felt forced to deny it, even though in reality Theo and Nicky were half-brothers. She wondered if Nick would be in contact with Doria to enquire about the baby he had fathered, but of course he had no idea where she was living. Eileen had telephoned Peter, in Wimbledon, to tell him he had a nephew, and he had promised to let her know should Nick try to get in touch with Doria there.

'I miss you,' he'd said. 'It's ages since we've seen each other. I don't fancy coming while Doria's there.'

She wanted to see him too. She hadn't forgotten how handsome he was, and rather fancied a bit of romance in her life, even if it wasn't the

275

passionate, breathless sort she had known with Nick. It would be a change to have someone tell her she looked pretty, someone who wasn't Brenda or Sheila; someone who admired her dress or the way she'd done her hair.

As the days and weeks passed, she continued to pray that Doria would soon disappear from her life, yet all the time she became fonder of Theo. She loved the way he snuggled his little head against her neck, just below her ear, and she could feel his baby heart beating near her own.

If only life would stop being so confusing!

It was August, and Phyllis had already received a Government Works Order requiring her to present herself at the Labour Exchange in Renshaw Street the week before her birthday. She arrived promptly for her appointment at 2 p.m., and announced that it was her wish to join the forces.

'The army is my favourite,' she emphasised to the fifty-ish woman behind the counter. 'I'd love to be posted to Normandy.'

'I'm afraid it's nothing to do with me, Miss Taylor,' the woman informed her. 'But wherever it is, and whatever you end up doing, it's bound to be interesting. I wish I were young enough to join up,' she said longingly. 'I wouldn't care where I was sent.'

'Well neither do I, not really,' Phyllis said. 'Anywhere will do.' She signed the appropriate forms and was told she'd hear back within a fortnight.

She was leaving the Labour Exchange when she came face to face with Doria, who was coming in.

'What on earth are you doing here?' she gasped.

'I have an appointment. I'm joining the army, like you.' Doria grabbed her shoulders, twisted her around and they did a little jig. 'I told you ages ago, didn't I, that that was what I intended doing. When you told me you'd made an appointment, I telephoned and made the one after yours.'

'But I never dreamt you *meant* it. What about Theo?'

'Eileen has agreed to look after him – we had a long discussion the other day. It's only until the war is over, then I'll come straight home, collect Theo, and we'll go and live somewhere in London; it's my favourite place.'

'And Eileen doesn't mind?'

'No, she adores Theo. Have you seen the look on her face when she nurses him?'

'Yes.' Phyllis thought it very sad. She wasn't surprised that Eileen had agreed to have Theo, even if it would only be for a matter of months. But she would find it even more difficult to part with him then than she would now. For all Phyllis considered Doria to be her best and closest friend, she thought she was being opportunistic, taking advantage of the woman who had offered her sanctuary in the last weeks of her pregnancy.

'Shall I wait for you here?' she asked outside the Labour Exchange.

'Yes *please*,' Doria said eagerly. 'Then we can go somewhere and have a coffee.'

They went to the Kardomah in Bold Street. 'I asked the woman behind the desk at the Labour Exchange if we could be sent to the same place

277

to do our training,' Doria said. 'I hope you don't mind.'

'Gosh, no. I think it would be marvellous if we stayed together.'

'She said it wasn't up to her, but as we were joining the army at exactly the same time, it was likely that we would.' She rubbed her hands together excitedly. 'I'm really looking forward to it. It's been a horrible year.'

'I wouldn't call it horrible ending up with a baby like Theobald,' Phyllis said primly.

'That's because you're so much nicer than me, much kinder, less selfish. But the day will come,' Doria said happily, 'when I shall be an absolutely perfect mother.'

'What about being a perfect wife as well?'

'A perfect wife, too.' Doria still had a few secrets her new friend had yet to learn about. 'Oh, and please don't mention to anyone about me joining up, will you? Eileen wants it to be kept a secret until it actually happens. She's worried that people might try and talk her out of it. And don't you speak to her either. She'll be annoyed I've told you.'

Phyllis promised she wouldn't breathe a word to a soul.

It was terribly sad. Sad that Winifred was obliged to move back to Beverley a few days before her daughter's birthday in August; sad for Lena Newton, who would only have Phyllis staying with her for a few days when she'd hoped she would be there for weeks. It was sad for everyone except Phyllis herself, who had received her call-up papers and was really looking forward to a new life in the army. She had to present herself at Colchester barracks in Essex in ten days' time before being directed to the place where she would be trained.

Doria had also received her call-up papers with the same instructions, but Phyllis was the only one who knew.

Nick Stephens had been living in a single-storey bed-and-breakfast establishment on the lonely Norfolk coast for close to six weeks. It was called Windward Ho and was run by a retired white-bearded naval man called Clarence Baines and his daughter, Mary, who was a potter. Her skilfully made vases, ornamental plates and statues were on sale in a shop-cum-studio at the rear of the premises. Customers could choose what to buy while watching Mary at work. She was a hefty, shapely woman with short curly hair that Nick had once witnessed her cutting herself without a mirror. He presumed she just wanted it short and didn't care what it looked like. Her face might have been regarded as beautiful if it hadn't been for the skin that had been roughened by too much sun, wind and rain over the years. She never wore make-up, and Nick doubted if she ever had. The contents of her wardrobe consisted of half a dozen home-made dirndl skirts, some hand-knitted jumpers and a man's pea jacket for when the days were chilly.

On sunny days, tables and chairs were set out on the shingle beach outside the shop, where tea, coffee, sandwiches and scones were on sale.

279

In the darkness of the night and when the sun rose and there was no one about, the tide could be heard coming in or going out, racing through the stones, making a subtle rattling noise that Nick found soothing, though he could imagine there was a time, only recently, when the noise would have driven him mad, because it never stopped; never.

In all the weeks he had been there, not another soul had taken advantage of the bed-and-breakfast side of the business. He had been the only guest, though plenty of holidaymakers visited the shop to buy Mary's attractive ornaments or partake of the refreshments.

'When will you be thinking of moving on, Nick?' Clarence enquired while they were having their evening meal one day late in August.

'I wasn't thinking of moving on.' Nick felt a moment of panic. Was the establishment closing for business now that the holiday season was nearing its end? He couldn't ever imagine wanting to leave this peaceful place.

Clarence hastened to reassure him. 'I was just expecting you to be off somewhere on your travels one day.' He had a faint Yorkshire accent, but had never talked about his past. Neither had Nick.

'One day, maybe; but not yet. I'm perfectly happy here.' Not ecstatically happy as he had once been with Eileen and Nicky, but quietly happy; relaxed.

'Well, me and Mary are perfectly happy having you.' Clarence held up a bottle of whisky, inviting Nick to have a sup, as he called it.

280

'No thanks.' In London, he had almost become a drunkard as his troubles piled on top of him. Now, looking back, the troubles didn't seem all that onerous. He worried, slightly, about his wife and son, but there were plenty of friends and relatives to care for them should they be needed. As for Doria, the Christmas he had spent with her in Wimbledon had shown that her parents were actually pleased that she was expecting his baby. He wondered if she'd had a boy or a girl, but didn't dwell on it for long.

Mary now spoke in her low, husky voice. She had made the meal, an extremely tasty fish pie with boiled potatoes and carrots. Although a plain cook, she was very good at it. 'Would you like another helping, Nick, or just a pudding?'

'Just a pudding, please. If I had second helpings every day, I'd be as big as a house in no time.'

At that, a hint of a smile came to her weather-beaten face. As far as Nick was concerned, she didn't possess an ounce of sex appeal. Indeed, he considered her rather mannish. 'Just a pudding, then.' She ladled jelly and custard into a bowl and handed it to him. Clarence accepted a second helping of fish pie. He was a small, slight individual who gave the impression of being half starved despite eating like a horse.

The meal over, Mary cleared the table, taking the dishes into the kitchen to wash. Clarence lit two oil lamps, placing one on a small table beside Nick and the other beside himself. He produced a book and began to read, and Nick did the same – a library book borrowed from Cromer library called *The Antiquary*, by Sir Walter Scott; it was

281

his intention to read all twelve of the author's Waverley novels. Mary didn't return, and the two men hardly exchanged a word until almost ten o'clock, when Nick put a marker in the book, closed it, and announced that he was ready for bed.

'Good night, lad,' Clarence said. 'See you in the morning. Oh, and don't forget to take that lamp with you in case you want to read upstairs.'

'I will,' Nick replied. They had the same exchange every single night. 'Good night, Clarence. And say good night to Mary when she comes back.'

Eileen woke to the sound of a baby crying. Unsurprisingly, it was coming from the next room, where Doria and Theo slept. She lay for quite a while wondering why Doria hadn't picked her son up to comfort him. It wasn't like her to sleep in.

Nicky had woken up too. 'Theo's upset, Mum. Can I go and talk to him?'

'All right, luv. We'll both go.'

She got out of bed and took Nicky's hand, and together they knocked on the door of the adjoining bedroom. Theo stopped crying for a second or so, then began again, even louder, when nothing happened. Eileen opened the door and they went in to find Doria's bed empty.

'She must be in the bathroom,' she muttered. In Nicky's old cot, Theo's little arms and legs were waving furiously and his face was red with anger. He ceased crying the minute Eileen picked him up and he buried his head in her neck.

'You little treasure,' she whispered.

'Was I a little treasure once, Mum?'

'Yes, and you're a bigger treasure now,' Eileen told her son. 'Let's try and find Doria.' She knocked on the bathroom door, but there was no answer and when she opened the door, the room was empty.

She was about to close the door, but paused. The bathroom looked unnaturally tidy and her heart lurched when she realised that all Doria's bits and pieces had gone off the windowsill, her jars and bottles of this and that, and her towel was no longer hanging on the hook behind the door.

She hurried back into the bedroom to find that most of Doria's clothes had gone too, as well as her suitcase. All that was left were the maternity clothes, which had been left in a heap in the bottom of the wardrobe.

Doria must have crept away in the middle of the night, leaving her baby with Eileen. When Eileen went downstairs, she found a note on the dining room table confirming her suspicious.

Dear Eileen, I hope you don't mind, but I have joined the army with Phyllis. We should be halfway to London on the train by the time you read this. I promise I shall return for Theobald the very minute the war is over.

With love and thanks for all you have done for me. Doria. xxx

'And all I am about to do,' Eileen added in a whisper.

'What a flaming cheek!' Sheila gasped when Eileen showed her the letter about two hours later. 'Would you have said no if she'd asked?' she enquired.

'Of course I would!' Eileen said indignantly. 'I'm not a bloody nursemaid. I wondered why she kept getting up early – she claimed she was waiting for a letter. A couple came, but she didn't say who they were from.'

'He's a lovely baby, though,' Sheila said. She reached out and chucked Theo under his little round chin.

'He is,' Eileen agreed. 'It's just that he's not *mine*. I'm already half in love with him. How will I feel when madam turns up in a year's time wanting him back?'

'There is that,' her sister agreed. 'Can I hold him a minute?'

'You can have him for more than a minute,' Eileen said. She transferred the baby to her sister's knee and immediately missed the weight, the feel and the smell of him. 'Oh,' she said. 'Give us him back. I feel I want to move somewhere like Australia so we won't be around when Doria comes to collect him.'

'It's an awful thing to happen,' Sheila said soberly. 'Messing about like that with your own kid's life. I suppose Phyllis must have known what Doria was up to. They became bosom friends within the first five minutes and they've joined up together.'

'I can't imagine Phyllis having anything to do with it, Sheil. She's far too nice and sensible.'

Eileen kissed Theo's red cheek – he was still pretty cross about what had happened that morning. 'Me dad'll have a fit when he finds out. He never liked Doria.'

'Only because she spoke posh,' Sheila said. 'He can't stand people who speak posh.'

'He liked Nick.'

'Nick spoke well, not posh. There's a difference. You know, Eil, Brenda needs to know about this. She doesn't like missing anything. I'll ask one of the kids to knock and tell her you're here.' She went to the front door. The house was unnaturally quiet at the moment. The Reilly children were enjoying the last days of the school summer holiday, and every single one of them, including Mollie, the baby, who was eighteen months old, were playing in the street, Nicky with them.

Sheila returned, and in no time at all, Brenda had joined them wearing a thimble. 'I've been doing a bit of embroidery,' she informed them.

For the second time that day, Eileen described the events of the morning, this time to Brenda, who was duly shocked and amazed. 'Oh well, there's none so strange as folk,' she said when Eileen had finished.

'It's "queer",' Sheila corrected her. '"There's none so *queer* as folk", not "strange".'

Brenda squinted. 'Are you sure, Sheila?'

'Sure I'm sure.'

'You're both wrong,' Eileen said, exasperated with the pair. 'It's "there's nowt so queer as folk", not "none". Anyroad, does it matter?'

'It doesn't matter in the least,' Brenda said, and Sheila agreed.

Chapter 17

Phyllis and Doria spent only three days in Colchester, along with four other girls of roughly the same age – three entirely wasted days where all they did was fill in forms and read pages of rules and regulations, which eventually had to be signed. They all had a successful medical and were issued with uniforms, including everything from peaked caps and massive overcoats to thick woollen stockings and hideous knee-length bloomers. The other girls came from all over the country: Glasgow, Birmingham, a little village somewhere in Cornwall and another village in Wales.

'I don't think I can walk in flat shoes.' Doria clumped across the dormitory, her footsteps extra loud on the wooden floor.

As Phyllis had never worn anything *but* sensible flat shoes, she wasn't bothered.

On the fourth day, they were told they were being sent to an Army Training Centre in Islington, London. All six recruits were delighted, having expected to be sent somewhere in the depths of the countryside.

Furthermore, they weren't travelling to London on the train, but in a lorry with a canvas cover and benches on each side. This, they considered when they climbed aboard wearing their uniforms for the first time, was to be their first real taste of army life. In fact, the journey was hideously uncomfortable: the benches were hard and the lorry's wheels had solid tyres, so every single bump in the road could be felt.

'I'm glad that's flamin' over,' said Hazel, the girl from Glasgow, when they alighted. 'Me bum's lost all sense of feeling.'

Even so, they had arrived in London feeling like proper soldiers, and that night they slept like logs.

Their first drill the following morning wearing khaki tops and shorts was little short of hopeless. The instructor, a tall man with the build of a heavyweight boxer and a moustache that made him look as if he was wearing a bow tie on his upper lip, became exceedingly cross. Doria was the first to giggle, and after that no one could stop. With every mistake they made, they only giggled more.

They returned in high spirits to the women's quarters, changed their clothes, ate lunch, and in the afternoon attended a lecture on map-reading, to which they listened attentively.

Doria, who was familiar with the centre of London, took them to a cinema in Leicester Square, where they saw *The Fleet's In* with William Holden, with whom they fell madly in love, and Dorothy Lamour, whose perfect figure they envied.

When they emerged, it had grown dark and they could hear people singing, not a wartime song for a change, but 'Somewhere Over the Rainbow'. They found that a big crowd had collected in a place that Doria said was called Piccadilly Circus.

'It's where tourists gather in peacetime,' she told them. 'There's usually a statue of Eros on

287

the top of the steps, but he's been put in a safe place in case he was struck by a bomb.'

They sat on the steps around the absent statue and joined in the singing, then caught a bus to a Lyons Corner House, where they had supper.

They were six healthy young women who were having the time of their lives, attracting smiles from members of the female population and admiring whistles from the men. Phyllis, however, found the unlit city streets spooky, much more so than in Bootle, where it was never this crowded. There was something distinctly nerve-racking about rubbing shoulders with so many complete strangers whose faces couldn't be seen. You'll get used to it, she told herself.

'Well, if this is the army,' Doria said on the bus back to Islington, 'I wouldn't mind being a female soldier for the rest of my life.'

The dormitory had enough beds for ten girls, but only the six who'd arrived the day before from Colchester were living there at present.

Phyllis was finding it hard to sleep after such an exciting day, but she also, much to her surprise, found herself shedding quite a few tears. She was badly missing her mother and, even more surprisingly, her ne'er-do-well father, and was thinking how nice it would be to be living in Beverley, where it wasn't even faintly exciting, with Mum and Dad asleep in the next bedroom. She could have gone to college and taken the new Higher Education Certificate in preparation for university.

She was doing her best to keep the tears as

unobtrusive as possible when she realised that the girl in the next bed – Doria was asleep on her other side – was crying quite noisily. It was the girl from Birmingham; Effie, her name was.

Phyllis slid out of bed and knelt on the floor beside her.

'What's the matter?' she whispered, as if she didn't know.

'I feel so miserable,' Effie whispered back. 'I really wish I hadn't joined up.'

It wasn't in Phyllis's nature to say 'So do I' and share the girl's misery. Instead she said stoutly, 'Don't worry. You'll soon get used to it. We all will.'

'I can't imagine ever liking it,' Effie sniffed.

'You will, I promise.' Phyllis squeezed her shoulder and hoped she was right. 'Another month and you'll be enjoying every minute. Shall we have a bet on it?'

The girl had stopped crying. 'A bet! If you like.'

'A shilling!' Phyllis chuckled. 'I bet you a shilling that four weeks today, life in the army won't exactly feel like a bed of roses, but you'll be laughing yourself to sleep at night, rather than crying.'

'Oh, all right then.' Effie brought her hand out from under the bedclothes and they shook on it.

Phyllis had only been back in bed a couple of minutes when she heard a noise as if a motorbike was on the dormitory roof, making the building reverberate. She raised her head, expecting the other girls to be awake, but none had moved, not even Effie, who must have fallen asleep instantly.

It was one of those pilotless V-1 planes! She'd

read about them in the paper and heard about them on the BBC news. Immediately after D-Day, just when everyone had thought the war was practically over, the evil, murderous V-1 had started to fall all over London. They'd been nicknamed 'doodlebugs' and had already killed hundreds of people.

She pulled the bedclothes over her head, as if a sheet and a few layers of blankets would protect her if the plane decided to drop on the barracks and explode, but after a while the noise faded and there was a subdued explosion some distance away. The doodlebug had found another target for its victims that night.

The following Sunday, Doria's brother Peter caught the first train out of Euston to Liverpool Lime Street, arriving at Eileen's cottage not long after eleven – Eileen had written and told him that his sister had joined up, leaving her baby behind. Once her family and friends in Bootle had been to Mass, they too would turn up, bringing contributions towards dinner. Jack Doyle was already there, having arrived on his bike at dawn. He was picking the fruit that was ripe enough, and would sweep up the autumn leaves later. It was a damp, sunless day, and he and a warmly wrapped Nicky, who was helping, appeared now and then like ghosts out of the shroud of fog that covered most of the garden.

A lamp had been switched on to make the living room look slightly more cheery. Eileen was hoping she wouldn't have to light a fire and use precious coal as early as September.

Peter was meeting his nephew for the first time. 'How old is he now?' he asked Eileen. The baby was sitting on his knee, scowling at him and the world in general.

'Ten weeks,' she told him.

'Does he always look this unhappy?'

'He's not unhappy; he's just not very pleased with things.'

'That sounds like unhappy to me,' Peter jigged the baby up and down. 'Did he miss Doria when she left?'

'He didn't give any sign of it.' Eileen shook her head. 'I mean, he's looked like that since he was born. I've taken him to the clinic and they confirmed he is a perfectly healthy baby. He might have three-month colic, in which case another few weeks and he'll be smiling at everybody.'

'It's nice being an uncle. I've never held a baby before.' He hoisted Theo on to his shoulder and stroked the back of his head. 'Now that he's actually born, and she has a flesh-and-blood grandson, my mother worries that she and Dad should be doing something about him.'

'Such as?' Eileen asked warily.

'I don't think they know, but they're pretty fed up with Doria and your precious husband.'

'There's no need for them to do anything,' Eileen told him firmly. 'Doria left him with me.' If there was any argument about it, she had Doria's note to prove it.

'You don't mind having him?'

'I love having him. Nicky does too. And don't forget, Theo has relatives here. Nicky is his half-brother.'

'Does that mean you and I are related in some remote way?' He was flirting with her. She could tell by the way his blue eyes sparkled and his mouth twisted in an appealing way that she was determined to resist.

'You and I aren't related in any way at all,' she informed him, and was relieved when her dad came into the kitchen with Nicky, wanting to know if there was a cup of tea going.

On reflection, Peter Mallory was much too young for her to have a relationship with, no matter how inconsequential. He was twenty-three and she was thirty-one, hardly old enough to be his mother, but old enough for it to matter.

She was even more relieved when Sheila, Brenda, Lena Newton and a whole crowd of children came marching up the path like an advancing army, and she could keep out of Peter's way for the rest of the day.

A few days later, Brenda Mahon woke up in Pearl Street to yet another dull morning. September was normally her favourite month, but this year it had let her down. She had always enjoyed kicking her way through the crisp golden leaves that had fallen from the trees in North Park, but now they would be all wet and limp and would stick to her shoes and she could easily slip over. She had taken the girls there in the pram when they were little.

She turned over in the double bed and wished there was a man in the other half. Not for a bit of nooky or anything like that, just for company, someone to talk to, share a joke or two. She cursed

292

Xavier, her husband, and wondered where he was. It was years since she'd heard from him – not surprising, given that she'd thrown him out after discovering he'd married another woman. He hadn't just been unfaithful, but a bigamist on top.

Xavier Mahon had been a miniature Adonis, a man with ten hats – or was it twelve? She'd forgotten. She actually wouldn't mind having him at home for a little while, just to prove to people that she had a husband. If she knew where he was, she'd write and invite him back for the weekend.

It gave her a fright when Tommy jumped on to the bed and began to lick her face. Well, at least there was one male in her life who she could talk to without any chance of an argument.

'What do you want?' she asked, sitting up and hoisting the pillow up behind her. Tommy crawled on to her knee and made himself comfortable 'I'll give you some milk in a minute.' It was about time cats were entitled to their own milk ration.

For some reason, she felt out of sorts this morning. Perhaps it was because the war had gone on too long, the entire country depressed and bored witless.

There was a glimmer of pale light between the blackout curtains. That meant she could turn on the gas light and draw back the curtains without some overzealous air-raid warden screaming, 'Put that light out!' She'd go downstairs soon and make some tea; as usual, she was dying for a cuppa.

The first thing she noticed when she opened the curtains was that there was activity across the

293

road at number 10 where the Taylors had lived; Winifred had returned to Yorkshire and Phyllis had joined the army. The woman Winifred had swapped jobs with hadn't wanted a whole house to live in, so number 10 had been empty for a few weeks.

Brenda had her nose pressed against the net curtains, trying to make out the new occupants, when the curtains upstairs were suddenly whisked back by a familiar figure in a blue dressing gown. Brenda's scream of delight caused Tommy to leap off the bed and hide underneath, while Monica and Muriel rushed into the room thinking their mother was being murdered.

'What's the matter, Mam?'

'Nothing!' Brenda yelled. 'Nothing's the matter.' She dragged on her clothes and stumbled across the road to Sheila's house, pulling the key through the letter box and letting herself in.

'You'll never guess who's moved into number ten,' she shouted. '*Never!*'

Sheila was still in her nightdress. Upstairs, the boys were having a fight and the girls were arguing. 'Clark Gable?' she guessed.

'No, idiot. Guess harder.'

'The King?'

'No, even better: Jessica Fleming.' Brenda spread her arms and stepped forward as if she'd just introduced the biggest star in the world to a grateful nation.

'The red-haired one?'

'What other Jessica Fleming do we know?'

'Blimey!' Sheila said. 'Don't forget, she's not Jess Fleming any more, but Jess Henningsen since she married that American captain – or is he a colonel? I wonder what she's doing back in Pearl Street.'

'Let's go and see.'

'Not in me nightie, Bren. We'll go when I've got dressed.'

Jessica Henningsen had been born in Bootle forty-six years ago. She was the only child of a rag-and-bone merchant, a shady character who became rich from the profits he made out of buying a precious piece of china or family heirloom from some poor old person who was ignorant of its real value as well as down on their luck and therefore desperate for a few bob. These items he would sell at a vast profit.

The business had done so well that Jessica and her father – her mother had passed away when she was a baby – had moved away from Pearl Street to live in the best part of Liverpool. After her father's death, Jessica's husband Arthur, a nice man but hopeless at business, had lost everything, and the couple had returned to Pearl Street, where Jessica owned several properties.

In the third year of the war, Arthur had joined the army and was killed in Egypt, and Jessica had married Major Gus Henningsen of the US Army Air Force. Now she was back in Pearl Street for the third time.

'For goodness' sake,' she laughed when she opened the door and found her two old friends outside, almost hysterically pleased to see her. She sat them down and made them tea.

'I'm just as pleased to see you too,' she told

them when they were seated around the table. She looked at Sheila. 'I thought I'd go and see your Eileen this afternoon. We've been writing to each other, but it's ages since I heard from her and she doesn't know I'd decided to come back – I only made up my mind at the last minute. Gus is being posted to France to join the American forces, so I'll probably not see him until the war is over.'

'I thought you had a really nice bungalow in Burtonwood?' Brenda cried.

'I have, but I hardly know anyone there and I decided I'd sooner spend my last months in England with my friends in Bootle than anywhere else in the world. We plan on moving to New York eventually, as you know.' Gus's family owned a chain of bakery shops there.

'Where's Penny?'

'In bed, fast asleep. Well, she was until you two attempted to knock the door down.'

Five-year-old Penny proved that she was now wide awake by entering the room, still in her nightdress. 'Hello,' she said, looking shyly at the newcomers.

'Hello, luv,' the women chorused, and Sheila added, 'The older she gets, the more your Penny looks like our Caitlin. They could be sisters.'

'Actually, Penny is very like my mother,' Jessica remarked. 'There's a photo of her somewhere. I'll show it you if I happen to come across it.'

'She hasn't got red hair.' Brenda glanced admiringly at Jessica's own head of glorious waves and curls.

'Neither had my mother. She had brown hair;

296

it was my father who was the redhead.'

Sheila decided it was time she went home. 'The kids'll be wondering where I've got to. Can you come round tonight for a chat, Jess? Bring Penny with you. Oh, and you'll find our Eileen has quite a surprise in store when you see her.'

'In that case, I'll go to Melling as soon as I can.'

Outside, Brenda said to Sheila, 'I woke up this morning feeling really down in the dumps. Now I feel as happy as a lark because Jess has arrived. The world's a funny place; what do you think, Sheil?'

'It's a funny place all right, Bren, particularly with people like you and me in it. Me dad says we remind him of those women on the wireless, Gert and Daisy.'

Brenda hooted. 'Oh well, cheerio, Gert.'

'Ta-ra, Daisy. I'll see you later.'

Five years ago, a mere few weeks after the start of the war, when Jessica had returned to Pearl Street, she and Eileen had started out as enemies, what with Jessica thinking she'd come down in the world, but had eventually become friends. It was therefore no surprise that Eileen's reaction when she opened the door was somewhat similar to Sheila and Brenda's earlier on.

'Jess!' she yelled. 'It's marvellous to see you. you're looking well. Oh, and Penny, you are prettier than ever. Come on in, luv, so I can kiss you. And after I've done that, I'll make us all a cup of tea.'

Nicky had arrived in the doorway and was hanging on to his mother's leg. He and Penny, who was two years older, had met before, but the chances were they wouldn't remember each other.

The fire had been lit, mainly with wood chopped from the trees in the garden. There was a fresh, flowery smell to the room that hinted of lavender.

Theo was propped up in a bed of cushions on the settee, staring into the fire with a strange expression on his face that was possibly a smile.

Seeing him, it was Jessica's turn to yell. 'You've had a baby – and no one told me, not even this morning when I saw your Sheila.'

'Don't be daft, Jess. This is Theo. Sit down while I make some tea, and then I'll tell you all about him and everything else that has happened since I last wrote.'

Jessica was almost too stunned to speak by the time Eileen had regaled her with the story of Nick and Doria, and how she'd ended up holding the baby while the main characters in this sorry tale had both disappeared. While they were speaking, Nicky and Penny had gone into the garden to gather the windfalls off the apple trees.

'I haven't an idea in the world where Nick is, or Doria, though I could find out about her easily enough if I wanted.' She explained that Doria had gone off with Phyllis, who had lived with her mother in Jessica's old house. 'Phyllis has promised to write to Lena Newton, who lives over the dairy. Not that I'm interested, mind you,' she said hastily. 'I'd be happy to keep Theo for ever – you know his real name is Theobald?'

'Never!' Jessica studied the baby. 'Can I give him a little cuddle?' she asked.

'Of course!'

'Oh, they do feel nice, don't they, babies?' She heaved a pleasurable sigh. 'When they're little, they fit in all the places outside your body just like they did inside.' She tucked Theo against her side, within the curve of her arm, then, without looking at her friend, she said, 'What are you going to do about Nick?'

Eileen watched the fire spit and crackle before answering, an expression of almost hopeless sadness on her face. 'I don't know, Jess,' she said eventually. 'I love him dearly most of the time, but other times I don't love him at all. I know something bad happened when he lost his arm, but it wasn't my fault. Not only that, but I loved him more after the accident than I'd done before – and I hadn't thought that was possible.'

'Love, babies, men and women.' Jessica stared into the fire. She looked staggeringly beautiful with the firelight reflected on her lovely face, her hair as brilliant as the flames and her green eyes soft and pensive. 'Life is just one long drama, and I bet it never stops. When we are both very old women, we'll have the same things to worry about – and I'll be there a long time before you. I was forty-six on my last birthday and I can't tell you how much I would love to have another child; girl or boy, I wouldn't care. Another one to hold as I'm holding this little one here.' She smiled at Theo, and Eileen could hardly believe it when he smiled back.

'You lost a child, didn't you, Jess?' she said softly. 'Not long after you met Gus.'

Jessica remembered the day with horror. It was

one of the worst of her life. 'Yes, it was Arthur's child, a brother or sister for Penny.'

Eileen didn't know it, but Jessica was lying through her teeth.

That night, Jack Doyle let himself into his daughter's house just around the corner from his own. He was only coming for a chat, to see how Sheila and the kids were. It was a while since Calum had been home, and it was clear for the whole world to see how much she loved and missed him.

There was more than a bit of noise coming from the living room; mainly screams of laughter, and he could make out a voice he didn't recognise – a woman who didn't have a Liverpool accent.

There was something going on in the parlour, too, though the voices in there were more subdued by far. He opened the door and saw that the best table had been pulled into the middle of the room and six children were sitting around it engrossed in a game of cards. It was Pairs, a game Jack had often played with his grandkids. It required enormous concentration that he was incapable of.

'Hello there,' he said.

'Hello, Grandad,' muttered Dominic. The other children ignored him, too involved in their game.

'Ta-ra, then.' He closed the door, his brow furrowed in thought. Sheila's three lads had been there, and he recognised Brenda's girls, but there'd been another girl, the youngest of the lot, brown-haired, pretty...

'Jaysus!' He actually whispered the word out

300

loud. 'Penny Fleming!'

So that was who the unknown voice belonged to: Penny's mother. He was amazed he hadn't recognised it straight away. Jessie Fleming was back in Bootle! What for this time? To haunt him and taunt him; to break his heart for the umpteenth time? And she'd brought their daughter with her.

Jack left the house, closing the door quietly behind him. He hoped Dominic wouldn't mention that his grandad had been and gone. If Sheila said anything, he'd just reply that seeing as she'd company, he'd thought it better not to disturb them.

He made his way rapidly to the King's Arms and ordered a whisky chaser with his first pint.

'Have you come up on the pools, Jack?' Mack the landlord enquired. 'You usually only treat yourself to a chaser on special occasions, like Christmas.'

'Just felt like one tonight,' Jack mumbled. He hid himself in a corner and hardly spoke to a soul the entire night. Word soon got round that Jack Doyle was in a mood and to leave him alone.

He left the pub before Mack rang the bell for closing time, and made his unsteady way back to Garnet Street. When he let himself in, he found a note on the mat just inside the door.

Jack, I need to see you urgently. Will you please come round as soon as you can. I'm back at number 10. Jessica

Chapter 18

Well, he wasn't going now, not straight away, not when he was more than a bit drunk and couldn't think straight. But he could never think straight when he was in the vicinity of Jessie Fleming.

Jack was a popular man and he knew it. He was also as straight as a die and could hold sway over a hundred men, two hundred, and bend them to his will. He was generally happy with his lot. His wife, Mollie, had died not long after Sean was born, but that was the way things happened. No one should expect life to be one big bed of roses. There was good, and there was bad. He drove his daughter Eileen mad going on like this, explaining everything away, reasoning, making sense of things, never allowing for the unexpected to happen. But Jessie Fleming was the unexpected; he would never be able to explain her away.

Next day, at work on the docks unloading a big dusty ship from India, he was bloody useless. He couldn't remember which was his right hand and which his left. He fell down the same ladder twice, fortunately not a very big one, and discovered he'd put lemon curd instead of mustard on the sarnies he'd made for his dinner.

He arrived home at six in a terrible tuck with himself. Should he go and see Jess now? Should he go and see her at all? How dare she just demand his presence as if she were the Queen of bloody England? Knowing Jess, though, she'd not take no for an answer; best to go now, before he went near the pub and got pissed out of his mind for the second night in a row.

He was tempted to go as he was, in his working clothes, smelling of God knows what had been in the crates and sacks he'd spent the day carrying off the ship. But a sense of pride made him change into a clean shirt and his second-best suit. He contemplated not wearing a collar and tie, but once again pride forced him into searching for his collar studs and picking out a tie – he only had two.

Ready! Now, which way should he go? It was still light outside, and tongues would wag if he was seen entering Jessie's house by the front door, all done up, like. Aggie Donovan's tongue would wag the most, and if Sheila discovered where he'd been, he would be subjected to the third degree, pinned against the wall while she shone a torch into his face and demanded to know what was going on. He would have to go down Amethyst Street, turn into Coral Street and go in Jessie's by the back way.

He looked at his reflection in the wardrobe mirror, bowed at himself from the waist and set off.

'Ah, there you are,' she said. She smoothed the lapels of his jacket by way of greeting and kissed him briefly on the cheek. She was wearing a long blue velvet garment; he wasn't sure if it was a dressing gown or an evening dress. It wasn't the sort of thing that Pearl Street women were usually seen wearing. He could smell the scent she'd used, which was subtler and softer than the stuff the other women he knew dabbed behind their ears. Straight away, instantly, he wanted to bury his face in her red hair. 'How have you been, Jack?'

'Very well,' he replied; his voice had just a touch of a croak in it. 'Very well indeed. Where's Penny?'

'Upstairs, fast asleep.' She smiled and said conversationally, 'I'm glad your Sean is so much better; almost completely, Eileen said. She told me before what a state he was in before. Almost like a coma.'

'Almost like a coma, yes, you're right. But he's much better. Wants to go back in the RAF, but they wouldn't take him in a million years.'

'You're right. He needs to be set up in his own business.'

At her words, Jack recovered himself just a little. 'His own business? Oh, that's a fine idea. I'll set one up for him tomorrer.'

Jess smiled. 'Good old Jack, as prickly as ever. Why don't you sit down and have something to drink?' She pointed to the easy chairs close together in front of the fire and he sat on the nearest. The room was fully furnished, and he wondered if it was Miss Brazier's furniture that she'd left behind when she went off and joined the army.

'I wouldn't mind a cup of tea.' There hadn't been time to make a pot at home while he'd been beautifying himself for her.

'I meant a real drink. There's everything imaginable available at the base. What would you like?

I've brought whisky, rum, gin, a couple of liqueurs. I even have half a dozen cans of beer.'

'Huh! It doesn't look as if your lot are suffering shortages like us on this side of the Atlantic,' he growled.

'They aren't. They brought loads of stuff over with them. And I don't know what you mean by "your lot", Jack. I married an American, but I didn't change my nationality.'

'Sorry,' he muttered. 'I'll have a whisky, then, neat.' It was his nature to pick a fight with anyone who appeared to be overprivileged. He'd had no end of battles with Jess's dad, the tight bastard, in the days when he'd lived in Pearl Street. 'Anyroad, what was it you wanted to see me about?'

She selected the whisky from the row of bottles on the sideboard, poured him a glass, then sat in the other chair. He was aware that her face had suddenly flushed. She was embarrassed about something. 'You've always known that Penny is your child, haven't you, Jack?'

It was his turn to flush. 'Yes.'

'Arthur must have had something wrong with him. We were married for almost twenty years, but I never became pregnant, although I'd always longed for children.' Her voice dropped to a whisper. 'There was just that one time with you – and nine months later I had Penny.'

Jack hung his head, embarrassed himself, and didn't speak. 'I became pregnant a second time. That was yours too, but I lost it.'

He hadn't known that and he was shocked. 'Lost it?'

'I had a miscarriage, a sort of accident.' She

305

moved her legs so that her knees touched his, and he wondered if she'd placed the chairs close together deliberately. 'Ever since, I've never stopped wanting another baby, Jack.'

'Aren't you getting a bit past it?' he said coarsely. 'And correct me if I'm wrong, but haven't you been married to your Yankee officer for the past two years? Is he another one like Arthur?'

'Gus is a widower; he has a son from his first marriage. No, there's nothing wrong with him, I just haven't been lucky enough to conceive, that's all. Now he's been posted to Europe; he only left the other day. I've no idea when I'll see him again.'

'What's that got to do with me?' Why on earth were they having this conversation? He reminded himself that it was Jess who'd introduced the subject of babies and how they were acquired.

'Can't you guess?' she said softly.

It took Jack a minute or so, and when he understood what she meant, his body went cold from head to toe in a way it had never done before. He stared at her with horror. 'You want me to...?' He couldn't think of a polite word for it on the spur of the moment.

'Yes.' She fell to her knees and laid her head in his lap. 'Please, Jack.'

Jack couldn't have described the emotions that ran like wildfire through his body right then, but he went from being very cold to very hot. He couldn't help himself. He slipped out of the chair so that they were kneeling together on the mat in front of the fire and buried his face in her beautiful hair. 'I love you, Jess,' he whispered.

'And I love you, Jack. I always have and I always will.'

He laid her down so that she was on the floor beneath him. The dressing gown thing fell open, exposing her white body and her luscious breasts. He kissed them greedily, then thrust his big hand between her legs...

Afterwards, they lay on the floor, exhausted, though Jack wasn't the sort of chap who could lie about naked in someone else's house and he had pulled his trousers back on. He wondered what had happened to Jess's blue garment as he stroked the curve of her hips and felt the softness of her breasts.

If she loved him as much as she said, why weren't they living together in the house in Garnet Street, where they could lie together like this whenever they liked – which as far as he was concerned would be every single night?

He didn't bother asking the question; he already knew what the answer would be, not that she'd spell it out in detail. He, a mere docker, living just round the corner from the house where she'd been born, wasn't nearly good enough or important enough for her. She was only prepared to take up with a professional man like Arthur, her first husband, who'd gone to university and had a degree in something or other, or the Yankee officer she was hooked up with now.

He grinned, and she said immediately, 'What are you smiling at?'

'I was thinking how I'm nothing but a bloody racehorse,' he said. 'A stud.'

'You should charge a fee,' she suggested, smiling back. 'It would have to be guineas, not pounds.'

A thought struck him. She wouldn't want the Yank knowing she'd been having it off with another man. If Jack was going to give her the baby she wanted, it'd have to be soon, within the next few weeks. It meant he'd have to get a move on. In fact, he felt up to it again right now.

He could do things to Jess, and she to him, that he'd never dreamt of doing with Mollie. He bent down and kissed her right breast, and she responded by arching her back and clasping his head in her hands. 'Don't stop, Jack,' she said hoarsely. 'Don't stop.'

In the King's Arms, quite a few of the customers were keeping an eye out for Jack Doyle. He hadn't felt well the night before, had actually gone home early, they recalled, and they were worried that he'd come down with something.

When it reached nine o'clock, Mack suggested that someone go and knock on his door, make sure he was all right.

The someone returned five minutes later and said there'd been no answer to his knock, 'I didn't like to go inside. Anyroad, if there's summat wrong with him, then his kids'd know and we'd have heard.'

Mack nodded. 'I reckon you're right. It seems that for once, Jack's got something more important to do tonight than prop up the bar.'

It was October; Christmas was approaching.

Would this be the last Christmas of the war? Everyone had wished for the same thing every Christmas since it had begun. Every time they had been wrong.

In the days before the war – it felt like an eternity ago – they'd made the cake and the puddings well in advance of Christmas, given them time to mature, like fine wine or posh cheese. But now it was a struggle to get most of the ingredients. Dried fruit was desperately hard to come by, eggs virtually impossible unless you were a child; margarine was needed for every day, not for an entire week's ration to be used in a cake, even if it was for Christmas. Candied peel, glacé cherries and almonds were but a distant memory; as well as nutmeg, unless you still had a bit left to grate from before the war.

Despite these handicaps, the women with children were determined that Christmas Day would turn out to be just fine. Half a dozen or so of them might well get together and make the cakes and puddings between them, each contributing something until most of the ingredients were available. Decorations, years old, would be brought down from lofts or up from cellars and used over and over again. Fathers and grandfathers would be called upon to make go-carts and scooters, though obtaining wheels proved a problem.

Sheila Reilly was desperate to find a skate – the sort with four wheels that you stood on, not the fish. The family already had one, and she would have loved the lads to have a pair between them. She had put a card in the window of the post office before now, but nothing had come of it.

Brenda Mahon was at her busiest, having had orders for dozens of bobble hats and scarf and glove sets. Customers had to provide their own wool, which was rationed and could only be obtained by using precious clothing coupons – or by undoing another knitted garment that had lost its shape.

The weather didn't help the national mood of mild dejection. The summer hadn't exactly been glorious, and the autumn was foggy and damp, with the sun mainly invisible as it hid behind the droopy grey clouds that seemed to be permanently overhead. It had been forecast that the winter was destined to be a cold one.

In addition to the nagging worry that the war might never be over, that things could possibly get even worse as time passed and they would never eat a proper Christmas cake again, or manage to obtain a skate, Eileen and Sheila were deeply concerned that their dad appeared to be coming down with something.

'He's dead quiet all the time,' Sheila complained to her sister. 'Even if you deliberately say something to rile him, he doesn't respond. I've encouraged him to see a doctor, but he says he doesn't believe in them.'

'Well, we've always known that,' Eileen said worriedly. 'It's ages since he came to do the garden. Mind you, it's not as if he's miserable. No matter how quiet he is, he always seems to have a bit of a smile on his face.'

'Do you think he's up to something, sis?'

'What on earth could he be up to that he wouldn't tell us about?'

Sheila shook her head. 'I can't think of a single thing.'

Phyllis Taylor wasn't enjoying being in the army nearly as much as she had expected. She was still missing her mum and dad, still feeling homesick, though it was two months since she had joined up.

And although Doria would always be her best friend, there were times when she wished she was best friends with someone else, someone who enjoyed sightseeing, say, who would like to go to museums and art galleries, theatres – though it would have to be the cheapest seats. (Some of these places might be closed due to the war, but it would be easy to find out.) Doria preferred dance halls and pubs crammed with servicemen, who would virtually leap upon them when they entered and insist on buying them drinks. Then Phyllis would have to confess she didn't drink.

'Just an orange juice,' she would insist. At first she wondered why the man offering the drink would instantly go off her, until she realised it meant he was most unlikely to get her drunk and therefore willing to go outside with him for a 'jolly good snog', as Doria called them.

It was all rather unpleasant. Even if Phyllis could bring herself to ditch Doria as a friend, she would never do it, because she felt obliged to protect her. The day might come when Doria would get into serious trouble with one of the men interested in having more than a snog, and who would rescue her if Phyllis wasn't around?

311

Phyllis and Doria were dancing in Trafalgar Square. It wasn't an official dance; there wasn't an orchestra, just three buskers – two with harmonicas and one with a banjo. The girls had been on their way to the Paramount Dance Hall in Tottenham Court Road on a brightly moonlit night, but had been distracted by the buskers and the couples – the men were American soldiers – who were jitterbugging like mad. It was the sort of occasion when women didn't mind dancing with each other, and Doria and Phyllis were trying to jitterbug but making quite a hash of it, Phyllis in particular because she was in uniform, whereas Doria was wearing something frilly and high-heeled shoes.

Suddenly Doria was whisked away by a dashing young American and Phyllis was left on her own. She didn't mind; she just backed into the watching crowds and, as so often happened, wondered what Mum and Dad were doing at this very minute in Beverley.

'You don't want to dance, do you?' said a voice.

Phyllis turned. A young man in civvies was standing beside her. He was quite clear in the moonlight and looked very young, eighteen or nineteen at the most. He had a lovely cheerful face, a half-grown moustache, and wore a pair of thick-rimmed spectacles. 'That's a strange thing to ask,' she said. 'I suppose you'll ask next if I don't want anything to eat. Do you always ask negative questions?'

He didn't look at all disconcerted. 'Not usually,' he said. 'It's just that when I saw that that American had taken over your friend, I felt I

312

had to talk to you but thought you would prefer to dance, and I'm afraid I can't dance a step.'

'I'm not very good at it either.'

He grasped her elbow and they moved further back into the crowd. 'Would you like a coffee? There's a Lyons not far away. My name's Martin Winters, by the way.'

'I'm Phyllis Taylor.' She would have loved a coffee with Martin Winters, but... 'I'm sorry,' she said. 'I must wait for my friend. I can't possibly desert her.'

'I understand, but would it be possible for you to desert her at some time in the foreseeable future, like tomorrow, for instance, and we could go for a coffee then?'

Well, it *should* be possible, Phyllis thought. She and Doria weren't Siamese twins. They didn't *have* to go out together every single night. The American Doria was dancing with might ask her out and this time Phyllis would say she didn't want to tag along like a gooseberry, or have the American bring along one of his pals for her – a blind date, it was called.

'I could go for a coffee tomorrow,' she told Martin Winters.

He raised his eyebrows and they disappeared behind the frame of his glasses. 'Half past seven in Lyons?' he suggested.

She said that would be fine, whereupon he smiled and demanded she tell him her entire life story in no more than a hundred words.

Phyllis laughed and said she wasn't prepared to try, but would tell him in as many words as it took. She briefly described her upbringing in

313

Beverley, adding that her mother was a nurse and her father a naval architect, but omitting the nonsense he'd got up to in Bootle. She told him what it was like living there and how much she'd loved it, then about joining the army as soon as she turned eighteen.

'That was two months ago,' she finished. 'Now, what about you?'

'Aged twenty-three,' he said crisply. 'Born in Coventry, no brothers and sisters, went to university, took French history. Wanted to fight for my country but turned down by army, navy and air force because my sight's not up to scratch. Work now as reporter for the *Daily Recorder*, due there at ten o'clock, in fact – I'm on the night shift. Oh, and my dad was killed in an air raid. Me and Mum miss him very much.'

'You poor thing,' Phyllis cried. Holding her elbow had somehow turned into holding her hand. 'I'm so sorry.'

'So's me and Mum,' he said with a heartfelt sigh.

'I'm an only child too,' she told him.

'It's quite nice sometimes, but not all the time,' he remarked, giving her hand a squeeze.

'And I've always been interested in French history. All those pompous kings and their mistresses – Madame de Pompadour...'

'And Madame du Barry. And the Revolution; I mean, that was a revolution and a half. They really went to town with the guillotine.' He shuddered.

'And Napoleon. I admired him, but I know I shouldn't because he wasn't really a very nice person.'

'Nor was Josephine,' Martin said with a grin. 'Do you know, since university, you're the first person I've ever talked to like this.'

He squeezed her hand again and she squeezed his back. They looked at each other and Phyllis knew that something truly remarkable had happened that night. It was a bit scary in a way and she was frightened to put it into words or even think about it too hard.

'I just knew, when I saw you,' Martin stammered. 'I just knew...' His voice faded and he pulled Phyllis close and kissed her on the forehead. 'I just knew something.'

'*There* you are!' Doria was standing in front of her. 'We're going to a proper dance. This is Henry.' Henry was behind her, leaning his chin on the top of her head. 'Henry, this is my friend Phyllis.' She ignored Phyllis's companion.

'Hi, Phyllis,' Henry drawled.

He sounded very drunk. If it hadn't been for that, Phyllis would have told Doria that she would rather have a coffee with Martin Winters than go dancing. But it seemed irresponsible to allow her friend to go off with a drunken American. Lord knows what might happen.

Anyway, Doria had just taken it for granted that Phyllis would come, and was in the process of dragging her away, still not having noticed the young man she was with.

Phyllis turned, 'Cheerio,' she called.

'See you tomorrow,' Martin called back.

The American grabbed Phyllis by the hand; he already had hold of Doria, who squealed as he pulled them both to the other side of Trafalgar Square, where the sound of drums drowned out the harmonicas and the banjo. He was whooping like a cowboy and Phyllis was annoyed that she had given up coffee with Martin for this! It dawned upon her that she had let Doria take over her life to the extent that she was no longer Phyllis Taylor but a slave who hadn't any will left of her own. It had to stop, and it would stop later tonight when they got back to barracks. She would tell Doria that she had had enough.

They stumbled up some steps, both girls by now attempting to free themselves, but the American's grip was like iron. At the top of the steps he seemed to think they were still in Trafalgar Square, and pulled them into the middle of what was in fact a very busy street full of fast-moving traffic. He seemed unaware of the double-decker bus that was bearing down on them. It knocked him down first, then the girls, who were one on each side of him and just a tiny bit behind.

Eileen received the official-looking letter from the army a few days later. It turned out that Doria had given her name as next of kin to be advised if anything unfortunate took place.

The letter told her that Miss Doria Caroline Mallory had died in a road accident in London and that her body was in a hospital close to where she had been killed. Did Mrs Stephens wish the army to go ahead with a funeral, or would her family sooner make the arrangements?

Eileen picked up Doria's baby and shed tears into his white knitted shawl. Theo woke up and gave her a lovely smile. He had got over his bad humour and smiled a lot these days. Sometimes life could be dead cruel, she thought sadly. Although Doria had got on her nerves, she had put up with having Nick's baby and his cruel desertion with remarkable good humour.

After a while, she telephoned Peter and gave him the bad news. 'You can come and see Theo whenever you want,' she added. In fact, she would sooner never see Peter Mallory again, but Theo was the first, possibly the only nephew he would ever have.

He was understandably upset by the news and said he would leave work immediately and go home and tell his parents.

Eileen hoped the Mallorys wouldn't decide that they wanted Theo in place of their daughter. They were, after all, blood relatives and had far more right to him than she did.

'I hope not,' she told the baby she had begun to think of as her own.

In Pearl Street, in the flat over the dairy, Lena Newton received a letter from Phyllis Taylor's mother, Winifred.

My daughter made so many friends when we lived in Bootle, and I think you were the closest. I am so sad to tell you that last week Phyllis died in a road accident in London. My husband and I are broken-hearted at the thought that we shall never see our bright, lovely daughter again. I hope you will think of her on Friday, the day of her cremation. Phyllis was a very modern young woman and had expressed a wish to be cremated when she died, something that I had never, ever imagined happening in my or my husband's lifetime.

In all the time Lena had worked at the company in Hope Street, she had never taken a single day off, but after reading the letter, she decided to give work a miss that day and go and see Eileen Stephens. More than anyone, Eileen would understand just how distraught she felt that the God she had always worshipped should allow Phyllis to die so casually.

'I'm so useless,' she wailed a few hours later in the living room of the cottage in Melling. Nicky watched from the table, where he was colouring in a book, clearing wondering what was wrong. 'I do nothing to make the world a better place. But Phyllis, she was so full of life. I just know she would have made a real impact on the world in one way or another. It's so very unfair. If only I had died and Phyllis had lived.'

'Oh, Lena!' Eileen sat beside the woman on the settee and stroked her hair. It was terrible that such a nice person should think so little of herself. 'Lena, you aren't useless. What an awful thing to say. Like so many people, you have done your bit towards the war. You should feel proud of yourself. And I'm sure God isn't sitting up in heaven choosing the people he wants to die. I mean, so many people have died since this awful war began; hundreds, thousands, even millions if it's true about these concentration camps that Hitler has established.' Jews were the prime victims of the camps, along with Gypsies, the handicapped, and socialists like her dad.

She was really saddened to hear about Phyllis. She assumed that she and Doria had died in the same accident, so it was a double blow: two young women with lives yet to live. So far, she was the only person who knew about Doria, and it seemed wise to tell Lena now, rather than having someone like Sheila or Brenda come out with it once they knew and upsetting her all over again.

Lena rocked silently back and forth when told about the other girl's death; she was already so distressed, it seemed almost too much for her to bear.

'Why not stay the weekend with me?' Eileen proposed. 'I did invite you months ago, but Doria turned up. After she went to join the army, I truly forgot to ask you again.'

Martin Winters had gone to the Lyons restaurant in Charing Cross Road expecting to meet Phyllis, the girl he knew he would marry one day. If she felt the same as he did, she would already be aware that they were made for each other.

He arrived early, half expecting her to be early too, but instead she was late, very late. In fact, she didn't come at all, much to his shock and dismay. It meant that the plans he had made over the last twenty-four hours for his future with Phyllis Taylor had been knocked off course before they could begin.

But of course, she was in the army. It could be that an emergency had arisen in another part of the world and she'd been posted abroad along with her friend. He clung on to that idea all night while on duty with the newspaper. Next day, he caught a bus to Islington, identified the whereabouts of the Army Training Centre and almost ran there.

There weren't any guards in sentry boxes outside, as he had expected; just a small building at the entrance with a young soldier sitting inside to identify visitors.

Martin explained why he was there, though he elaborated rather, thinking that to merely say he'd been let down on a date wasn't sufficient reason for him to be given the information he wanted.

'I promised,' he said fervently to the fresh-faced private, 'really promised that I would go and see her sick mother in Beverley – that's in Yorkshire – this weekend. My job's taking me up that way, but I lost the mother's address.' He managed to include a note of real anguish in his voice.

'I'll see what I can do, mate.' The soldier picked up the phone and dialled a number. If it turned out that Phyllis had merely not wanted anything to do with him, thought Martin, then it would be a terrible blow.

After a long conversation that seemed to get quieter and quieter until Martin could scarcely hear a word, the soldier put the receiver back in its cradle and turned to face him. His expression was grave.

'Sorry, mate, but I'm afraid there's been an accident. Private Phyllis Taylor is dead.'

Chapter 19

It had been a wearing weekend, what with discovering that both Doria and Phyllis were dead and dealing with Lena Newton's distress. Eileen hoped it wasn't selfish, hard-hearted even, to be pleased when Monday came and she could attempt to think of something else. Lena had returned to Bootle, and apart from two small children and a cat, she had the house to herself. It was a crisp, sunny day with a strong breeze and not all that cold for late October.

In times gone by when she had felt stressed, she had immersed herself in a baking spree, turning out trays of jam tarts, fairy cakes, scones, and possibly a sponge cake, which Tony would help her to decorate. Most of it was presented to her family and friends in Pearl Street. But with rationing, these days such an extravagance was out of the question. Instead, she indulged herself in doing the laundry, in the boiler and by hand, the only expense being a small amount of Persil soap powder. She washed everything: clothes, bedding, any bits and pieces she could get her hands on; even things that weren't faintly dirty, merely in need of ironing.

Although washing helped to take her mind off her worries, the thing that helped most was hanging it out on the line and watching it blow in the wind. If there was a good gust, the sheets

321

would become almost horizontal, collapsing limply until the breeze got its strength back and they took off again. Nicky enjoyed it too. They sat at the bottom of the garden on the bench that she thought of as her dad's, and he clapped and cheered when the washing almost became airborne and her stockings wound themselves round and round the line. Theo sat on her knee, warmly wrapped up, as much entertained by the acrobatic washing as she and Nicky were, while Napoleon regarded it as a challenge, as if he was wondering how he could possibly get his claws into a garment and swing on it.

She was wishing there was someone there who could take their photograph – the woman, the little boy, the baby and the cat, something to keep for ever as a reminder of a strange day at a strange time – when a man came in through the wooden gate at the side of the house. He wore a matching jacket and trousers made of rough brown material. She knew straight away what he was – an Italian prisoner of war. There was a camp somewhere in Kirkby and the prisoners were being dispatched about the countryside to help their captors with their farms and gardens.

Eileen got to her feet. 'Stay there,' she ordered Nicky before she went towards the man, Theo in her arms, with a slight feeling of trepidation. The next house was quite some distance away.

'Good morning.' He bowed slightly from the waist. 'Would you like me to tidy your garden?'

'No thank you,' she said nicely. 'Me dad keeps it tidy for me.'

The man glanced around the garden, frowning,

and she realised that it looked a mess. It was a good month since Jack had set foot in it; the grass needed cutting, the vegetable patch was full of weeds and there were autumn leaves everywhere that required brushing up. She should really have kept an eye on it herself.

'Do you live here alone?' the man enquired.

'No, me husband will be home around five o'clock.' The man frowned at the line of washing, just as he had frowned at the messy garden. It didn't contain a single item of men's clothing. He had no doubt guessed that she was lying.

'Are you sure you wouldn't like me to do the garden for you?' He was smiling at her pleasantly. Nicky had arrived and took hold of his mother's hand.

'Oh, all right. You can if you like.' Lord knew when Dad would come again.

It was only then that the penny dropped and she realised he'd been speaking to her in English when he was supposed to be Italian. 'You speak English,' she said, which was an awfully stupid remark.

'I am an actor,' he said. 'My company toured European theatres with our plays. I joined the army as an interpreter.'

'That's handy.' Another stupid remark. 'The things are in the shed.' She pointed to the building that her father and Peter Mallory had rebuilt the previous year.

He bowed again. 'Then I will begin,' he said stiffly.

'When you've finished, I'll make you a cup of tea.' Clutching Nicky and Theo, she fled into the house, locked the kitchen door and watched through the lace curtain, aware for the first time of just how attractive the man was – quite literally tall, dark and handsome, not all that surprising when he was an actor and an Italian.

He pulled the lawnmower out of the shed, removed his jacket, rolled up his sleeves and began to cut the grass. She wondered what Dad's reaction would be when she told him that an Italian prisoner of war, one of the enemy, had actually touched his precious garden.

She would tell him that it was his own fault. There was nothing wrong with their father according to Sheila, who said he just walked about with a gloating look on his face. 'Though what he's got to gloat about, I've no idea.'

Well, something had been keeping him busy over the last few weeks, thought Eileen, and it wasn't her garden.

She watched until the lawn was finished. It was always fascinating to see the stripes appear, some so very much darker than others, yet all the same grass. It became less interesting when the man began to weed, though she held Nicky up to see when the leaves were brushed into a heap beside the shed. They wouldn't stay still and flew all over the place because of the wind. She made herself go outside and tell the man that there was a compost heap at the bottom of the garden where her father usually put them.

'There's a wheelbarrow in the shed,' she informed him. He bowed again and thanked her. Then she hurried back inside and telephoned Cicily Dean, to tell her there was an Italian prisoner of war at work in her garden.

'I just wanted someone to know that he's here,' she said. 'In case anything happens.'

'If something happens, then it'll be too late to do anything about it,' Cicily pointed out. 'Would you like it if I came round?'

'No, it's all right. I just feel better having told someone.'

'I understand they're very polite and helpful.'

'Well this one seems to be.'

Eileen rang off and looked through the window again. The garden had never looked so tidy. The man was in the throes of rolling down his sleeves and putting on his jacket. He glanced at the window, and either saw her watching through the lace curtain or just assumed that she was, because he raised his hand in a gesture of farewell and looked as if he was about to leave.

Eileen opened the door. 'I promised you a cup of tea,' she said. She had almost let him go, relieved at the idea of seeing the back of him, but that would have been unfair and a little bit cowardly. 'The garden looks lovely. Thank you very much.' She stood back to let him in. 'Sit down,' she said. 'What's your name?'

'Vincenzo Conti.'

'I'm Eileen Stephens, this is Nicky, and the baby is called Theo.'

Nicky was seated at the kitchen table, and Theo was propped up in his pram in the corner of the room. The kettle was already boiling.

'I suppose you must have a lovely garden at home,' she said, with false brightness as well as a false smile. Close up, he was just as attractive –

325

and it was a nice face as well as handsome. If she had been single, she would have been even more impressed.

'I do, yes, but I never touch it. We have a gardener.' He was hunched over the table and gave no sign of smiling back.

'If that's the case, you've done very well for a non-gardener.'

'Thank you.' There was a touch of sarcasm in his voice.

It irritated Eileen. Having made the tea, she put a cup in front of him. 'Do you take sugar?'

'No thank you.'

'Would you like a sarnie – a sandwich?'

'No, but thank you very much for offering.'

'That's all right.'

He straightened up in the chair, as if he was pulling himself together. 'I'm sorry. You are the first person who has been polite to me, and I am being very rude.'

'But you're the enemy,' she pointed out. 'Some people are bound to be impolite. They might have lost relatives in the war, or had their homes ruined by a bomb. In fact, I'm not sure why I'm being polite meself.'

'Did you have relatives killed?'

'Yes, I lost me husband and me little boy.' She felt a rush of tears when she thought about Tony.

'I have never killed anybody,' he said quietly.

'Well, somebody killed my son, and the bomb wasn't made in England. It was just dropped here.' She felt like asking him to leave. How dare he come into her home and argue the rights and wrongs of war? Well, sort of.

He stood, the tea hardly touched. 'I'm sorry. There is every reason for you to hate me. It's just that...' For a minute, he looked quite desolate. 'When I came into your garden and saw you, it was such a delightful picture: a mother with her two sons, and a cat, and the washing blowing on the line. A picture showing a perfectly happy family. Yet I expected you to shout at me to go away, even hit me as some people have done. It made me realise that I no longer belong to the normal world. It's as if I have caught a plague, become untouchable.'

Eileen ordered him to sit down again and he meekly complied. 'Drink your tea,' she said sternly. 'In a little while, I'll make you a sarnie. It's only natural that people will shout at you. You can't expect kisses when you don't deserve them.' And the perfectly happy family was a lie. There should have been two little boys and a baby; the baby's mother was dead, and she had no idea what had happened to the father of the children who were still alive.

Any day now, thought Jack, Jess would tell him not to come any more because she was pregnant, or because it was too late for her to become pregnant without that Yank of hers guessing she'd been having it off with someone else.

And if the truth be known, Jack was becoming exhausted, and just a trifle bored. He was beginning to miss arguing with his mates, holding up the bar in the King's Arms. He'd been too tired to go to the footie the last two Saturdays.

One evening towards the end of October, he

arrived at her house at seven, the usual time. In the past at this time of year there'd be kids coming round asking for a penny for the guy, but that hadn't happened since the war began. The guy had to go on top of a bonfire, and kids today probably had no idea what a bonfire was.

He went in the back way. To his surprise, Jess was sitting in front of the fire with a sleeping Penny on her knee.

'Don't come near,' she warned him. 'She's caught something, her temperature's very high. The doctor will be here soon.'

'I'll go now.'

He turned to leave, but she said, 'Don't go, Jack. I need to talk to you.'

He sat at the table rather than in the chair in front of the fire. 'I suppose it's all over. It's time, isn't it, Jess?'

'For us to be over?' She smiled sadly. 'Yes, it is.' Her hair hadn't been combed, and it lay in untidy waves and curls around her face. For once, she hadn't used any lipstick or the stuff she put on her eyes or her cheeks. She looked pale and tired and also, for the first time, as if she were getting on a bit. But in his eyes she had never been more beautiful or desirable.

'Are you...?' He couldn't think of the right word. 'Pregnant' sounded a bit raw, a bit too obvious. But she said it for him.

'Pregnant? No, Jack. It's a bit too soon to know, but I very much doubt it.'

'I'm sorry.' He felt quite forlorn. This was what he'd wanted, but it had happened too suddenly. He needed time to get used to the idea of Jess disappearing out of his life.

'Oh, Jack, don't be sorry.' Her green eyes twinkled. 'I know you did your best.'

'I did my utmost,' he was saying when the front door opened, and the doctor came in. Jack departed in a hurry and went straight to the King's Arms, where he didn't enjoy himself nearly as much as he'd expected. He left early, and when he'd gone, his mates remarked to each other that it was obvious that Jack Doyle was still in a mood.

Just as Jack's affair came to a sad, though inevitable end, his son-in-law, Nick Stephens, found himself involved with a woman for the first time since he had left London.

He was still living on the Norfolk coast with Clarence Baines and his daughter Mary. He was still enjoying the peace and tranquillity of his new life. Planes occasionally flew over the area, both British and American, but apart from that, there was no sign of the war. At night, he was able to draw back the curtains and stare out at the dense blackness of the sky, or watch the moon shine down on the inky water or slip in and out of the clouds, creating perfect examples of a silver lining. The view at all times was spectacular.

He was lying in bed one night in the run-up to Christmas, imagining what the day would be like here, knowing it would be different to every other Christmas he had ever known. After breakfast, unless it was too stormy, he would walk on the beach. Clarence or Mary, or both, might come with him. Mary had been promised a chicken – the family were friendly with local farmers, and eggs or small cuts of meat were often available without the need for ration books.

He was thinking that this would be the strangest Christmas he had ever known when he heard the click of the bedroom door opening, followed by soft footsteps on the wooden floor, and suddenly Mary Baines was in the bed with him.

At first, he was too astonished to respond or say a word. He had never felt attracted to her, but when she touched him, he was unable to resist. He lay there while she virtually took him, roughly, so that it hurt, but it was a new and titilating experience for him, deeply thrilling.

When it was over, she got out of bed and returned to her own room. She hadn't uttered a single word. The next day, she acted as if nothing had happened and was her same rather withdrawn self. Nick wondered if she remembered the night before, or whether it was some strange form of sleepwalking, but the same thing happened that night, and the night after. It would seem that Nick had ended up in some sort of earthly paradise.

Sheila Reilly never felt there was anything extraordinary about having seven children. In years gone by, it was customary for women to have as many as a dozen kids, even more, so seven didn't seem all that many in comparison. The only time it felt like a trial was at Christmas; obtaining seven decent presents wasn't easy when there was a war on.

It was a relief when, ten days before Christmas,

she managed to buy a rusty Meccano set from Mike Harris's second-hand shop in Strand Road, thus completing the presents for the boys, then a pretty little lace shawl that Caitlin would love that only needed a bit of a soak in Lux soap flakes to get the dirt out.

She was about to leave the shop when Mike called her back.

'Mrs Reilly, aren't you the one who asked if I'd keep me eye out for a pair of skates, like?'

Sheila's heart performed a somersault. 'I did, yes,' she said in an awed voice. This couldn't be happening.

'Well, I've got them in the back of the shop, luv. They're in good nick, so I suggest five bob for the pair.'

A whole pair! As Sheila said to Brenda later, 'Putting aside the day I married our Calum and when I had each one of me kids, I've never known a day as beautiful as this one.'

'Beautiful!' Brenda pulled a face. 'It's only a pair of skates, Sheil.'

'I know, but you don't know what they mean to me.' She would have to draw up a chart giving the boys turns of half an hour each. Of course, the girls might insist on having a go too, but she'd cross that bridge when she came to it.

The following day, she heard from Cal that he'd be home for a whole week at Christmas. For Sheila, life couldn't have been more perfect.

It was impossible for most people to be miserable now that Christmas was so close. The children's excitement was like a tonic for their parents, cheering them up no end.

As far as the hateful war went, there was a terrific battle going on in Belgium, the Battle of the Bulge, it was called. Some people referred to it as Hitler's Last Stand. Others wondered why there was fighting in Belgium when it was more than six months since the Allies had landed in France. Germany must be much further away than they'd thought.

At home, the air raids weren't over, not for the people of London, who were now on the receiving end of the murderous V-2 rockets that had replaced the doodlebugs.

At Dunnings factory in Melling, since there was no longer an urgent need for parts for Spitfires and Lancasters and other wartime aircraft, a staff party was held on Christmas Eve and Eileen Stephens was an honoured guest.

'It's so lovely to see you,' she cried, hugging and kissing the women she'd worked with during the first year of the war, who had become as close as sisters: tall, willowy Pauline; Doris, who still wore too much orange make-up and was waving a diamond engagement ring on the third finger of her left hand; Carmel, well over sixty and, as ever, without a full set of teeth. A few had left; one, Theresa, had died in an air raid while Eileen had been working there. And she'd been at Dunnings when she'd met Nick. The girls had all come to her wedding.

'Oh, he's fine,' she told them when she was asked, over and over, how he was. 'He works in London and he comes home most weekends.'

332

She didn't want them knowing that the wonderful romance they had all been so envious of was over, and she wasn't sure if she would ever see him again.

She arrived home to find Jessica and Penny at the cottage with Lena Newton, who had Christmas Eve off and had stayed the night in order to look after Nicky and Theo that morning. Eileen and the children were expected at Jessica's house in Pearl Street the next day for Christmas dinner. As a little pre-Christmas treat, Jess had brought half a dozen iced cup cakes that she'd bought from the American shop in the camp at Burtonwood that morning.

'Did you know,' Eileen informed her, 'that it's against the law to ice a cake in this country while there's a war on, because icing uses up too much sugar?'

'So we are, in effect, breaking the law by eating these cakes?' Jessica put the colourfully iced cakes on the table in a row while Penny, Nicky and Napoleon watched with interest. 'Even the children?'

'And the cat,' Eileen told her. 'Nevertheless, I think I shall eat that pink and white one with the cherry on top and hope I don't end up in jail. Lena, are you willing to risk it?'

'I am.' Lena remembered Phyllis Taylor saying that she would quite like to go to jail, 'just to see what it's like'. She missed Phyllis like nobody's business, and always would.

'I think I'll risk it too.' Jessica laughed. 'Penny, Nicky, what colour would you like? Oh, and Eileen, I've brought tea bags with me, save using

333

your own tea.'

'Tea *bags?*' Eileen and Lena said together.

Jessica held up a little square bag for them to scrutinise. 'They're extremely convenient,' she said. 'They were invented in New York, not far from where we will live.'

Lena went home at four o'clock, refusing to stay to tea. 'I'm worried about Godfrey,' she said. 'He wasn't home by the time I left to come and see you.'

'Who is Godfrey?' Jessica asked after the woman had gone. She didn't know Lena all that well.

'Her cat.' Eileen wrinkled her nose. 'Poor soul, she has a terrible inferiority complex. What's more, her husband has done a disappearing act, same as Nick. Luckily, she doesn't mind. It wasn't a very happy marriage, but she's been left without a relative in the world.'

'Well, much as I feel sorry for her, I'm glad she's gone. I've something to tell you. But before I do, will you please tell me what a film star is doing sweeping up your garden?'

Eileen glanced through the window. 'That's Vincenzo, he's Italian and comes once a week to tidy up. Me dad's been neglecting things a bit lately. Have you seen much of him since you came back, Jess?'

'Not much, no,' Jess said casually. 'Can I tell you my news now?'

Such was the expression on her friend's face – a mixture of joy and mischief, achievement and surprise – that Eileen was able to guess what the something was.

'You're pregnant!' she said in astonishment. She frowned. 'I'm about to do my Aggie Donovan impersonation – how have you managed that without the presence of your husband?'

'Gus left for France three months ago, in September, only days before I came back to Bootle. It is now December, and I've just discovered I'm pregnant. It's all perfectly legitimate, Aggie.'

'Whew!' Eileen made a pretence of looking relieved. 'In that case, congratulations, Jessica. I bet you're thrilled to bits.'

'I'm over the moon.'

Christmas Day turned out to be very ordinary, neither sunny nor dull, warm nor cold, just a little bit wet, but mostly dry. It was more or less the same throughout the British Isles.

Surely, the pessimists complained, surely this had to be the last Christmas of this flaming war. If it wasn't, then by this time next year there'd be nothing left to eat, no presents left to buy, no clothes left to wear. Curtains would fall to bits, furniture would rot, houses would decay for want of maintenance.

Don't be such a miserable shower of gits, the optimists would cry. We're not going to let them Jerries get us down. The country had kept going for more than five tortuous years and would keep going for another five, another fifty if necessary. After all, as the song said, 'There'll always be an England...'

Dominic was more inclined to let his mates have a go on the skates than his brothers. On Christ-

335

mas morning, a small war broke out outside the Reillys' house, though so far there hadn't been any casualties.

Calum kept control until Jack Doyle called for him on his way to the King's Arms. There being no conceivable way in which Calum would miss downing a few pints in his favourite pub on Christmas morning, Sheila was left to control the children herself. She managed this by deliberately bursting into tears and claiming she was at the end of her tether, whereupon Dominic burst into tears himself, handed the skates to Niall, and promptly began to set the table.

Godfrey still hadn't returned home. Lena had bought two ounces of ham for his Christmas dinner. She had hers with Brenda and her girls, where Tommy, Godfrey's brother, was fast asleep beneath the home-made tree.

'Oh, he'll come back,' Brenda assured her. 'He's just finding his feet, sowing his oats, that sort of thing. Probably got a lady cat tucked away somewhere. You should have got him neutered, Lena, if you didn't want him going out on the town, as it were.'

'Neutered?' Lena had never heard of the word.

Brenda looked at her girls, who were busy eating, and mouthed 'castrated' at the other woman.

'Oh!' Lena swallowed hard. 'Is it too late to have it done now?'

'I don't think so. You could talk it over with the vet. It would mean poor Godfrey would be forever denied the joys off...' She mouthed the word 'sex'.

'Oh dearie me!' Lena was horrified. 'Would it

336

hurt?' she asked.

Brenda looked at her with amusement. 'Think about it, Lena,' she snorted. 'Just imagine if you had balls and someone cut them off with a knife. Of course it would hurt, daft girl.'

Across the street at Jessica's house, she and Eileen were having a good laugh. Nicky and Penny were playing in the street with Sheila's children. Eileen was wondering why she was enjoying herself so much when this was the first Christmas she'd spent since the war had begun without there being any chance of seeing Nick. Even last year, he'd managed to come home for a few days, despite the fact that he was in the throes of his affair with Doria. She was sorry now, though it was much too late to do anything about it, that she hadn't had it out with him, had a really furious row, got things off her chest. Sometimes I am much too nice, she told herself.

What if she never saw him again? What if he was dead too? At least she was all right for money. Gosh, that was a horrible thing to think, but she had the children to care for. Both of them were Nick's sons, and if he were dead she would be entitled to the cottage. She had a widow's pension for her first husband and she would get one for Nick.

'Cheers, Eileen.' Jessica had raised her glass containing the very best sherry.

Eileen picked up her own. 'Cheers, Jess.'

'May all our worries be little ones.'

It's much too late for that, Eileen thought cynically.

337

In the small town of Beverley, Winifred and Leslie Taylor's house was completely devoid of decorations, and they hadn't bothered with Christmas dinner. They'd eaten very little since they'd heard that Phyllis had died.

They sat staring into the fire, reminiscing. Leslie blamed himself for the tragedy. 'If I hadn't behaved so damn stupidly, you and Phyllis wouldn't have had to go to Liverpool,' he moaned. He said the same thing almost every day. 'Things would have been very different.'

'She would still have wanted to join the army,' Winifred pointed out. Like him, she also said the same thing daily.

'Yes, but it would have been under different circumstances. She might not have been sent to London.'

Winifred agreed. She blamed him totally for their daughter's death, but had never said it outright. She had thought of leaving him, but wasn't sure if she could cope on her own, not yet.

'Shall we go and say a prayer, Win? A Christmas prayer for our little girl?' He'd become quite soppy. If Phyllis could have heard him, she would have laughed her head off. Our little girl!

'Yes.' She got eagerly to her feet. They went every day to Beverley Minster, a great, glorious house of prayer more than eight hundred years old. It was the only place where they felt at peace.

Nick couldn't recall having gone to bed before midnight on Christmas Day in his life, not even when he was a child. But go to bed he did at ten

338

o'clock after a quiet day spent walking along the beach, where a crisp wind blew and the sky was dark and full of menacing clouds. Just before dinner, he and Clarence had visited the local pub, which looked and felt as if it had been carved out of a giant tree.

Dinner was, as expected, totally delicious. The chicken Mary had obtained had been roasted to perfection, along with the potatoes. The vegetables had been cooked so that they were neither too hard nor too soft. A memory flickered through his brain of Christmas at the cottage, when Jack Doyle had so proudly picked the Brussels sprouts a mere half-hour before they would be eaten.

Memories of the cottage and Pearl Street kept returning throughout the day, like scenes from a film. After dinner had been eaten, Clarence produced a bottle of rum and they drank half of it between them. Nick wondered if Clarence had memories of his own that he wished to remember, or preferred to forget. There were chicken sandwiches for tea, more Christmas pudding, more rum.

When Nick went to bed, he wasn't quite sure which world he occupied, the one in Liverpool or the one in Norfolk. It wasn't until he heard the door open and footsteps approaching his bed that he remembered it was the one in Norfolk.

When Eileen returned to the cottage the following day, she found an attractive pot on the back step containing a single plant. She wasn't very knowledgeable about plants, but she thought it might be a hyacinth. It had a card attached; 'Buon

Natale, Vincenzo', it read.

The handsome Italian prisoner of war had been thinking about her over Christmas.

Chapter 20

1945

One Monday late in February, two unexpected visitors arrived at the cottage in Melling: Mr and Mrs Mallory, Doria's parents. At least they thought they were unexpected, but Eileen had received a phone call earlier that morning from Peter telling her they were on their way.

'They want to take you by surprise for some reason.' She imagined him shrugging at the other end of the line. She was glad *he* hadn't turned up over Christmas, and hoped their relationship from now on would just be occasional visits to see his nephew.

At first Eileen had considered spending the day in Pearl Street – she was irritated that the Mallorys had taken it for granted that she would be at home – but if she did that, they might stay in Liverpool and keep on calling until they found her in. Perhaps they wanted take her unawares to ensure that she kept a clean house and that their grandson was properly clothed and fed. She hoped and prayed there would be no suggestion of them taking him back with them.

They arrived just before half past one and refused anything to eat or drink. Although they introduced themselves, they didn't shake her hand. Eileen had expected them to be in their forties, but they looked much older; in their fifties, or even early sixties.

Theo, seven months old by now, was produced, a healthy, active baby with an adorable smile. He looked as much like his mother as he looked like Nick.

'Would you like to hold him?' She held the baby out to Mrs Mallory, who shook her head. Her hair was almost completely grey and she wore a beaver coney fur coat and a hat with a black veil.

'No thank you. I just wanted to see him, that's all.'

Eileen looked at Mr Mallory, who had not even sat down, but he also shook his head, saying, 'We wanted to make sure he was being looked after properly.'

'I can assure you that he is,' Eileen said levelly.

'Do you not feel the least resentment that he is your husband's child by another woman?' Mrs Mallory asked curiously.

'How could anyone possibly feel resentment towards a baby? The circumstances of Theo's birth are hardly his fault.'

Mr Mallory spoke. 'Not all people think that way. Some schools, good ones, require a birth certificate; friends and neighbours ask questions. It's easy for someone to become *persona non grata*, as it were.'

'I see.' She understood. Even in her own working-class world, an illegitimate baby could end up having a hard time as he or she grew up. She was absolutely certain she could protect Theo from that sort of unpleasantness, even if it meant moving house.

342

'She ... Doria,' for the first time Mrs Mallory's expressionless face bore the suggestion of a smile, 'had a teddy bear called Theobald when she was a child. He still sits in her wardrobe to this very day.'

'Would you mind sending him to me? At some time in the future I can tell Theo it once belonged to his mother.'

Eileen could have kicked herself when the woman looked as if she might cry. Until then, she and her husband had given the impression that they didn't give a damn about Theo, but maybe she was wrong.

'I'm sorry,' she said. 'I shouldn't have asked.'

'We'll send it.' Mr Mallory helped his wife to her feet and she smoothed her skirt and touched her hat as if it had gone askew. 'It's only sitting in the wardrobe. We will also send a monthly cheque towards Theo's care.'

'There's no need,' Eileen assured him.

'It's what my wife and I would prefer.'

'As you wish. Would you like me to send photographs over the years?'

'No thank you.'

As they were walking towards the gate, Mrs Mallory turned. 'Tell me, Mrs Stephens, where is your husband now?'

'I have absolutely no idea. I haven't seen him since the Christmas before last.'

'That's the last time we saw him too.'

Mr Mallory closed the gate behind him and Eileen shut the door. The couple had been in the house for less than half an hour. She would never see them again.

The war was undoubtedly being won. In March, the advancing Allied armies, led by General Montgomery, joined hands in Germany with the Russians coming from the east and the Americans from the west. In the Pacific, islands captured by the Japanese were slowly being liberated.

Despite this, V-2 rockets continued to fall on London, one landing in the middle of Smithfield Market killing more than a hundred souls and injuring even more.

To lift the nation's heart a tiny bit, dim lighting was introduced, a milder form of blackout, meaning the headlights on vehicles became slightly brighter and ugly blackout curtains could be taken down, usually accompanied by clouds of dust and dead insects.

At the end of March, Eileen held what she fully anticipated would be the final garden party of the war. Strangely enough, she felt little enthusiasm for it. Nor, it seemed, did those who'd helped since the first party five years before. It would appear there was little left for people to get rid of. The white elephant stall was virtually empty, people having run out of rubbish to give away; no one felt like embroidering a tray cloth or making scarves or gloves for the handicraft stall, in particular Brenda Mahon, who vowed never to knit another scarf for as long as she lived. Not a single toy was contributed; only a few cakes appeared, and very little home-made jam.

People came, though. They came in their dozens to sit and drink tea and talk, comparing dates, assessing headlines, making predictions. It would be over by mid-April, by the end of April; no, it would be May. Could it possibly go on until June?

And what about the other war, the one the Brits had taken little part in, the war with Japan? When would *that* come to an end so that the brave Americans could go home to their families?

Once that had happened, the entire world would be at peace again. And afterwards, who in their right mind would ever want to start another war?

Friends and family remained at the cottage until it was almost dusk and the sky was a pink blush, gradually growing darker. Cider had been brought in jugs from a nearby pub.

Jack Doyle watched Jess, who was clearly several months pregnant. I am responsible for that, he thought proudly and with the most enormous grin. He'd best not drink any more cider, else he might be tempted to make a public announcement.

Jessica saw his glances and wished that her life had gone differently and she'd been married to Jack all this time and had half a dozen kids. But although she'd been born in Pearl Street, it had never been her destiny to stay. She needed more out of life. She needed what she was about to have, a life in New York with her American husband and all that that could offer.

Sheila Reilly kept counting her children, making sure all seven were present and safe. Calum had promised that when the war was over they would have another baby. She was a woman born to have babies; the more the merrier as far as she was concerned.

I'm drinking too much, Brenda told herself as she finished off her second glass of cider. Oh, but it's such a lovely feeling. It makes me want to sing me head off. Next week, she would make herself a frock out of that bright red taffeta stuff she'd seen in Scottie Road market the other Saturday. And dresses for the girls out of the same stuff. They'd wear them at the street party that the women of Pearl Street had already planned to celebrate the end of the war.

Perched on a tree at the bottom of the garden, Sheila's son and Brenda's daughter were sitting side by side.

'Where will we live when we're married, Dom?' Monica asked her future husband.

'In Pearl Street, where else?' Dominic said. 'We'll get a house next to your mam, or mine. I don't mind.'

Brenda couldn't resist it. She jumped to her feet and began to sing: 'There'll be bluebirds over...'

Everyone joined in immediately, as if they'd been waiting to do it all night, standing and singing full throttle, 'Tomorrow, just you wait and see...'

Their voices could be heard for miles and miles, getting fainter and fainter until a point was reached where nothing could be heard at all.

It had happened!

It was over!

On 1 May, Hitler had killed himself and his girlfriend, Eva Braun.

The following day, it was announced on the BBC that the Germans still fighting in Italy had surrendered, and later that day that Berlin had fallen.

Even so, peace had not been officially declared. People who had a wireless sat crouching over it waiting for news. In shops, offices and factories, on the stroke of every hour a crowd would gather around the set, only to be disappointed when the headline was about something humdrum and without interest.

Eventually it was announced that the following day, Tuesday, would be designated as VE Day, and Wednesday 9 May would be a national holiday for the entire country to celebrate the end of the bloodiest war that Europe had ever known.

When Eileen woke up early on Wednesday morning, the sun was already shining and the telephone was ringing. She leapt out of bed and ran downstairs.

'Hello,' she said breathlessly. She usually gave the number, but today she couldn't remember what it was.

'Eileen?'

She recognised the voice immediately. After all, she'd been married to its owner for more than four years. 'Nick?'

'I shall be coming back sometime today, quite late, I should imagine. About seven o'clock or eight.' He spoke pleasantly, but not fondly. He didn't sound over the moon or as if he'd missed her terribly since they'd last met.

'I look forward to seeing you,' Eileen said in a

similar tone; not cold, but not exactly warm, either.

'See you later, then. Cheerio.'

'Ta-ra, Nick.' But he had rung off and didn't hear her response.

Eileen stared at the receiver in her hand and wondered what on earth had got into her once loving husband.

As he came out of the telephone box on Norwich station, Nick Stephens wondered the same thing. That had been a bit abrupt on his part, hadn't it? He would apologise to Eileen when they met.

For the past year, he'd scarcely been part of the human race, had hardly spoken to anyone other than Clarence and Mary Baines. He'd actually lost the art of conversation. Even the pub where he and Clarence occasionally went was full of grumpy old men whose main interest seemed to be smoking their evil-smelling pipes.

He was finding it hard to connect with the atmosphere of gaiety and even merriment present in the other would-be travellers on the station and, he discovered, on the train to London after he'd boarded and it was on its way.

Instead of the carriage being full of people apparently determined not to speak to anyone else, as was usually the way with the English, these passengers seemed unable to stop talking to each other, describing exactly where they'd been and what they'd been doing when they'd heard the news that the war was over at last, followed by their reaction to it. Nor were they dressed in the manner of the normal London-bound commuter, but wore sports jackets, flannels and check shirts.

Nick remembered that today was a national holiday, and it turned out that his fellow travellers were on their way to share the day with their brother in Ipswich or their friends in Colchester, or going all the way to London to see their 'jolly old mum and dad', as one man put it.

'And where were you, young man, when you heard that the whole ghastly business had finally been done with?' he was asked by a chap sitting opposite, a florid individual in a green tweed suit.

'About to have a bath,' Nick said abruptly, which caused some merriment, though he couldn't think why. At Windward Ho, Clarence had worn down the batteries on the wireless for days, listening to every word.

Just now, Nick was feeling rather uncomfortable with himself. He'd always been a sociable man, with plenty of friends. He supposed a person was bound to change if they cut themselves off from the world as he had done. And he would become even more unsociable once he returned to Windward Ho and married Mary. There would be no need to mix with anyone except Clarence and his daughter, which would suit him fine. He had proposed to Mary the other night while they were making love with the sound of the rippling tide in the background, anticipating a future of unalloyed tranquillity.

But first he had to see Eileen, ask for a divorce and tell her that the cottage would always belong to her. Oh, and say goodbye to Nicky. Doria would have given birth to his other child months ago – he didn't know if it was a boy or a girl – and

349

would be in Wimbledon with her parents, but he wouldn't bother going there. A letter would do.

In Pearl Street, the children's party was already half over by mid-afternoon. The rows of tables on each side of the street were full of crumbs and spilt lemonade. The cakes were yet to come. The mothers couldn't help but compare today with the last time they had thrown such a big, lavish party in the street.

'It was when Mary and Joey Flaherty were leaving for Canada,' Brenda said. 'Our Monica and Muriel were only half the size they are now.' She and her girls wore identical scarlet taffeta frocks with loads of frills that she'd made herself. They looked too old for the girls and too young for their mother, but nobody cared. It was too wonderful a day to mind about piffling little things like clothes.

Gladys Tutty remembered the other party well – Eileen Costello, as she was then, had knocked on her door and invited Freda and Dicky to the party. She cringed, recalling the state the house and her kids had been in those days. Everything and everyone dead filthy, and she'd probably been as drunk as a lord on top.

There was no denying that as far as the Tuttys were concerned, the war had turned out to be a good thing. The kids had been evacuated to some dead posh house in Southport and it had been an entirely different Freda who'd come back, determined to change their lives.

And there she was, her Freda, across the street, talking to some new woman who'd just moved in.

350

Nearly seventeen and as pretty as a picture. When she left Seafield Convent next year, she was going – Gladys could hardly believe it was true – to Cambridge University to study English! Her heart began to pound so loud and fast at the sheer enormity of it that she feared she might faint.

'I bet you're proud, Gladys.' It was the red-haired woman, Jessica, whose dad had lived in the end house and been a rag-and-bone man. 'Freda is a credit to you.'

'No, she's a credit to herself,' Gladys said. She felt pretty sure that once Freda got as far as Cambridge University, she and Dicky wouldn't see much of her any more, but she didn't care.

Using the last of virtually everything in their larder, someone had made dozens of fairy cakes and, as an act of sheer rebellion, had iced every single one. It was to be assumed that icing sugar was still banned, so every person who ate a cake, including the children, was breaking the law.

Bunting criss-crossed the street, fluttering in the soft breeze, the sun shone brilliantly, balloons floated in the air, flags hung from the windows, blackout curtains had disappeared. Everyone, young and old, felt mad with happiness and excitement.

Women appeared with trays of jelly and custard sprinkled with some very old hundreds and thousands, a packet of which had been found at the back of someone's cupboard. The children leapt up and grabbed them with joy.

The window of Jessica's house was wide open and a gramophone was playing 'You Were Never

351

Lovelier'. It was being sung by a man with a voice like melting chocolate. A few couples had started to dance.

Eileen remembered dancing with Nick to the same song. It was the weekend they'd spent in London. What was he up to? she wondered. Why else would he be coming back now the war was over if it wasn't for good? And would she take him back? Of course she would, no matter what he'd done, because she loved him and always would.

Lena Newton listened to the song. It was so romantic. She and Maurice had never danced, so she had no idea what it must be like, the feeling of having a man's arms around you in that particular way.

She had been talking to a man at work a few weeks ago. 'What are you going to do after the war?' he'd asked. 'You were posted here, weren't you? You don't belong in Liverpool.'

'I hadn't thought about it.' She had supposed that she would stay on in Liverpool, but on reflection, there was nothing here for her except Godfrey, her cat, and a few friends. She had no real ties.

'What are you going to do?' she'd asked the man.

'Me and the wife intend emigrating to Australia,' he'd replied. 'It's a new country, very different from here, loads of space, different climate. It'll be a big change as well as a challenge.'

Emigrating! She'd never heard the word before. And she quite fancied a change and a challenge. Her first thought was of Godfrey, but she knew

352

Brenda would be willing to have him.

The man advised her to write to the Australian Embassy in London and ask them to send information as well as the appropriate forms. 'That's what I did,' he said, adding with a grin, 'You never know, Mrs Newton, one of these days we might catch up with one another on the other side of the world.'

Lena had received the forms and filled them in, and was now waiting for an answer. She had told no one about her plans.

As it began to grow dark, the lamplighter came and the gas lights flickered on for the first time in almost six years. A great cheer went up.

'When the lights go on again,' they sang, 'all over the world.'

The King's Arms was full to overflowing. Some customers were forced to sit outside on the pavement, but they didn't mind. Nobody minded anything; the war was over and nothing else mattered.

Jack Doyle came and gave a short speech, saying how stupid war was and promising personally that there would never be another.

Someone suggested they all meet again at the turn of the century. 'It's going to be called Millennium Eve.'

'We'll all be dead by then,' someone laughed.

'*I* won't.' It was Sean Doyle speaking. 'I'll only be seventy-seven.'

The same person laughed again. '*Only!*'

When Eileen noticed how late it was, she realised it was time she went home. She didn't want Nick coming back to an empty cottage. She left Nicky and Theo with Brenda and said she would come back for them early tomorrow. She told no one why she was leaving, just kissed everyone in sight and returned to Melling.

Nick was on the train from Euston to Liverpool. At some time or other, the uniqueness of the day had come to him: that this was the sort of day when you did talk to strangers. Chances were he would never experience another day like this in his lifetime.

When he'd got off the train at Liverpool Street station, it was more like a ballroom or a music hall. In the ticket hall, people were dancing. By the exit, they were singing. He wished he were an artist and could have painted the scene. Feeling rather out of things and much too sober, he went into a bar and ordered two pints of beer and a double whisky.

That was better! He patted his stomach cheerfully and went outside, where he realised there wasn't a chance in hell of getting a taxi. He went on the underground instead and lost his way. By the time he arrived at Euston station, it was later than he'd planned. Not that it mattered.

The Liverpool train was already crowded when he got on, and every single soul appeared to be singing. There were no seats available, but that didn't matter either. He hadn't yet drunk enough to join in the singing, but there was a bar on board where he ordered another two beers and more whisky. Thus fortified, he joined in one of the inevitable sing-songs in a corridor full of troops.

354

'I used to be in the air force,' he told a young man in naval uniform. He felt slightly ashamed at being in civvies.

'How come you got out before the war ended?' the young man enquired.

'Lost my arm.' Nick giggled. He turned and showed the sleeve of his jacket neatly tucked inside the pocket.

'Jesus, I'm really sorry.' The young man touched him gently on the shoulder.

'That's all right,' Nick said gaily. 'Everything's all right. In fact, everything is absolutely top-hole.'

He'd been playing a part over the last year. He wasn't really the sort of fellow who wanted to listen to the tide for the rest of his life, and make love nightly to a woman he didn't actually fancy and who insisted on making love to him. As for Clarence, he wasn't exactly stimulating company.

No, what he wanted, who he wanted, was Eileen and Nicky, his wife and his son, and to live with them in the cottage in Melling. Together, the three of them would take whatever life had to throw at them.

'Eileen!' he shouted. 'I love you.'

No one was taking a blind bit of notice. A soldier had opened the train door, was actually swinging on it; in and out, in and out. The train was hurtling along, rocking violently, making a monumental noise.

'Don't be a damn fool,' someone shouted.

Someone else pushed past Nick, desperate to get to the toilet. In an effort to move out of the way, Nick tripped over a khaki haversack that had been left on the floor. He put out his left arm to prevent himself from falling, entirely forgetting that he no longer had a left arm. Unable to stop himself, he fell out of the open door.

The train must have travelled another mile before someone thought to pull the communication cord.

In Melling, Eileen sat alone in the cottage, waiting to hear the sound of Nick's footsteps on the path; waiting and waiting.

The parties were over. The centre of Liverpool was wreathed in silence. It was that hour when the moon was fading and the sun had yet to appear, when it was neither night nor morning. The city had been bombed ferociously during the war that had just ended, but its people were unconquerable and would never be beaten. Any minute now, a new day would dawn. Who knows, the old streets might still be there, in another thousand years.

Epilogue

Millennium Eve

They arrived at the cottage at about half past seven. It was nothing like Penny remembered. The dark country lane had been widened to become a busy road, and there were now houses on either side, mostly detached, mostly bungalows, all brightly lit, with neat gardens, garages and cars parked outside.

And Penny was sure it hadn't had a name before. Now there was a slice of varnished wood hanging over the front door, with *Autumn Cottage* painted on it. The place was also considerably bigger, with an extension almost as large as the original cottage built on the side.

'Have they moved it?' she asked Caitlin. 'Is this really the same cottage in the same road?'

'Liverpool's changed drastically over the last fifty-five years, Pen,' Caitlin said. 'It's expanded; most cities have. This is definitely me Auntie Eileen's cottage.'

'If Liverpool's expanded, then what's happened to the docks? There was nothing left of them when I looked this afternoon.' Penny felt genuinely upset. All her memories of Bootle were being drastically altered.

Caitlin parked her car on the drive leading to the garage, and they both got out. 'Nowadays,'

357

she said, 'there are what are called container ports. Cargo doesn't have to be unloaded by real human beings, like in Grandad's day. Bootle isn't a container port, so the docks have died a death.'

What a terrible shame, Penny thought sadly.

The curtains hadn't been drawn in the front room, which was already full of people, mainly standing. Music was playing loudly. Caitlin knocked on the window and then rang the front door bell.

The door was opened by a woman of about fifty. 'Oh there you are, sis!' she cried, and threw her arms around Caitlin and kissed her on both cheeks. Then she did the same to Penny. 'I don't know who you are, but welcome,' she said, pulling them both inside.

'This,' Caitlin said a trifle portentously, 'is your Auntie Penny. Penny, this is your niece, Lillian. She was me mam's tenth and final child, born five years after the war was over.'

'How do you do?' Penny murmured. She clearly recalled Sheila Reilly and her vast brood of children.

'Let's get something to drink.' Caitlin led her into a huge modern kitchen that had replaced the rather stark, old-fashioned one that Penny remembered. 'There's only wine, red and white, and beer – and it's very limited. We didn't want people getting drunk when they had to drive home. What a way to start the new century – in the ozzie or a police cell.'

'Or the morgue,' Lillian suggested drily. 'Can I have your coats to take upstairs? Ugh! Is this mink?' She was only prepared to hold Penny's fur

358

coat by the lining. 'Poor little minks,' she said sadly. 'They're so sweet when they're alive.'

'They also stink something horrible,' Caitlin told her. 'Our Lil's a vegan,' she added to Penny when Lillian had gone upstairs. 'I like your dress. You suit red. It goes well with your hair.'

'They're both new, the dress and the hair.' Her fair hair had grown darker with the years and was turning grey. Perhaps it was Steve's decision to exchange her for a younger model that had inspired her to have it dyed Marilyn Monroe silver and buy a simply styled dress in eye-blinking red. 'Do I look fifty-nine?' she asked Caitlin, who responded with, 'No, you only look fifty-eight and a half – and you still haven't said what you want to drink.'

'Orange juice, please.' She still had a touch of jet lag. Everything and everywhere felt extraordinarily odd.

It felt odder still when they went into the front room and Caitlin clapped her hands, demanding attention. Without actually counting, Penny reckoned there were about thirty or forty people there. Apparently there were more to come, all connected in some way or other to Pearl Street.

'Quiet, everyone,' Caitlin shouted.

'Yes, miss,' a few voices remarked sarcastically.

'Stand to attention,' someone else called.

'Be quiet, the lot of you,' Caitlin answered with a grin. 'I'd like to introduce this lady. Some of you have never met her before, and for those who have, it was fifty-five years ago. This is Penny O'Hagen, née Henningsen, née Fleming, though in actual fact,' she went on dramatically, 'if she went by her real father's name, she would be Penny Doyle.'

359

'What?' queried a couple of voices.

Penny wanted to sink through the floor. Every eye in the room was upon her.

Caitlin continued, 'It wasn't until Penny's mother Jessica died – she of the wonderful red hair; I'm sure lots of you remember her. Any-road, Jessica passed on in 1985, but not before telling Penny that her real father was Jack Doyle.'

At this, there was a chorus of 'I don't believe it' and 'By Jove'.

'Yes, isn't it amazing?' Caitlin was almost dancing on the spot. 'During the war, our strait-laced, stiff-backed, extremely moral grandad'd an affair with gorgeous Jessica Fleming, resulting in Penelope here, who is related in some way to virtually everyone in this room. What is more, folks, this wasn't just a flash-in-the pan affair. Jessica also had a son, Bernard, by our sexy old grandad, born straight after the war. Now, where's Uncle Sean?'

'Here!' A grey-haired man with a short beard waved from across the room.

'You've just acquired a half-sister.'

'Jaysus, Mary and Joseph!' said Uncle Sean, pretending to swoon. 'We'll have a jangle later, Penny, luv.'

Penny nodded weakly. She became aware that the music was nothing but wartime songs. Presently, the Andrews Sisters were singing 'Don't Sit Under the Apple Tree'. A few people had joined in. The noise was tremendous. She found herself surrounded by people who recalled her, or her mother and her lovely hair.

'I remember you well,' a woman a few years older than her said. 'I was Monica Mahon in those

360

days and we used to play together. I married Dominic Reilly, but we got divorced not long afterwards. You might not know this, but Dominic became quite a famous football player. Loads of girls were after him and he couldn't bring himself to turn a single one away.' She laughed as if she'd been over the experience a long time. 'He's a manager now and still can't turn the girls away.'

More people came and spoke to her. 'Hello, Penny, I'm Niall Reilly.'

'I'm Muriel Mahon.'

'I'm Edward Doyle – so you're my auntie,' chuckled a slim, handsome man a bit younger than herself. 'Sean Doyle is me dad.'

'What happened to Eileen who used to live here?' Penny asked. It was Eileen, her mother's friend, who she remembered the best, and playing with her little boy, Nicky, in the garden of this very cottage. It had been most odd to discover, years later, that Eileen had been her half-sister.

'After the war was over,' Edward said, 'Eileen married Vincenzo Conti, the gardener. She died quite young, in her forties, but not before she'd had two daughters. Vincenzo took them with him to live in Italy.'

'Where's Nicky, her son?'

Edward glanced around the room, which seemed to be getting more crowded by the minute. 'I can't see him, but he's probably somewhere.'

Caitlin was making another announcement. 'As you know,' she shouted, 'I've been busy preparing for this party for years, tracking people down, like, seeing if they wanted to come if they

361

were still around. Well, one I found was Lena Newton, who lived over the dairy in Pearl Street during the war. She lives in Australia and she's in her nineties and can't be with us, but she's actually sent a letter wishing us good luck. She married a sheep farmer, had five kids, went into politics and became a member of the government of New South Wales. I'll put the letter on the sideboard in case anyone wants to read it.'

'I've brought something.' A long-haired man of about thirty wearing jeans and a fluorescent sweatshirt stepped forward holding a book. 'Me dad used to live in Pearl Street; his name was Dicky Tutty. He lived a good life, worked hard, paid his taxes, but his sister, me Auntie Freda, became a lawyer and was quite famous – she took up lost causes and represented hopeless cases. She retired ten years ago and lives in London with her husband. She had a book written about her.' He held it up for everyone to see. The front cover showed a stern-faced woman grimacing at the camera below the title *Left of Left, The Life of Freda Owens*.

'I've heard of her,' gasped Caitlin. 'I never dreamt she was our Freda from Pearl Street.'

'Well she was,' Freda's nephew said proudly.

Penny was feeling uncomfortably hot. She left the room and discovered that people were gathered in the hall and on the stairs. No doubt she was related to them all in some way; their great-aunt or second cousin once removed, whatever that meant. The kitchen was crowded too.

She thought about her girls, her daughters, her real flesh and blood, and wished she was with them in Breckenridge, Colorado, rather than with these people to whom she was related, yet who were mostly total strangers.

There was a door to her left, which she opened in the hope that it was a place where she could be alone for a while to shed a few silent tears; a broom cupboard would do, a bathroom, a laundry room, anything. Instead she found herself in a small office, where a man was seated behind a desk feeding paper into a fax machine.

'I'm sorry.' It came out like a sob. 'I didn't realise...' She was about to leave, but the man got to his feet and came towards her. He was tall, blond, with slightly greying sideboards and a world-weary expression in his blue eyes. He laid his hand on her arm.

'Don't go, sit down a minute. You're too gorgeous to leave straight away.' He smiled at her appreciatively. 'Is it getting to you out there? It's making me as depressed as hell. That song they're playing now was my mother's favourite.'

'We'll Meet Again' was being sung by a woman with a voice like an angel. 'Would you like some coffee?'

Penny sank into a chair. He'd called her gorgeous – and that smile! 'I'd love coffee,' she conceded with a massive sigh, 'but the kitchen's full to suffocation.'

'Aha! Well I thought that might happen, so I have my own supply.' He pointed to a coffee machine on a bookshelf beside the desk and switched it on. 'I'm a columnist with the *Guardian* newspaper and had an urgent article to get to London before midnight,' he explained, 'which is why I've secreted myself in here. I'll join the fray in a minute, but not before you and I have had a cup of coffee. Fortunately, I have another cup.'

It dawned on Penny that this must be Nicky Stephens, who she'd played with often when they were children. For some reason this knowledge came as an enormous disappointment. She was wondering why when she remembered that she was his aunt, and no matter how gorgeous he found her and she him, they were out of bounds to each other.

'I'm Penny Henningsen,' she said. 'If you remember at all, it will be as Penny Fleming. Your mom and mine were best friends.'

The coffee had boiled and he was pouring it out. 'Do you take milk and sugar?' he asked.

'Cream, if you've got it, no sugar.'

'All I have is some grotty powdered milk.'

'Grotty powdered milk will do.'

He brought the drink across. 'Eileen Stephens wasn't my real mother,' he said. 'I'm Theo Stephens; Nicky is my half-brother and he's not going to be here till later. My real mother died in the war, but I couldn't have had a better substitute than Eileen.'

'I don't remember you.'

'I wasn't quite a year old when the war ended.'

Penny sipped the coffee. She didn't want to think any more. In the living room, they were having a loud argument about the attributes of Margaret Thatcher compared to the present prime minister, Tony Blair.

Theo Stephens was also listening. 'I don't like either of them,' he remarked. 'And I feel sorry for

364

you lot across the Atlantic having elected George W. Bush as your next president.'

'I feel sorry for us too,' Penny said. 'We voted for Al Gore.'

'Who's "we"?' he asked quickly.

'Me and my husband; we're separated.'

He grinned. 'I'm sorry to hear it.' He didn't look it.

'What about you?' she asked.

'Divorced. Three sons. Three grandchildren. All living in London.'

'I have two daughters, Laura and Elaine. And five grandchildren.'

They stared at each other, neither saying a word, while Penny thought of all the love, the pain and the drama that went into a few words describing two people's lives.

There was sudden activity in other parts of the house. It would seem everyone was going into the garden, brimming over with excitement. The television was on loud as it chimed in the new year – the new millennium.

The chimes couldn't be heard outside. In the garden, Penny and Theo were holding hands, and she wondered how long it would continue. Just until the century changed from the twentieth to the twenty-first? Or afterwards?

Voices began to count down: 'Eight, seven, six, five, four, three, two...'

The 'one' went unheard as the world exploded into a roar of sound and the sky became a mad canvas of lights and colour, with fireworks soaring upwards, spilling stars and sparks and streamers in their wake.

'*Happy New Year!*' people screamed.
'*No it's Happy New Millennium!*'
They danced and laughed until Caitlin's voice could be heard above all the others.
'Let's make a toast!' she yelled.
'What to?' they yelled back.
'To Pearl Street. That's why we're here. Raise your glasses to Pearl Street.'
'To Pearl Street!' everyone shouted, and they laughed, cried and shouted even more.

The publishers hope that this book has given you enjoyable reading. Large Print Books are especially designed to be as easy to see and hold as possible. If you wish a complete list of our books please ask at your local library or write directly to:

Magna Large Print Books
Magna House, Long Preston,
Skipton, North Yorkshire.
BD23 4ND

This Large Print Book for the partially sighted, who cannot read normal print, is published under the auspices of

THE ULVERSCROFT FOUNDATION